Dangerously Dark

COLETTE LONDON

KENSINGTON PUBLISHING CORP.
http://www.kensingtonbooks.com

KENSINGTON BOOKS are published by

Kensington Publishing Corp.
119 West 40th Street
New York, NY 10018

All Kensington Titles, Imprints, and Distributed Lines are available at special quantity discounts for bulk purchases for sales promotions, premiums, fund-raising, and educational or institutional use. Special book excerpts or customized printings can also be created to fit specific needs. For details, write or phone the office of the Kensington special sales manager: Kensington Publishing Corp., 119 West 40th Street, New York, NY 10018, attn: Special Sales Department, Phone: 1-800-221-2647.

Kensington and the K logo Reg. U.S. Pat & TM Off.

ISBN-13: 978-1-61773-347-5
ISBN-10: 1-61773-347-4
First Kensington Mass Market Edition: October 2015

eISBN-13: 978-1-61773-348-2
eISBN-10: 1-61773-348-2

First Kensington Electronic Edition: October 2015

10 9 8 7 6 5 4 3 2 1

Printed in the United States of America

To John Plumley, with all my love.

One

You should probably know one thing about me right up front: I'm not a morning person. Never have been, never will be. If it's too early for traffic jams, tequila, and at least 50 percent of the taxi drivers in any given metropolis to be plying their trade, then it's too early for me. End of story. But sometimes I have to make exceptions. Doesn't everyone?

The fact of the matter is, I don't always set my own hours. Sometimes my clients do that for me. That's because I'm a freelancer—a freelance chocolate whisperer. You might not have heard of me. I'm the first of my kind. My clients would probably prefer you don't know I exist. But I definitely do.

My work takes me around the world, where I use my expertise with *Theobroma cacao* to solve problems (on the QT) for my influential clients. Usually, they find me by referral. I'm not exactly a household name; I don't want to be. But the downside of working on an on-demand basis is that I don't always work when I want to.

For instance, consulting for bakeries means getting up with the roosters (because bakers are lunatics). Consulting for multinational corporations means crossing multiple time zones (because CEOs are relentless). Consulting for mega chocolatiers (some of the biggest in the biz) who are desperate for me to troubleshoot their gloopy ganaches and freaky frappés means working around the clock. But that's okay, because chocolatiers are *wonderful*—truly some of my favorite people in the world.

So *sometimes* I'm up at dawn. While I'm working, at least.

For the most part, though, the whole early-bird routine isn't for me. Neither is planning too far ahead, taking on clients who won't reveal who referred them to me, or passing up any chance I get to taste a new single-origin varietal chocolate (preferably around 72 percent dark). But after the consultation-gone-wrong that I'd just had, all bets were off.

After everything that had gone down with Lemaître Chocolates in San Francisco, I was ready for a change of pace.

Ordinarily, after finishing one hush-hush assignment for a client, I'm off and running to the next. Partly because it suits me—I grew up rough-traveling the world with a pair of globe-trotting parents who wore out passports the way other parents wore out their suburban SUVs' tires, so gridskipping feels like walking around the block to me—and partly because if I don't . . .

Well, my financial advisor—steady, sexy-voiced Travis Turner—could fill you in on the consequences of what happens if I *don't* keep my duffel bag and always-packed wheelie suitcase at the ready. Suffice it to say, it's in my best interest to keep moving, which I do by fixing problems with my clients' cocoa-butter-filled cookies, cakes, and confections. I like chocolate. It likes me. Together we make magic. For money.

Don't tell anyone, but I'd do it for free. In a heartbeat. I'd just rather not do it before noon, if possible.

That's why, if I'd been a celebrity, there would have been paparazzi present to document my arrival at PDX in Portland, Oregon (since my plane touched down at the earlyish hour of 8:00 A.M.). If I'd been an endangered monkey (instead of a woman with a rampant monkey mind), there would have been a Sir David Attenborough–style voice-over to narrate my transfer from the terminal to the car-rental counter to the highway leading into the city. That's just how unusual it was to find me, mobile and agile, drinking excellent cappuccino while squinting into the sunshine *before* eleven o'clock or so. But since I was just me, ordinary Hayden Mundy Moore—thirty, single, possessed of an unusually talented set of taste buds and an admittedly oversize collection of Moleskine notebooks (home of my omnipresent to-do lists)—there wasn't anyone around to remark upon the fact that I was voluntarily up early. On purpose. Playing hooky.

After leaving Maison Lemaître and its disastrous consultation-turned-murder behind (don't ask), I'd planned to visit Seattle to meet Travis. In person. For the first time ever. Because I'd (technically) risked my life while bayside, and that kind of thing had a way of re-ordering a girl's priorities. I wanted to *see* the man who (along with my security expert, Danny Jamieson) had helped me sidestep disaster. So I'd booked a ticket online, headed for SFO . . . and gotten a call from Travis just as I'd climbed into a taxi to leave for the airport.

"Seattle, huh?" he'd asked in that memorably husky murmur of his, sounding *almost* as though he'd set down his calculator and spreadsheets for the occasion. "What's in Seattle, Hayden?"

"Well, he's tall, dark, handsome, planephobic—"

"If you're talking about me, I'm blond."

How would I know? I'd never so much as seen a photo of him. Travis was notoriously private. On the other hand . . . I had him.

"Who says I mean *you*?" Of course I meant him. I'd been angling to meet Travis for a long time now—practically from the day he'd taken over for his less enigmatic (and less intriguing) predecessor. A meeting had never worked out for us, though. I was always on the run. Travis was the ultimate homebody.

Danny had met him. In fact, they were archenemies.

I didn't know why they didn't get along. They wouldn't say.

"You can't come to Seattle," Travis said. "Not today."

"Sure, I can." Stubbornness is my middle name. Except I like to call it persistence. "I already have a ticket. I'm coming."

That's why Travis had called, of course. To stop me. He must have seen the airfare purchase show up in my bank account.

See, that was the trouble with my otherwise workable setup with Travis. Stealthiness was tricky to pull off when the person you were trying to surprise could—and did—track your every move.

For the first time, it occurred to me to wonder if Travis had thwarted me this way before. Maybe he wasn't really gripped by an intense (and, to me, inexplicable) fear of flying. Maybe he was simply determined to keep our relationship professional.

Boringly, frustratingly, *professional*.

Where was the fun in that?

"No, I mean you can't come to Seattle today because you're supposed to be in Portland." Travis could have been consulting a complex FBI database instead of a simple shared online calendar. That's how focused he sounded. Which was what I got for having someone as detail-oriented as a CPA keeping my schedule for me. "For your friend's engagement party. You can't have forgotten."

"I . . . might have forgotten." *Rats.* Foiled again.

"Hayden." Travis sounded disappointed. "You forgot?"

"Hey, I was just almost *murdered* via hot-cocoa mud bath at Maison Lemaître, remember?" Thinking about it, I couldn't help shuddering. Of all the ways to die, biting it via chocolate-themed spa service would have lacked a certain dignity. On the other hand, my complexion would have looked *fabulous*. "Cut me a little slack."

Instead, Travis had gotten back down to business. Even as I'd watched the busy streets of Nob Hill sliding past the taxi's window, my financial advisor had squashed my plans.

"I'll send you the Evite again with the details," he'd said, typing in the background. "And book you another flight."

I'd remembered that hot-pink electronic party invitation and made a face. "I can book my own flight, Travis."

"It's already done. I'm texting you the details."

Now, several hours and roughly 550 air miles later, I was on my way to my friend Carissa Jenkins's engagement party weekend. I was happy for Carissa—and her fiancé, Declan Murphy—who'd shared a whirlwind romance the likes of which usually only happened in the movies. But I wasn't thrilled about being rerouted through an early-bird flight, and despite wanting to support my friend, I wasn't over the moon about the prospect of a few days spent in hypergirly mode, oohing and aahing over diamond rings and flower arrangements.

I'm not the girly-girl type, prone to all things foofy, fussy, or bejeweled. I spend my days with burly, chain-smoking line cooks and tattooed back-of-house staff. That kind of thing tends to crush a person's girlier tendencies. I was about as likely to wear pink willingly as I was to leave my chopsticks upright in my rice during a dinner in Osaka (a serious no-no).

On the bright side, though, I'd probably make it out of Carissa's party weekend alive, I figured as I crested I-5 and caught sight of the city's iconic White Stag PORTLAND OREGON sign perched over the cloud-gray skyline. That was more than I (almost) could say about my stay at chichi Maison Lemaître.

The chances of something dangerously deadly happening in the Pacific Northwest were slim. Portland was known for its roses and bridges, brewpubs and bicycles, tattooed baristas and cutting-edge indie restaurateurs. (And rain.) Not for *murder.*

As it was, a getaway to someplace scenic and safe sounded pretty good to me. I'd had enough of threats and surprises, of sneaking around and of suspecting strangers, of playing amateur Sherlock Holmes, minus one deer-stalker hat and/or one Benedict Cumberbatch and/or one Jonny Lee Miller and/or one Robert Downey, Jr. (take your pick.) For one weekend, at least, I wanted to forget about my foray into catching a killer. If Travis wouldn't help me accomplish that goal (and he obviously wouldn't), then Carissa, her fiancé, and her friends would have to do so.

This weekend, I didn't want to spend any time thinking about criminal behavior. Or even chocolate, for that matter.

Danny Jamieson, my oldest friend and newly hired

protection expert, would have said I was dodging the facts. He would have said that my plan to visit Travis and my trip to "PDX" (a nickname for Portland) were both procrastinatory detours from what really needed to be done: dealing with what had happened to me at Maison Lemaître.

He might have had a point. Because even though justice had been served and things had ended well, I was still shaken up. I still felt unsettled. Vulnerable, even. But who wouldn't? It wasn't every day that a person showed up to troubleshoot some nutraceutical truffles for one of San Francisco's most venerable chocolatiering families and wound up dealing with a killer.

I was proud of the way I'd handled my inexpert sleuthing. But I *didn't* want to repeat the experience. Not even for the sake of cozying up to Danny again—and we *had* gotten cozy.

Nothing serious had happened. Just a night of brainstorming in a dive bar in the Tenderloin. Just drinking, joking around, and being reminded of good times past. Just sharing a few saucy remarks. That's it. We both knew better than to take it further. But I'd been tempted. If you met Danny—all muscular, macho, and ready to get down to business—you would have been, too. The thing was, I was supposed to know better.

I *did* know better. But some nonnegotiable time apart—while Danny stayed in California and I partied down with Carissa's bridal party in the "Rose City"— sounded like a sensible idea.

I was being so responsible, it was downright saintly.

Travis would have been thrilled. But my financial advisor didn't know everything about Danny and me, and I wanted to keep it that way. For now, Travis's objections to Danny were limited to opposing paying his salary as my bodyguard-on-retainer. That, and balking at Danny's light-fingered way of getting evidence, of course. Travis wasn't thrilled with Danny's shady past.

But I believed in giving people second chances, which was part of the reason I was in "Stumptown" in the first place. And before you get confused, let me clue you in: Portland has a number of nicknames—"Bridgetown," "Stumptown," "Rose City," "PDX," and (because of its many brewpubs) "Beervana." The rallying cry of the city's residents is *"Keep Portland Weird!"* and it works.

Portland is one of my favorite places. It has greenery, mild weather, friendly residents, the winding Willamette River, and one of the most up-and-coming food scenes anywhere. Sure, it has its gritty side. And its stodgy side. And yes, it sometimes trends too hard toward hipster haven. But the thing about Portland is that it's *earnest.* In my life, there's too little earnestness. Wandering the world can make you cynical.

I can be cynical. Which was probably (along with the aforementioned murder) why I'd forgotten Carissa's engagement party weekend. We'd known each other in college, during my parents' brief fling with academia at a New England university. We'd gotten close. Then Carissa had pledged to a sorority, I'd (strenuously) objected in the way that only a self-styled emo kid could do (don't laugh—you've probably got a few embarrassing memories from college yourself), and that had been that. Not long after, I'd left for a sojourn in Belgium.

Surprisingly, distance had only brought us closer— probably because living on separate continents had a way of shrinking our differences. It had been tricky to stay in touch, but Carissa and I had been devoted. We'd emailed and shared, Instagrammed and video chatted. We'd managed.

I was grateful to hang on to a friend who connected me to my onetime Ivy League past, and Carissa . . .

Well, Carissa now lived someplace that hadn't been touched since Norman Rockwell dabbled with Crayolas. Driving toward the food cart pod, where Carissa and Declan both worked—where I'd arranged to meet Carissa for a "surprise" (her word, not mine)—I passed Tudor-style cottages and Craftsman bungalows, California ranch homes and modern post-and-beam Rummers, foursquares with dormer windows and well-kept Colonials. I was Airbnb-ing it in the surrounding neighborhood, but rather than check in to my accommodations, I decided to go straight to Cartorama instead.

That was the name of Carissa's cart pod: Cartorama. I had to say, its kitschy moniker suited the neighborhood. I passed a few corners where construction crews appeared to have torn down an old gas station or a block of care-worn houses and were turning one plot or another into apartment buildings. Aside from that, the whole place looked as though it could have doubled as a set from an old Technicolor movie. It was downright charming.

It was also going away quickly. Gentrification was de rigueur in Portland. Thanks to the city's "no-sprawl" edict—which limited development to a designated urban-growth boundary—anyone who wanted to live or conduct business in the area had to squeeze into older houses or remodel dated business sites or, in the case of the cart pod, pay rents to park their food service trailers on an otherwise unused (for now) parking lot.

Demand was high. Availability wasn't. My own Airbnb hosts had cashed in on the demand themselves. They no longer lived in their once-affordable 1920s foursquare, instead using the fees they earned to finance their larger house in a nearby suburb.

I was glad, for once, that I didn't have a home base of my own to worry about. I could afford a mortgage, a husband, 2.2 kids, and a golden retriever (for instance), but I wasn't in the market for domesticity. I couldn't be. Thanks to my eccentric uncle Ross and the trust fund he left me (to be administered by Travis, my hyperintelligent keeper), I had no choice except to . . .

. . . snag the handy street-side parking space that suddenly became free and swerve my rental Honda Civic into it. Score!

My parking job was haphazard at best. I cut the engine and grabbed my gear, anyway—my excuse being that I don't drive much.

I prefer to walk, take the Metro, Tube, or U-Bahn, or grab a cab during my worldwide travels. That means I'm fairly rusty when it comes to expertise behind the wheel. If catching that killer in San Francisco (technically, the Marin Headlands, but who's quibbling?) had depended upon me making sharp U-turns and navigating the Bay Area's notoriously hilly streets . . . Well, let's just say I'm glad it didn't and leave it at that.

Clambering out of the car, dressed in my go-to uniform of jeans, a slim gray T-shirt, and Converse sneakers (plus a jacket, my concession to the brisk prenoon weather), I headed toward Cartorama. The cart pod was easy to spot. It occupied what appeared to be the very last empty-corner parking lot in the area. Directly across the street from me stood a freshly built high-rise apartment building. Its banner outside boasted about its über-high-speed Internet, eco-friendly construction materials, and tricked-out "community gathering place," aka fancified rec room. Next to that, a row of buildings hunkered down straight out of the Eisenhower era, sporting a variety of indie storefronts and looking especially geriatric (but charming, in a funky way) next to their sleek, new neighbor.

The whole thing was a lesson in new supplanting old, but I didn't have time to wax philosophical about time marching on. I'd agreed to meet Carissa for her "surprise," but between my scheduled and rescheduled flights (and my usual A.M. fogginess), our plans had gotten jumbled. I wasn't sure how long it would take for Carissa to arrive, but I wanted to look around before she did.

Up close, the unopened cart pod reminded me of an after-hours amusement park. Or a deserted carnival, cut loose from its clowns and barkers. All of the food carts were different—one was housed in a cheerfully painted lumber shack, one in a repurposed metal storage container, one in a vintage VW bus, one in an Airstream trailer—and most were closed for the morning. Since Cartorama specialized in everything chocolate (or so Carissa had told me), the pod wouldn't see much business until lunchtime.

The chocolate whisperer in me knew that someone ought to bring in a chocolate-themed donut cart or a mobile *boulangerie* specializing in *pain au chocolat*—something to lure in customers during the morning hours. But I wasn't here to work, I reminded myself. I was here to reconnect with my long-lost friend.

Despite Cartorama's momentary lack of customers, though, the place had definite appeal. The gimmick of offering all chocolate, all the time, was working on me. I was hungry already.

If you're not familiar with the food-truck phenomenon, let me explain: We're not talking ho-hum spinner dogs and dodgy kebabs served on the sidewalk in Anytown, USA. We're talking delicious, locally sourced fare from innovative restaurateurs, served up without pretension but with plenty of imagination and verve. Everyone from the *New York Times* to Anthony Bourdain has raved about Portland's food cart scene, and with good reason.

At Cartorama, the kitschy carts were parked facing an inner courtyard of sorts, which featured scrubbed wooden picnic tables beneath a sheltering awning. The awning's canopy cover was tied back—probably on account of the clear weather—but the whole getup looked as though it could be covered quickly if diners needed protection from the elements. Overhead, strings of festival lights were hung with industrial-chic Edison bulbs, all of them dark for now. At the edges of the pod, tall oaks and graceful Japanese maples swayed in the breeze, playing host to what sounded like a whole Hitchcock movie's worth of birds.

Birds. I shivered and kept moving.

Birds and I don't get along. Maybe because of that aforementioned (terrifying) Hitchcock film. (Speaking of which . . . do you know what creepy old Hitch used as a stand-in for blood in *Psycho*? Chocolate sauce. Yep. What a waste, right?)

Anyway, I don't like birds. Maybe that's because I'm a city dweller at heart, used to seeing pigeons and seagulls for what they are: rats with wings. Either way, those birds put a crimp in the whole sunshiny springtime vibe I'd been enjoying.

I could feel their beady little eyes on me as I wandered toward the cart pod's inner courtyard. Their avian shrieks sounded like warnings. But that was probably just me, feeling easily (and unreasonably) spooked after Maison Lemaître.

I was fine. Everything was fine. It was *fine*.

Hoping to assure myself of that, I texted Carissa that I'd arrived, then distracted myself by exploring the pod further. I watched as a few vendors began setting up for the day. I was interested to see how their various carts unfolded and opened (Transformers style) into mobile kitchens and service areas. One by-product of my vocation is that I'm curious. Just then, I was curious about Carissa's work at Cartorama with Declan.

She'd been playing it coy so far. But if I'd guessed right, my old friend's new career likely involved something social, uncomplicated, and fairly frivolous. Something like advising the cart entrepreneurs on installing fab new décor. Or writing a gossip column for a local blog. Or doing PR. Carissa would have been good at any (or all) of those things. She'd always been outgoing. Popular. Able to talk anyone into anything.

Even me. I was there in Portland instead of cornering Travis in Seattle for some one-on-one time, wasn't I?

"Hayden!" someone yelled from nearby. "Woooo!"

I recognized that unmistakable feminine squeal. *Carissa.* I turned to see my old friend bustling toward me, all toothy grin and long auburn hair, dressed in ankle boots and a boho-cool, direct-from-Etsy ensemble, with her arms outstretched. A few dainty footsteps later, she engulfed me in a hug. "Hiiii!"

Simultaneously, the scents of her hair products and perfume engulfed me. So did a jolt of girlish exuberance. My friend was nothing if not excitable. And strong. Freakishly strong for a woman so thin. I hugged Carissa warmly, complimented her cute boots (girlspeak for *"Hello"*—I could do it, I just didn't indulge often), then extricated myself long enough to catch my breath.

Seeing her hurtled me back to my college days. Not that it was that long ago, but a lot's happened to me since then.

"Ohmigod! Look at you!" Carissa marveled at me, her

face pretty and pale behind her geek-chic tortoiseshell glasses. "I *love* your hair! And your jacket! And your Chucks! I'm *all* about that nouveau-retro look. Hey, you cut back on the eyeliner!"

I grinned and shook my head at her reference to my short-lived emo past. "When you're backpacking through Kazakhstan, a face full of L'Oréal doesn't cut it." These days, I tended toward lip gloss and (maybe) mascara. Combined with my shoulder-length brown hair and (aforementioned) Converse sneakers, it made for a low-key look—one that traveled as well to Beijing as it did to Thessaloniki. "Congratulations on your engagement!"

That incited a fresh squeal. Carissa thrust her left hand forward, then waggled her fingers. "Thanks! See? Isn't it fab?"

I dutifully examined her engagement ring. But when you've gotten up close and personal with the Crown Jewels at the Tower of London, ordinary baubles have a tough time competing.

I couldn't think of much to say about it. Sometimes my globe-trotting upbringing leaves gaps. "Pretty!" I gushed.

Carissa sighed, then hugged her ring finger, obviously disappointed . . . but willing to wait for me to rally. I sensed a long weekend ahead of me. What else was I supposed to say?

"It's so big!" I tried. Hey, it worked on men, didn't it?

My friend brightened with pleasure. "I know, right? Declan is *so* generous with me. He's a sweetheart. *Really,* he is."

I couldn't help thinking that, generally, people who temper their statements with "really" or "honestly" or "actually" (or similar qualifiers) are hiding something. Which only made me wonder . . .

"Do you think he's 'the one,' Carissa?" I asked. "This

has all happened so fast. You haven't been dating all that long—"

"Declan is *totally* the one," Carissa interrupted with certainty, literally waving away my question. "He's sweet and caring and *super*handsome! And, okay, so sometimes when I text him an 'I love you' and he texts back 'U2,' I get a little stabby"—here she broke into a wider grin—"but overall, Declan is fantastic!" Carissa inhaled. "What about you? Seeing anyone?"

Ugh. It was the question dreaded by singles everywhere.

I'd been seeing several people, actually, across a couple of continents. But that made me sound flighty at best and promiscuous at worst—neither of which was accurate (and that's before you add in my three ex-fiancés). It's just that I'm a people person. That tends to lead to a lot of dates.

"We can get to that later." It was my turn to wave off a query. I gazed around at Cartorama. "So, what's your surprise?"

"You'll *never* guess."

That's what people said when they *wanted* you to guess. It was a tendency that traveled to the far corners. So I did my best. "You're doing interior decorating at one of the carts?"

Carissa gawked at me, disappointed again. "*That's* what you think of me? That I'm good for nothing but decorating?"

Hastily, I backpedaled. "You're writing a blog?"

Wisely, I omitted "gossip" blog. I learn quickly.

"I'm running a cart!" Carissa shook her head, then grabbed my arm. Again, I was reminded of her surprising strength. "An ice-cream cart. It's called Churn PDX. It's a budding chain. You know, as in Churn PDX, Churn LA, Churn Las Vegas, Churn Tokyo. . . ."

I bumped along in her wake, letting myself be towed toward the vintage Airstream trailer I'd noticed earlier, while Carissa described the food cart she'd founded and hoped to expand to the aforementioned cities. She was dreaming big. But why not?

I've known other food entrepreneurs who've succeeded fantastically, even with admittedly niche products. Ice cream sounded like a slam dunk to me. Who doesn't like ice cream?

"Who doesn't like ice cream?" Carissa echoed my thoughts as she set up an awning at the business side of the trailer, then pushed out a locked rolling service counter. "My ice cream is even better than most, though. It's *scientifically* better."

The sorority girl I'd known at university had joked about "paying a nerd" to take Chemistry 101 for her while she pursued a degree in design. "Tell me another one, Einstein," I joked.

To my surprise, she did. "My ice cream is frozen with liquid nitrogen," Carissa explained as she went on setting up.

Her cart had all sorts of cleverly designed features crafted to be stowed away for the night, then set up the next morning. In no time flat, she'd established a work space without even needing to go inside the trailer. I envisioned a *Punk'd*-style camera crew hiding in there, stifling guffaws as they waited to see if Carissa's old college friend bought the idea of her as an ice-cream impresario who rattled off details like the boiling point of liquid nitrogen (-321 degrees Fahrenheit) and its dielectric constant (1.43) as easily as she'd once nailed the names of fashion designers and reality-TV celebs.

Formerly ditzy Carissa wound up her spiel with a slightly more down-to-earth reference to British culinary wunderkind Heston Blumenthal, but by then I was already agog.

"So, what flavor would you like?" she asked. "We only serve chocolate—of course—but we've got bittersweet chocolate, white chocolate, malted chocolate, mocha swirl, chocolate caramel—"

"Bittersweet." It's my once-and-forever *amore.* I like my chocolate dark—dangerously dark. The darker, the better.

Not that there isn't room in my heart for a mellow milk chocolate. Of course there is. But if we're talking favorites . . .

"Coming right up!" Carissa grabbed an aluminum container, then busied herself adding a chocolaty-liquid ice-cream base to it. "I designed the churning machine myself," she went on as she fixed the container beneath a spiroid paddle. The whole outfit was reminiscent of the KitchenAid stand mixer you might have at home—with an important difference: one wrong move and this one could give its user irreversible frostbite. "I designed and patented custom software to calibrate precisely how much liquid nitrogen to use for each batch. Faster freezing means fewer—"

"Ice crystals!" I blurted, eager to atone for my gaffe with her ring. *This* subject I could ace, unlike engagement ring etiquette. "Which means smoother ice cream and fresher flavor."

With ice cream, as with chocolate, it's all about details.

Carissa brightened. "That's right! Most people zone out when I talk about the technical stuff. Or they laugh.

I don't know why people insist on thinking I'm dumb!
It's *infuriating*!"

She pouted over the idea. I gave an inward wince,
knowing I'd doubted her intelligence myself just minutes
ago. Bygones.

"I'm a culinary professional," I reminded her, side-
stepping the issue of her newfound aptitude for science
for the time being. "I can connect the dots. I'm impressed,
Carissa."

I was. I've known a lot of people who've followed their
dreams—and a lot *more* people who've wanted to but
never tried. Carissa was part of the first group. My hat
was off to her.

She tossed me a grateful smile, then turned back to the
churning machine. "Get ready for this to knock your
socks off!"

Dramatically, she flipped a switch. Nothing happened.

She frowned. "I said, 'Get ready for this to—'"

Another flip. Again, nothing. Carissa muttered a
swearword.

With forced brightness, she regrouped. "Okay. Something must be wrong with the tanks inside. Pretend this
never happened. I'll be back in a sec, and then you'll
really be amazed!"

Carissa unzipped her messenger bag to search for her
keys. I waited, mouth watering in anticipation of tasting
chocolate. (I'm predictable that way.) Even early in the
morning, bittersweet-chocolate ice cream sounded *très
délicieuse* to me.

Come on . . . you can't tell me *you* wouldn't eat ice
cream at 10:00 A.M. It's made from milk and eggs, right?
Practically breakfast.

I scanned Cartorama, then wandered a short distance
away to watch another vendor begin setting up for the day.

That whole "Go-Go-Gadget" thing the food carts had going on was fascinating. Behind me, Carissa unearthed her keys. They jangled as she used them to unlock her trailer's door, step inside . . .

. . . *and scream.* Her shriek made all the birds take flight.

An instant later, I heard a sickening thud. *Carissa.*

I wheeled around and headed for her trailer, hoping I wasn't too late to deal with whatever had just happened to my friend.

Two

You would think that once you've stumbled upon an honest-to-god murder, you'd be prepared for anything, right? No matter how ghastly or unlikely. But I wasn't prepared for what greeted me inside Carissa's Airstream trailer. I wasn't prepared at all.

I vaulted inside, heart pounding, and glimpsed Carissa collapsed on the floor. She seemed to have fallen on top of . . . *something*. Something bulky and long. Bags of sugar, maybe?

Trying to see what it was, I edged closer. I couldn't see clearly, though. A ghostly vapor filled the space where Carissa kept her equipment and inventory, partly obscuring my vision.

Plus, I felt downright woozy. Short of breath, too. Spots swam before my eyes. I was terrified a homicidal maniac might burst from a dark corner at any moment. After all, *someone* must have gotten in here. On the alert for a potential attacker, I blinked and moved closer, shivering from the chill. It was as if the Airstream was refrigerated—and now so was I. Shakily veering from side to side, I tried not to think of haunted houses and horror movies, dead bodies and killers lurking in the shadows.

It didn't work. *Murder* was all I could think of.

"Carissa!" I crouched beside my unmoving friend. I touched her limp arm. I peered at her face. Her stillness scared me.

A faint hissing sound filled the trailer. My raspy breath overrode it. I was freaked out and not afraid to admit it. At least now the mist was subsiding. That meant I could see.

In that moment, I almost wished I couldn't.

"Carissa?" Gently, I tried to jostle her, feeling on the verge of tears. I'm not a crybaby, but these were extraordinary circumstances. I swallowed hard. "Carissa, are you okay?"

Clearly, she wasn't. Confused about what might have happened in here, I grabbed her arm, hoping I could drag her outside the same way she'd good-naturedly lugged me to Churn PDX. Or maybe just hoping I could make her wake up. *Wake up!*

That's when I caught sight of what Carissa had fallen on top of: *a body.* Startled, I tottered backward, almost tripping on the metal Dewars scattered on the floor. I gawked at the man sprawled beneath my friend. His face was squished into the industrial rubber kitchen mat underfoot in an awkward way that *definitely* suggested he wasn't here innocently napping.

Surely, he wasn't *dead*, though, my jumbled thoughts insisted. I mean, he couldn't be, could he? For one thing, what were the odds I'd stumble upon two dead bodies inside of one week? They had to be infinitesimal. Maybe he was drunk. Maybe he was a tanked-up, nicely dressed homeless man who'd startled Carissa and made her faint from shock, that's all. Sure. Okay.

He looks too handsome to be dead. I couldn't help trying to reassure myself. But I wasn't having it. I rebutted: *Nobody who's livin'* la vida loca *lies facedown that way.*

I was about to scream for help—the way Carissa had done—when the whole trailer swayed. Someone clomped inside behind me.

I surged upright, high on adrenaline, and confronted the man who stood there. I'm roughly average size for a woman, about five-six sans my sneakers. But I've got my share of tricks. If the new arrival wanted a taste of my go-to self-defense moves (hey, they'd thwarted a would-be mugger in Barcelona), then all he had to do was take another step.

He seemed to realize it, because he put up both hands.

"Whoa! I'm here to help." He eyed my ready stance, then boldly came closer. But now I could see that he was hardly threatening. Husky, flannel-shirted, and bearded? *Yes.* Capable of murder? *Probably not.* I relaxed a fraction—but only that.

I recognized him as the vendor I'd seen setting up earlier.

"We've got to call for help," I said, taking charge.

"We've got to get her out of here," he disagreed. "Now."

The whole incident—from hearing Carissa scream to entering the trailer to meeting Beardy—probably took twenty seconds, tops. But it seemed to be happening in super slo-mo.

At least to me, it did. Beardy was another story. He didn't have any problem operating in real time. He knelt beside Carissa with evident concern, then hoisted her in his massive arms. He turned, looked around, then galumphed down the steps with an involuntary grunt. The trailer shuddered again. I followed him outside, just in time to watch him lay Carissa on the ground.

Beardy stripped off his flannel shirt, heedless of the onlookers who'd begun gathering (other vendors, I surmised). Dressed only in his undershirt and baggy jeans, he bundled up his flannel button-down, then tenderly placed it beneath Carissa's head for a pillow. She moaned, then began to stir.

Thank God. She wasn't dead. Shaking and feeling faint with what I assumed was leftover adrenaline, I hurried to her while digging for my cell phone. We still needed help. We needed an ambulance, paramedics, someone knowledgeable about killer vapor. . . .

Even as I had that ludicrous thought (*killer vapor?*), a siren cut through the springtime air. Help was already coming for Carissa, probably thanks to one of the other Cartorama vendors. *She'll be fine, she'll be fine* ran through my head like a comforting litany—then hit an awful, unsettling speed bump.

"The man! Inside!" I gestured wildly toward the trailer. "We've got to go back and get him. He's still in there."

Beardy pursed his lips and very faintly shook his head. His pale face and drawn expression were trying to tell me something. In my fraught state, I didn't know what. I looked around at the onlookers, then singled out one person who appeared capable—a stocky, thirtyish blond woman wearing a T-shirt featuring a screen-printed piglet and the scripted words BACON HAD A MOM.

Hey, if she was compassionate toward animals, she'd help.

"You." I pointed. "Help me carry him out of there."

"No!" Beardy heaved himself to his feet. He wiped his hands on his jeans-covered backside, then cast an apprehensive glance at Carissa. "I haven't turned off the safety valve yet."

He was wasting time. I peeled off toward the Airstream trailer anyway, trusting my designated helper to follow me.

She didn't. I only made it a few steps before realizing as much. I glanced backward. Her face was as pale as Beardy's.

"Is it . . ." She faltered and knit her brow. "Who's in there?"

This was no time for discussion. Yet everyone around me seemed to be frozen in shock. The piglet T-shirt woman. Another vendor nearby, who was headed our way wearing a va-va-voom skintight vintage dress and an armful of tattoos. Even a tall, hipster-y man who'd wandered out of a nearby building, frowning at us with his arms crossed over his deep-V-necked T-shirt.

What was wrong with all of them? Couldn't they see this was an emergency? Ordinarily, people listen to me. When I'm on a consultation job, I'm the expert. Clients pay for my opinion, so they tend to comply with it. But here, I might as well have been invisible. I was no match for the stunned inertia around me.

Whatever. I didn't care if these people wanted to stand idly by in a crisis. *I* didn't. I'd drag out that man myself, one inch at a time, if I had to. There was no time to waste.

But just as I took another step, Carissa's voice pierced the sounds of distant traffic. "Declan?" she asked brokenly.

Oh no. Beardy turned to her. I couldn't see his face.

Carissa could. The sight made her burst into tears.

"Declan!" Muzzily, she lurched to her feet. With an awful wail, Carissa ran back to her trailer. She staggered inside.

My gaze met Beardy's. He looked dazed, sad . . . and *guilty*?

What the. . . ? Before I could pursue that line of thought, I realized the awful truth. Carissa had just stumbled upon her fiancé's dead body. *Declan Murphy was dead.* I had to go to her.

Part of me didn't want to. I'm not proud of it, but it's true. It had been one thing when I'd thought the man merely needed to be helped out for some first aid. It was another now that I knew he was beyond first aid. Permanently.

Poor Carissa. I heard her keening from inside her trailer and I was in motion before I could think up any reason not to be.

"Carissa?" I stepped into the tiny Airstream trailer through the open door, squinting to see in the gloom. It was still so cold in there.

Declan Murphy was still so unmoving. Handsome and lifeless.

I couldn't believe it. I suppose I was in shock. So was Carissa. She lay over Declan, her arms wrapped around him, sobbing against his big, broad, completely immobile chest.

"No, no, no," she murmured in a shattered voice. "Please—"

Whatever she was about to plead for was drowned out by the sound of Beardy lurching into the trailer behind me. I turned to him, annoyed that he'd intrude on Carissa's heartbreak.

The look on his face stopped me. He appeared devastated.

Humbled, I watched as he moved across the trailer, past bags of sugar, containers of cocoa, and ten-pound blocks of chocolate arranged in tidy stacks. Comically, he appeared to be tiptoeing across the space, but he wasn't built for stealth. The whole place rumbled vaguely beneath his ungainly footsteps.

He hunched his undershirt-covered shoulders, looking embarrassed. But Carissa seemed to neither notice nor care.

Poor Carissa. I went to her, then laid my hand on her shoulder. Comfortingly, I patted her. "I'm so sorry, Carissa."

She sniffled, her thin shoulders shuddering. She looked up at me. When her gaze met mine, it was damp with tears, yet oddly bright with hope. "He'll be okay. Really, Declan is tough."

It was the "really" that broke my heart. Carissa's hopefulness couldn't have been more obvious—or more agonizing.

I could see actual *frost* on Declan's waxy, slightly yellowed face. The situation was grim.

"We should all get out of here," Beardy broke in, standing over both of us with a helpless mien. "Carissa, you know how dangerous the nitro is. I've got the safety valve shut now—"

He looked younger than me—probably in his midtwenties—but he seemed knowledgeable about the science involved. I couldn't forget his guilty expression earlier, though. What did it mean?

"—but it was totally hashed, and I don't know how stable my fix is." Beardy spoke faster now as he gestured for us both to move. "It's better with the door open, but until all the nitro has dissipated, there's still a serious risk of displacement."

It was all Greek to me. I'd majored in . . . well, a little of everything, really. You won't be surprised to learn that I wasn't the most decisive college student. Unlike Carissa, who'd seemed to have found her métier early on in art and design, I'd dabbled in all kinds of things. Eventually, chocolate found me.

But that's a story for another, less tragic day.

"I'm not leaving him." Carissa nudged aside her glasses to wipe her teary eyes. The gesture made her look like a toddler—one who wanted no part of the nap that would help her feel better. "It's our engagement weekend! How can I leave him?"

Sobered by that, I went still. But Beardy didn't.

He came to Carissa, then took her arm. "Come on. Please."

Outside, the siren I'd heard drew closer. I could hear what had to be an ambulance's doors banging shut. Footsteps neared.

"Just come outside for some fresh air," Beardy insisted.

His stalwart stance reminded me of Danny. He and Carissa's friend couldn't have been more different, but this was exactly the way Danny had reacted when Adrienne Dowling had been found dead, only steps away from me, at Maison Lemaître. His strong and protective presence had helped me enormously that night.

There was never a good time to encounter your first dead body. It helped to have someone less emotionally invested on hand. Taking Beardy's lead, I patted Carissa's shoulder again.

"Come outside with us," I urged. "There's help coming

for Declan. We'll need to be out of the way of the paramedics."

That seemed to get Carissa's attention. Her desperate gaze swerved to mine. Held. I thought I was getting through to her.

Then, "*They* can't help with Chocolate After Dark."

I frowned. "'Chocolate After Dark'?"

Carissa nodded. Her hair shielded her face. "Declan's—"

She wept, unable to continue. I looked to Beardy.

"Declan's culinary tour," he explained, sotto voce, casting Carissa a fretful look. He clenched and unclenched his hands, shaking his head. "It was supposed to launch on Monday."

"Not 'was.' *Is!*" Carissa exclaimed heatedly. She jerked up her chin, even as voices outside penetrated the trailer. The Cartorama vendors, I assumed, directing the paramedics to the emergency. "It *is* launching on Monday! Declan's worked so hard for it! Chocolate After Dark *has* to go forward. It has to!"

Gloom fell over the trailer's interior as one of the EMTs stopped in the doorway. It was time to get serious.

"Yes," I told Carissa. "Yes, of course it will go forward!"

"It can't without Declan!" Her scattered gaze flashed to the paramedics. She gulped. "*You* do it, Hayden. *You* do the tour. Just until things are . . . settled with Declan. Okay?" She focused in on me. "Promise me you will. *Please* do it."

I wasn't sure what doing "it" involved. But under the circumstances, there was only one thing to say. I squeezed Carissa's hand. "I'll do whatever you need me to," I promised.

Like magic, my words got Carissa upright. She took in

the waiting paramedics, glanced at anxious Beardy, then returned her attention to me. Like a frail ghost of her formerly cheerful self, she tried to smile. All she could muster was a lip wobble.

Carissa was being *so* brave. I teared up all over again.

If my would-be fiancé turned up dead during my engagement party weekend, I would have hoped to have behaved just as admirably as Carissa was, I decided as I helped her outside—me with one arm, and Beardy with the other. Carissa was remarkable.

And okay, so her fixation with making sure Declan's culinary tour launched on time was a little odd. But there was no telling how people would react to trauma. I knew that. Sometimes people focused on random details during a catastrophe, as a way of momentarily escaping whatever ordeal was at hand. By this time tomorrow, probably, Carissa would have forgotten all about the way she'd talked about the Chocolate After Dark tour.

She'd have forgotten about my promise to launch it, too, more than likely. Not that that's what I was thinking about over the next half hour or so, as we all—vendors, visitors, and neighborhood residents alike—waited for the EMTs' pronouncement.

The paramedics checked out Carissa, then released her to us. The Portland police arrived and took statements—from me, from Beardy, and from Carissa. A local TV-news satellite van parked across the street behind my rented Civic, disgorged its crew, then grabbed footage of the goings-on, even as Deep V-Neck—the wiry, frowning man I'd noticed earlier—crossed the street and berated them for it. He scowled, dark and intense.

I couldn't hear what he was saying, but body language didn't lie. Whoever he was, he wasn't pleased with Oregon's news media invading Cartorama during its moment of misfortune.

All too soon, Declan's body was carried out of the trailer on a scoop stretcher, hideously zipped into a large plastic bag. By then, I think we were all becoming numbed to the proceedings. Hugging Carissa tightly, I watched as the EMTs loaded Declan's body into their waiting ambulance. The controlled, purposeful activity of the past thirty minutes felt like a dream.

Well, technically, it felt like a nightmare. Especially for Carissa. She couldn't stop crying. Everyone had rallied around her, exchanging worried, teary-eyed glances and helpless words of sympathy. None of us knew what to do or how to do it.

The surprising thing about tragedy is, life goes on— and so do you, one moment at a time. Maybe by numbing out. Maybe by clinging to a routine. Maybe by becoming cynical or angry—or by engaging in some unprecedented sleuthing. I'd learned that after seeing someone close to me die unexpectedly in San Francisco.

Then, I'd helped bring some justice to the situation. Now, I just wanted to be there for Carissa, in any way I could.

Not that my sentiments were shared by *everyone,* I couldn't help observing. The vivacious-looking brunette I'd noticed earlier had vanished shortly after the EMTs had arrived. I'd last glimpsed the short (but not especially petite) piglet T-shirt wearer at about the same time. Not everyone was good in a crisis. Me? I'm usually on the move myself. But not this time.

"Carissa, I'm going to be in town awhile," I told her as gently as I could, deciding in that moment to stay as long as was necessary. "If there's *anything* I can do to help—"

"Just get Chocolate After Dark off the ground," she

said in a desperate tone. "For me. For Declan. For all of us. Okay?"

Her teary gaze swept Cartorama and its vendors. Everyone around me seemed to shift uneasily. Then Carissa pushed away, hauled in a deep breath, and followed the EMTs to the ambulance.

Her slender shoulders trembled as she peeked inside it. Then she climbed in beside Declan Murphy's lifeless body, the ambulance doors closed behind her, and Carissa was gone.

As soon as the ambulance pulled away—moving with an awful slowness that told everyone at Cartorama there was no help for Declan Murphy now—I wished I'd gotten into it with Carissa.

"One of us should have gone with her." Beardy stood nearby me, clenching his cast-off flannel shirt in his fist as he watched the ambulance disappear down the tree-lined street. "Carissa shouldn't be alone right now. Not after all this."

His emotional tone was heartbreaking. He was obviously upset by the events of the morning—and *I'd* callously thought he'd seemed guilty earlier. What was the matter with me?

I couldn't let what had happened at Maison Lemaître color my whole life in shades of gray. That was no way to go forward.

There weren't killers around every corner, I reminded myself. The paramedics had told us Declan's death had seemed to be an accident. The police had agreed. It helped. A little.

"She won't be alone," I told Beardy, taking refuge in

that fact. One of the vendors had already called Carissa's
parents. They'd be meeting her soon. "You were really
amazing," I added, meaning it. "Thanks for all you did
this morning. I don't know how I'd have gotten Carissa
out without you." I held out my hand to him. "I'm
Carissa's friend from college, Hayden Mundy Moore."

I'm here for Carissa's engagement party, I was about
to say. But he cut me off before I could explain my presence
there.

"You're the chocolate expert. Yeah, Carissa told us about
you." Warmly, he clasped my hand. "I'm Austin Martin."

Austin stopped, seeming to wait for something. I
didn't know what. He gave a fleeting, puzzled frown, then
went on.

"I run The Chocolate Bar cart next door." He angled
his burly shoulder toward the small, brightly painted
building I'd noticed earlier. It stood partly open with its
counter bare. "I specialize in imported, nostalgia, and
hard-to-find candy bars."

"Do you stock Kit Kat Chunky?" I couldn't help
asking, taking refuge in normalcy. I needed the comfort
just then. "Cadbury Double Decker? Flakes?" I inhaled,
then, *"Maltesers?"*

Those were among my international favorites. Austin's
eyes brightened. "Of course. Plus, Terry's Chocolate
Orange. Kinder Bueno. Mars bars. Aero bars. *Every* kind
of Kit Kat. The works."

My eyes widened at the possibilities. You might not
know this, but Nestlé makes Kit Kat bars in all kinds of
flavors, all over the world. Strawberry in Japan. Cookie
dough in Australia. Banana in Canada. I don't know
why those flavors don't play in the States. They just
don't. They're not exactly artisanal chocolates made of

extra-spendy, ultra-rare Criollo cocoa beans and handmade praline, but they're pretty tasty, all the same.

"Sometimes I get a wicked craving for a nice Matcha Kit Kat," I confessed. "I'll have to hit up your cart sometime."

We both smiled, momentarily connecting over something less traumatic than Declan's death. The other vendors and neighborhood residents still milled around, murmuring in groups of two or three. It was awkward, but also consoling. I guess none of us wanted to be alone just then. It felt heartless to go back to ordinary life while Carissa was facing such a crisis. Maybe that's why I lingered. Even though I didn't know anyone there, I didn't want to be alone. Not then. Not after . . . everything.

"So you really were great with Carissa," I told Austin, feeling inexorably drawn back to those events. "Without you—"

"Carissa would have been asphyxiated. Just like Declan."

I didn't understand. "Asphyxiated? In her trailer?" That's what one of the EMTs had alluded to earlier, but it still didn't make sense to me. "But Carissa was alone. I checked."

Foolishly, I recalled. A wave of nausea rolled over me at the memory. I still felt overwhelmed. Light-headed too. You know that feeling you get when you've mainlined six espressos standing at the counter in a Naples caffe? No? Well, it involves a lot of shakiness, buzzy thoughts, dry mouth, and queasiness.

Overall, it's not pleasant. But at least *I* was alive.

Poor Declan. How could he have been asphyxiated? Aside from the frost on his face, he'd seemed to be the picture of health.

I wished I could have met him earlier. Seen him and Carissa together. Helped them embark on their married life together.

Now that would never happen. *Poor Carissa.*

"It's not *who* attacked Carissa. It's *what*," Austin told me. "The air in that trailer was dangerously low on oxygen. Carissa must have rushed in there and been overcome almost instantly."

I remembered her haste to impress me. I nodded. "She did."

"It's a good thing you followed her. Another minute or two without sufficient oxygen, and she would have been in serious trouble. I'm guessing that the open trailer door let in enough air to keep you upright and Carissa okay— once she was outside."

But not Declan. I frowned. "Whatever got to Declan is the same thing that made Carissa pass out? Like a poison?"

I wasn't sure how that meshed with the asphyxiation theory.

"Sort of. Do you know much about liquid nitrogen?"

I shook my head. "My oeuvre is chocolate. That's it."

"Well, liquid nitrogen is a cryogenic liquefied gas." Austin gave me a watchful look. "That means it gets—"

"Really cold. I don't need the kindergarten version."

He almost smiled at that. I was starting to like him— flannel shirt, shaggy hair, Portland-style beard, and all.

"Right. Well, aside from being cold, liquid nitrogen is also colorless, odorless, tasteless, noncorrosive, and nonflammable. Ordinarily, it's nontoxic and inert—"

"Which is why it's used for freezing ice cream," I surmised, "and in molecular gastronomy." In certain Michelin-starred restaurants, I knew, fancy foams and flavored orbs were all the rage. I still didn't get how it led to suffocation.

"Yes." Austin nodded. "But in certain circumstances, it can also produce tissue damage, cause cold contact burns—"

I remembered the frost on Declan's face and shivered.

"—or act as a simple asphyxiant. One with no early-warning system." Austin's tone suggested I should be following along.

I appreciated the vote of confidence, but . . . "You lost me."

"Okay. Let's put it this way. Atmospheric air—the air we breathe—is a mixture of oxygen and inert nitrogen, plus small amounts of other gases and water vapor. Make sense so far?"

I was getting antsy. It had been a long day already.

Plus, after hearing Carissa ramble on about science while she'd been describing Churn PDX, I was beginning to feel like the mental midget in the crowd. Did everyone around here kick it Mr. Wizard style? Since when did making food require a Ph.D.?

Austin was a slacker type, but he seemed brilliant.

"If allowed into the air we breathe, liquid nitrogen expands rapidly," he explained, seemingly deciding to skip a few steps to get to the point. "One liter of liquid nitrogen becomes 24.6 cubic feet of nitrogen gas. So if it's released without adequate ventilation—say, in a small, enclosed trailer—"

My gaze shot to Carissa's Airstream. I shivered again.

"—it can displace oxygen in the air and cause suffoca-tion."

Aha. Yikes. "*How* do you know all this?"

Modestly, Austin shrugged off my question.

"If that's true," I pushed, "why would anyone use it?"

"With the proper protective gear and safety devices, it's fine. Laboratories across the country use it with no problem. Even beginner medical students use it to work with tissue samples and things."

"Yeah," someone said. "Bars use it with no problem, too."

Startled, I looked to the side. The dark-haired man I'd noticed berating the news crew earlier stood there, evidently having listened to Austin's scientific spiel without comment.

Until now. "Which is where I suggest we go," the newcomer suggested with a compassionate look. "The drinks are on me. Let's all hash this over in private at Muddle + Spade."

His emphasis on "in private" couldn't be missed. Neither could his distinctive cadence (an Eastern European flatness to his vowels) or his overall aura of charisma. Just being around him made me feel a little better somehow. I'd been too busy reacting to the events of the day to notice before (and I was slightly appalled to be noticing now), but he was *gorgeous*.

You know, in a "sexy starving artist" kind of way. If he was a guitarist in an indie band that played at Cartorama, or a sculptor who showed his pieces at a nearby gallery, I wouldn't have been surprised. He had that bedraggled-but-sensitive look about him. Tall, broad-shouldered, and sinewy. Dressed in a deep-V-necked T-shirt, jeans rolled up at the hems, and vintage oxfords. A few tattoos, some silvery chains in his chest hair, and icy blue eyes. Not to mention, cheekbones to die for.

Whoops. Scratch that. "To die for" is a terrible idiom. Austin wasn't impressed. Not by the new guy's modelesque good looks or by his magnetism. My new friend kept talking.

"The first signs that displacement is happening are dizziness, headaches, fatigue, and nausea," Austin lectured on.

He went on to describe something called the Leidenfrost effect, but I was busy immediately experiencing all of the symptoms he'd mentioned—just as I had, I remembered, when I'd stepped into Carissa's trailer. I felt unsteady and lost, sorry I hadn't done more to help. Probably, Austin did, too. It was clear that he dealt with trauma by taking refuge in facts. We had that in common. I hadn't been able to stop cataloguing Cartorama and its residents since hearing Carissa's scream.

My gaze wandered back to Deep V-Neck. Held.

He'd somehow persuaded the local TV-news crew to leave earlier than they otherwise would have, I recalled. He'd started out enraged—as evidenced by his waving arms and forbidding expression—but by the end of his encounter with the reporters, everyone had been on friendly terms. Now I understood why.

As far as protectors went, Cartorama could have done worse. It was sweet that he'd come charging to the pod's rescue, hoping to spare Cartorama and its vendors further upset.

". . . but for some people, the first sign of trouble is unconsciousness." Austin broke into my reverie. "That's all. Death isn't necessarily painful or traumatic. It just *is*."

This whole conversation was macabre. I couldn't help being interested, though. I wanted answers. Austin seemed to have them.

"Not 'painful or traumatic'? Speak for yourself, dude," someone blurted from nearby. "I'm plenty traumatized."

It was the blond woman in the piglet T-shirt. She was back.

So was the sultry brunette in the tight vintage dress. While I'd been listening to Austin's explanation, they'd both appeared out of nowhere. I wondered where they'd gone. And why.

"As far as Declan knew, he just fell asleep." Austin shrugged, seeming heartened by that fact. I wanted to be, too. But I wasn't. "In fact, death by critical hypoxia is sometimes recommended as a more humane means of capital punishment. When arterial oxygen saturation falls below sixty percent, it—"

"Dude!" The blond piglet–T-shirt girl looked aghast. "Shut up!"

"That's enough science for now." Deep V-Neck put his hand on Austin's shoulder, steadying him—and silencing him, too. He gave a reassuring glance to the gathering vendors. By now, I saw, the area's residents had left, doubtless to get on with their days, leaving only the Cartorama sellers. Jokingly, he jostled Austin's shoulder before letting go. "And here we all thought you were only interested in finding obscure candy bars and becoming head goblin in that MMORPG you play, Austin."

I knew what "obscure candy bars" were (delicious) and what "MMORPG" were (massively multiplayer online role-playing games—think Dungeons & Dragons played as a video game in an online virtual world: nirvana for nerds), but I didn't know why Deep V-Neck was (subtly) making fun of Austin for playing them.

Maybe it was just the handiest means of distraction— a way to help the T-shirt woman in the same way he'd protected Cartorama and its vendors. Because he *had* to want to dissect what had gone on this morning, just the way I did.

Searching for understanding was human nature. It was why we were all still there, talking about what had happened to Declan Murphy. Searching for meaning in what felt like catastrophe.

I faced him, momentarily distracted from his dreaminess by my own curiosity—and my (inexplicable) urge to defend Austin.

"Almost seven million people play World of Warcraft," I pointed out with a private hat tip to my friend Eduardo in Sao Paulo. He'd used the voice-acted version of the *Mists of Pandaria* expansion to teach me Portuguese. Let's just say I had a pretty unusual grasp of the language at this point. (*Obrigado,* Eduardo!) "There's nothing wrong with MMORPGs."

Beside me, Austin stood straighter. Good. All the same . . .

"Don't you want to find out what happened?" I asked.

"Yeah, don't you want to know?" Austin prodded, defensively squaring his shoulders in a way that reminded me how young he seemed, despite his grasp of science. "Plus, I'm a goblin engineer, Berk. I deal with explosives, not leadership."

I didn't think the most important task here was reaching an understanding of Austin's MMORPG role, but Berk only smiled.

"You're right. Sorry, Austin." He turned to me. "That reminds me that you haven't met any of the rest of us."

He took it upon himself to perform the introductions. I couldn't help noticing how smoothly and likably he did so—starting with himself. He put his hand on his chest and bowed.

Yes, it was a little cheesy. But it worked. You had to be there to understand the effect that an Old World/ New World man—especially one with a searching smile— could have on a person.

"I'm Tomasz Berk." He clasped my hand. "You're Hayden?"

"Hayden Mundy Moore." I omitted my usual *chocolate whisperer* label. It wasn't relevant here. "Didn't I hear you say something about drinks?"

"You did." His smile broadened, but his eyes stayed sad. "I guess you're one of us now, Hayden. Why don't you come on over to my place?"

I followed his head tilt toward a nearby building, right alongside everyone else. And that's how I became an honorary member of the Cartorama cart pod, melded into the family like a Venezuelan dark chocolate into a bitter soufflé of trauma, confusion, and the vagaries of a technology I didn't understand.

I did know one thing for sure, though. After today, it was going to be a very long time before I wanted another ice cream.

Three

If you've worked in the food service industry, then I don't need to tell you that the staff quickly tend to become a family. If you *haven't* slung hash or waited tables, picture the most mismatched, dysfunctional, fiercely loyal crowd of egomaniacs and malcontents you can imagine, then add fire and sharp knives.

Voilà! That's a restaurant kitchen, patisserie, or confectioner for you. Tempers flare. Egos run amok. Differences of opinion become bitter rivalries, stoked by day-to-day demands and the need to make money in a low-margin, high-risk business.

At Cartorama, I learned that afternoon while sampling chocolate porter at Muddle + Spade, things were much the same.

There were still temperamental head chefs, sulky servers, demanding line cooks, and grumbling cleanup crews at the cart pod—but they all tended to be the same person, filling each of those roles at once. Each food cart was a microcosm of a typical restaurant, usually with a stressed-out entrepreneur at its helm. There was Austin

Martin and The Chocolate Bar. Carissa and Churn PDX.
Tomasz Berk and his bar adjacent to Cartorama.

Muddle + Spade was the epitome of a Bridgetown
watering hole. Decked out in modern-meets-steampunk
style (with a dash of lumberjack thrown in), it occupied a
renovated warehouse next door to Cartorama. There were
antlers on the walls, antique penny farthings in the rafters,
and ironwork on the bar. Scraped maple flooring lay
underfoot. Mullioned windows were draped with white
Christmas lights, but for now we enjoyed the afternoon
sunshine. It was cozy, quirky, and edgy, all at the same
time.

True to his word, Tomasz served us all drinks on the
house. That's how I came to be savoring my creamy
chocolate porter at lunchtime without a single qualm.
(Hey, it had been a hard morning.)

As the handwritten A-stand outside had boasted,
Tomasz's bar featured artisanal cocktails made with
muddled herbs, homemade simple syrups, tangy vinegar-
based shrubs, and cacao essences (along with food, of
course). My needs were simple. I needed to steady my
nerves. I needed to know if Carissa was okay (or at least
as okay as she could be, given the circumstances). I
needed to know who else was part of the Cartorama
family.

They were all my suspects, I decided as I gripped my
condensation-beaded bar glass, giving everyone a wary
eye. I had to be on my guard. Now more than ever (after
Maison Lemaître), I understood that sometimes appearances could be deceiving.

Take the dishy temptress in the body-hugging dress,
for instance, I thought as I watched her chat with Austin.
She *seemed* to be a burlesque performer transported from

the fifties to present-day Muddle + Spade—one who'd stopped downtown for some tattoos on the way. But, in fact, she was *probably* a murderous, scheming . . .

. . . friend of Declan's, who was devastated to have lost him, I relented as I watched her blow her nose into a tissue. Her mascara ran. Her scarlet lipstick was smudged. She looked utterly lost and alone, and I just couldn't remain suspicious of her. The contrast between her almost costumey appearance and her genuine air of distress was too jarring. I felt sorry for her, instead.

Hearing her husky voice rise over the bar's murmur, I leaned closer, hoping to break into the conversation. Tomasz had introduced her to me as Lauren Greene— proprietress of Sweet Seductions, a food cart featuring treats with risqué names and an over-the-top, indulgent slant—but we hadn't spoken at length.

Looking at her now, I didn't doubt Lauren knew how to stir up a craving—for chocolate *or* herself. Her knee-length dress showcased plenty of cleavage but left the rest of her assets to the imagination. I would have been envious of her bodacious look, but the fact is, that kind of over-the-top femininity is so far outside my wheelhouse that I could only marvel at it.

Would I have *liked* to make men drool over me the way Austin currently was salivating over Lauren? Sure. Some of the time. But I have my own charms. Plus (usually) a cache of chocolate samples from grateful clients to sweeten my allure. I do okay.

Sniffling, Lauren wadded up her tissue. She nodded blankly. Beside her, Austin patted her hand in a comforting fashion.

At that, Lauren seemed to notice him for the first time. She stared at his hand on hers, then recoiled violently.

"No. I can't do this." She slid off her bar stool and left.

I watched her make her way across the bar, wiggling past other vendors as they quaffed cocktails and craft beers. Her walk was a spectacle, equal parts promise and tease. Men stared, including Tomasz. So did the girl in the piglet T-shirt.

Janel White, I reminded myself. That was her name.

She wasn't one of the Cartorama vendors. Unlike the other people at Muddle + Spade, Janel hadn't sold smoked salt pretzel bark or gianduia-stuffed beignets at one of the pod's carts. She was (as I understood it) strictly a customer—and an outsider?

I could relate, actually. Now that the immediate crisis was past (and the cocktails had begun flowing in earnest), everyone had assembled into what appeared to be their usual cliques. Chocolate candy people gathered near the bar's vintage coin-operated video games. Chocolate bakers held court near the pool tables. Chocolate "artisans" (who created fusion goods combining chocolate with bacon, chiles, herbs, or other ingredients) perched at tables near Muddle + Spade's kitchens, where they could glimpse what came from the ovens and critique it.

I didn't see how anyone could find fault with the spread Tomasz had provided. There were grilled brioche sandwiches filled with melted chocolate and sea salt (surgically quartered for easy noshing), delectable cocoa crumb tartlets with sweet mascarpone filling and marion-berry jam (all locally sourced), and a plate offering cinnamon-spiked churros with chocolate and caramelized cajeta dipping sauce (house made, naturally).

The only thing there *wasn't* was any camaraderie being extended to Janel White. Maybe the foodies resented her T-shirt? Portland's culinary scene was a meat-centric one, but that didn't mean there wasn't plenty of room for veggie lovers who eschewed everything pork-filled, beef-stuffed, and/or garnished with a duck's, quail's, or chicken's egg. Why was she alone?

The newfound crime-solving side of me piped up to suggest that Janel was being shunned because she was a *murderer.* I told my suspicions to take a hike and went to talk with her, instead.

I started with my never-fail opener.

"Hi! Do you mind if I sit here?"

(I never said it was fancy. Just effective.)

Looking frazzled, Janel frowned more intensely at her laptop. Surrounding it were books and notebooks, scattered pens, and an open backpack. On the laptop itself was one of those peel-and-stick decorative "skins" depicting a burst of red and pink hearts and fireworks. Janel White was a romantic, then.

My mission to make her feel included ought to be easy.

"I don't really know anybody here," I persisted with a winning smile. "It's getting kind of awkward, to be honest."

She finally looked up. "Why don't you leave, then?"

So much for friendliness. "I want to pay my respects."

"You didn't even know Declan." Upon saying his name, Janel choked up. Her eyes swam with tears. She rapidly blinked them back, then cleared her throat. Her gaze wandered to the people clumped at the bar. "But then nobody here did. Not really."

At the oddly smug half smile she gave, I was hooked. Janel White was a little weird, but that didn't mean she was wrong.

It was possible Janel knew something no one else did.

I took a swig of my second porter. (But who's counting

on a day like today?) "What do you mean, 'nobody here' knew Declan?"

Janel shook her head. "It doesn't matter anymore."

"Sure, it does. Declan matters to everyone here."

Her frown returned. Deepened. "Not to you."

She had a point. Carissa's fiancé and I hadn't even met. But now that Janel was being so resistant, I was digging in my heels. I don't excel at my chocolate-consulting business for nothing. My work demands talent, intuition, and a thick skin for criticism. Plus persistence. Lots and lots of persistence.

I can be tenacious, is what I'm saying.

"Unless you're *another* one." Janel groaned, then rolled her eyes. Distractedly, she looked past me. "Does Carissa know? I know she knew about Lauren, no matter what she said, but—"

Now I was really mystified. "Know what?"

"That you were hooking up with Declan too." Candidly, Janel eyed me up and down. The endeavor seemed to cheer her up. "We should come up with a name, a logo, and a theme song."

I didn't follow. "A theme song?"

"For our club." Janel frowned. "Declan's Dates?" She made a face. "No, that sounds like fruit. Maybe Declan's Dozen?"

Was she saying there were a *dozen* women who'd slept with Carissa's dearly departed fiancé? "Declan was getting married."

Janel shrugged. "Maybe he was. Maybe he wasn't."

"Carissa's engagement party weekend says he was."

"I'll admit, he seemed pretty close to going through with it," Janel grudgingly allowed. She sipped her rhubarb shrub. "The thing is, Declan had a hard time saying no to people."

"Unlike you." I slid into the booth and sat opposite her without waiting for permission. Her reaction to my intrusion was a knowing glance at my chocolate porter as I took another drink. That's it. I was in. "How did *you* know him so well?"

She gave me a look that said *three guesses*. I only needed one. But I didn't believe it. *Janel had slept with Declan?*

If the telltale glimmer in her eyes could be believed, *yes*.

Janel wasn't unattractive, per se. I believe there's beauty in everyone. (Thank God, Danny wasn't there to hear me think that—he'd have died laughing over my supposed naïveté.) But it was true. Janel had wavy blond hair in a loose bob. Intelligent blue eyes. Even features and a slightly turned-up nose. All the requisite curves, packaged in a slightly stout, doughty form.

To the right man, Janel would have been perfectly appealing. But to Declan Murphy? Who supposedly loved picture-perfect Carissa to distraction? I somehow thought he'd be immune.

Not that I didn't get it. I was starting to like Janel myself. She was spunky. After being pals with Danny for so long, I have a soft spot for anyone who's outspoken. I have to.

Janel chuckled—probably at my incredulous expression.

"Declan was kind of a slut," she told me. "It's better you find out now, believe me. I learned the hard way. At first, he was so sweet. So attentive. He liked all the same things I did. Anime, farmers markets, vegan ice cream, Wes Anderson movies—even cycling. We biked all the way up Mount Tabor once."

No wonder she was distraught over losing him. They'd really bonded. I nodded, commiserating. "Then he met Carissa?"

"Then he realized I *couldn't* teach him anything about chocolate." She glanced at her stack of notebooks. "That was my bad, though. Declan asked me what I was working on so hard all the time. I told him chocolate, because I knew he was into it."

I shook my head. "You can't learn about chocolate from a book." With cacao, it's all about being there. Experiencing the rich, chocolaty flavor. The lush, complex aromas. The soft, sensual mouthfeel as the chocolate melts in your mouth precisely at body temperature. There's nothing like it. Nothing better.

"You know that. I know that. Declan? Not so bright. He was always looking for a shortcut. I wasn't the only one he hit up for help. At one time or another, he cozied up to everybody."

"For chocolate help?" That was forgivable. Technically, everyone was a beginner once. But most beginners didn't launch their own chocolate-themed culinary tours, the way Declan had apparently been about to do with Chocolate After Dark.

I hoped I hadn't signed on to help launch a substandard tour. Word travels fast in the culinary world—in the chocolate world. I didn't want to dent my reputation. I relied on it.

Janel nodded. "Yeah. Or for a fast Humpty Dumpty in one of the carts. Those things really shake if you get after it."

I laughed. I couldn't help it. Then I reconsidered the fact that she was describing sex in a place where food prep happened.

"Ew." I grimaced. "Tell me that never happened."

"It's not even the grossest thing that ever happened." Janel leaned nearer. I think she liked me, too. "Not long after Declan dumped me, I saw him chowing down on a double burger with porkstrami and dirty fries at Lardo, on the west side." Her grimace matched mine. "Have you heard of it? They put 'pork scraps' on those fries, dude. It's a major Meatpocalypse."

I nodded at her piglet T-shirt. I assumed it meant Janel was vegan or vegetarian. "That must have been a deal breaker."

She only looked away, shuddering at the memory. "I'll tell you one thing—Declan was way more into that porkfest than he ever was into me. That's not a euphemism, either."

I laughed again. Janel was blunt, busty, and bawdy. Danny would have loved her. I almost wished he were there with me.

Almost, but not quite. Danny would have said suspecting someone as straightforward as Janel was a waste of time. I didn't want to hear it. I needed a security blanket, especially after what I'd been through in San Francisco. Conducting a minor investigation—as I was doing by talking with Janel—was it.

If you think I was overreacting, well . . . maybe you're right. But you weren't there when Adrienne Dowling died. I was.

I still couldn't quit seeing Declan Murphy's yellow, frost-tinged face. It haunted me. I wanted to know more about him.

"If that's true"—*and Declan wanted bacon more than he wanted you*—"then maybe being 'dumped' by Declan was the best thing that ever happened to you." I raised my chocolate porter in a toast. "Good for you for rallying. That's not always easy."

Janel's expression turned sardonic. "It's easier when the guy you're into turns out *not* to be who you thought he was."

"Better to know sooner than later, though, right?" I have my share of exes. We're on friendly terms, but I've never had to deal with one of them being dead. I sobered. "I'm sorry, Janel. I don't mean to be flip. Sometimes I go glib under pressure."

"Me too." She clinked glasses with me, then drank.

I guessed we were all good. So . . . "It probably wouldn't have lasted between you and Declan, anyway," I surmised with a nod at her telling T-shirt. "Him with the Meatpocalypse, you at the PETA rally. . . ." I paused, searching for an appropriate analogy.

But Janel was having none of it. "There's more to veganism than PETA, dude. It's about avoiding suffering, not ending fun." As evidence, she lifted her (animal-free) rhubarb shrub. *Most liquor was indeed vegan,* I realized, *however accidentally.* More importantly, so was chocolate. Especially dark chocolate.

I felt a sudden craving to do something nice for the animal kingdom—such as snack on a scrumptious peppermint truffle.

"Okay, point made," I said. "You must be a real rebel."

Janel cocked her head at me, looking puzzled.

"Your Midwestern accent," I clarified. "Wisconsin?"

"The land of cheese," she confirmed with a laugh. "A lot of Portlanders are transplants to the area. My cheesehead parents still think not scarfing dairy is responsible for stunting my growth." She caught my glance at her small stature and shook her head. "My mom is five-two, at most. My dad, five-eight. My short-but-deadly ways are all natural, dude. Believe me."

"And Declan? Where was he from?" I asked casually, fishing for more. "Was he a 'transplant,' too?"

Janel wasn't biting. "You were never with him, were you?" She studied me. "Why all the questions?"

I'm concerned there might be a killer on the loose. Again.

No. That only made me sound paranoid, however true it was.

"Carissa is one of my oldest friends," I said instead. Honestly. "I'm curious about the man she was going to marry."

I stumbled over the sentence, remembering only too late that the wedding was now off. After Declan's tragic death, there wouldn't be any engagement party weekend. It would be canceled, starting with the gala engagement brunch that was supposed to take place—privately—at Muddle + Spade tomorrow morning.

Janel seemed taken aback. "Carissa didn't fill you in on Declan? I'm surprised she didn't tell you everything about him, right down to his preferred underwear style and size."

I raised my eyebrows. Questioningly.

Janel played along. "Boxer briefs. Medium."

I wasn't surprised she remembered. She seemed smart.

Shouldn't she have been more rancorous about her breakup with Declan, though? It was obvious she still had feelings for him. Her tears when she'd first said his name told me so.

"Carissa told me about Declan." *But online isn't real life, and emails aren't heart-to-heart chats.* "But I was looking forward to meeting him in person." I explained to Janel about my past with Carissa and our long-distance friendship. "I was looking forward to spending time with Carissa in person, too."

I fell silent, realizing that might never happen now. At least not for a while. Carissa would doubtless be too upset to reminisce with me about our university days.

"That's handy," Janel observed. "You being here just when Declan could use some advice from a veteran chocolate expert."

To launch Chocolate After Dark, I realized, catching her drift. As a transplant to the area, Janel was probably more cynical than the average earnest Oregonian. But I disagreed.

"I wasn't here for that. This was strictly a fun weekend for me. I'm here to support Carissa, not consult with anyone."

"Hmm." Janel seemed unconvinced. "Too bad for Declan."

"You're not really suggesting that Carissa contacted me just to line up a free consultation for Declan, are you?"

I would have done Carissa that favor if she'd asked.

I figured there was no point beating around the bush with Janel. She and Danny weren't the only ones who could be forthright. I could be, too, given the right circumstances.

"Maybe. Did you know that you're the *only* one of Carissa's friends from college to be invited this weekend?" Janel studied me. "Don't you think that's weird? No childhood friends, no work colleagues—aside from us Cartoramians, of course—no cousins, no sorority sisters . . . No one else from Carissa's past was invited."

"Well, she and Declan *did* get engaged in a hurry. They had a whirlwind romance." I had to defend Carissa. I'm loyal to a fault. Just ask Danny. Or his former parole officer. Frankly, I wouldn't have invited Carissa's daffy sorority sisters, either. "Maybe Carissa didn't have time to organize anything bigger."

Janel disagreed. "Carissa had time for everything that really mattered to her. Some of the time, it was Declan."

Some of the time? I silently repeated. Her resentful tone could not be missed.

On a ten-second delay, the obvious answer hit me.

"You weren't invited, either, were you?" I asked Janel in a gentle voice. I didn't want to hurt her. All I wanted was to find the truth. "That's why you're over here, all on your own."

I was right about her. She was an outsider.

Janel raised her chin. "I'm 'over here' because I'm busy." She nodded at her laptop, books, and notebooks. "I have a lot to do, and not nearly enough time to do it all in. Especially now—"

"You're 'over here' because you spent the night here last night, and you know it," Tomasz interrupted, showing up with another chocolate porter for me and an expertly made rhubarb shrub for Janel. "This place is practically your second home."

He gave us both a genial smile, then slid into the booth beside me. At his arrival, Janel brightened. I guess I wasn't the only one who found him attractive. But only one of us had actually *spent the night here last night, and you know it.*

I was too busy boggling over Tomasz's casual statement to register anything else at first. Were he and Janel a twosome? Muddle + Spade was his place. If Janel had stayed at the bar last night, that definitely suggested they were an item.

And Janel had had the nerve to call Declan a "slut" a

few minutes ago. It looked as though she got around herself.

A second later, Tomasz's warmth touched me. So did his left thigh. My thoughts scattered like chocolate jimmies on an ice-cream sundae. Maybe I was tipsy, but I knew what had to be done.

Reluctantly but responsibly, I slid away, moving a fraction closer to the wall. This was practically an improvised wake for Declan. I had to show some respect. Now wasn't the time to get all hot and bothered over a soulful bartender with perfectly groomed beard stubble and an excess of personal magnetism. No matter how much I wanted to. And I did want to. After all, *I* wasn't in mourning for Declan. I was just sad that he'd been lost so tragically. And suspiciously. I was more than ripe for distraction in the form of one Tomasz Berk. Starting now.

Have I mentioned I have a knack for procrastination?

It's possible that my ninja-level ability to stall on necessary tasks was working overtime just then. Because I was *supposed* to be getting ready to lead the Chocolate After Dark tour in a couple of days. It would have been sensible to leave Muddle + Spade and start preparing my tour guide patter. Or, given my concerns over encountering *another* potential crime scene, it might have been smart to investigate more diligently.

Say, by cornering Lauren Greene and questioning her.

Ogling Tomasz was a lot more fun, though. It was too bad he was (maybe) spoken for. I liked his shoulder-length bohemian hair. His oceanic blue eyes. And his knack for caretaking, too.

He must have noticed things were getting tense between me and Janel. So he'd whipped up some drinks and intervened.

Not that I minded. That chocolate porter was delicious.

He eyed us both with bonhomie. "What are we talking about?"

"Declan," I said loudly, to be heard over the crowd.

"You and your excellent timing," Janel wisecracked at the same time. She raised her shrub (containing fruity drinking vinegar spiked with spirits, in case you've never tried one) and nodded. "You're going to go broke spoiling us all, Berk."

Aha. No wonder Tomasz was well-liked in the neighborhood, if today's largesse was any indication of the kind of man he was. Everyone liked the guy who picked up the tab. I'd leaned on that shortcut myself a time or two, especially in the early days of my inheritance. I couldn't fault Tomasz for treating us.

Or Janel for appreciating the gesture. I didn't think she was wearing patched-up jeans with her piglet T-shirt as a fashion statement. I thought she was too thrifty to give up clothing that still (technically) functioned. I've been there.

Not recently, but still. I understood her position.

However (and more interestingly), Janel's use of that man-to-man nickname (Berk, the same as Austin had used) didn't sound romantic to me. It didn't sound like a pet name lovers would use, for instance. I felt more uncertain about them than ever. Seeing Tomasz and Janel together didn't enlighten me, either.

Her up-front demeanor didn't change. She didn't go all flirty and giggly, the way some women did when a man entered the picture. But maybe Janel was just too down-to-earth for that?

Tomasz nudged his knee almost imperceptibly closer to mine. That move was no accident. Neither was the way his gaze touched me. "It feels good to be generous," he said with a shrug. "I like treating everyone. Here at Cartorama, we're a family."

I scooted another inch farther away and distracted myself by thinking that it was a good thing Travis wasn't there. He would have pointed out to Tomasz that the members of a self-made "family" didn't qualify as tax-deductible dependents.

Sometimes my financial advisor can be a little *too* literal. Travis is lovable, anyway, though. He's always got my back.

Especially if I need advice on derivative instruments.

"Have you always been close at Cartorama?" I asked, tuning back into the conversation with another tasty sip of porter.

"Sure. For the most part. We were almost split up last year, though," Tomasz confided, pulling a sad face. "A group of real-estate developers tried to buy out the property that all our food carts are parked on. They wanted to build one of those huge apartment complexes on our corner." He aimed a grateful smile at Janel. "Janel led the effort to save us all."

She actually blushed. I couldn't believe it. She got tongue-tied, too. "Well, maybe. I mean, okay, kind of," Janel stammered. "I guess. But I couldn't let our stupid landlord sell out and take away my only means to see Declan, could I?"

I swear, my eyebrows reached my hairline. Janel noticed.

"Settle down, dude. He's on my mind today. *Obviously,* I meant my only means to get chocolate stuff at Cartorama."

She gave a derisive snort, then gulped down some shrub.

I examined her a minute, then let it go. If she was

obsessed with her ex-boyfriend, she wouldn't be the only one. Oftentimes people have trouble letting go of lost relationships.

I wasn't immune myself. I'd hung onto Carissa all these years, hadn't I?

I wondered how she was doing. If her parents were with her.

But we'd been apart for too long for me to be the one to lead the charge to her doorstep with a wreath of flowers and a sympathetic shoulder to cry on. We weren't that close anymore.

"How did you stop the developers?" I asked instead.

"Petitions. Protests. Media pressure." Tomasz ticked off those tactics on his fingertips—his evocative, skilled-looking fingertips. "The usual. Oregonians have a history of battling unwanted developments and winning—if properly led, of course."

His affectionate glance at Janel was ambiguous at best. I still couldn't tell if they were more than friends.

"Our landlord was hard to get to—they're a consortium called Common Grounds, not really a single person we could target. The whole thing dragged on awhile," Janel told me. "We were all pretty nervous. Vendors rely on cheap rents for spaces to park their food carts. If they had to pay the full costs of running traditional restaurants, most of them wouldn't make it."

Tomasz nodded, glancing somberly between the two of us.

I was glad for them, but . . . "The land must be worth a lot more now than it used to be, though," I pointed out, remembering all the construction I'd seen earlier. "I can't believe your landlord didn't decide to cash in. This area is booming."

"It is," Tomasz agreed. "But in the end, Common

Grounds decided against any more negative publicity. And that was that."

I couldn't let it go. "Are you *sure* that was that?"

They both frowned at me. Quizzically.

I thumbed my chocolate porter, turning it around on the table. I wiped away the condensation on the glass. "What if . . ."

I trailed off, feeling ridiculous. Also, light-headed again.

"Yes?" Tomasz urged in a silky, sexy voice.

"Spit it out," Janel commanded. "Sheesh. If you're this tentative when 'chocolate whispering,' I don't know how you ever get anything done. Is your reputation all smoke and mirrors?"

That did it. I couldn't stand for having my reputation maligned. "What if Common Grounds—or the developers—*didn't* give up?" I asked. "What if one of them killed Declan? To scare all the Cartorama vendors into abandoning their leases?"

A momentary silence fell between us. Faintly, I heard the pinging of video games. People talking at the pool tables. Music from somewhere. It all seemed very far away from me.

Then Tomasz and Janel burst out laughing. Guffawing, really.

I was offended. "It's a reasonable theory! Undermine the cart pod. Dissolve it from within. Take over through fear."

Danny had told me once that the best motive for murder was greed. At the time, I'd disagreed. But now I thought I might be onto something. It all made sense. Especially if, in a limited market, Cartorama's land was worth as much as I thought it was.

Tomasz and Janel didn't agree, to say the least.

"That's it. You're cut off." Tomasz took my porter. Then he called me a cab, Janel grabbed my things, and they bundled me away to my Airbnb accommodations without even taking seriously the idea that someone could have deliberately murdered Declan.

"You are *crazy*," Janel said, firing up my indignation.

"But *cute* crazy," Tomasz added, firing up my . . . Never mind.

Maybe it was all the chocolate porter talking. Maybe it was the stressful day. Maybe it was the fact that I'd only just recently caught my first murderer. San Francisco was fresh on my mind, and so was everything that had happened there. I couldn't let go of the idea that Declan may have been killed on purpose.

Janel and Tomasz's denials only lent credence to my fears.

That's why, later, snug in my Airbnb accommodations—a cute foursquare in the rapidly gentrifying Northeast neighborhood—I picked up my cell phone. I dialed. Woozily, I waited.

A familiar, sexy voice came over the line.

"Hey, Travis!" I shouted, feeling elated to hear him. Also, admittedly tipsy. I don't usually drink much, especially on a nearly empty stomach. But after stumbling over another dead body today, sampling Tomasz's excellent craft brew had seemed like a superb idea. "I've got a problem," I told my financial advisor. "A big one. But first . . . what are you wearing right now?"

Four

When I woke up the next day, I honestly didn't know where I was. Not that that was strictly unusual for me. I travel so often and so widely that I might at any time (for instance) wake up in a capsule hotel in Singapore, a "tree house" hotel in Harads, or a penthouse in Manhattan. I have friends all over the world. Waking up to an unfamiliar ceiling is de rigueur for me.

This time, though, the experience was more unsettling than normal. Mostly because, as I blinked up at my room's white-painted crown molding and mullioned widows (I apparently hadn't even closed the curtains last night before collapsing into bed), I couldn't remember, for an instant, how I'd gotten there.

Alarmed, I sat bolt upright in bed. The motion made the room spin. My head ached, too. With a groan, I sank backward.

I felt *awful*. If this was what came of drinking chocolate porter at noon, I needed to put the kibosh on that activity, stat. It didn't seem likely that a mere three or four drinks could have created a hangover this severe, but I could barely tolerate opening my eyes to examine my surroundings again.

Warily and painfully, I did so, anyway. I glimpsed my jeans and sneakers, cast off to the gleaming hardwood floor. I saw my stand-in purse (a lame-duck substitute for my beloved—and lost—crossbody bag) on an upholstered armchair nearby. I saw my jacket draped haphazardly on the bed's footboard, half on and half off the mattress. I saw the twisted coverlet on the bed.

Clearly, I'd spent a restless night here. But before that . . .

In a flash, it all came flooding back to me. The cab ride. The drinks at Muddle + Spade. The police, the EMTs, the ghastly sight of Declan Murphy dead on the floor of Carissa's trailer.

I remembered my own gruesome theory involving the real-estate developers, who'd wanted to build on the property, and/or the landlord, who would have stood to benefit from that.

What if one of them killed Declan? I'd hypothesized to Tomasz and Janel. *To scare all the Cartorama vendors into abandoning their leases?*

They had laughed at my explanation for Declan's "accidental" death. But maybe that was *because they were in on it.* Maybe they wanted to throw me off. Maybe they'd cozied up to me yesterday to find out what I knew . . . and then silence me.

Maybe Tomasz *hadn't* innocently brought me and Janel fresh drinks. Maybe he'd *poisoned me,* the same way someone might have poisoned Declan. Maybe that's why I felt so awful.

Reeling at the possibility, I made myself crawl out from beneath the covers. Squinting at the sunlight, I stood. Dizzily, I'll admit. But when was the last time *you* confronted your own possible homicidal poisoning? It was a lot to take in.

I lurched to the armchair and grabbed my bag, intending to call Danny. He was my protection expert—my on-call bodyguard. If there was ever a time to make Danny quit putting his muscular bod on the line for Hollywood types at premieres and red-carpet events, it was now. He could leave the skeleton-style, two-way radio earpiece and designer tux at home. For this job, all he'd need were muscles, his badass former-thug instincts, and a willingness to put both of those things on the line for me.

I knew he'd do it. Danny and I went way back. He'd known me before I lucked into my inheritance, before I turned my knack for chocolate into a full-time, freelance consulting gig . . . before I nabbed my first cocoa-covered killer while ostensibly on the job. Shivering at the memory, I rooted around for my cell phone.

It was gone. Launched into a full-blown panic by its absence, I staggered toward the next room. Its serenity stood strictly at odds with my jumpy state of mind. Barefoot and clad only in yesterday's T-shirt and the men's boxers I like to sleep in (sorry if that's oversharing), I careened throughout my Airbnb lodgings, looking for my phone so I could send up an SOS.

Very quickly, I wished I'd instructed Travis *not* to go whole hog on my accommodations this time. Left to his own devices, Travis has a tendency to treat me *too* well. You'd think that as guardian of my finances and an expert in all things fiduciary, he would have leaned toward the skinflint side, right? Well, nope. You'd be wrong. Because, for whatever reason, Travis insists that I deserve the best. Exemplary views. Prime locations. Frette linens, designer amenities, and (I'm not making this up) sometimes a private butler of my very own.

Ordinarily, I can't fault Travis's insistence on pampering me. Frankly, I like that about him. Who wouldn't? But this time, in Portland, Travis's occasional yen to indulge me was too much.

My (temporary) two-and-a-half-story authentic four-square house was charming, lovingly restored, and large enough for a family (not surprisingly) of four. Its four boxy rooms per floor (hence, the name) took ages to careen through, tossing throw pillows and scrabbling through built-in Craftsman cabinets and woodwork. I couldn't find *a thing*. There wasn't even an old-fashioned landline that I could have used to summon the police—not that I wanted to see Portland's finest again with the grisly events of yesterday still so fresh in my headachy mind.

Queasy and concerned, I stopped downstairs in the kitchen—a vintage number with butcher-block countertops, nickel hardware, and original 1913 cabinets—and tried to catch my breath. The kitchen was adorable (if way too capacious for one person, just like the rest of the place). I didn't even plan to cook while I was in town. I didn't know what Travis had been thinking to arrange such comically gargantuan accommodations, but I could see why the house's original owners had been eager to rent out the place via Airbnb. They were probably making three times their mortgage payments in rental fees each month. In Portland's inflated real-estate market, cashing in was only smart.

Unfortunately, the idea of *cashing in* only sent me into another concern spiral. I recalled the conversation I'd had with Tomasz and Janel about the developers who'd attempted to take advantage of Cartorama's prime location, about the landlord who'd given up on making a fortune (far too readily, if you asked me), and about the way the pod's vendors had triumphed.

I was all in favor of community action. For picketing and protesting and exerting some well-earned media pressure. But seriously? It sounded as though Janel had circulated a few petitions to save Cartorama from development, the local newscast had aired a segment on the beleaguered pod being pressured by greedy developers, and the whole endeavor had simply collapsed.

That didn't seem likely to me. Maybe the Cartorama vendors didn't have much experience with big business, but I did. The corporate world doesn't lay down for a bunch of hippies with protest signs and handwoven hemp beanies. There's too much at stake for that. I doubted any real-estate development company worth its salt would have gone after Cartorama's land without a solid strategy— and a couple of contingency plans, too.

If one of those contingency plans had involved *killing* one of Cartorama's vendors and scaring everyone else into leaving . . .

Well, if it had, then I'd stumbled upon it a little too publicly last night. Which was why Tomasz and/or Janel had decided to dose me with whatever poisonous substance had me swerving, sweating, and seeing double just then. I grabbed the countertop and waited for the next wave of nausea to subside.

That's when, blearily, I glimpsed my cell phone. Its screen winked at me from amid the folds of a plush cable-knit throw, lying on my (short-term) house's living-room sofa. I was saved.

I reeled toward it while the room continued rotating. Chills raised goose bumps on my arms and legs. My mouth tasted swampy, my tongue cottony, my teeth fuzzy. *Yuck.* It was just like a murderer to target my taste buds. What if this attempt on my life destroyed my ability to discern a Venezuelan single-varietal chocolate from a

Tanzanian Grand Cru blend? I'd be out of a job, out of free chocolates, out of my mind with boredom.

Of course I'd be *dead,* so I probably wouldn't mind.

But if I somehow survived, would my vaunted palate come through unscathed? What if it didn't? What would I do for fun, for treats, for a much-needed sense of mastery in my life?

What would I do for a funeral? I didn't even know where my own memorial should be held, I realized as I picked up my cell phone in my clumsy hands. I peered at its screen, trying to decide if I'd rather be remembered at a beachside ash scattering or a full-out burial at sea, if I'd prefer to be interred in the poppy fields of Normandy or laid to rest in the good ole USA.

I didn't really have a home, I remembered as my head went on pounding too hard for me to read my phone's screen properly. I'd been traveling for as long as I could remember—first with my parents, then on my own. Did I belong *anywhere*? Maybe I'd missed my chance to settle down in a comfy house like this one, with someone special by my side and a cocker spaniel at my feet.

The thought made me hyperventilate. Or maybe that was just another symptom of my (potential) poisoning. I wasn't sure.

Have I mentioned that my mind tends to gallop in a million directions at once? At the best of times, I've got a rampant monkey mind. Now, on the verge of a nefarious "accidental" death, I couldn't help touching on every possible scenario. How eloquently Travis would eulogize me. How sadly Danny would break down over my grave. How my family would mourn me, and how . . .

Wait a minute. Was that *movement* outside my living-room window?

Startled out of my morbid daydreams, I went still. If someone was out there, it had to be Tomasz or Janel, come to find out if I'd succumbed to whatever they'd dosed me with.

Well, if they weren't merely murderers but *gloating* murderers, they were going to be disappointed. Because there was nothing like a genuine emergency, I learned, to jolt a person out of an imaginary disaster. With someone seemingly creeping right outside my front door, I found the strength to fight back.

I dropped my phone on the sofa's throw again and picked up a poker from the fireplace instead. Hefting it in my trembling hand, I crept toward the curtained window to have a better look.

Almost there, I heard the *clunk* of footsteps on the front porch. I froze again, listening hard. I tried to picture the front of the house, hoping to pinpoint the intruder's position.

All that came to mind were muzzy memories of treacherously steep stairs leading to a wide porch—and a solid door with a stubbornly uncooperative dead bolt. I grumbled to myself at the memory of it. Yesterday my key hadn't worked to unlock it.

Although Tomasz had had no trouble opening the door and ushering me inside beneath my foursquare's hipped roof and center dormer, I recalled. So maybe the dead bolt's balkiness owed more to (tipsy) operator error than inherent faultiness.

Humph. If I *wasn't* fatally dosed with some lethal poison, then I *really* had to watch it with the porter in the future.

Another scrape of footsteps jerked me straight back to the present. Very cautiously, I leaned sideways. Through the window, I glimpsed someone standing on my porch. I couldn't see who it was. From my vantage point, all I could make out was a sliver of a be-jeaned form, a slice of red-and-black checked coat, and a hint of Fair Isle knitwear. Maybe a beanie? I wasn't sure.

What were the chances—honestly—that a murderous intruder would wear a cap that could have been knit by his or her grammy?

I strode to the front door and wrenched it open.

Austin Martin stood on my house's welcome mat. Or, more accurately, he jumped sky-high on my house's welcome mat.

"Urgh!" he burbled. "Hayden! Hey! I was just about to knock. You scared me."

I'd scared *him*? That was funny. But Austin's pale round face (at least what I could see above his scruffy facial hair) and jittery laugh confirmed it. My bravado vanished.

My headache, unfortunately, didn't.

Maybe this was a devious, slow-acting poison? Given the way I felt just then, I would have believed it. I swear I could feel my eyeballs shriveling in my skull. I was unnaturally conscious of my roiling intestines, too. I had *definitely* been poisoned yesterday. There was no other explanation for the way I felt.

Suffused with relief to see another (harmless) human being, I gave him a cheery "Austin! Hi!" It came out as a croak.

He widened his eyes. "You, uh . . ." He pointed, backing up a step. He gazed fixedly at my doorbell. "You're busy," Austin finally blurted. "I'll come back later. Sorry to bug you."

He was already scampering down the steps, trailing wool fibers and the scent of one of those noxious after-shaves (the ones with names like BOLT! and CHISELED!), before I wised up.

The chilly springtime breeze helped with that. Because a draft suddenly ruffled the T-shirt and boxers I'd slept in, making me remember that I was nowhere near decent for company.

But I *was* interested in finding out if Austin thought I'd been poisoned. I might need him to call an ambulance, too.

Setting aside my makeshift fireplace-poker weapon near the Craftsman-style inglenook, I yelled to him. "Austin, wait! Don't leave. Just stay right there. I'll be back in a minute!"

Then I shut the door, picked up my cell phone again, and went to put on some appropriate clothes. My rampant bedhead hair would have to wait, though. I had to prioritize. Before opening that door again, my priority was calling Danny.

Danny didn't pick up. That was unusual.

My burly bodyguard is willing to text or email, if necessary. (Who isn't? It's not the Stone Age.) But he prefers a face-to-face conversation. Or an old-timey phone call. For him, texting comes in at a solid third place. I don't like it (I'm all about the masterful thumb work), but that's the way it is.

Danny insists there are things he can discern from voices and body language that don't carry over any other medium—things that are valuable in his line of work. Since he's not the least bit woo-woo in any other capacity, I have to believe him.

Plus, it's not as though Danny doesn't use technology. He does; he's only thirty-two. We both grew up with Super Nintendo controllers in one hand and Tamagotchis in the other. (Don't tell me you don't remember that '90s toy craze. We weren't the only ones who took those digital pets everywhere we went.)

Stymied in my SOS plan, I dithered with the phone in my hand. Leaving a voice mail would have been downright archaic (not to mention ineffective—who listens to those things?), so I shot Danny a quick text before shimmying into my jeans, throwing on a bra and a fresh T-shirt before returning to my front door to let in Austin Martin.

That was the moment I recognized the pun in his name.

Austin Martin was pretty close to *Aston Martin*! My mom would have loved knowing I'd met someone with almost the same name as one of her favorite cars. She's crazy about all things British, anyway, but she's also a big auto buff. I can't tell you how many international auto museums exist in the world. (Too many, that's how many, and I've toured them all.) That's how I know that James Bond drove an Aston Martin DB5 in *Goldfinger*.

But as a person with an unusual triple moniker myself, I wasn't about to give Austin a hard time about his name. I didn't intend to try to be "funny" about it, either. I've been on the other side of that scenario. (And no, I'm not telling you the top ten "jokes" I've heard while people were riffing on Hayden.)

Seriously, stop trying to come up with one. I can guarantee you, someone has already beaten you to it.

"Sorry about that, Austin." I stepped back and invited him inside, trying not to jostle my painful head. "I'm not at my best this morning, I'm afraid. It was a tough day yesterday."

"Yeah. That's why I'm here." He moved past me, then turned. His owlish face was solemn. I couldn't help being comforted by his sympathetic demeanor. "I heard you left

Muddle + Spade sort of abruptly yesterday. I wanted to make sure you were okay."

I'm possibly poisoned. "Don't I look okay?"

"Well . . ." Austin scrutinized me. For an insultingly long time. I might have been hypothetically dosed to death, but I didn't like thinking I *looked* bad. "You look kinda hungover, actually."

Humph. I scoured the neighborhood outside my front door with a suspicious glance. All I saw were newly leafed green trees, similar foursquare houses, sidewalks, and parked cars.

I shut the door. "You could have at least brought me a coffee, then," I cracked, still feeling shaky. "I could have—"

Used some wake-up assistance. I spied his face and stopped.

Austin looked appalled. "Coffee to go? No way. I wouldn't do that to you." He shook his head. "It would be awful. I mean, assuming you wanted a pour over, brewed with the water at two hundred seven degrees Fahrenheit, you'd still get subpar results once wetting, dissolution, and diffusion took place. That's for a medium to light roast, too. With a dark roast coming in at ten degrees cooler, you're talking about . . ." He caught *my* expression and weakly trailed off. ". . . a major loss of flavor after transport had taken place."

I smiled. "Sorry. I forgot I was in a serious coffee town." To Portlanders, java was a beverage, a hobby, a way of life. It made sense, given the drizzle. "Anyway, what I've got feels *worse* than a hangover," I confided. "I think I might have been—" *Poisoned.* I stopped. "Hey, how did you know where to find me?"

I certainly hadn't given Austin my address yesterday.

As a woman traveling alone, I tended to be cautious with that intel.

"Your address was on Cartorama's group page. Online." Austin described the social-networking site all the vendors used to keep in touch and arrange special events, something started by Janel for the Save Cartorama movement. "Carissa told us you don't drive much. We thought we might need to take turns picking you up and dropping you off, so—" He broke off, belatedly catching sight of my face. "Don't worry. It's private."

I didn't feel reassured. *Everyone* at Cartorama had access to my temporary local address? "That needs to come down."

"I'll ask Janel to do it. She's the one who maintains the site for us, along with Cartorama's Instagram, Facebook page, and Twitter feed." Austin gestured to the sofa. "Maybe you should chill for a sec. You look a little unsteady."

He gently helped me to the sofa, then tucked me onto the cushions with the cable-knit throw, generously if not adroitly. I couldn't help thinking that of all the Cartorama vendors who might have come to check up on me today, Austin was my favorite.

Danny would have said I was being gullible. I knew I wasn't. I decided to try out a quasi interrogation, to be sure.

But first . . . "You look a little unsteady yourself, Austin." I studied his beanie-wearing self with concern. "Are you okay?"

His face twisted. I thought he might be about to cry.

I hoped not. I wanted to maintain some distance from him and the others at Cartorama. If I was going to investigate things—and I increasingly thought I might be, since I appeared to have been targeted, too—I had to be impartial. I couldn't be misled by Austin's teddy bear demeanor and red-rimmed eyes.

"I just spent the morning notifying everyone about Declan, that's all." Austin's voice was hoarse with emotion. "I've got to say, it was one of the hardest things I've ever done."

Distractedly, he lowered himself onto the sofa beside me, then stared at the unlit fireplace, probably looking for a diversion from his gloomy feelings. He let his gaze travel along my armchairs, then meander to the kitchen and stairway.

Danny would have said he was casing the place. Maybe for an attack later. I scoffed inwardly and gave Austin a pat on the knee. "I'm sorry. At least you got through it, right?"

He sniffled and nodded, making his beanie shake.

"Shouldn't Carissa have done that, though?" I didn't want to be insensitive, but I couldn't help wondering about it. "I mean, Declan's family was going to be her family, too. It would only make sense for her to have made those phone calls."

Poor Carissa. What awful calls they'd have been, too.

"Oh, they weren't phone calls. They were posts. On a different private message board. A couple of texts, too."

Okay, me getting an Evite for this weekend was one thing. Austin notifying Declan's next of kin via kilobyte was something else again. "You texted Declan's family about his death?"

"No." Austin scoffed. He smiled, shaking his head. "I told his gamer group. Well, *my* gamer group. Declan doesn't play much anymore. But everyone really liked him. They were pretty upset."

I was still confused. "I can imagine."

"That's how I met Declan. We were both big into online gaming." Austin reminisced about the various games they'd played. "Declan came to town for Comic Con Portland last year. We had a real-world meetup with some of the other players. I took everyone over to Cartorama, Declan met Carissa, and . . ."

Austin trailed off, his expression turning distant— and bitter, too. I was reminded of his guilty look from yesterday.

I'd never met anyone as outwardly guileless as Austin before, though. I didn't think he could keep a secret for long.

"And?" I prompted, watching him for clues.

He blinked. "And the rest was history. Declan moved to Portland, started seeing Carissa, and started making chocolate."

"Making chocolate? I thought Declan's thing was the tour."

"Chocolate After Dark? Yeah. It is now," Austin confirmed, "but first he tried the whole bean-to-bar routine. He lucked into a big hit with his first candy bar—kind of a bacon-y take on a Snickers. Lots of local places stocked it. He made a bunch of connections. He was a big-time wunderkind for a while there."

That explained how Declan knew enough about the area and its chocolatiers to launch a culinary tour of his own.

"How did he go from bacon-y boy wonder to tour guide?"

"He couldn't cut it as a chocolatier. Even Carissa had Declan whipped when it came to the science of it all."

I couldn't miss Austin's mildly dismissive tone. I'd be lying if I said I wasn't a little gratified to have my own skepticism of my friend's newfound scientific expertise confirmed. Especially by someone like Austin, who would know.

"But Carissa developed all the equipment necessary to

freeze her ice cream at Churn PDX herself," I protested with an inner bat of my eyelashes. I don't like playing dumb, but sometimes it's useful. "Wouldn't that take a lot of brainpower?"

"Technically, yes," Austin said. "But the rumor going around Cartorama is that Declan designed that equipment for her."

"Really?" I breathed, gawking at him. "*Declan* did it?"

Carissa would have flipped her lid to hear Austin say so.

It would explain a lot, though—the disconnect between the (self-admitted) airhead I'd known at university and the smarty-pants I'd hugged hello just twenty-four hours ago, for one thing. But it would also make it less likely that Declan would make a mistake while refilling Carissa's liquid nitrogen tanks yesterday, which was the current explanation for why he'd been in her trailer. If he'd designed the valves and ventilation, he would have known how to use all of them safely, wouldn't he?

"I'm pretty sure *Declan* started the rumor," Austin added.

"Oh." I frowned. "Wow. Carissa would have *hated* that."

"Yeah. Declan could be kind of a dick to her sometimes."

"That doesn't sound like a devoted friend talking."

"Well, he could be a *tremendous* dick to *me* sometimes." Austin gave a sarcastic grin. I was reminded he wasn't *all* flannel-and-bearded good humor. "That's just the way he was."

So far, Declan Murphy didn't sound like the most stand-up guy. I mean, I was sorry he was dead. But he'd slept with Janel and broken her heart, started a rumor that disparaged his own fiancée's intelligence, and maybe cheated on Carissa. He was no prince, it seemed. Yet everyone had liked him. Why?

"You'd think remembering Declan's shittier qualities would make me miss him less, wouldn't you?" Austin grumbled, choking on a laugh. He wiped his watery eyes with the heel of his hand. "But the funny thing is, I miss that bastard. I really do."

"*Aw.* Of course you do." I patted his knee again.

He realized what I was doing and shifted subtly on the sofa, very much the way I'd done when Tomasz had pressed his thigh against mine yesterday in our booth at Muddle + Spade. It seemed evident to me that Austin was keeping his distance.

But why? Did he have a girlfriend he was devoted to?

He sucked in a huge breath, then shook his head. His smile broadened, enlivening his shaggy-hair-framed face. "The funny thing is, I came here to make sure *you* were okay. Now *I'm* not."

"There's no telling how grief will affect you," I assured him, wishing I weren't speaking from experience. "It'll take some time. Declan didn't have to be perfect to be lovable, you know."

Austin snorted. "Declan wasn't perfect. Not by a long shot. But he liked all the same things I did. Gaming. *Tacos de lengua.* Vinyl record stores. Coffee. Nintendocore." He noticed my baffled look and explained. "It's metal music influenced by video game soundtracks. It's kind of obscure. But Declan *got it.*"

I remembered Janel similarly reciting a list of the things she and Declan had had in common. It had been vastly different.

After all, it didn't get much less vegetarian than *tacos de lengua.* Who *was* Declan Murphy, anyway?

"Well, he *did* move here to Portland, right? So you two—"

"He didn't do that for *me.*" Austin held up his hand.

"That was all for Carissa. Declan left some cushy job in Seattle real estate to do it, too. The market is totally booming there now."

Warning bells clanged in my head. Declan had worked in real estate? Just like the developers pursuing Cartorama's land?

"Or maybe it was a tech company he worked at," Austin amended, frowning. "I can't remember for sure now." He gave me an abashed look. "Most of our conversations centered on gaming."

Oh, well, so much for that brilliant theory of mine.

"At least they did until Declan got 'too busy' to keep up his end of things." Austin made air quotes with his fingers. "I think he just didn't want anyone here to know he was a gamer."

I felt bad for him. "That must have hurt your feelings."

Austin chuckled, surprising me. "Nah, dude. I mean, I appreciate you jumping in to defend the honor of the nerd herd yesterday, but I get it. Declan wanted to impress Carissa. If I'd had a shot with her, I would have done the same thing."

I appreciated his honesty. In my experience, it's too rare.

"Actually, I *did* have a shot with her," Austin mused, "but all I got out of it was a chance to troubleshoot her equipment."

I grinned. "If that's some kind of double entendre—"

His laughter was heartening. "It's not. I mean *I'm* the one who designed Carissa's liquid nitrogen equipment for her. The software component, at least. There were a lot of late nights spent debugging that thing. If it was going to happen with us . . ."

". . . it would have." I understood. "But you have someone now?"

Austin angled his head, confused. "Nope. Why?"

"Oh . . ." I remembered the way he'd deliberately avoided my (innocent) hand on his knee, but decided not to pursue it. "I just thought you would. You know, a nice guy like you."

"Don't you know? Nice guys *never* finish first." With his hands on his knees, Austin pushed upward. "So you're okay, then? No lasting effects from yesterday's debauchery?"

Belatedly, I remembered his reason for coming over. I'd been so busy talking with him, I hadn't thought about my (alleged) poisoning symptoms for several minutes. "You know, I think I'll be fine, actually." I was relieved to realize it.

"Good. Then I'll leave you to it. I need to get down to Muddle + Spade. It's getting pretty late." He trod toward the front door. "Next time," he warned, winking, "take it easy."

I followed him to the front door, still chatting away. I get that way sometimes. A respite from death makes me talkative.

"Hey! I only drank a few beers." *And they destroyed me.*

"Oh yeah? What did you try? Berk has some good IPAs and stouts on tap, plus some limited-edition hard ciders and perrys."

"Chocolate porter. It was good, but it packed a wallop."

"Ah, that explains it." Austin grinned at me. "At Berk's place, chocolate porter isn't just beer brewed with cacao nibs added to the mash. It's porter *plus* added chocolate liqueur."

That explained it. I'd essentially been downing two-for-one drinks yesterday. I was far too much of a lightweight for that.

It was possible that I'd gotten carried away with my

murder theory. Most likely, no one in the Rose City was after me.

At the door, Austin stopped. "Just so you don't worry about it, Carissa's parents were going to contact Declan's family."

Tardily remembering our exchange about that earlier, I angled my head inquiringly. "Really? How do you know?"

"They told me. We've been in touch. I'm the one who called them yesterday." Austin looked away, seemingly absorbed in the homey, hand-wrought details of my entryway. I was onto his distraction technique, though. I figured he was upset. "You know," he said, "so they could be there to meet Carissa."

After Declan's body was brought to the morgue. Neither of us wanted to say it. It was too horrible to contemplate.

"I'm the one who called the ambulance, too." Austin lifted his chin. "I was right next door. I heard Carissa's scream."

Our gazes met in what I imagined was mutual sympathy.

Of course it was mutual sympathy. Otherwise, I'd be suggesting that cuddly Austin was some kind of gentle sociopath.

"It's a good thing you did," I told him.

But I couldn't help thinking, as I showed Austin out the door and watched him galumph good-naturedly down the steps, that that's exactly what someone would have done if they'd *known* that Declan was already dead—known that Carissa would be screaming after finding his lifeless body. Otherwise, wouldn't Austin have come to find out what was wrong first, before calling for help?

Something about Austin's story didn't jibe. If Declan had really been murdered yesterday, I contemplated as I waved good-bye to Austin, there weren't only real-estate developers and landlords to consider. There were also fellow Cartoramians, too.

Like Tomasz Berk. Janel White. And Austin Martin.

I shivered and shut the door; then I went to track down my rental car. Austin had offered to give me a ride, but after everything that had happened, I'd decided it was safer to call a cab rather than hop into a car with a (relative) stranger.

This day wasn't going to start itself. Neither was my makeshift stint as a Bridgetown chocolate-tour guide. I had to get all the details about Declan's tour—and maybe call Travis again, too. I couldn't quite recall what I'd said to him when I'd drunk-dialed him yesterday.

Knowing me, it might have been a doozy.

Five

Remember how I wondered what I might have tipsily said to Travis? (Besides a pseudosultry "What are you wearing?", my standard greeting for him?) Well, even as I exited the cab I'd taken to Cartorama, paid the driver, and strode into the middle of the cart pod, I still didn't know. For once, Travis had been "unavailable" to take my call. It was unprecedented.

Concerned over the way that *both* of my go-to guys seemed to be dodging me at the moment, I shrugged into my jacket and looked around. None of the carts were open. That was odd. After yesterday, someone at least should have been here setting up.

Maybe everyone had decided to stay closed today, out of respect for Declan? But I doubted any of the vendors could afford that kind of sentimentality. Their carts were popular, sure—but they were hardly deluxe. A few of them were basically held together with duct tape and determination. Their entrepreneur owners spent their limited resources on things that were more important than aesthetics, like scrumptious triple-chocolate cookies and down-home chocolate cream pie.

Finding myself alone amid the unopened carts, I

frowned in confusion. My rental car was right where I'd left it parked on the street, but nothing else was as I expected it to be.

It was hard not to feel spooked. Sure, there was still construction going on in the distance—heavy equipment beeping as it backed up and workers shouting while clanking things—but here at Cartorama, all was silent. Eerily silent. Even the birds were quiet, leaving only the sound of wind to ruffle the trees.

Nope. Wait a second. The birds were there, chirping away in that brainless way they do. Okay, I was getting carried away again, creating a threatening atmosphere where none existed.

But I've told you about the eerie deserted-carnival vibe at the cart pod. It wasn't that difficult to talk myself into being creeped out. Especially when I glanced toward Churn PDX and the trailer where Declan had drawn his last chilly breaths.

Why had he been there so early (or so late)? Surely, topping off Carissa's equipment with liquid nitrogen wasn't a task that typically happened in the wee hours of the morning, was it?

Inescapably lured closer, I switched directions and veered toward Carissa's Airstream trailer. There was no one around to see me snooping, so the timing was right. Plus, my philosophy is that if something scares you, you have to confront it.

Unless you're talking about birds. In that case, run.

Holding my breath, I circled the trailer. There wasn't any sign that anything unusual had happened there yesterday. There wasn't even any police tape surrounding it. The authorities had determined that Declan's death was an accident. With no evidence to suggest otherwise, they'd had no reason to investigate.

That didn't mean *I* didn't. Nosily, I tried the trailer's door. Disappointingly, its latch held firm. I couldn't open it.

What I needed was Danny, plus his lock-picking skills.

Officially, of course, I disapproved of him using his less-than-lawful talents, especially on my behalf. But I couldn't deny that Danny's expertise came in handy sometimes. Thwarted in my quest to examine the inside of Carissa's trailer, I looked around.

No one was in sight. With a flash of inspiration, I bent and turned over a rock, looking for a spare key. Carissa *must* have stashed one nearby. She'd never been the most organized of college students, so she'd have wanted a backup. You know that recurring nightmare you have, where you're back in school and you've forgotten an exam—maybe even forgotten to attend an entire class for a whole semester? Well, that was Carissa in a nutshell. Scatterbrained but lovable . . . and always able to talk even the most hard-nosed professors into giving her more time.

Unfortunately, all I unearthed were a couple of worms and some topsoil. I muttered a swearword and straightened, brushing my hands on the back of my jeans. Yuck. Not only was I was no closer to getting into the trailer, but I was dirty now, too.

I turned to leave and almost stepped on something. Something *furry.* I yelped. It screeched, then streaked away.

Almost upended by my attempts *not* to step on whatever it was, I flailed my arms. My heart pounded. I put my hand on my chest and breathed hard, wondering if surprise could be fatal.

"What are you up to out here?" someone asked behind me.

Tomasz Berk. I turned to face him. Shakily.

He must have seen the whole embarrassing thing.

I had no excuse for my snooping. So I did what anyone

would have done. I went on the offensive. "What are *you* doing out here?" I demanded, hands on my hips.

He gave a lazy grin, then lifted something in his right hand. A plastic bowl. "Feeding the pod's resident cat, Chow."

It had been a cat I'd almost tromped on. Whew. "Of course you're feeding the cat, cat chow. What else would it eat?"

"No, her name is Chow. She's a stray, but we feed her."

Of course they did. Of course *he* did. Just the way Tomasz looked out for Cartorama's vendors, he cared for the cat, too.

It was hard not to like a guy with those credentials.

He gazed at me. Affably. "What are you hoping to find?"

I remembered my blatant, inexcusable attempt to either break into Churn PDX or locate Carissa's spare key and let myself inside. What was *wrong* with me? One murder (maybe two) and I'm not myself anymore. Usually, I'm a live-and-let-live type. Frankly, I'm on the road too much to get overinvolved.

It seemed that suspicious deaths had a way of bringing out my nosy side. I wasn't proud of it. But I couldn't deny it.

"I think I dropped my earring over here yesterday," I lied.

Yep, not proud of that, either. Until I knew more, it was better to keep my cards close to my chest. I hadn't done that at Maison Lemaître, and it had gotten me into trouble. Not that I suspected Tomasz of any particular wrongdoing. I didn't want to.

Especially not when he was looking at me that way, all warm and interested, with his finely muscled forearms showcased by his rolled-up shirtsleeves. Today's barman ensemble featured skinny black pants, a button-down shirt, and a dapper vest, plus excellent brogues. I'd say one thing for Tomasz—he had superior taste in men's footwear. The rest of him said *thrift store,* but his feet said they'd been custom shod on Savile Row in London.

Or maybe I was just channeling my mom's Anglophilia, dressing up Tomasz Berk in exactly the clothing that would have impressed her. Which was dumb, really. I wasn't going to bring a Portland mixologist home to meet my parents. For one thing, my mom and dad have developed a pretty solid (and understandable) skepticism about my transient urges to settle down with someone.

They know it won't last. But I'm always an optimist.

"Aha, I noticed you looking around for something." Tomasz bought my fabrication without blinking. He hooked his thumb toward Muddle + Spade. "My windows overlook the cart pod. See?"

I glanced at those pristine renovated-warehouse windows and wanted to scamper away like the stray cat, Chow, had. Tomasz really had seen everything. I might have fancied myself an amateur sleuth, but I had a long way to go before I had any idea how to "investigate" matters with any degree of stealth.

Right now, hunches were all I had. That, and dead ends. For all my prowling around, I hadn't turned up any information yet.

On the other hand, that could change quickly, I knew.

"You're coming inside, though, right?" Tomasz's eyes twinkled at me. "Everybody's already there, having brunch."

Carissa's engagement brunch. "It's still happening?"

I'd thought it would be canceled. But if it was on, that explained why Austin had been in a hurry to get to the bar.

I'd been so busy suspecting him, I hadn't questioned

that. Or gotten myself ready to attend the same event. My skulking-around clothes weren't exactly dressy. I was geared up for a regular Sunday in the Pacific Northwest, not a gala brunch.

"Well, now it's more of a memorial for Declan than anything else." Tomasz put his hands in his pockets, then glanced up at me from beneath his dark brows. "The funeral's tomorrow."

At that, I felt suffused with sorrow. And shame. Plus regret. Carissa was dealing with the realities of her fiancé's death, and I was goofing around, pretending to be Miss Marple.

But there was still time to set things right. I had to stop overdramatizing everything and start being there for my friend.

"Of course I'm coming inside." I bent and scooped up a pebble (aka my "earring") for the sake of maintaining my alibi. Then I marched off toward Muddle + Spade, leaving Tomasz to catch up with me.

Inside Muddle + Spade, I expected to find sadness and shock, anecdotes about Declan, and reminiscences of times past.

Instead, I walked into a riot of laughter and feasting, togetherness and mutual support. Everyone was there. Carissa sat at the center, with Austin, Lauren, some vendors I recognized from yesterday but hadn't met, and (now) me and Tomasz gathered around her. Even Janel was involved—circulating with a pitcher of mimosas like a waitress, sure—but still, she was included.

They were all seated at one of the bar's big, rough-hewn communal tables, with a row of Mason jars full of lighted candles for a centerpiece and plates of food all around. The aromas wafting upward from the spread—savory, sweet, spicy, and everything in between—made my stomach rumble. I was reminded that I'd been so eager to get to Cartorama (and make sure my rental car hadn't been towed or sabotaged) that I hadn't stopped for a nosh. It looked as though Tomasz's kitchen staff had the cure for that, though. I spied skillet scrambles, plates of French toast, pastries and fruit bowls, granola, and juice.

And coffee. Lots and lots of coffee. (Hurray!)

Everything was being served tapas-style, to be shared. It was plain that everyone was used to that custom, because they didn't hesitate to dig right in. Sunshine streamed in through the bar's windows. Indie music played subtly in the background. Everyone chattered away, their conversations creating a low hum.

If I hadn't known better—if I'd arrived today instead of yesterday—I'd have sworn nothing tragic had happened at all.

"Well, I guess now I can blow off my diet!" Carissa dug into a plate of chocolate chip pancakes, forking two of them onto her plate. "Sayonara, custom-fitted wedding dress!"

Her manic glee didn't bother anyone else, but I swear I felt the hairs on the back of my neck stand up. I realized that Carissa might have been crash dieting in preparation for her wedding—so she was probably legitimately hungry—but shouldn't she have been a little more, I don't know, *grief-stricken*?

Concerned, I went straight to her. "Carissa, how are you?"

"Starving!" She hugged me tightly, then pulled back. "You?"

I couldn't believe she was asking me that, just as

though this were any ordinary day. I struggled to regroup. Carissa merely blinked at me, her face fixed in a pleasant expression.

My gaze darted to Austin. Without saying a word, he gave me the universal *drinky-drinky* symbol, pantomiming someone knocking back alcohol.

I frowned. Austin nodded, almost imperceptibly.

I understood. Carissa's amiable mood had been helped along by something, likely antidepressants prescribed by her doctor. Or a few of Janel's mimosas. Or maybe (unwisely) both.

"I'm fine." Truly, I was worried about Carissa. Her face looked slightly drawn, her eyes swollen, her cheeks pale. I searched for something to do to help, not wanting to fall back on the old *"what can I do for you?"* routine, which put the onus on the grieving to orchestrate their own relief. "More mimosa?"

Argh. I wanted to smack myself on the forehead. The last thing (possibly medicated) Carissa needed was to get hammered.

I searched the table for another tactic, but I was too late.

"Yes, thanks!" My friend held out her glass to me.

Unprepared, I looked for Janel with the mimosa pitcher. Instead, amid all the frivolity and sociability, I saw *Danny.*

I blinked. I had to be imagining things.

But no. There he was, all burnished muscles, militarily short dark hair, and perceptive eyes. Right now, his eyes were sizing me up, undoubtedly seeing all the tumult I'd put myself through so far this morning. Danny knows me like no one else.

He could *see* that I'd woken up a wreck. That I'd already been rebuffed by a kindly nerd. That I'd been discovered while trying (and failing) to stage a clue-gathering trailer break-in.

Danny gave me a nod, then returned his attention to Lauren.

He was seated next to her, sure, but that was no excuse.

As I tried to process all that, Janel swooped in to refill Carissa's mimosa. I caught her eye and mouthed a thank you.

"You didn't tell me you were bringing a plus-one!" Carissa beamed at me. I began to have doubts about her doctor's judgment in prescribing anything for her. She seemed . . . agitated. Leaning nearer, Carissa gestured for me to stoop closer. I did.

"Especially one who's so cute!" she bellowed with a wink at Danny, my supposed "date" for the occasion.

I'm not going to sugarcoat things. Carissa's elation was kind of unnerving. I got goose bumps all over again.

"After this, Declan's funeral is going to be a major downer!" Carissa chortled. She quaffed her drink. "More, please!"

Janel rushed to oblige, but I couldn't take any more.

"Sorry. I'll be right back," I muttered, then I made my escape to the ladies' room and left the macabre party behind me.

If I knew Danny, he'd catch my signal and follow me. I wanted to know what he was doing there, but I didn't want to cause a scene—or interrupt his tête-à-tête with Lauren.

At least now I knew why he'd been unreachable earlier, though: because he'd been on a plane on his way to see *me*.

I was trying to shake out a second (and hopefully more effective) dose of an over-the-counter analgesic from the bottle in my bag when the door to the ladies' room whooshed open behind me.

I dropped everything in fright. My bottle of painkillers clattered to the floor, spilling extra-strength caplets like confetti. My purse followed, dropping like a stone into a soapy splash of water on the floor, just as someone walked in.

I swore and bent to retrieve everything. I'd perched my bag on the edge of Muddle + Spade's square, polished-concrete sink basin. That obviously meant it hadn't had a chance. Wishing I still owned my trusty crossbody bag—which had seen me through more countries than I could count without nose-diving into some soapsuds—I scooped my things into my inferior backup bag.

This was why restaurants should quit installing those trendy, unusual-shaped sinks. They were impractical at best and nonfunctional at worst. A sink that failed at the essential job of helping to hold up your possessions while you washed your hands was no good to anyone. *You had one job, sink,* I thought as I glowered up at it. *Now I can't even take care of my headache.*

I didn't think a single caplet had stayed in the bottle.

"Oh, I'm so sorry! Did I startle you?" The newcomer bent alongside me to gather a few strays. "Here, let me help you."

Lauren. I recognized her seductive, striptease-worthy voice. Not to mention her high, pointy-toe pumps and the 1950s-era spangled dress that went swimmingly with it. On anyone without her verve, the whole ensemble would have looked silly.

On her, with her bodacious bod, it looked fantastic. I'm not the sequins-and-sparkles type, but I almost wanted to be.

I couldn't help wondering if she'd purposefully followed me to keep me and Danny apart a little longer. They'd looked *really* cozy earlier. Lauren obviously hadn't cared that my erstwhile bodyguard had announced himself as my date for the brunch.

"Lauren! Thanks, but don't worry. I've got this."

She helped me anyway, cheerfully risking her flawless manicure in the process. I couldn't stop sneaking glimpses at her equally impeccable hair and makeup. The effect was artificial, sure, but coupled with Lauren's genuine aura of vulnerability and kindness, it somehow worked. I wanted to dismiss her as a cosplay Dita Von Teese, but I couldn't do it.

"Here. Take some of mine." While I'd been dissecting her look, Lauren had been searching in her own vintage handbag for something. She pressed a couple of pain reliever tablets into my palm, then gave my fingers a gentle squeeze. Her fretful gaze met mine. "Let me guess, rough night last night?"

"I'd say so—or I would, if I remembered it more clearly."

I'd apparently whooped it up all afternoon, then slept all night and partway into the morning to make up for it.

Lauren gave me a sympathetic, red-lipsticked moue. "You've got to watch it when Tommy's tending bar. He's been known to mix the drinks a little stronger—or weaker—depending on the needs of the day." She gave me a commiserating look. "He's our very own *gorgeous* Dr. Feelgood," she purred, "making sure we all feel just as good as we possibly can. He's sweet that way."

"Yeah, *sweet*." I risked swallowing the analgesic she'd given me, reasoning that nobody would try to kill me *now,* just steps away from where Declan had (maybe) been murdered. It would look too suspicious. "I'd rather have known about Tomasz's unconventional bartending theories *before* he served me, though."

"Oh, Tommy doesn't roll that way. Not if he's decided you're one of us." Gaily, Lauren waved. Her slightly husky voice wrapped me in its sultry embrace, making "Tommy's" philosophy sound perfectly reasonable. Considerate, even. "It's his way of taking care of everybody. You get used to it after a while."

Maybe. But I didn't think I'd get used to Lauren calling a grown man "Tommy." Berk probably liked it, though. Some men went in for that baby-talk routine. Even men . . . like Danny? He'd seemed pretty into Lauren a few minutes ago at the brunch table.

As soon as we were out of here, he owed me some answers.

"So . . ." Lauren glanced over her shoulder, her husky voice echoing off all the porcelain, concrete, and tile in the bathroom. "I just thought I'd sneak in here to warn you—you know, girl to girl." Her voice lowered to an even more intimate timbre. "Watch out for Austin, okay? You don't know him, but—"

I burst out laughing. I couldn't help it. *"Austin?"*

I couldn't imagine what I had to fear from helpful, endearing, guy-next-door Austin Martin. I mean, yes, I'd been suspicious of him earlier, that's true. But hearing Lauren voice similar reservations somehow laid all mine to rest.

"He's not someone you want to mess around with," Lauren insisted. "Carissa's already had more than one run-in with Austin. He seems harmless, but he tends to get attached easily. *Too* easily. Then, when a girl doesn't return his feelings . . ."

She let her voice trail away ominously, leaving me to draw my own (seemingly inevitable) conclusions.

Was she intimating that Austin was *dangerous*?

"I wouldn't have said anything," Lauren assured me, "except I saw the familiar way you two looked at one another out there."

I remembered Austin giving me the *drinky-drinky* sign to let me know he thought Carissa had taken something to get her through today's brunch. I wasn't sure how he would know that, though.

Unless Carissa had friend-zoned him. Then Austin would know all the details of how Carissa was coping. Or maybe Austin's acquaintance with Declan's family meant he had the inside scoop?

Lauren edged closer, frowning at me. She could probably tell that I wasn't taking her seriously. I'm afraid that putting a polite front on my disbelief was impossible for me, especially on an empty stomach. I don't exactly sport a poker face.

What *I* have is a "tell me everything" face—a face that seems to invite friends, strangers, people on buses, workers in airports, and everyone in between to confide in me. It's a useful quality when drumming up business or troubleshooting a particularly recalcitrant brownie recipe, but under circumstances like these, I wished I looked more forbidding.

I didn't want to gossip with Lauren about someone I liked.

"Austin told us about how he went over to your place this morning," Lauren added. "He looks harmless, I know. But I really think he might have *killed* Declan!" she stage-whispered, letting her serious gaze search mine. Her breath feathered across my face, smelling strongly of champagne and orange juice. "After yesterday, I don't want anything to happen to anyone else."

I had to ask: "Why would Austin have killed Declan?"

"Because he wanted Carissa for himself," Lauren told me in another harsh whisper—even though it was unlikely we'd be overheard. "He wanted Declan out of the way. Believe me, I know when a man is into a woman. Austin is *way* into Carissa."

"But she doesn't feel the same way," I said, playing along.

A nod. "Be serious. Who would?"

Well, that was kind of mean. My estimation of Lauren went down a notch. There was no reason to take potshots at Austin.

"Every man has the potential to go a little crazy if the woman he has the hots for doesn't feel the same way about him," Lauren went on, undeterred by my non-response. "You *must* have run into that scenario a few times. I mean, just *look* at you!"

She did exactly that, at length, then waved her arm in apparent acknowledgment of my . . . irresistibility, I'm guessing?

Was Lauren *flirting* with me? I was flattered, but not interested. "Fine. I'll be on the lookout," I promised.

"Don't accidentally lead him on," Lauren cautioned. She seemed serious. "It's still possible that Austin meant to kill Carissa and got Declan, instead." She looked away. "Poor Declan."

For a heartbeat, Lauren's composure faltered. I recalled that I'd detected champagne on her breath not sixty seconds ago. It was probable that Carissa wasn't the only one who'd needed chemical assistance to get through Declan's memorial brunch.

If Lauren was this upset over Declan's death, that meant that the Cartorama vendors were even closer than I'd thought. Because while Lauren looked more pulled together today than she had yesterday when she'd been crying at the bar, she still seemed distraught. I could detect puffiness near her eyes. She'd probably been crying. Her shoulders slumped slightly, too, as though she was over-tired. From weeping instead of sleeping?

When she caught me studying her, she straightened. Her smile shined out at me, vivid and practiced. I wondered if she *did* perform burlesque somewhere in Portland. She had a performer's knack for putting on a happy face, no matter what.

Either that or Lauren was (maybe) a sociopathic killer.

I shivered, watching as she pulled out a compact to powder her nose. After that, she reapplied her scarlet lipstick.

If Lauren really *was* secretly dangerous, there was something I had to do. So I whipped out my own "lipstick" (it's ordinary clear lip balm, let's be real) and applied it while meeting Lauren's gaze in the mirror, just-us-girls style.

"So while we're sharing warnings, you should probably stay away from Danny." Casually, I recapped my lip balm. "He just got out of jail." It was a minor fib—an exaggeration. He's been out five or six years now. He's completed his parole and everything.

Still, when warning away a prospective murderer, details could be finessed. Now Danny would be safe. Thanks to me.

After all, most women bugged out when they heard "ex-con."

Lauren brightened. "Really? Where? My uncle did some time at Columbia River Correctional Institution. Now he's on parole."

Oops. Her upbeat tone jarred me. It was as if I'd made Danny *more* attractive to her, not less. Maybe Lauren was into the whole "bad boy" thing. Or maybe she was just extremely open-minded, given her family circumstances. What were the odds?

I wish I could have told you that Lauren's uncle's jail

time made no difference to my opinion of her. But under the circumstances, it did. I know it's not fair to stereotype people (especially based on their family ties), but what's that saying? "The apple doesn't fall far from the tree"? That's a truism for a reason. Maybe, I decided, *Lauren* was the dangerous one here.

Maybe *she'd* liked Declan and he hadn't liked *her.* Maybe all her theories about Austin were actually veiled hints about her own pain, her own motivations, and her own killer impulses.

Maybe Lauren was throwing shade on Austin to deflect attention from her own guilt. It could happen.

Stuck, I made up something about where Danny had served time. He'd be furious if he ever found out about what I'd done. It wasn't that he was embarrassed by his wrong-side-of-the-tracks upbringing or the various (sometimes illegal) ways he'd coped with it. It was that Danny was private. Super private.

Even as I attempted to fib my way out of trouble without giving myself away by breaking out in hives, I remembered what Janel had said to me yesterday. It had major implications here.

I know she knew about Lauren, Janel had quipped about Carissa before suggesting a name, a logo, and a theme song for the women who'd slept with Declan. *No matter what she said.*

It was obvious what Janel had been alluding to, but before I could gather any further intel, Lauren snapped shut her compact. She stowed it away, then smiled brightly at me.

"Good talk," she said. "Try the mocha-chocolate-chunk muffins. They're *fab.* Tommy gets them delivered from a local bakery."

Then she touched up her hair, gave me another smile, and whisked herself away with me still gawking behind her, wondering exactly how many women there were in Declan's Dozen—and how many of those women might have wanted Declan dead because of it.

Six

It wasn't easy trying to keep up with a woman who was stress-eating her way through an erstwhile engagement brunch. But for Carissa's sake, I did my best. I wanted to support my friend: to be there, to listen to her, to comfort her. But the more I tried to talk to Carissa about how she was coping, the more food she piled onto my plate. It was getting ridiculous.

"Ooh! You haven't tried the chocolate-swirl sweet rolls yet? You *must*." Carissa plucked a spiraled roll from a Jadeite glass cake plate, then added it to my overflowing plate amid the chocolate chip pancake, chocolate-stuffed French toast, *pain au chocolat,* and ramekin of brûléed steel-cut oats with cocoa, which she'd already served me. "They're *so* good. I can't get enough."

Dutifully, I took a bite. The roll *was* delicious, but it seemed to turn to chocolaty sawdust in my mouth. I was worried about Carissa. Too worried to enjoy Declan's memorial brunch.

"Come on!" she urged perkily. "You're in Portland now—home of some of the most decadent food ever created! It's time to cut loose, Hayden." She waved at my plate. "Do it for Declan."

I stopped chewing, appalled. *Was she serious?*

"Let's *all* do it for Declan!" Carissa smiled at her friends, waving her arms to include them all. *"Mangia! Mangia!"*

"Was Declan Italian?" I asked when she'd returned to me.

I was hoping to coax Carissa into sharing some more details about her fiancé. I thought remembering Declan might help her feel better. But she seemed to be doing fine without me.

"Declan? Nope. I don't think so." She made a face. "Umm—"

"Irish?" Declan Murphy was an Irish name, after all.

"Sure. Probably." Carissa shrugged, unbothered. She forked up another bite of waffles covered in chocolate sauce and whipped cream. "Declan and I didn't talk much about our pasts."

Her tone was carefree. Her expression, however, wasn't.

Tellingly, Carissa's gaze swerved to Lauren. Narrowed.

Had Lauren and Declan slept together? *Did* Carissa know? If so, that would explain why she seemed less than heartbroken today over Declan's death. It was probably easier to cope with the loss of an unrepentant cheater. On the other hand, Carissa *had* been prepared to marry Declan in a few weeks' time, so maybe all my conjecture was misguided. It wouldn't be the first time.

"You and Declan didn't talk about the past? Why not?" I asked lightly. "Declan wasn't into Greek life?"

As far as I knew, that had been the focus of Carissa's life on campus after I'd gone to Bruges. But now she disagreed.

My friend snorted. "I'm *more* than a sorority sister now, Hayden. Please. Give me a little more credit."

"Of course." I glanced at Danny, wishing I'd had a

chance to confront him about his sudden arrival. When I'd returned from the ladies' room, he'd been chatting with Tomasz. Now he was listening raptly to Lauren. "Declan wasn't in a fraternity, then?"

I don't know what made me harp on the subject. I might have been knocked for a loop by my bodyguard's apparent fascination with sequins, scarlet lipstick, and dual sleeves of tattoos. (Lauren had more visible tattoos than Danny did.) Plus, I was still flummoxed by his presence there. Despite what he must have told Carissa (sparking her *"You didn't tell me you were bringing a plus-one! Especially a cute one!"* comments when I'd arrived), I *hadn't* invited Danny. I'd left him in northern California.

"I don't know. Declan and I were happy to leave the past behind us." Nonchalantly, Carissa knocked back her mimosa. She waved her glass for more. With gusto, she added in an aside to me, "I know it sounds bad, but I'm *so* glad not to be dieting anymore. I swear, it was killing me working around all this chocolate every day and not having any of it. But Declan wanted us to look our best for the debut of Chocolate After Dark."

I blinked, startled. "You mean for the wedding?"

She frowned. "That's what I said."

"No, you said—" I was about to clarify when Tomasz arrived. He did *not* bring another mimosa refill for Carissa, despite her appeals for more alcohol. Instead, he set a wonderfully aromatic cup of coffee in front of her. I guessed he was caretaking again. I watched as he squeezed Carissa's shoulder, then slipped away. "Was Declan dieting, too?" I asked, wondering about him.

I still didn't know if he was good to Carissa or a chronic philanderer, if he was hopelessly vain or simply blessed with good looks. I was starting to share Janel's surprise that Carissa hadn't gushed more about the man she'd planned to marry.

Carissa chortled. "Declan didn't have to diet, the bastard. Nothing he ate stuck to him. Of course, he *did* work out, so that's probably why. I mean, you don't get to be that shredded by accident." She gave a wistful sigh. "I'll miss those abs."

I must have stared at her in dismay, because she amended herself right away. "I mean, I'll miss *him,* of course! I will."

She dug into her plate of food again, then elbowed me with her mouth full. She nodded at my chocolate roll—akin to a cinnamon roll, but with chocolaty filling—something like an individual chocolate babka. She gestured for me to eat more.

Unwillingly, I took another bite. I wanted to help her, but I didn't know how. It seemed that Carissa was still in shock. She simply couldn't—or wouldn't—accept that Declan was gone.

I wondered what it would be like to love someone that much.

I found myself glancing at Danny again, then rolled my eyes as Lauren cooed something in his ear. Surely, he wasn't falling for her bombshell shtick? He was smarter than that.

Evidently, Tomasz—aka Tommy—thought so, too. I noticed him watching Danny and Lauren with an expression of amusement. Maybe this wasn't the first time Tomasz had witnessed Lauren's seduction routine in action. Maybe she'd used it on the barman. Or on Declan. Tomasz Berk probably knew *everything* that went on at Cartorama. Muddle + Spade seemed to be the cart pod's preferred gathering place. I bet dramas unfolded here regularly.

If I were clever, I'd ask him about a few of them, I realized. I caught Tomasz's eye. He winked at me. I smiled.

No, I *wasn't* planning to talk to Tomasz just because I thought he was good-looking. I was *investigating*. Intelligently.

"Speaking of Declan, I brought his iPad for you." Carissa withdrew a darkened iPad from the tote bag she'd slung on the back of her chair. She handed it to me. "I couldn't find his phone to get the contacts for you the easy way, but everything is on here for Chocolate After Dark. The reservations list, the investor mailing list, the schedule of culinary-tour stops, all of it. Plus all the financial software for walk-ins and people who didn't pay in advance. It's dead easy to process payments."

I nodded, accepting the iPad while trying not to think about Carissa's (probably unconscious) use of the words "dead easy." Earlier, she'd said that not eating chocolate was "killing" her. That lingo couldn't be accidental. She was obviously troubled. I wished I could do more. "You must have been close, if Declan shared so many details of his business with you."

It wasn't my best effort, but I was commiserating with her.

"Of course we were close." Carissa's annoyed gaze shifted from me to Janel, who was still circulating—shortly and blondly—with the mimosas. She frowned at her. "We were getting married."

"Yes! I'm sorry. I didn't mean to upset you." I wondered if she was giving Janel the stink eye because she knew that Declan had slept with her. Once. More? The timeline was admittedly fuzzy. "I just mean, sometimes couples keep their work lives separate."

"Declan and I could never do that."

"Because Declan was helping you with Churn PDX?"

I didn't mean it the way it sounded. I swear I didn't. I was only continuing our (admittedly stilted) conversation.

"Declan and I worked together, yes," Carissa said heatedly. "But despite what you may have heard, he did *not* do all the brainwork. I came up with my liquid nitrogen machine myself."

She shot a disgruntled glance at Austin. He noticed and shrank in his chair with comical oversolicitousness, slurping away at an avocado smoothie with candied cacao nibs and muddled mint.

The rumor going around Cartorama is that Declan designed that equipment for her, Austin had told me that morning. *I'm pretty sure Declan started the rumor.* Undoubtedly, Carissa knew that Austin had been to see me. They probably all did.

"How did you do it?" I asked. "It sounds so technical."

But Carissa was in no mood to satisfy my curiosity.

"You can't believe everything *some people* say," she told me. "Around here, the gossip gets pretty thick. Some people don't have anything better to do. It's sad, really."

Wow. That was mean. Why all the enmity toward Austin?

Belatedly, I noticed Janel White hovering over Carissa's shoulder. Clearly, she'd been about to refill her mimosa.

She'd overheard her rant instead. Janel stomped away, then set down the mimosa pitcher on the bar with a thud that made Tomasz glance up in surprise. He watched with evident concern as Janel beelined toward what had to be Muddle + Spade's back room.

Janel was really at home here at the bar. That was interesting, especially for an apparent outsider at Cartorama.

Tomasz quit making the Bloody Mary he'd been preparing. He wiped his hands on a bar towel, then frowned and went in back.

Oblivious to the drama around her, Carissa sighed. "I just wish I could rewind the clock, you know?" She glanced at me, her eyes brimming with tears. Her lower lip trembled. She nudged away her brunch plate. "I was so mean to Declan the last time we saw each other. I can't believe that's the last thing I'll ever say to him. I mean, how am I supposed to get past that?"

Her heartache touched me. "He knew you didn't mean it."

"But I *did* mean it!" Carissa's gaze wandered to Lauren again—maybe just because that tattooed temptress was laughing loudly while touching Danny's knee. "I was *so* mad at Declan."

"Wedding planning is stressful," I comforted Carissa. "Believe me, I know." I'd never gotten past it. "It's normal."

I told her a little about my three exes. She perked up.

"I forgot all about them! That makes me feel better, Hayden. Thanks." Carissa gave me a sniffly smile. "I mean, you seem to have it all together these days. So if *you've* struggled with this relationship stuff, that gives me hope."

"The trick is to remember the good times." I felt hungrier now that I was helping her. I tried some of the chocolate chip pancakes. *Yum.* "I'm still good friends with my exes. I just couldn't settle down with any of them, that's all."

I should have left it at that. I know I should have.

But I couldn't. I had to try investigating a bit more. Otherwise, how was I supposed to find any peace of mind?

"You and Declan must have had a lot in common," I mused.

"Oh, we did." Carissa snapped up the bait I'd shamelessly dangled. "Declan liked all the same things as me. Romantic comedies. Broadway musicals. Shopping. Doing DIY around the house. Even eating soul food!" I remembered that Carissa was originally from Mississippi. "You wouldn't have expected it of a guy like him, but Declan could really polish off a plate of fried chicken, biscuits and gravy, hush puppies, okra, and a big ole mess of greens, with sweet potato pie for dessert." She gave a nostalgic sigh. "Like I said, he worked out a lot, though."

I had the feeling Carissa was mourning the loss of Declan's muscles again. I didn't enjoy thinking my friend was so shallow.

But if the shoe fit . . . I nodded, equipped with yet another (disparate) list of Declan Murphy's likes and dislikes. How could one man have produced so many conflicting opinions?

"Anyway, I'm *so* glad you're taking over the tour temporarily, Hayden. Now all of Declan's advance publicity efforts won't go to waste. His customers and investors won't be disappointed, either!" Carissa broke into my thoughts with a new sense of vitality. Maybe I'd helped her feel better? I hoped so. "We'd brainstormed about maybe bringing in experts, like you, to guest host the tours sometime later, after Chocolate After Dark was established. Declan didn't want to do it, though."

"So you talked him into it?" I joked fondly, remembering Carissa's knack for persuading professors to give her more time to complete assignments when we were at university together.

I wished we could have had the reunion I'd hoped for. I'd been busy crisscrossing the globe, but I'd still missed her—despite our success at keeping in touch via bits and bytes.

Carissa chuckled, then tossed her auburn hair. "Chocolate After Dark was Declan's baby. I tried not to interfere— even when he was on the verge of doing something *really* boneheaded."

I smiled. "That couldn't have been easy. It's tough to stand idly by while someone you love does something dumb."

My gaze meandered to Danny and Lauren. I couldn't help it.

Carissa noticed. She waggled her brows. "You? And Danny?"

I got a grip on myself. I scoffed. "No, it's not like that between us. We're just friends. I've known Danny for forever."

"I hear friends make the best lovers," Carissa sing-songed.

I think I blushed. I know my face felt hot. Needing a diversion, I grabbed Declan's iPad and tucked it securely into my bag. "I'll take good care of this, I promise. I'll make sure the first few tours go off without a hitch, too. After that—"

"I can do it!" Austin piped up. He nodded at my bag, where I'd stowed all the culinary-tour information. His eager gaze moved to Carissa. "Declan told me about the tour. I can close The Chocolate Bar early and help out. I'd be happy to do it."

If looks could have killed, Carissa would have machine-gunned Austin on the spot . . . and he would have been happy to bite the bullet for her, too. I didn't understand her enmity toward him.

"I think *you've* done quite enough for Declan already," Carissa said. Then she got up in a huff and swerved toward the ladies' room, still obviously feeling tipsy (and/or drugged).

Austin and I exchanged an awkward look.

"She's really upset," he said by way of an excuse.

"She's not herself today," I added, hoping to bolster it.

Then I glanced down at my (almost empty) plate and realized I'd made a mistake. Carissa *was* herself today, if the crumbs and chocolate-sauce smears on my plate were any indication. Prompted by Carissa, I'd polished off more food than I'd intended.

Plainly, she still had her knack for persuasion. I hadn't even noticed myself chowing down while we'd talked— that's just how effective Carissa was at dropping hints, making suggestions, and (subtly) getting her own way. It was her superpower.

I couldn't believe she hadn't used it on Declan. Especially if she'd thought he was making mistakes. Had Carissa truly resisted interfering with Declan's decisions, the way she'd claimed? Or had Declan Murphy been the only person in the known universe who'd successfully thwarted Carissa's wishes?

If he had, had he paid for that mistake with his life? Could Carissa have changed *that* much, that she'd killed him?

I realized the unpleasant direction my thoughts had taken and jolted myself onto another course. I refused to think of my friend that way. No matter what tragic things were going on, Carissa had to be innocent. She simply had to be. That was it.

The brunch broke up a short while later, with Carissa's friends and fellow Cartorama vendors milling around in genial clumps, busing their own plates and offering their sympathies to Carissa. It turned out that the engagement brunch-turned-memorial was partly catered by Muddle + Spade and partly potlucked by all the Cartoramians. They'd pitched in to bring their specialties. It was heart-warming how close they all were.

You know . . . unless one of them was secretly a murderer.

But the consensus among everyone except me was that Declan had died accidentally. That he'd doubled back to Churn PDX on the night in question, opened the liquid nitrogen tanks to do Carissa's prep for her for the next day (as he sometimes did), then passed out before realizing that anything was wrong with the safety valves and/or ventilation in the trailer.

As ways to die went, Declan's could have been worse. That didn't mean it wasn't awful, though. Especially since he'd been trying to be nice at the time. That hurt, even if Declan *had* sometimes been a "tremendous jerk" (to use Austin's words).

Declan's funeral was set for the next morning. Since I wasn't due to kick off the first Chocolate After Dark session until the evening—its gimmick being that it began at twilight and featured adults-only cocktails among its stops—I was invited to the service, too.

"Please come, Hayden." Carissa emerged and hugged me, just as though she *hadn't* huffed off in a bad temper earlier. Since she was going through such a hard time, some volatility was to be expected from her, I reasoned. "Do it for Declan."

"Declan and I never even met," I pointed out gently. "You'll be happier with your family around you. You'll be fine."

"But I want *you*." Carissa pouted, one step short of stomping her foot. "How else will I be able to brag to everyone that I know a real, live, world-famous chocolate whisperer?"

That was very much beside the point.

Also, I wasn't the type to network at a memorial service.

"Don't worry," I assured her. "I'll be in town awhile."

"Oh, all right." Carissa relented, then turned to Austin. "I'm sorry about before," she baby-talked, standing pigeon-toed before him. "You know I never mean it, don't you, sweetie?"

The expression on Austin's face when Carissa carelessly dropped that endearment said it all. He hadn't avoided touching me on my sofa because he had a girlfriend. He'd done it because his heart belonged to Carissa . . . whether she wanted it or not.

Poor Austin. Declan had moved to Portland and immediately pretended he and Austin *hadn't* played hours upon hours of online video games together. Carissa had allowed Austin to troubleshoot her liquid nitrogen software, then—for an encore—planted him squarely in the friend zone. I doubted she even knew she'd done it. It wasn't something most women thought consciously about doing when it came to men they weren't interested in dating. It just . . . happened. Even now, Austin and Carissa's unfortunate dynamic was playing out all over again. She hugged him good-bye. He held on just a *little* too tightly, for a *little* too long.

"Are you *sure* you don't want me to lend a hand with the tour?" Austin asked when they'd finally parted. He gazed into Carissa's face like a starving man looking at a life-saving *taco de lengua*. "I don't mind. I can do it. Declan's not the only one who was good with people. I am, too." Austin searched Carissa's expression. "Plus, I know chocolate *a lot* better than he did."

His casual boast silenced the room. Everyone in the bar turned to watch. Even Danny could tell that something was about to go down, and he'd just arrived that morning. It was probably his magical body-language mojo at work, alerting him somehow.

But everyone was disappointed. Because Carissa only patted Austin's arm and said, "You keep doing *you,* Austin. It's cute. But the fact is, Hayden is better at chocolate than all of us."

Every gaze in Muddle + Spade pinned itself on me. Austin, especially, looked as though he wished I'd vaporize on the spot.

Et tu, Austin? I tossed him an apologetic headshake. It didn't help. Maybe Austin was more malevolent than I thought.

Danny almost exploded trying not to laugh outright at my self-effacing headshake. He knew me too well to believe my show of "Who, me?" humility was authentic.

"It's a mystery to me why Declan didn't jump on the chance to have Hayden consult for him," Carissa added, oblivious to the target she was painting on my back. "Her expertise would have done wonders for Chocolate After Dark, and *I* totally had an in."

Several gazes swerved speculatively to me. I shrugged.

"Someone on her last job wound up murdered," Tomasz said.

What the. . . ? He hadn't even been part of the conversation.

For a chaser, he blithely pulled a bar towel from his shoulder and set to work wiping down the polished bar. It was as if Tomasz's to-do list for the day had read: *(1)*

make the bar perfectly spic and span, and *(2) destroy Hayden Mundy Moore's credibility.* He'd accomplished both. I didn't appreciate his stirring the pot. Indie Superstud or not, he was out of line.

I held up my hands, about to explain, then thought better of it. I could do that later. "Carissa, I'm happy to step down if you're not comfortable with me leading the tour."

"Or *I* could do it, instead," Janel piped up. I wondered when she'd returned from the bar's back room. "I'm the one who suggested a bunch of the stops to Declan in the first place."

It was as if she hadn't spoken. No one even looked at her.

That was harsh. Sure, Janel was a little lacking in social graces, but there was nothing wrong with outspokenness.

Into the resounding, uncomfortable silence that followed, Carissa suddenly squealed, "So thanks for a wonderful party, you guys!" She held out her arms as though to hug everyone—everyone except Janel, I assumed. "It's been so, *so* fantastic!"

Hmm. That was a lot of enthusiasm for what was essentially Declan's wake. Carissa bounced up and down in between hugging each person good-bye, looking for all the world like me at fourteen: the NSYNC fan club years. I was shaken by her erratic emotions—but not as shaken as I was by the way she hugged *me.*

Carissa's grip was viselike. I couldn't breathe.

"Don't let me down, Hay!" my friend commanded, using one of those (unwanted) nicknames I've told you about. "I'll be watching you! Don't mess up Declan's tour and make me break both your legs!"

She tittered and released me, grinning oddly. I've been to a few engagement- and wedding-related parties. I didn't recall ever being threatened, Mafia don style, at any of them before.

Still, I was sympathetic to Carissa's heart-rending position. So I did what I could to play along. "You don't fool me," I joked after drawing in a much-needed breath. "You won't do the job yourself. You'll have your enforcer do it for you."

I aimed a flippant glance at Austin, underlining my wisecrack. But the look on his face truly gave me chills. *Austin would kill for Carissa,* I thought as I looked into his bleak eyes. The question was . . . had he done so already?

I shuddered and made my getaway. It was time to retrieve Danny and get down to the business of catching a killer. Again.

Seven

When I went to grab Danny, I couldn't find him.

It was as if he was ditching me on purpose. If this continued—with my protection expert *and* with Travis—I was going to develop a complex. They'd never avoided me simultaneously.

Frowning with bewilderment, I made my way through the lingering Cartorama vendors (none of whom seemed in a hurry to open their carts for the day), peering beyond Muddle + Spade's northwest décor to the faces of everyone present. No dice. No one there was tall enough, broadshouldered enough, or anywhere near tough enough to be my oldest friend, Danny Jamieson.

At first, I wasn't worried. I thought Danny had probably slipped away with Lauren for a more intimate tête-à-tête. The two of them had been canoodling pretty heavily. But then I glimpsed Lauren huskily laughing at one of Tomasz's jokes and got concerned.

People were dropping dead. I couldn't risk losing Danny.

With my heart rate kicking into high gear, I shouldered my bag and headed outside. I felt the weight and rectangular solidity of Declan's iPad thumping against my ribs, reminding me of all the promises I'd made to Carissa. I didn't know if I could successfully lead the Chocolate After Dark tour. I'd need to do some homework first—brush up on any new chocolatiers who'd opened up shop in Stumptown since I'd last been there. . . . probably a year or so ago, by now, I recalled as I left the bar's warehouse-y exterior and traveled across the parking lot to Cartorama.

I'd been to Portland several times before—most notably for the city's annual ChocolateFest, which brought together cacao lovers, confectioners, wineries, distilleries, and chocolate purveyors of all types for an extravaganza of chocolate sampling, competing, and tasting. There were cookies, cakes, fudge, and truffles, plus vinegars, oils, and hand-harvested salts. Also, beverages—hot chocolate, liqueurs, wines, and more.

Most cities host a similar event these days, but Portland's ChocolateFest was special. So, to me, was Danny. Where was he?

The cart pod was still quiet as I made my way past its center picnic tables. On the narrow neighborhood street beyond, a few cars chugged past. Overhead, blue skies and clouds sailed over the trees surrounding Cartorama's lot. I could see why the pod's location was in demand. It was peaceful and cozy, the kind of place developers tried to mimic with planned communities but couldn't quite nail down. A woman walked by pushing a baby in a stroller; a middle-aged man jogged past, panting "hello" to her.

It was all so quaint, *I* practically wanted to live there. Especially once I glimpsed Chow the cat, sunning herself nearby. Ordinarily, I'm a dog person. But that black cat's attitude of calm composure lured me in. Despite being (technically) homeless, Chow appeared absolutely zen. I could have used some of that serenity. Plus, what's not to like about cuddling a cat?

But succumbing to retro nostalgia (and my own sporadic yearnings for a pet and/or home base to chill out in) wouldn't help me find Danny. I stopped outside a coffeehouse that occupied a vintage Routemaster double-decker bus, with seating in the top and a kitchen and ordering area in the bottom, then frowned.

Frustrated, I scanned the bus. It was repainted green, so it wasn't the iconic Bus Red color that tourists would have recognized around Piccadilly Circus or Westminster, but its charm remained intact. My Anglophile mom would have disagreed, of course. But since not all of us currently live in Mayfair, we can't all be quite so picky about our vintage-bus situations.

A rustling sound nearby caught my attention. I started.

A *clunk* came next, followed by the creak of a door.

I wheeled around, temporarily forgetting about finding Danny. I trod mostly silently against the paved blacktop in the middle of the pod, following those sounds toward . . . Carissa's Airstream trailer? Just as I realized what I was looking at, the door swung open a little farther. Instinctively, I ducked.

Whoa! I almost bashed my head on the menu board hanging off Lauren's cart. I winced, belatedly noticing Sweet Seductions' listing of available treats: Slutty Brownies were fairly self-explanatory, but Screaming Chocolate Orgasm wasn't. Neither were Cherry Bombs, Lick Sticks, or Choco Bliss Bites.

Equating the pleasure of chocolate with sex is pretty common, but it's not my thing. Chocolate is *amazing*. So is sex (of course). But the two of them together? No, thanks (no way). Getting my sheets all gooey with hot fudge or gunking them up with cookie crumbs is not for me. Besides, those edible "chocolate" body paints generally *aren't*. Enjoyably edible, that is.

I once consulted for a company that made that stuff. I still have nightmares about it sometimes. Don't ask me what's in it. I'd rather not say. But *maybe* you should steer clear.

The sound of footsteps thumped back into my consciousness, dragging me out of my mental roundabout. I snapped back to alertness and peeked around Sweet Seductions' menu board.

Janel White hurried in the opposite direction, carrying a bundle of something clear and crinkly in her hands. It looked like . . . a giant wad of plastic wrap? That she'd taken out of Carissa's Airstream trailer? Perplexed, I tried to examine it more closely. Janel was moving too quickly for me to make out details like printed logos or labels, but it was definitely plastic wrap. The foodservice variety was longer, wider, and more durable than the stuff you might buy for your home kitchen, but it's otherwise identical— unmistakable in broad daylight.

Janel wasn't managing one of the food carts. She certainly didn't work at Churn PDX with Carissa. I'd have been surprised if she had a key to the trailer—I knew firsthand how tricky they were to come by. If Janel was strictly a *fan* of Cartorama (and she was), what was she doing with an obvious foodservice item?

"So this is what you're doing for fun now," Danny said.

His deep voice startled me. I lurched, my heart pounding.

A few feet away, Janel jerked up her head, then ran faster. She must have heard Danny's voice and decided to skedaddle. Now I might never know what she was doing or why she was doing it.

I'd have bet my emergency stash of bittersweet chocolate *carrés* (four-gram individual squares, perfect for a pick-me-up when a whole chocolate bar was too much) that it was something nefarious. That was just the way my week was going so far.

". . . spying on innocent people," my lunkheaded body-guard continued, oblivious to the (potential) drama he'd interrupted.

What had Janel been doing with that plastic wrap? More importantly, why had she appeared so *guilty* about having it?

I gave Danny a shove. "Thanks a lot, Captain Oblivious! You scared her away before I could find out more."

"More about what? How to keep food fresh?" Danny chuckled, rebounding with ease. He's light on his feet, like Chow the cat—only a lot less skittish. He seemed pleased to see me. "There are at least half a dozen food carts within shouting distance. People are bound to have plastic wrap around here."

He didn't understand. "Didn't you see how *suspicious* she looked?" I flailed my arm, exasperated. I watched as Janel disappeared. "That might have been an important clue."

"*Plastic wrap* might have been an important clue?" Danny crossed his arms, appearing unconvinced. He studied me, unsmiling now. "Travis was right. I was right to come here."

"Wait a minute." Incredulous, I stared at him. "Did you just say, 'Travis was right'?" I shook my head, pantomiming knocking something out of my ear with the heel of my hand. "I must be hearing things, because that's impossible."

"He was right to call me. I was right to come here."

"You—" I broke off, speechless with confusion. "You

never agree with Travis. He *never* agrees with you. Those are laws of nature, like 'water is wet' and 'gravity is constant.'"

"And 'Hayden is procrastinating.'" Danny had the audacity to smile at me. But I didn't want to trade jabs just then.

"Or 'Danny is late again.'" *Okay, maybe I did.*

Then I realized that Danny *wasn't* dead, and I *wasn't* going to stumble across his lifeless body the way I had Declan's yesterday. All the fight went out of me. Temporarily, at least.

Just seeing someone familiar made me realize how tightly wound I'd been. Hoping Danny wouldn't notice my lapse into sentimentality, I scowled at him. Elaborately. With gusto.

He laughed and shook his head, catching on instantly. "You quit arguing pretty quickly there, boss. It's that bad, huh?"

Darn him and his perspicacity. I suddenly felt like crying. That's what being understood does to me. Being truly *known* is pretty rare in my life, given all the places I travel and the strangers I meet. I'm proud of my independence. I cherish my freedom. But Danny knows how to get to me like no one else does.

"So, what's with you and the dead bodies all of a sudden, huh?" Danny's dark-eyed gaze roved over me, seeing all. "Travis said you stumbled onto another one and called him all aflutter."

"Aflutter?" Now I was really offended. "I was *never* 'aflutter.' Concerned, yes. Freaked-out, okay. But 'aflutter'? *No.*"

"Granted, he also said you sounded pretty loaded at the time," Danny went on nonchalantly. A few of the Cartorama vendors emerged from Muddle + Spade and began walking toward the pod. "Even so, we both decided it would be best if I—"

"Hang on." I held up my palm. "You 'both decided'?" This didn't compute. I must have misheard him, just as I had thirty seconds ago. "Are you and Travis *collaborating* on something?"

Danny scoffed. Then he shrugged. "Well, actually—"

"Oh, my god. You are. The apocalypse has begun."

"—we're collaborating on *you*," Danny finished with a quirk of his mouth. Some women would have found it attractive. I knew better. "It seems pretty obvious that you're struggling."

"I don't have to listen to this." My mind raced a zillion miles an hour. Danny and Travis had *collaborated*? But they were sworn enemies. They always had been. My world had tilted. Nothing good could come of this. I started walking, kidding myself I could somehow outrun it. "You shouldn't have come."

I remembered the SFPD detective he'd started seeing in San Francisco. She'd been nice. Now I'd accidentally taken Danny away from her—and all for a nonsense mission that he and Travis had concocted. They were too protective of me sometimes.

"I'm here because you need some help. Some perspective." Danny broke into a jog, easily keeping up with my tromping footsteps. "Maybe some relaxation. Like a trip. A nice, relaxing trip to Aruba."

I keeled to a stop at the sidewalk. Behind us both, the cart pod was gradually coming to life, its vendors unaware of the world-shattering event happening just a few yards away.

Danny and Travis really were getting along. What the . . . what?

"Aruba is where Travis has always dreamed of traveling," I broke in, crossing my arms. "You know, if he ever shakes his rampant airplane phobia. Exactly what's going on, Danny?"

He hauled in a deep breath. "We both think you need—"

"You 'both think'?" I groaned, then stomped onward.

"—a vacation." Danny pursued me. His athletic strides ate up the ground between us. He'd taken up running while in San Francisco (or sometime before), and it showed. He cornered me at my rented Civic, pinning me between his arms and the driver's-side door. "You've been under a lot of stress lately," he told me. "That's why you're seeing *murder* around every corner. You need a break."

"You need to quit being so patronizing."

"You need to quit being so defensive."

"Stop overreacting!"

"You go first." My sometime bodyguard gave me a headshake. "Repeat after me, 'Nobody was murdered here yesterday.'"

He had a lot of nerve. "You don't know that."

"I'm pretty sure I *do know* that," Danny disagreed. "Clue number one? There aren't any police investigating."

"They didn't investigate Adrienne's death, either."

"Clue number two? The odds of you stumbling onto two murders in two weeks are infinitesimal. You know that."

I did. I'd had exactly that same thought myself. Still . . .

"There was an actual death here yesterday! I saw it."

"And that's why you called Travis. You wanted one of us to intervene—to reassure you before you got carried away." Danny gave me a sympathetic look. "What happened at Maison Lemaître would have gotten to anyone. You need time to process it. Then the world will stop seeming like such a big, scary place."

It was my turn to scoff. "I'm not making any of this up."

"You're upset. I see that." His voice wound around me, hitting up all the familiar soft spots. "Come on. Let me help."

I wanted him to. But I didn't trust this unprecedented alliance between Danny and his sworn nemesis. Exactly *what,* I wondered, had I said to Travis on the phone last night?

It had definitely gone beyond "What are you wearing?"

I wished I could take it all back. I wished I'd been warier about letting Tomasz mix up superstrength drinks for me.

"Fine." I raised my chin. "You want to help? Then get in the car. Let's go."

"When I said I wanted to help," Danny grumbled to me sometime later that afternoon, "this *wasn't* what I meant."

Disgruntled, he eyed the blowout on the table between us at a local chocolate shop. We'd ordered two flights of drinking chocolate—premium milk, white chocolate orange peel, and spicy Mayan for Danny, and delicious dark, cinnamon masala, and cardamom rose petal for me—plus an assortment of goodies to share. So far, we'd sampled a "firecracker" chocolate bar made with chipotle chiles and exploding Pop Rocks candy, a pretzel toffee swirl bar, and a honeycomb bar with crystallized ginger.

"Well, that's too bad for you," I told him, trying to sound contrite (and probably failing—I was a little miffed). "This is what I need help with. If I'm going to lead Declan's culinary tour tomorrow, I have to bone up on the tour stops."

"What happened to your die-hard procrastination streak?"

"I never had one."

Danny almost broke his ribs laughing at that. He knew me too well—well enough to know I was avoiding a confrontation with him. He wanted a reaction. He was pretty close to getting it.

I had to say, though, the chocolate we'd tried was going a long way toward assuaging my soured mood. I might not have wanted Danny acting as an on-demand babysitter (courtesy of Travis), but I didn't mind having company as I ate and drank my way through some of the best chocolate-themed foods in PDX.

This was our third stop. So far, I felt okay about taking on Declan's chocolate tour. I was more ready than I'd thought.

"I've had enough." Danny shook his head, pretending to voice a serious objection for a change. "I'm getting fat."

I eyed his taut midsection and laughed. "As if."

"I don't even like this stuff!" he complained. "Ugh. It's all so . . . *chocolaty*. What they did to those chipotle chiles was sacrilege. They belong in a freaking burrito. End of story."

I attempted to give him a conciliatory look. "That's not true. Chiles and chocolate are both tropical New World fruits. Pairing them showcases their inherent richness. Or sometimes their fruity or smoky flavors. I would have preferred a nice guajillo chile to offset the floral flavors of the cacao, but—"

"Enough!" Danny groaned and gave me a time-out signal.

"—chipotles are more accessible," I continued. "The lemon and grapefruit notes in my Bolivian cacao beans are nicely highlighted by the flavors in my cinnamon masala blend, though, so I'm scoring this one an A minus. How's your white chocolate?"

"Sweet." Danny's face suggested that was a criminal

offense. "Why don't any of these places serve suicide hot wings? Vindaloo pork? *Sichuan huo guo?* You know, actual *food*?"

"You are a masochist. Food shouldn't bite back."

"Nah. That's where the adventure is." Danny's eyes gleamed as he recalled some of our previous trips together. "Remember when I ate that phall curry in Birmingham?"

I did remember that dish. The Brummies typically made it with nine or ten different chiles, including habaneros and notorious bhut jolokia peppers—aka "ghost chiles."

"There's a reason the Indian military has weaponized those ghost chiles," I informed him. They'd turned them into tear-gas-like hand grenades to fight terrorism. "They are *not* food."

"The chef *did* wear a gas mask while cooking it."

"My point exactly." But we were getting sidetracked. I nodded at my cinnamon masala drinking chocolate, redolent of black pepper, cardamom, coriander, and ginger. "Maybe you should have some of this. The cinnamon in it is good for you. It regulates blood sugar, reduces inflammation, boosts memory—"

"Yeah . . . who are you again?"

"Ha, ha. And it improves digestion, too."

Danny sprawled in his chair, as comfortable in an upscale chocolate salon as he was in a street fight. He regarded me with his usual patience. "Are you done getting the upper hand yet?"

"I don't know what you mean," I lied unconvincingly. Then, "Anyway, no. Which you might realize if you drank more of your chocolate. Go ahead. Take a big whiff," I directed in my best professorial tone. "Did you know that the smell of chocolate increases theta brain waves, which promote relaxation?"

"I'm practically asleep already," Danny drawled.

"Good. Because when I tell you what's been going on at Cartorama, you are going to freak out," I warned him.

"I doubt it. By the way, Travis says you should cut down on the booze." Danny fiddled with his demitasse cup of chocolate, appearing to have no intention of imbibing more. "I'm pretty sure he's conducting an audit of your liquor budget right now."

That sounded about right. "What he should be doing is cutting back on my lodging budget. You should see the Airbnb that Travis set up for me this time. It's ridiculous."

"Show me." Danny aimed his chin at the door. "Let's go."

"No way. I'm onto you, pal." I tasted more of my cardamom rose petal chocolate. Its Middle Eastern notes were intriguing, if a tiny bit reminiscent of Grandma's linen cupboard. "You want to go there to get my things and hustle me out of town. I'm not leaving, Danny." I was beginning to feel dizzy, thanks to all the sugar and high-test chocolate. "I mean, sure. Maybe it would be smart to just grab my suitcase"—it was always packed, anyway—"scratch 'become a chocolate-tour guide' off my bucket list, and jet off to someplace less deadly," I began.

"Good idea." Danny nodded. "Let's make that happen."

"But I can't abandon Carissa! Not now. She needs me," I protested. "I'm her friend. I'm not the kind of person who skips out on a friend when the going gets tough. You know that."

I'd finally gotten through to him. I could tell.

"I would agree," Danny said, "if you weren't seeing *murders* around every corner." He pronounced "murders" as if it had show lights and a Broadway marquee behind it. "You're overwrought. The fact that you can't tell you're overwrought only proves it."

I hesitated for a second, *almost* buying that argument.

"'Overwrought'?" I arched my eyebrow. "Have you been reading Jane Austen or something?" Then I got it. "*Aha.* Travis."

Danny nodded, infinitely patient. That was one of his better qualities. At least it was when it wasn't aimed at convincing me I was hallucinating Declan's potential murder.

"I understand *murder* is unlikely," I whispered, glancing around the mostly deserted chocolate shop as I tried to summon a modicum of patience myself. "That doesn't mean it can't happen."

"It usually means it *didn't* happen, the law of averages being what it is." Danny ignored the chocolate on the table between us in favor of studying my face. "I'm serious. Leave."

"*I'm* serious. No." I sipped my dark chocolate, crooking my pinkie to show I still had fight left in me. "Drink up."

My protection expert didn't. "You hired me to advise you."

"Right. You've advised me there's no risk here. So, what's the problem? I'm staying."

Danny almost growled. "If there was really a murder—"

"You'd stay? And help me figure out whodunit?"

"This isn't a joke, Hayden. Why are you digging in?"

He'd used my given name. He was serious. I sobered up. "I already told you—I'm staying for Carissa. To support her. To help her launch Chocolate After Dark. Plus, I think I'm uniquely qualified to figure out who might have killed Declan. People open up to me, Danny. You know that. And, anyway, I'm already involved. I think someone might have *poisoned* me yesterday."

My exaggerated ghoulishness only elicited a sigh.

"'Tommy' mixed your drink too strong. You were hungover, that's all."

Lauren. I silently cursed her knowledge of Cartorama, Muddle + Spade, and me. "It felt worse than a hangover."

"But you're staying, anyway? Like I said, Travis was right."

"I'm fine now. No worries. Now that *you're* here, you can help me." After Maison Lemaître, I'd asked Travis to put Danny's freelance-security-expert services on retainer. I didn't want to pull rank with him, but . . . "You're going to help me, right?"

He eyed me with evident reluctance. "It wasn't exactly a barrel of laughs last time. You got hurt, remember?"

I pooh-poohed to show I wasn't scared. But I was.

I would feel a lot better with Danny backing me up.

"This is my second time sleuthing," I informed him assuredly. "I'm a quick study. I'll have improved a lot by now."

"How much better could you be? It's only been a few days."

He was right. Not much time had elapsed since my adventures with homicide in the Marin Headlands. That was why Danny and Travis thought I was seeing shadows. I was sympathetic to their position (minimally), but that didn't change my intentions.

Or my suspicions. "My suspects are the Cartorama vendors." No reason not to jump in with both feet, right? "Especially Janel, Austin, Tomasz, and Lauren. They were closest to Declan."

"Lauren didn't do it."

I grinned. "Too sexy to be a killer?"

Danny reconsidered. "Although she *was* sleeping with

the deceased," he mused. "Behind Carissa's back, too,
so—"

"How could you possibly know that?"

He shrugged. "I coaxed. I deduced. I won. I know. Did
you think I was just drooling over Lauren like a lovesick
idiot?"

"If it walks like a duck and quacks like a duck . . ."

"I was getting the lay of the land. Just in case."

"Then you *did* think there might be trouble at Cartorama?"

Despite Danny's lip service to the law of averages,
he'd taken the time to gather information. I found that
heartening.

Even if he *had* dropped in on me out of the blue.

"What about Carissa?" Danny asked. "She's a suspect."

"She is not!" I was appalled. "She's grief-stricken."

"She's acting pretty strangely," Danny disagreed. "Of
everyone, Carissa has the most reason to mourn Declan.
But she seems pretty freaking psyched that the wedding
is off."

I couldn't *entirely* disagree. "I think she's medicated."

We discussed the likelihood of that, downing more
chocolate as we got into the swing of things. Even my
bodyguard noshed on more of the sweet stuff I'd selected
for him, although he—like Declan—probably would
show no signs of indulging later.

Men. Was it possible that Carissa had offed Declan just
because he'd made a mockery of her relentless need to
diet? *Nah . . .*

"What about everyone else?" Danny named a few
other vendors in the cart pod. Evidently, he'd gotten to
know everyone at brunch while I'd been outside snooping.

If only we'd teamed up earlier. "Did anyone else have a reason to want Declan dead?"

"Not that I can tell so far," I admitted, glancing at the chocolate shop's pierced, hipster worker. "But with you as my trusty assistant, I'll be able to cover a lot more ground."

"Hang on. I'm going along with this, *this one time.*" Danny delivered that edict in no uncertain terms. "But only to prove to you that there *aren't* boogeymen hiding around every corner."

"Mmm-hmm." I nodded, knowing he'd bend later, if I needed him to. I couldn't risk looking him in the eye. Otherwise I might accidentally chortle with triumph. "Of course."

"You need to stop seeing *murder* everywhere you look," he insisted. "I don't intend to make a habit of this stuff."

I appreciated his motives. I did. "Neither do I."

I meant it. It's not as though I *like* murder and mayhem.

"Good. Then we understand one another." Danny waited a beat. Toyed with the Pop Rocks bar. Eyed me. "I hate to speak ill of the dead, but Declan Murphy sounds like a real tool."

I was glad he agreed. I was glad he was on board, too. If Danny was willing to analyze the people involved in the deadly goings-on at Cartorama, then he was committed to helping me. Once he was committed, Danny was (like me) too stubborn to quit.

"Yes! A complete jerk!" I marveled at our synchronicity. Then I realized I'd accidentally blurted out that comment with a lot more delight than the situation called for. "I mean, I never met Declan," I told Danny in a more

subdued tone, "but from what I can tell, he wasn't very
nice—to Carissa or to anyone else."

I told Danny about Austin's history with Declan. And
about Declan's habit of responding to Carissa's "I love
you" texts by typing "U2" . . . which she'd said made her
"get a little stabby."

"'Stabby'?" Danny raised his dark brows with con-
sternation. "She said that? And she's still not a suspect
because . . . ?"

"Because she's my friend. She's not a killer."

"You're too nice, Ms. Mundy Moore. As usual."

I ignored that misguided remark and went on. "Janel
told me Declan had a whole posse of women he'd slept
with and discarded. Maybe including Lauren. Even if we
know for sure they were seeing one another, we don't
know how long they'd been together. Maybe they'd split."
I trusted Danny's intuition, but I wanted to verify for
myself. "That makes Lauren and Janel suspects."

"Agreed. Did you see the way Berk followed Janel into
the back room earlier?" Danny glanced at the ceiling,
remembering it. "If I didn't know better, I'd think he was
tapping that."

I made a face. "Classy, Mr. Jamieson." *Ugh.* Also, "Why
couldn't he and Janel be an item? Maybe Tomasz killed
Declan because he was jealous. Or maybe Tomasz
resented Declan for callously breaking Janel's heart after
they hooked up."

Danny's face told me he didn't agree—probably because Janel wasn't conventionally pretty. I thought that
was shortsighted. People fell in love—or lust—for all
kinds of reasons.

"Then you think love was the motive?" Danny asked.

I did. I'd believed the same thing at Maison Lemaître.

"Why not?" I asked. "There were a lot of intrigues

going on at Cartorama. People sleeping around, trying to keep secrets—"

"No one can keep a secret forever." Danny sounded as though he had experience in the area. There were things about my security expert I didn't know—and didn't want to know. "Nobody."

I shivered. "Or maybe the motive was money," I suggested, purposely distracting myself. I told Danny about the real-estate developers who'd tried to take over Cartorama's property. "Maybe they—or the pod's landlord—haven't given up yet?"

"It would be easy enough to find out. I'll tap—"

"Travis. Ask Travis." I didn't want Danny interacting with any of his shady friends from his past, not even for the sake of quickly gathering intel. "He can run a background check."

"If Janel's protest efforts were that effective, it ought to be easy to find a record of who the development company was." Danny gave me a knowing look. "And I was going to say 'Travis,'" he informed me with a wiseass grin. "We're best buds now."

"Ha. That'll be the day." Something else occurred to me a moment after that—something that made me feel instantly better. "This collaboration thing you and Travis have going on explains why he's been ducking my phone calls lately, doesn't it?"

Danny nodded. "He didn't want you to catch wind of what we were up to and bug out before I got here. I doubt a straight arrow like him trusts himself to talk to you *and* keep a secret at the same time."

"Well, it wouldn't have been easy. I know Travis pretty well by now." Reminded of what I'd learned about Declan and the people who thought they knew *him,* I told Danny about Declan's disparate likes and dislikes. "The weird thing is," I explained, "everyone I talked to believed that Declan spontaneously loved all *their* favorite things just as much as they did. *Everyone.*"

My longtime friend nodded. "There's a reason for that. Ask any con artist. People open their wallets faster if they think they're dealing with someone who's similar to them."

"And their hearts? Do they open them faster, too?"

Declan hadn't wanted money from anyone. Not that I knew of.

Danny shrugged. His silence made me think unhappy thoughts about his past, his unusual skill set, and my own (occasional) susceptibility to his bad-boy charms. Then, "Yeah. They do."

"But then I'm always the romantic in a crowd," I joked at the same time, moving on deliberately. "Just ask my exes."

"I don't have to," Danny said. "I have reason to know."

His meaningful tone made me look away. I picked up my third demitasse of chocolate—the darkly delicious one—and drained it.

My cup clattered back into its tiny saucer. "Let's jet."

I was on my feet and tossing down a tip before Danny could even blink. That's how I operated. On the move. Not tied down.

Not even to Danny. Or to Travis . . . and his sexy, sexy voice.

"Hold up, hotshot." Danny grabbed my arm to stop me. *Uh-oh.* I straightened my spine. "Yeah?"

If Danny intended to slow me down again, I was going to bolt. I'd already spent enough time dithering about whether I should be concerned with murder or not. Now I had more practical matters to think about—such as finishing vetting the stops on Declan's Chocolate After

Dark tour. I didn't want to implicitly endorse any place I didn't personally approve of. My reputation is all I have. In my business, credibility means everything.

After doing that, I intended to find a way to exculpate Carissa. I needed proof of her innocence. For Danny. Not for me.

I knew my old university friend was in the clear. But if I wanted to avoid going twelve rounds with Danny about it, I had to have some answers to trade. I needed to find out more about Carissa and Declan. I couldn't do that if Danny waylaid me now.

"Now what's the problem?" I asked him, hands on hips.

Declan's iPad swung in my bag, thumping me on the side.

"You tipped a hundred bucks." Danny stuffed the bill back in my hand, giving me an inquisitive look. "You don't need to make it rain. You didn't even get a lap dance out of the deal."

I shrugged, then brandished the money he'd returned. I strode to the table, dropped off the Benjamin, then smiled at the chocolate worker. "Have a good one," I told her.

I would rather have died than admit I'd only meant to leave five dollars. Especially to Danny. He was touchy about my unearned inheritance. It was a sore spot between us. The least said about it, the better, I decided as I sailed back out again.

Besides, I could definitely afford it. It was no big deal. Even if I *did* feel vaguely, inexplicably *guilty* about all of it.

Out on the sidewalk in one of Portland's tawdry-but-appealing up-and-coming neighborhoods, I gestured through the window to Danny. He looked at the tip I'd left, plainly still bothered by it. Then he frowned and followed me out.

"I think you should drive the tour van," I told him.

"I think you shouldn't push your luck," he replied.

But I knew that was Danny's way of agreeing with me. I was glad. We were on our way to solving Declan's murder—as longtime friends, first-time tour guides, and two-time sleuths—together.

Eight

If you've never been to a funeral, I envy you.

At the best of times, in my experience, a memorial service is a sad blend of melancholy, remembrance, and regret—all stirred up with a heaping helping of unfamiliar formality, which leaves the mourners utterly off balance, uncertain of where to go or how to act or even what to say in those difficult moments.

Under those circumstances, inevitably, someone decides to stage-direct the whole thing, causing relief and hard feelings in equal measure. Once you drop in a few long-lost friends and estranged relatives, then add the horrible element of a young man "accidentally" dying unexpectedly, you've got a recipe for . . .

. . . well, for what happened at Declan Murphy's funeral, actually. Because it was, hands down, the weirdest service I've ever attended.

The first sign that something might go wrong was when I spotted Janel White, somberly dressed in head-to-toe black, lingering near the entryway of the funeral home. She was holding an elaborate bouquet of white stargazer lilies—one almost as tall as she was. As I approached in my own muted black dress and flats, my shoulder-length brown hair whisked into a subdued ponytail at my nape, I noticed the other mourners who were standing nearby her. As they moved, Janel jerked up her flowers to cover her face. Her lilies trembled as she hid behind them.

Then, as the other mourners began making their way into the funeral home together, Janel quickly crab-walked inside amongst them. I blinked and stared as she vanished into the mortuary. It seemed Janel was using Declan's loved ones as *cover.* But why?

Deciding I'd probably misunderstood what I'd seen, I headed up the funeral home's stairs. Inside, I heard organ music and low voices. Then one particular voice rose above them all.

"Okay, let's get this show on the road, everyone!"

Carissa. Apparently, *she'd* taken on the role of stage director. As I stepped inside and bowed my head amid the mourners, wondering if I should have come at all, I heard her clap her hands for attention. "Come on! Declan wouldn't have wanted us all to be so sad!" Carissa urged in a hearty voice.

There were a few grumbles in response to that. Some apprehensive looks, too. I spied Carissa at the far end of the room. She stood near Declan's casket, dressed in a chic black dress that even I (who don't shop much) could tell was new.

Her auburn hair was wound up in a tasteful chignon, and she'd switched out her geeky tortoiseshell glasses for a pair of suitably serious black-framed specs. Her diamond engagement ring gleamed on her left hand, noticeable even at a distance.

"We still have the graveside committal service to get to!" Carissa called out, holding her hands protectively in front of her chest. "If we don't start soon, we'll ruin our schedule."

I stopped, aghast at her seeming callousness. There were probably three dozen bereaved people there to pay their respects to Declan. It was a sizable turnout on behalf of a young man who'd only moved to Portland in the past year or so. Now, every one of them gaped at Carissa. An older woman near me glared.

I heard muttered complaints from farther away and rushed to my old friend's side. Because that's when I *also* noticed the tremor in Carissa's beseeching hands, the redness around her eyes, and the tautness in her neck. She held herself so rigidly, it looked as if her neck might snap at the slightest breeze.

Mourning Declan was clearly very difficult for Carissa. No wonder she seemed insensitive to everyone else. She couldn't help it. None of them knew her the way I did.

"Carissa." I enfolded her in my arms, inhaling hair spray and perfume along with the funeral home's background aroma of candles and commercial cleaning solution. It was a nice place, as houses of mourning went, I guess, but I didn't want to think too carefully about what went on behind the closed doors I'd seen. "I'm so sorry. I'm here for you. How are you holding up?"

"Well . . ." Carissa's voice broke. She dabbed her teary eyes. "I've been better," she struggled to say. Her next shuddering inhale seemed to restore her composure a bit. "How are you?"

"I'm . . ." *Heartbroken for you.* "I'm worried about you."

As social niceties went, hers were both unnecessary and tragic. Her forced cheeriness reminded me, in an uncanny way, of the Carissa Jenkins I remembered from university—a woman who'd rushed her eventual sorority with glee, led the school's Spirit Week festivities, and jumped on any chance to have a good time.

But this new Carissa—the woman who'd lost her fiancé just weeks before her wedding—now looked pale and broken, nothing like the student I'd known *or* the upbeat ice-cream vendor with an unforeseen knack for manipulating liquid nitrogen I'd met.

It occurred to me that I didn't even know if Carissa had gotten along with Declan's family. Maybe there was some discord between them, and that's why she seemed so tense today?

Carissa blinked, then focused on me. "How are the tour preparations going? Did you have a chance to visit all the stops?"

I understood. She wanted distraction from her grief.

I obliged . . . even as I spied Austin trundling down the aisle between the folding chairs that had been set up for the viewing, dressed in a poorly fitting suit and another knit beanie—a black one, this time.

"Declan's tour is fine," I assured Carissa. "I've met all the shop owners." There had been only a few I hadn't known already. "I've tried all the best chocolates at all the stops."

Carissa nodded, looking heartened. "Then you were able to access all the information on Declan's iPad?"

Ruefully, I shifted. Danny hadn't been wrong about my procrastinatory tendencies. I hadn't even turned on that iPad.

"Don't worry. I have everything I need," I hedged.

A frown. "Really? Because some of the info was password protected. Even I didn't know Declan's password," Carissa said.

I didn't want to get trapped by details. The important thing was reassuring Carissa and helping her feel better. My excuses for delaying my necessary pretour prep could wait.

"I've got it covered," I told her. "Really. Don't worry."

It was true. I'd find a way, I knew. I always did.

Around us, the funeral home was filling up. People were taking their places in the folding chairs, gathering to talk, and occasionally hugging. There was crying. There was music.

There was Austin, nearly prostrate at Declan's coffin.

"Oh no!" I exclaimed, nodding. "Look at Austin."

Carissa frowned at him. "What's he doing?"

A sob rent the air. It came from Austin.

"*Ugh*. He barely knew Declan." Carissa sounded annoyed. She rolled her eyes, then cast Austin an impatient glance. "Some people will do anything for attention, won't they?"

"I don't think that's it." I squeezed her arm, gazing into her (irked) face. I guessed Declan really *had* kept his gamer-geek friendship with Austin under wraps from everyone at Cartorama. "Maybe I can help him. Will you be okay?"

"Sure. Go ahead." She waved me off. "We'll talk later."

Her apathetic tone left me dismayed. How could Carissa feel this indifferent to her friend Austin's suffering?

Unless Austin *wasn't* really suffering. Unless he really *was* grandstanding, as she'd suggested just now. Who would know better, me (who'd just met him) or Carissa (who knew him)?

I didn't want to think the worst of Austin, though. For the sake of keeping the peace (if nothing else), I hurried to his side. Behind Austin, the other bereaved waited their turns.

I tiptoed up to him, then hunched to peek at his face. It was almost obscured by his shaggy hair and beard. The sounds of sniffling and sobbing kept me on course. I felt sorry for him.

"Hey, Austin." Gently, I put my hand on his shuddering back. His suit felt slippery and new beneath my palm. "Hi."

He gave a mighty sniffle, then glanced at me. His whole face sort of *blubbered* in my direction. His eyes overflowed with tears. He fisted them away, then heaved a sigh. *Poor Austin.*

"It was my fault," he croaked. "I shouldn't have let him—"

"Shh. It wasn't your fault." I put my arms around his shoulders, then lightly tugged him away from Declan's casket. "It wasn't anybody's fault. It was a terrible, awful accident."

Even if it wasn't, this wasn't the time to debate it.

"I'll never forgive myself!" Austin protested hoarsely. He searched his pockets for a tissue, then produced one. "I can't."

In the distance, Carissa rolled her eyes at us again. It was clear that grieving didn't bring out the best in my friend. I couldn't hold it against her, though. Losing someone is hard.

"Come on, Austin. Why don't we go over here?" I murmured.

He let me nudge him to the side. As we moved to allow other mourners access to the casket, I caught a glimpse of Declan's body inside. At the sight, my stomach somersaulted. For the past day or so, Declan's death had become sort of a puzzle to me. I'd almost forgotten that there was real loss—real *tragedy*—here.

If Declan had been murdered, I thought, the people who loved him deserved answers. They deserved justice, too.

But was I capable of giving it to them? I was just a globe-trotting chocolate whisperer, there to celebrate a wedding that wasn't. Despite my experience at Maison Lemaître, I wasn't the kind of person who poked her nose into other people's business.

Maybe, I knew, I ought to listen to Danny and Travis. Maybe I ought to launch Chocolate After Dark, then bow out gracefully. Maybe I ought to let Austin and Carissa grieve the way they wanted to, no matter how messy or inappropriate it seemed to be.

I decided that's what I'd do . . . until about fifteen seconds later, when things got even *more* messy and inappropriate.

"You!" Someone's voice boomed across the room, full of anger and outrage. "What do you think *you're* doing here?"

Everyone hushed, including Austin. I craned my neck to see who'd spoken and saw an older woman, maybe in her late fifties, dressed in a knee-length black sheath dress and slingbacks. At her side stood a dignified-looking man of similar age, wearing a charcoal suit and laced-up oxfords. He reached for her hand.

"Carissa's parents," Austin explained in a low tone, all but reading my mind. Mrs. Jenkins's outburst seemed to have diverted him from his own sorrow. "They *loved* Declan."

That seemed reasonable. But it didn't quite explain what came next. "*You* can't be here!" Mrs. Jenkins pointed at someone, her face a mask of fury. "This is unwanted contact! A hundred and fifty feet! That's what the civil protection order said. You can't come within a hundred and fifty feet of him."

She strode closer to whoever she was confronting. The other mourners edged aside to make room, murmuring and pointing. When they parted, I saw that Janel White stood at the center of the mêlée, looking as if she'd been shot in the heart. Her pale face was tear streaked, her blond bob a mess, her posture defiant.

"Declan's *stalker* has no place here!" Mrs. Jenkins cried.

Janel was Declan's stalker? I darted a glance at Austin. He was busy gazing mournfully (and hungrily) at Carissa. *Uh-oh.*

"That restraining order was a mistake." Janel's voice quavered. She held her head high, her stargazer-lily smokescreen clasped in her hand. Those flowers now hung uselessly at her side. "Declan never wanted that. Carissa made him get it."

"You liar!" Carissa came forward, eyes flashing. "I can't believe you had the nerve to show up here. Get out. *Get out!*"

Janel held her ground. "I just want to say good-bye."

"Declan said good-bye to *you* a long time ago," Carissa sneered. Her mother frowned and hugged her closer. "Just go!"

All the Jenkinses stood united against Janel. Mr. Jenkins—autocratic, gray-haired, and imposing—drew himself up.

"Young lady, I'd suggest you leave immediately," he said.

Janel wavered. She glanced at Declan's coffin as though considering making a run toward it. Animosity bristled from the Jenkinses to her. I have to say, I was confused by all the drama.

I'd never had a chance to meet Carissa's family while we were at uni together. Now I was glad about that. They were scary, at least while being protective of their daughter.

Although this new "stalker" information *did* explain why almost everyone at Muddle + Spade ignored Janel. They had all adored Declan, believing *he* adored them and their favorite things. They were plainly on the anti-Janel side of this argument.

I'd thought when meeting Janel that she was a little peculiar, but *this*? Was Janel really Declan's stalker?

If she was, was she truly dangerous enough to warrant a restraining order? The whole thing seemed like overkill to me.

"You'll be sorry for this, Carissa," Janel vowed. "Someday you'll regret *everything* you've done. I swear you will."

Then she marched to Declan's casket, lay her white stargazer lilies on its closed lower half, and drew in a breath. Oblivious to the onlookers, Janel leaned down and kissed Declan's waxy face.

"I'll *never* stop, Dec," she murmured. "I promise."

Then, with that choked-up oath delivered, Janel turned her stocky body toward the other mourners, flipped them a matched set of middle-finger salutes, and left the service behind.

Janel's appearance at Declan's funeral left me with more questions than answers—and left everyone else with a month's worth of gossip, besides. I could tell, after Janel stormed out, that everyone present was eager to chatter about what had just taken place. But the sad situation required more decorum than that, so those conversations took place in whispers, between nods and sniffles and exchanges of much-needed tissues.

Everyone was *shocked,* they murmured. *The nerve,* they added. But I couldn't help admiring Janel's spirit and dedication, if not the way she'd upset everyone. She'd found a means to say good-bye to Declan, despite plenty of resistance, and she'd done it *her* way, besides. At her exit, Austin actually laughed.

No one else did. It wasn't appropriate, especially at a funeral. But Janel's newsworthy arrival (and departure) loosened up Declan's memorial viewing in a way that nothing else could have. Different mourners came together to express their outrage. Carissa basked in an outpouring of sympathy. Mr. and Mrs. Jenkins stood at the center of it all—with Declan's parents, who apparently lived in Portland, too—indignant and protective.

I sat in the rearmost row of folding chairs with Austin, next to a row of flickering lighted candles, at a respectful distance from Declan's casket, wondering why—if a protective order had really been necessary against Janel—Carissa's parents knew so much about it. I mean, some parents were more involved in their children's lives than others. But that seemed . . . weird.

"They're both lawyers," Austin informed me when I asked him. He seemed to be feeling better. I was glad. In a low voice, he added, "As soon as Carissa complained to them about Janel, they lowered the boom but quick. Declan was barely involved."

Interesting. "Was Janel really stalking him?"

"If by 'really stalking him,' you mean 'really, *really* wanting to be his girlfriend,' then yes," Austin said. "She was."

"But surely Declan didn't actually need a protection

order? He was a pretty big guy. Janel is a lot smaller than he was."

"Sometimes it's not about strength." Austin's gaze wandered to Carissa. Locked on. Held. "It's about persistence."

I was starting to think *he* seemed like a stalker himself.

Hoping I'd misread him, I gave his shoulder a companionable nudge. I nodded toward Carissa. "You're worried about her."

"Aren't you?" His attention transferred back to me. "She's acting strangely. I mean, maybe that's the antidepressants talking. Who knows? But I hardly recognize Carissa anymore."

That was surprising. "Really? In what way?"

"Shush!" A grandfatherly type turned to quiet us. The glare he delivered from beneath his bushy gray eyebrows was fearsome.

The minute he turned to the front again, Austin and I collapsed into silent, shared giggles. That was a compulsorily solemn occasion for you. Sometimes it brought on inadvertent rebellion. Not that I was at risk of doing a full Janel-style, flying-middle-finger salute. I wasn't. I had control of myself.

"Carissa used to be really positive," Austin told me, seeming to take comfort in our conversation. "Bubbly, even."

That meshed with what I remembered of my friend.

"But the last couple of months—" Austin shook his head, his face sorrowful. "She hasn't seemed like herself. Some of the time, Declan *really* seemed to get on her nerves, you know?"

I did know. I knew that must have given Austin unwarranted hope that he and Carissa might eventually be together, too.

I nodded. "Prewedding jitters, maybe?" I guessed.

"Maybe." Austin fussed with his funereal black beanie. "I think it was more than that, though. I know it sounds crazy now, but I think Carissa was going to break it off with Declan."

I didn't think so. But as I reconsidered Carissa's palpable relief at not having to diet to fit into her wedding dress, plus her glee at the brunch-turned-wake yesterday, I had my doubts.

Carissa sometimes seemed more *angry* with Declan than anything else. That would have fit with Austin's theory. But maybe she was simply angry with Declan for leaving her.

"If so," I settled on saying, "she wouldn't have been the first person to ever call off a wedding at the last minute."

Austin gave me a speculative look. Wisely, I clammed up.

At least I did until I saw Tomasz and Lauren near the other set of chairs, that is. He was outfitted in an immaculate black suit that *had* to be borrowed, because I doubted a mostly broke barman could afford such a thing. Despite my gypsy upbringing, I *do* understand the finer things in life, so I recognized the trademarks of the house of Arnys, on the Rive Gauche in Paris.

Arnys's bespoke tailoring stands out in the same way that fingerprints do, especially to someone who's seen it before (like me, via Uncle Ross). Tomasz's suit wasn't an Armani or a Gucci; it didn't carry an obvious label. Recognizing an Arnys garment is more subtle than that. Let's just say, this was the suit that Clark Kent would have worn if his alter ego had been James Bond instead of Superman. It was the suit that an international man of mystery would have worn to go undercover, stylishly and perfectly. Not that I thought Tomasz understood as much.

He was wearing that suit as if it came from Goodwill,

with zero reverence for its tailoring and quality fabrication. It was endearing, actually. Where another man might have subtly (or subconsciously) peacocked around, soaking up admiring glances, Tomasz turned all the attention onto other people instead. It was almost as if he didn't *want* to be seen looking so fantastic.

Ahem. In a sad, funereal context, I mean. Of course.

Beside him, Lauren really *was* wearing clothes from a thrift store. She looked typically theatrical in a close-fitting black dress, high-heeled pumps, and (I'm not making this up) a pillbox hat with a veil. Think "sexy Jackie Kennedy," and you've got it.

The whole getup made her look as if she had something to hide. I mean, let's be real—a veil is meant to *conceal.* That's its entire raison d'être. Lauren was keeping something hidden.

Was it her affair with Declan? Or something more sinister?

I didn't know when the two of them had slipped in to pay their respects to Declan. I wasn't surprised Tomasz had shown up with Lauren, though—or that he was currently in the midst of making introductions while the viewing continued. Berk seemed to be a classic "connector"—a person who thrived on creating links between people—so, naturally, he would have felt at home anywhere.

"Hmm, they're arriving late," I mused to Austin, trying to lead him into giving me more Cartorama gossip.

"I'm surprised Lauren is here at all," he muttered darkly.

I sensed more info on its way and leaned nearer to catch it while watching Lauren and Tomasz. "Really? Why's that?"

Silence. Confounded, I glanced at Austin beside me.

His malicious glare was back. It was focused on *me.*

"You obviously already know." His tone was low and menacing, his voice shaky. "So, why keep playing dumb?"

His vehemence shocked me. "I'm not playing dumb! I'm—"

Investigating. I couldn't very well say that, could I?

Regardless, I never had the chance. Because Austin shot me another killing look, then burst upward from his chair.

It tottered in his wake. He swore and kicked it. *Hard.*

Since Austin wasn't an inconsiderably sized man, the chair practically crumpled as it fell backward, leaving me stunned.

Its crash against the floor drew every gaze in the place. By then, though, Austin was already stomping away. He didn't care. Lauren did, however. At least I thought she did—her veiled face turned toward Austin as he marched out of the funeral home.

An instant later, she whispered to Tomasz, then followed.

That was *definitely* my cue. I checked to make sure Carissa was okay—since it seemed almost time to begin the eulogizing portion of Declan's memorial service—then made a beeline for the mortuary's door, following Lauren. I couldn't add much to the fond remembrances of Declan's family and friends. But with a little effort, I might be able to learn who'd wanted him dead.

In the long run, that was more valuable. Grateful for my practical flat shoes (honestly, most of the time, I'm wearing kitchen clogs, so I don't get all atwitter about footwear), I followed the same path that Austin (and then Lauren) had.

Halfway there, someone stepped in my way. *Tomasz*.

I can't say I was 100 percent unhappy to see him. I mean, sure, he was technically thwarting my nascent investigation. But honestly, he was doing it in a pretty easy-on-the-eyes way.

Maybe, it occurred to me, stress had messed up my usual equanimity. Because it wasn't typical of me to go all gaga over a guy—or anything else for that matter. I'm pretty even-keeled.

Most of the time, I know what to do and how to do it— and I get on with doing it, wherever I happen to be. For example, I wouldn't order a Lyon wine while consulting on a chocolate job in Burgundy. While in Burgundy, similarly, I wouldn't think of offering fewer than four cheek-to-cheek kisses to someone. That's just the custom, no matter how it's done elsewhere in France. (FYI, if you're in Paris, *deux bises* are expected.)

On the same note, I don't tip after meals in Japan (it's considered an insult), and I don't *ever* jaywalk in Düssel-dorf. The Germans don't do jaywalking—they do rules. Just like me.

What I'm saying is, when it comes to cultural mores, I'm capable of fitting in. Except sometimes, of course. Say, if those mores insist I be unaffected by the tall, rakishly handsome bartender who'd just stopped me to say hello.

Tomasz took a look at (what must have appeared to be) my distraught expression (since I knew Austin and Lauren were getting away) and pulled me in for a sympathy hug. I melted.

Unlike Carissa, Tomasz Berk didn't smell like hair spray and perfume. He smelled like soap and expensive wool, mingled with what my finely honed chocolate-whispering senses told me was a trace of chocolate. I'd never seen him eating any delicious cocoa treats, but that obviously didn't mean Tomasz never did.

That whiff of chocolate reminded me, unfortunately, of everything else that was on my agenda for the day. Declan's funeral, a check-in phone call to Travis, a consult with Danny, and then—much later—my inaugural Chocolate After Dark tour.

I didn't have time to waste. So I pulled back, then patted Tomasz on the lapel of his fancy suit. "Nice Arnys," I said.

Then I winked and headed outside, knowing—the way a woman always does—that the probable riddle of what I'd just said (and the mysterious French way I'd said it) would make Tomasz wonder what I'd meant all day long. Exactly the way I wanted him to do.

That would teach him, I decided as I stepped into the fresh springtime air outside, *not* to know the provenance of his suit. Because while Arnys was now closed, its excellence appeared to live on—just as my ambitions to find Declan's killer did.

In the end, I stumbled upon Lauren and Austin outside the funeral home much sooner than I'd expected. That's because, this being Portland (aka the epicenter of bike culture), Austin had put on his black suit and black beanie and ridden his bicycle to Declan's memorial service. Even now, as Lauren stood over him in her ultradramatic funeral garb and harangued him, Austin fumbled with his bike's U-lock, trying to get away.

". . . can't *believe* you actually showed up here!" Lauren shrieked as I approached. "If you hadn't gotten on your high horse about covering for us, Declan would still be alive!"

Austin's shoulders slumped. Oblivious to me, the street full of parked cars, and the rest of the world, he finally wrenched open his U-lock. He pulled it free. Not looking at Lauren, he wheeled out his blue road bike from its parking spot. He pulled on the nylon backpack he'd dropped at his feet, then straightened. His getaway was clear. Still, he hesitated.

So did I. I wanted to hear what he said. I slowed down. Then I realized I should smarten up my gumshoe game, in case he or Lauren noticed me. I ducked and fussed with my shoe.

"If *you'd* taken no for an answer," Austin said through what sounded like gritted teeth, "Declan wouldn't have been scrambling at the last minute like that. He would have paid more attention to the nitro tanks! He would have seen—"

"It wasn't *my* fault!" Lauren interrupted. "I never asked Declan to sneak around. I asked him *not* to! Didn't he tell you?"

"He never had a chance to," Austin protested.

"All I wanted," Lauren said, "was for him to be with *me*."

"Well, he didn't want to be with *you,* did he?" Austin shot back, hard and fast. "Not when it came down to it, he didn't. If you'd realized that, like, two days earlier, he'd be here now."

The venom in his voice startled me. I wanted to believe Austin was a nice guy. But just then, he didn't sound very nice.

Neither did Lauren. "It could have worked out for both of us," she jeered. "Just the way we wanted. But *you* had to go and get cold feet. Now Declan's dead and everything is horrible."

She burst into tears. In response, Austin muttered

something I couldn't hear clearly. I probably didn't want to, either.

I straightened anyway, giving up the pretense of fixing my shoe for the sake of getting a better look at what was going on. What can I say? Lauren's misery had sounded authentic. So had Austin's anger. I wanted to know what they'd been conspiring to do together. Whatever it was, it sounded as though its failure had been costly for both of them—and deadly for Declan.

If I could only *see* them clearly, I thought, maybe I—

—could be interrupted by Tomasz again. *Argh.* He'd followed me.

"The viewing is winding down. They're gathering everyone so the service can start." Tomasz gazed at me from his much greater height, his eyes as blue as the sky. Against that backdrop, with his dark hair ruffled by the breeze and his black suit stark against the trees, he belonged on an album cover. *The Greatest Hits of Indie Men,* maybe. "I thought you'd want to know."

"I do. Thanks." It was the truth. I didn't want to let my inexpert info-gathering interfere with supporting Carissa.

Tomasz's gaze tracked Lauren and Austin. His brow furrowed.

Given how much he liked taking care of everyone at Cartorama, I figured he was troubled by any hint of discord.

"Emotions run high on a day like today," I misled him, hoping to spare his feelings—and thwart any attempt to intervene, the way he seemed liable to do. "Austin and Lauren will be hugging it out in no time. Just wait and see."

Tomasz quirked his mouth, looking doubtful. It was, I realized, the same expression Danny often gave me. He and Tomasz were a lot alike. Both were tall, dark, good with their hands. . . .

"Fine!" Lauren screeched. "Just get away from me!"

She gave an unintelligible grunt. Tomasz and I both looked back toward her, pulled by that sound. At the same instant, Austin veered into the street, half on and half off his bike.

Was he getting away? Or being pushed away?

I glimpsed a flash of metallic gray. *An oncoming car.*

Frozen in shock and horror, I watched as Austin wobbled on his bike, bulky and graceless. He leaned sideways, off balance.

No, not off balance, I saw. He was trying to snatch away the beanie that had slipped down his shaggy hair. He was blind.

"Austin!" I found my voice and my feet at the same time. I pounded toward him, heart thudding with fear. "Look out!"

The thing I'd forgotten about Portland, though, was that *because* it's a bicyclist's nirvana, it's also home to a very healthy "share the road" campaign for safe bicycling. That's probably why, even as I reached the curb, the driver of the oncoming car spotted Austin, slowed way down, and crept past.

I expected a rolled-down window and a string of expletives for Austin's "carelessness." Instead, I watched as the attentive driver peered through his passenger-side window at Austin, saw that he was unhurt, and then gave him—all of us—a cheery wave.

Limp with relief and spent adrenaline, I reached Austin. My legs felt rubbery, but my voice worked. "Are you okay?"

I searched his bearded face for signs of distress—and

found them in abundance. Austin might have narrowly escaped being seriously injured, but that didn't mean he was overflowing with the joy of existence. He was distressed, all right. The proof of it was in the murderous glance he aimed at Lauren.

"Nice try," he growled. "But *I'm* not as easy to kill as Declan." Then Austin swung onto his bike and pedaled away, leaving all of us—or at least me—wondering what he'd meant.

Nine

After attending Declan's funeral, watching Austin almost get pancaked by a late-model Subaru, and firing up Declan's iPad for an eleventh-hour pretour cramming session (only to discover that parts of it really *were* password protected, just as Carissa had told me earlier), I was kind of a wreck. "That's what you get for waiting until the last minute, Procrastination Queen," Danny would have told me . . . except he wasn't at my cozy foursquare Airbnb house with me just then.

He *was* staying there—but only because (I'm convinced) Travis had told him *not* to do that. Because when Danny had called up my financial advisor (presumably to tell "Harvard" their scheme to "protect" me had succeeded—and maybe to kvetch about my over-the-top accommodations), they'd immediately started bickering.

Paradoxically, their argument had reassured me. Because if Danny and Travis were sworn enemies again, that meant they both thought the danger to me was past. That was excellent news.

Less excellent was the realization that, if I wanted to ace my first Chocolate After Dark tour, I'd have to rely on nothing more than my own expertise. While I'm totally comfortable with that (because if I'm not going to believe in me, who will?), I wasn't exactly at my best that afternoon. Already it had been an emotional, exhausting, confusing day—and it was only half over. If I was going to excel later, I'd need a boost.

But I couldn't go straight to the good stuff. That was no way to work my way through my to-do list. So first, I did all the things I usually do when setting up a temporary home base in a new city. Since arriving in Bridgetown, I'd neglected (for various reasons) my habitual post-check-in ritual, but now it gave me comfort to get everything all set up for maximum hominess.

I didn't bother unpacking my wheelie suitcase or my duffel bag. (Are you kidding?) There's no point, when I'll be moving on before long. But I *did* take out my favorite fig-scented candle and set it beside the bed, where I could light it to feel at home. I did arrange all my framed photos in strategic spots throughout the house, so I could see the smiling faces of my family and friends. And I did lay my trusty pashmina on a corner of my living-room sofa, where I could grab it if I got cold.

Padding around, still restless in the too-large space Travis had chosen for me, I cast a disgruntled glance at Declan's iPad. Thanks to its password protection, it was as good as useless. If it had run out of battery life or Internet connectivity as well, it would have been nothing more than a fancy slab of aluminosilicate glass, anodized aluminum, and assorted rare earths—essentially, a gigantic drinks coaster.

That's why I relied on paper for everything important. My Moleskine notebooks aren't fancy, but they *always* work. They don't demand that I track down Wi-Fi coverage in the middle of a remote village or find a plug, converter, and/or appropriate transformer just to access my upcoming chocolate consultations. My friends often nagged me to transfer my to-do lists to my smartphone, but I was comfortable with my routine as it was.

Speaking of which, it was time for my favorite part of that routine: calling Travis. Full of anticipation for the boost I'd been purposely delaying until now, I settled in on the sofa.

My call connected almost immediately. To my delight, Travis's smooth, sexy, ultradeep voice came over the line.

"I hope you're sober this time," my advisor said.

You know . . . *sexily.* It was the only way Travis said anything. He couldn't help it. With his Barry White depth and raspy delivery, he could (and did) make things like spreadsheets and stock options sound appealing. As far as I was concerned, it was the secret of his success—along with his human-calculator brain.

Distracted for a second, I pictured all the admins and associates at his Seattle firm stopping whatever they were doing every time Travis spoke. I imagined them all swooning.

Just like me. What can I say? I like what I like.

Mostly, I like having Travis (literally) on call. I snuggled into my sofa cushions and cradled the phone, unable to resist smiling. "Hey, Travis. What are you wearing right now?"

His sigh traveled along the line. But I could swear I sensed him smiling, too. Just like me. "An expression of relief," he said. "If you're calling me, you must need an exit strategy. I already have holds on airfare and accommodations."

"*Hmmph.* Presumptuous, much? I'm not leaving, Travis."

"Not because *Danny* asked you to, no," he agreed with

a knowing ken. "I didn't expect you would. He's just the muscle."

"What, to make sure I get on the plane?" Hypothetically, that was—*if* I accepted the escape hatch Travis was dangling.

"If necessary," Travis said amiably . . . almost seductively.

Who am I kidding? *Of course* he said it seductively. He couldn't help it. He was Travis. But he was also mistaken.

"You already spoke with Danny," I reminded him. I'd been nearby, but I hadn't butted in. I'd wanted my own private time with Travis. "Didn't he tell you I was staying in Portland?"

"I understand he was unable to convince you to leave."

At his unassuming tone, I almost laughed. That was one way to put it. "Nobody makes me do anything. You know that."

"It's possible you can be persuaded."

By you? "Maybe."

But Travis knew I was toying with him. "Leave, Hayden. If that muscle head couldn't convince you, let me. Just leave."

"Nope. Also, I've got to say, so far, your approach is identical to Danny's." I paused. "I expected better from you."

He must have shifted in his chair, pondering his next move, because the sound of pinstripes on leather traveled over the line—at least in my imagination, it did. I pictured Travis in his deluxe high-rise office near Puget Sound, holding a pen in his talented fingertips, leaning back in his desk chair . . . wearing a suit, an air of command, and a surplus of intelligence.

I knew he looked forward to our conversations as much as I did. How could he not? It couldn't be *all* responsible transfers of itineraries, client details, and fiscal data between us.

"You have other commitments this week." Travis detailed them, running through my calendar with practiced ease. "Leave."

Or maybe it could be *just the facts* between us. I was disappointed by his lack of imagination.

"No problem," I said. "Those things can be rescheduled. I'm staying." I glanced around my impermanent living room, feeling enlivened. It was good to banter with Travis. "Next?"

I expected him to counter with financial concerns. Or maybe a demand that I consider my business reputation. Portland was an emerging culinary destination, but it couldn't yet compare to conventional foodie hot spots like London, Paris, or New York.

Or Barcelona, Copenhagen, or Tokyo. Or even Melbourne.

Hmm, maybe I ought to leave soon.

"What happened to you at Maison Lemaître was traumatic," Travis said calmly. "You need time to process it. It's natural that you might feel vulnerable. That you might imagine similar crimes happening in other places. I understand that. But—"

"Still sounding like Danny," I broke in. "I'm telling you, Travis—things are suspicious around here. Declan Murphy was killed. On purpose. I'm not imagining that. I wish I were."

His rumble of frustration gave me goose bumps. The good kind. Despite being (temporarily) at odds with my "keeper," I felt better than ever. Travis's voice and calm demeanor worked on me like nothing else. Danny might have that bad-boy appeal going for him, but Travis has everything else—security, stability, the ability to nurture houseplants and home life.

With Danny, I could have adventure. With Travis, I could have the prototypical house, kids, and a basket of puppies.

Not that I'm on the hunt for a capital-R "Relationship." I'm not. But if I had been, Travis would have been a contender—if not for his crippling air-travel phobia, at least. That was a deal breaker, for sure. Otherwise, he had everything I craved.

On the other hand, Danny and I had been together for ages. Much of that time we'd spent as (mostly) platonic pals, trying *not* to give in to the (perfectly natural) attraction between us. The rest of the time . . . Well, I was too busy talking with Travis to think about it just then. Reminding myself of that, I regrouped.

"You might as well give up, Travis. I'm assembling proof that Declan Murphy was murdered." Where my talk with Danny had focused on motives, my talk with Travis needed to center on practical matters. Danny was the motive guy; Travis was the means man. I'd just decided it. "What happened to Declan should have been impossible," I pointed out. "There were safety measures—"

"I'm not indulging you with this."

"—time constraints, issues with access—"

"You're out of your depth."

"—questions involving the timeline and liquid nitrogen—"

"I know as little about solving crimes as you do," Travis protested, sounding exasperated. "This *cannot* be happening."

"Please help me, Travis. Please, please, please, please." I hauled in a breath. "If you don't, I'll have no choice but to brainstorm exclusively with Danny." I purposely injected a note of uncertainty into my voice. "While that worked last time—"

"Hey! *I* helped last time. I was *instrumental*."

Boom. I had him. "I knew you had some ego in there."

"You can't expect to malign a man's contributions and get away with it." Travis exhaled. I pictured him loosening his tie. Rolling up his shirtsleeves. Getting ready to do exactly what I wanted to do, exactly the way I wanted to do it. "If I help you figure out what *might* have happened in Portland, will you agree never to chase a hypothetical murderer ever again?"

Unlikely as it was, I'd just encountered two suspicious deaths in two weeks. That wasn't a promise I could make.

"Do you know anything about liquid nitrogen?" I asked instead. "That's essentially the murder weapon."

I went on to explain to Travis what I knew about the stuff Carissa had been using to fast-freeze her custom ice creams. I described its benefits, its dangers, and its unique qualities.

"Only someone with very specific knowledge would have known how to set up Carissa's trailer so that Declan would suffocate to death while filling the tanks," I explained. "Unfortunately, that doesn't narrow down the suspects much. At least one of them helped design the custom software used to dispense the liquid nitrogen." *Austin.* "Another had complete access to the trailer." *Janel.* "Actually, maybe several people had access to it."

Was it possible that Lauren and Declan had had rendezvous there? It would have been convenient, with her Sweet Seductions cart only steps away (but too dinky to canoodle in). If so, Declan might have given her a key. Carissa sure wouldn't have.

As I'd hoped, Travis didn't seem to notice that I *hadn't*

promised not to try to track down any future murderers. While I hoped that wasn't an issue that would ever come up again, I valued my relationship with him. I didn't want to break a promise. Unlike (maybe) Austin had. Or Carissa.

You'll be sorry for this, Carissa, Janel had vowed at the funeral. *Someday you'll regret everything you've done.*

That certainly sounded as though Carissa had broken a promise. Or, you know, done something pretty reprehensible.

From Janel's viewpoint, I reminded myself, Carissa was the enemy. She was the one who'd taken away Declan—kept him away, too, by getting engaged to be married to him. Maybe Carissa's engagement party weekend had driven Janel over the edge.

"The person with the most access would be Carissa," Travis said. His blunt statement jarred me out of my reverie.

"Carissa could have manipulated her trailer any way she wanted to," he went on. "She could have tampered with the safety on the liquid nitrogen tanks. Or blocked the ventilation."

That was true. Technically. "Why does everyone want to blame Carissa? She's essentially the grieving widow. She had no reason to want her fiancé dead." *Unless she knew about his flings with Janel and Lauren,* I amended privately . . . uncomfortably. But I didn't want to discuss suspects with Travis. I'd already done that with Danny. "Carissa loved Declan. She nearly died trying to save him! She would have known better than to go inside the trailer if she was the one who'd sabotaged it."

"From her viewpoint, going inside would have been a reasonable gamble—and an excellent way to deflect suspicion," Travis argued. "The two of you were meeting that morning. She knew you would be there if and when she needed to be rescued."

"I almost *wasn't* there, remember? Besides, that's hardly a foolproof plan. I couldn't even drag out Carissa all by myself," I reminded him. "Austin helped me. I was lucky he was nearby."

"Were you lucky? Or was Carissa right? Maybe she knew Austin would be there. She had to have known his schedule."

I still refused to believe my friend could be a killer.

"Everyone knows everyone else's schedule at the cart pod," I debated. "That doesn't narrow the field much."

Although it did remind me that Tomasz's windows at the bar overlooked Cartorama. Maybe he'd seen something suspicious?

I made a mental note to ask him, then moved on.

"You know what this means, don't you?" Travis asked.

"That it's going to be difficult to catch the killer?"

"That there probably *wasn't* a killer. You said the police ruled this an accidental death—"

"They said the same thing about Adrienne Dowling."

"—so while it's technically correct that unregulated liquid nitrogen could cause enough oxygen displacement in a small, enclosed space to asphyxiate someone, that doesn't mean—"

There's a murderer on the loose. I didn't want to hear it.

"Why am I not surprised you already knew all the science-y details?" I broke in. Although I'd only just briefly described what I'd remembered Austin telling me about liquid nitrogen, Travis seemed to be well-versed in the subject. I was impressed, but perplexed. How did people get to know this kind of stuff, anyway? The only topic that had ever *really* interested me long enough to get into it was cacao, its flavor, and all its myriad permutations. "You need to get out more. Have some fun."

"I am having fun." *Talking to you.* Sure, I added that particular spin on his statement myself, but I didn't think I was wrong. Travis's husky tone confirmed it—and upped the pleasurability quotient for me, too. "But I don't believe Declan was murdered," he said. "The proof just isn't there."

"It could be. I've barely started looking." I pulled over my cashmere pashmina for warmth, just as someone came striding up my provisional front porch. I glimpsed Danny through the window. "I'll find something. Just wait and see."

"I'd focus on Carissa if I were you," Travis advised.

I suppressed a grumble of frustration. I was getting tired of everyone pointing the finger at my old college friend. Now I needed proof of Carissa's innocence for Danny *and* for Travis.

"You're too nice, Hayden," my financial advisor went on, sounding uncannily similar to my protection expert. "You hate to think the worst of people. That tends to cause blind spots."

"Blind spots? You mean I've been missing something all this time? Do you have a deep, dark secret, Travis?" I teased, completely willing to entertain *that* idea. "Does it involve body art? Illegitimate children? Overdue library books?"

I liked the idea of Travis being less than perfect.

He scoffed. Then . . . "I did accidentally kill a guppy once."

"Travis!" I tsk-tsked, feigning outrage.

"I was seven at the time. I overfed it. A lot."

He still sounded broken up about it. That was adorable.

I couldn't help picturing a tiny (bizarrely Barry White–voiced) Travis at seven years old, eagerly sprinkling fish food.

"That's why, after I got my next fish, I started using a microbalance to weigh out precise amounts of fish meal, shrimp meal, plankton, and freeze-dried daphnia for them to eat."

"Wait a minute." My delightful picture of teeny Travis (and his inexplicable access to lab equipment) faded. Probably, he'd asked Santa for pipettes, a microbalance, and dental floss instead of toy trucks, Legos, and a football for Christmas. "Did you just say 'fish meal'? You made your guppies *cannibals*?"

As Danny came inside our (now) shared foursquare, he shot me an understandably bemused look. He sprawled in an easy chair.

"No, guppies naturally eat fish," Travis told me. Casually.

What? This *horror* was what I got for wanting to glimpse my financial advisor's less-buttoned-up side. I was appalled.

"Well, at least 'daphnia' sounds nice," I tried. "Is that some kind of sea flower or something? You know, like dessert?"

"Leave it to you to want to treat the guppies to something sweet." Was Travis joking? "Daphnia are freshwater fleas."

Revolted, I gripped the phone, unwilling to admit defeat and hang up. If my idealized notions of aquatic life had to go down, they were going down swinging. "But *Finding Nemo*," I objected. "Nemo and his dad—they wouldn't—they couldn't—"

Eat other fish. I just couldn't say it out loud.

"Clownfish eat algae," Travis informed me reliably.

I sank back onto the sofa cushions, full of relief.

"Also, plankton, mollusks, and crustaceans, like shrimp."

That meant meat. Ugh. "No!" I howled, joking. Mostly.

"Hey, eat lunch or be lunch." Travis sounded terrifyingly matter-of-fact. "For someone who's determined to investigate a murder, you're pretty squeamish. Sure you won't reconsider?"

Aha. "This has all been a ruse?" I gawked. "You—"

His laughter cut off the rude epithet I had in mind.

I never would have expected Travis to be tougher on me than Danny had been. Evidently, my keeper had untapped depths *and* a willingness to plumb them. I'd have to keep that in mind for next time. If there was one. I really hoped there wasn't one.

Part of me just wanted to go back to perfecting brownies.

"Admit it, Hayden," he said. "You're in over your head."

"Never." Carissa was counting on me. Plus, I couldn't simply leave the question of Declan's death unanswered. I like to know the hows and whys of things. That's why I'm so good at troubleshooting chocolate. I like to solve riddles. I have the ability to stick with that process when the going gets tough.

On the easy chair nearby, Danny caught my eye. He waggled an unfamiliar set of keys, fixed to a monogrammed leather fob.

"You're not a detective," Travis said, more seriously now. "San Francisco was a fluke, that's all. You can't do this."

Well, if he had wanted to make me double down and try, he'd just stumbled upon the best way to do it. I dug in my heels.

"I'm going to do this," I informed him tersely, "and I'm going to start by clearing your prime suspect—Carissa."

Danny quit jangling his keys. He frowned at me. But I knew what I had to do. If Carissa had sabotaged her own Churn PDX trailer, there would be signs. All I had to do was find them.

So that's exactly what I intended to do. Or not do. Because, you know, I actually wanted to come away with nothing.

"Gotta run, Travis. I have things to do. Bye!"

As I disconnected the call, Danny eyed me warily.

He was right to look at me that way. I jumped up and grabbed those keys.

"Are you coming or not?" I asked him.

He grinned, probably thinking he was putting one over on me. Just like Travis. "*Those* aren't your rental car keys."

"I know." Jauntily, I tossed them in the air. "These belong to the Chocolate After Dark tour van you just picked up." That's why I'd been alone to chat with Travis. "I'd rather not argue about where we're going, though. That's why *I'm* driving."

For this leg, I wouldn't be talking—regaling tourists and chocolate-loving Portlanders with infotainment about cacao. That left me free to execute my plan ASAP. I pulled on my jacket.

"No, you're not driving. *I'm* driving." Lazily, Danny got to his feet. He always moved like molasses when *I* was in charge of things. That had to change. "That was the plan. We're supposed to be starting the first chocolate tour in an hour."

"Yep. That's why this is the *perfect* time to go somewhere else first." I grabbed my replacement purse, still missing my original crossbody bag. (RIP, little buddy.)

"Nobody will expect to see us anywhere else." I paused. "Well? Are you coming?"

He hesitated. I crossed my fingers. I needed him for this.

Finally, Danny relented. "I can't believe Travis got you all wound up this way, then left you for *me* to deal with."

His complaining was par for the course. I didn't mind. It was how I knew he was already on board with my idea.

I headed out, trusting Danny to follow me onto the porch.

"By the way," I said, "do you know anything about cracking passwords?" I pulled out Declan's iPad and handed it over. "Because I'm going to need to get into this thing in—"

"In about an hour?" my smart-alecky bodyguard guessed.

But I was too busy staring at the Chocolate After Dark tour van to answer right away. I blinked and refocused, then frowned.

Past my Airbnb's front porch, past its small grassy lawn, parked on the street, was our designated van. Declan's tour van. The entire thing—a van that could probably seat nine to twelve people, including the driver—was covered in one of those full-color vinyl vehicle wraps. All over. It looked like . . .

Well, the words "chocolate orgy" came to mind.

"I can see why someone wanted to kill Declan," I said.

"Yeah," Danny mused. "I wasn't going to argue with you too hard about who got to drive the Choco Mobile." He gave me a mischievous, knowing grin. "This one's all yours, chief."

"I'm not sure it's legal to drive this thing." Cautiously, I approached it, keys still in hand. I shielded my eyes as the sunshine glinted off the van's custom photographic images.

I swear it was taunting me. Remember how I said I'm not especially keen on equating chocolate with sex? Well, evidently, Declan hadn't felt the same way. Either that, or he'd taken the "after dark" aspect of his Chocolate After Dark tour name a *lot* too literally. I'd hoped the van would improve up close, but it didn't. Near or far, Declan's tour van was emblazoned with lascivious images of busty, suggestive, larger-than-life women, all in various stages of tasting chocolate, wearing chocolate, or having chocolate (you guessed it) poured all over them.

On the plus side, if appearances could be believed, they'd all been dreaming of such a moment their entire (nude) lives.

It was as if Declan had never imagined that anyone except a horny frat boy would ever embark on his culinary tour. I'd seen classier come-ons in Vegas. It lacked subtlety, taste, *and* inclusiveness. There wasn't even a representative naked man.

Not that that would have helped much. But still. Equality matters. So did proper use of (non-hot-pink) fonts. Yuck.

"I think *I'd* like to kill Declan." I shook my head, feeling dwarfed by the oversize cacao-covered breasts and butts on our van. "This is the vehicle a traveling porn circus would use."

"It's the vehicle a chocolate fetishists convention would use to shuttle conventioneers to the airport." Danny peered at it. "Why not just go for an X rating? Go big or go home."

I didn't agree. I was glad the chocolate (barely) preserved

the models' modesty. "I'm going to get arrested driving this."

"You might never work as a chocolate whisperer again, that's for sure." In the midst of taking out his phone for a commemorative snapshot, Danny hesitated. "Speaking of which, I think I recognize that 'chocolate.'" He made (justifiable) air quotes with his fingers. "Remember that body-paint consult?"

He waggled his eyebrows with sham lecherousness, trying to remind me. I smacked his shoulder. "I've been trying to forget."

Danny aimed his cell phone. Sighted the Choco Monster.

"If you Instagram that picture, I'll make you regret it."

But my security expert only laughed and clicked away.

That was the moment I almost gave up. Being horrifically hungover (maybe poisoned—I still had my suspicions) had been bad enough. Attending Declan's tense funeral had been no walk in the park, either. But hearing Danny's photo app whirr as his phone took our van's picture—with *me* standing with the keys in front of it, naturally—and rocketed it to the cloud for sharing was *the worst.* I know I've told you before that my reputation is all I have. Now I was officially risking it for Carissa's sake.

I hoped I was right about her. Now more than ever.

All that remained was finding out for sure.

I hauled in a breath and took a leap of faith. Even if it hurt, I was going to help Carissa—and, by extension, Declan. "Get in the van, Instagram. I'm leaving with or without you."

Then I unlocked the doors, got in the driver's seat of our van, and prepared to take off. If I could have, I would have closed my eyes. The inside of Declan's Chocolate After Dark van was just as atrocious as the outside. The entire interior was customized with brown and hot-pink upholstered seats, plenty of neon accents, a tricked-out A/V system, and a small wet bar.

It was as if *Playboy* magazine and Hershey's chocolate had somehow had a baby, and that baby was a Mercedes-Benz Sprinter.

I didn't doubt it was expensive. I didn't doubt the customizer had personalized it to Declan's exact specifications. But I *did* doubt that Declan had any business acumen. Austin had let slip that Declan had had a "cushy" job at a Seattle real-estate company (or maybe a tech company). So how could he have ordered this tour van and approved it? Was this one of the "really boneheaded" things Carissa had said Declan had done?

An ugly, sexist van wasn't the worst thing in the world.

But it wasn't the best thing, either. Not by a long shot.

"You know," Danny said as he slung himself into the passenger seat, "if I were one of those douchey party guys, I would think this van was *awesome.*" He craned his neck to take in all the garish dude-bro touches inside. "This kind of thing doesn't happen by accident. This is strategy, right here."

I remained skeptical. "Strategic ugly exclusionism, maybe. Doesn't it ever occur to men like Declan that there might be *women* in their target audience, too? Women who don't necessarily like looking at naked women?" I turned the ignition. Surprisingly, the van's engine purred like a sports car's. "I mean, if the chocolate companies I work for excluded half of their customer base, right from the get-go, with bad packaging . . ."

Wait a minute. Danny was right. This had to be strategy.

"Declan *was* trying to reach someone with all this." I stopped with the van idling and time ticking. "But who?"

Danny and I gazed at each other, pondering it.

"Newspeople?" My bodyguard looked dubious. "If Declan made this thing indecent enough, it could stir up local controversy."

"*And* attention," I added, riding his train of thought to its logical destination. "That would result in free advertising. If Declan had a limited budget to launch Chocolate After Dark—"

"That would explain why he didn't take advantage of your consulting services." *The way Carissa had alluded to at brunch.* Danny gave me a look. "Your expertise is stupidly pricey."

"It's ridiculously valuable, you mean," I rebutted automatically. I have my good points, but humility isn't one of them. "I wonder what Declan's financials were like?"

Our gazes swerved in unison to Declan's iPad. I'd asked Travis to look into my suspects' backgrounds, but it would be a while before my financial advisor sent me anything usable.

"There's only one way to find out." Danny turned it on.

I wasn't optimistic about his chances of cracking Declan's password. Danny has a lot of skills, but mostly they have to do with real-world, hands-on illicit encounters. Thievery. Forgery. Bar brawls. Pickpocketing. Lock picking. Criminally high levels of confidence and felonious amounts of machismo. The usual.

I didn't think "hacker" was one of Danny's alter egos.

"It's okay if you can't crack the password," I told him as I finally pulled away from the curb and drove the "Chocolate Orgy" into traffic. I tried not to cringe. "I have a plan B."

"You don't need a plan B. It distracts from plan A."

I liked his confidence, but . . . "Seriously, Danny. I can always—"

"Call Travis?" Danny muttered a swearword. *No way* was the subtext. As usual. Things were back to normal between them.

"Okay, but put your charm attack on standby," I warned him, "because if we get stopped in this moving monstrosity—"

"I'll handle it." His grin flashed at me. "Like always."

"—or, God forbid, stalled at a construction site—"

I pictured dozens of burly construction workers cat-calling our Chocolate After Dark van. "It would be a nightmare situation."

Danny laughed outright. "I'll take care of that, too."

"Good." He thought he was winning. I knew I was buttering him up for later. This way, we both (sort of) won. "Thanks, D."

"Anytime. You know that." Danny looked touched by my old nickname for him. I'd used it back in the day, while trawling dodgy SoCal bars with him. We'd been each other's wingman.

Back then, we'd been dealing with argumentative drunks and would-be lotharios, inexpert pool hustlers and overly handsy dance partners. Now, we were dealing with a potential murderer. But the more things changed, the more they stayed the same, right? Because whatever we were facing, we took it head on.

With a side of subterfuge, whenever necessary.

Our history together was why, when Danny and I arrived at our destination a short while later, just as the Oregon sun was setting, I was able to look him straight in the eye and casually say, "Later we're going to pretend this never happened. But right now, I need you to pick a lock for me. Okay? Let's go."

He didn't move. "You must have me confused with someone else. Someone you *don't* constantly badger about law and order."

He had a point. I was concerned about Danny relapsing into unlawful behavior. Still . . . "We have twenty-four minutes. Go!"

"Sorry." Wryly, Danny patted his jeans pockets. "I must have left my bump key and torsion wrench in my other pants."

"Har, har. Pretend *not* to be a criminal another time."

He looked hurt. "I've reformed. That's what you wanted."

"Right now, I want you bad, sneaky, and capable of getting into Carissa's Churn PDX trailer so I can have a look around."

"Oh, is that all?" Danny's cocky grin reappeared. "You should have said so. I thought this was an ethics test." He nodded. "Give me four minutes, then meet me at Carissa's trailer." He returned Declan's iPad to me, opened the van's door, then paused before getting out. "Try to be cool."

"I'm always cool!"

My bodyguard cast me a skeptical look, then got out of the van. I swear, he swaggered all the way there, from my street-side parking spot to Cartorama, four whole blocks away.

The minute Danny disappeared from sight, I grabbed my bag, got out of the world's ugliest tour van, and followed him. I was impatient to get going, sure. We were on a tight schedule. But mostly I was worried that if I sat there, I'd draw a crowd of confused kids who'd mistake my van for an ice-cream truck.

The last thing I needed was a pack of hungry kids and a rioting throng of angry parents getting between me and what I was there for—any evidence I could find (or, more to the point, *not find*) to clear Carissa of suspicion. Because if I heard one more person cast doubt on my friend from college, it would be too soon.

Ten

I was late claiming my designated four minutes from Danny.

I had a good excuse, though. Because despite my bodyguard's advice, I opted to create a plan B for us. Maybe streetwise Danny was comfortable winging it, but I wasn't. After all, there was a killer on the loose. We had to be smart. If we got caught snooping around Carissa's trailer without a valid excuse (and the murderer noticed), *we* could wind up the next targets.

Thinking fast, I headed to Muddle + Spade first thing. Inside, Tomasz was busy at the bar. I gave him an artless wave and pretended to be going to the ladies' room. It was the only refuge I could think of. The cart pod provided bathrooms, but since Cartorama was essentially a parking lot with an assortment of vehicles parked on it, the pod's accommodations consisted of two Porta-Potties—*not* my preferred option for a comfort break.

I strode to the ladies' room, site of my encounter with Lauren. As you might have expected, there was a line of women waiting to use the facilities. (That's happy hour at a bar for you.) I wanted to stash Declan's iPad someplace that *wasn't* the chocolate-tour van. That way, if anyone challenged me about being in Carissa's trailer, I could claim to be looking for Declan's iPad. It was necessary for the tour, so it was a good excuse—just as long as Carissa wasn't the one doing the questioning. But she would be at home, mourning, right?

Biting my lip, I turned around, looking for a less busy location. I didn't want anyone else to find Declan's iPad during the few minutes I'd be leaving it. Decisively, I followed the path I'd noticed Janel taking to the bar's back room.

Yes. With front-of-house service in full swing, no one was around to see me. I slung off my purse, took out Declan's iPad, and searched the spacious former warehouse for a hiding place.

To my right was a small, tidy office; to my left were a walk-in refrigerator and walk-in freezer. In front of me were rows of freestanding shelving units holding local and commercial foodstuffs, along with beverages. I moved toward them, mentally inventorying beer kegs, cases of wine, liquors, and food items. I was in a hurry, but I wasn't blind. It looked as though Muddle + Spade did a flourishing business. The bar even kept sixty-kilo burlap bags of cacao beans on hand. I noticed them stacked shoulder-high on the floor next to an antique continuous roaster.

Mmm . . . I inhaled the aroma of roasted *Theobroma cacao* that lingered on the air. Those burlap bags of beans were just as picturesque as you'd envision, too, printed with their weight, their varietal, and their farm or wholesaler in rustic fonts. Unlike the antique bicycles and wooden stag heads out front, though, those bags and that roaster were being used. That telltale aroma said so. Most likely, I figured, the Cartorama vendors had pooled their resources to buy everything I saw, ensuring themselves a steady supply of high-quality chocolate.

Making bean-to-bar chocolate requires work and expertise—it's not something a casual chocolate lover can DIY. Cacao beans have to be removed from their football-size fruits and fermented (aged, but for a much briefer time than wine or coffee). After that, they still needed to undergo roasting, cracking, and winnowing—separating the flavorful nibs from the inedible shell. After that comes grinding, flavoring, conching, and tempering.

The process is labor intensive, sure, but the resulting aroma is *fantastic*. That's what went on in Muddle + Spade's back room. Maybe it was even what Janel had scurried in here to tend to the other day, since she'd mentioned having an interest in chocolate—an interest that had led to Declan's interest in *her*.

Maybe chocolate making was what Janel was studying in her ever-present books and on her laptop. When we'd hung out in the bar together, I hadn't thought to take a good look at Janel's belongings for clues. She could have been downloading bank statements, learning to code JavaScript, or writing a potboiler.

For all I knew, a few days earlier, she could have been studying the uses and abuses of liquid nitrogen, boning up on how to freeze and suffocate Declan to death as revenge for his not wanting to see her anymore.

Just as I had that bleak thought, I almost stepped on some fallen cacao beans (they look similar to gigantic coffee beans) and experienced a burst of nostalgia for my less-complicated ordinary life as a chocolate whisperer. I didn't know how I kept getting mixed up in these dangerous situations, but I did.

The sound of footsteps interrupted my mental digression into my more carefree chocolate-filled days. I looked over my shoulder. Someone was coming. Out of time, I stashed Declan's iPad between the massive stack of cacao bean bags and the former warehouse's brickwork wall. I straightened just in time.

Tomasz walked in, a bar towel draped over his shoulder and a preoccupied expression on his face. He started with surprise.

"Hayden." He smiled at me. "What are you doing back here?"

He seemed so pleased, I thought he might have gotten the idea I'd come there to seduce him—to create a *real* "happy hour" for us. He clearly had me confused with Lauren, in that case.

I had to think fast. "Janel told me about your roaster." I gestured toward it. I hoped Tomasz couldn't see my hand shaking with urgency and pent-up jumpiness. Danny was still waiting for me. "I wanted to see it for myself. It's a nice specimen."

It stood next to the more prosaic dal grinder that had been pressed into service for cracking the roasted beans and the nineteenth-century conching machine that used time, aeration, heat (and a set of heavy rollers set inside its predictably shell-shaped basin) to develop the chocolate's flavors. The roaster was the only possible one of the three that could have doubled as an attraction—even for a chocolate nerd like me.

"Ah." Tomasz nodded. "I almost forgot your background in chocolate. I'm afraid that, to me, you're Carissa's superhot friend first and an expert second." His smile broadened.

I didn't know whether to be flattered (he'd called me "superhot") or insulted (he'd forgotten I had a brain).

Tomasz's vivid smile nudged me toward the *flattered* end of the spectrum.

"I'd be happy to show you how it works sometime," he told me. "We all own it in common. The vendors take turns using it."

"Hmm, maybe." I looked around offhandedly, hoping I'd stashed Declan's iPad with sufficient stealth. "That depends."

"On what?"

"On whether you're making that offer to chocolate-whispering me or superhot me." I nailed him with a look. "Which is it?"

Tomasz appeared trapped. With good reason. "Um, both?"

"Good answer." I was tempted to flirt with him and enjoy myself a little, but I didn't have time. I clutched my purse, acutely aware of its diminished weight now that Declan's iPad was no longer inside it—*and* acutely aware of Danny waiting for me at Churn PDX. "Superhot me accepts your offer. Tonight after close?" I was a night owl, anyway. "What do you say?"

"I say it's a date. Last call's at two, though."

If Tomasz expected to scare me off with the late hour, he was disappointed. His schedule and mine meshed perfectly.

I nodded. "No problem. I'll be there."

His smile promised I would celebrate that decision later. He withdrew something shiny from his pocket. A key on a ring. "Here. Let yourself in if I don't hear you at the door."

"I will." I took the key. "That's trusting of you."

"You seem like a safe bet to me. Besides, now I've got you—I'm pretty sure your taking that key means we're going steady."

"Hm. How do you know I'm not afraid of commitment?"

A grin. "Because you're holding my bar key."

Did that sound like a double entendre to anyone but me?

"Well, you don't know how much I like a good artisanal bean-to-bar operations tour," I disagreed, just to keep him guessing. It was true. I did like a bean-to-bar operations tour. I also liked a chocolate tasting, a chocolate-recipe-development session, a chocolate product launch, an all-chocolate brunch. . . .

Despite all the trauma at Maison Lemaître, I'd always have fond memories of the resort's delectable all-chocolate brunch. Not to mention the spa's cacao-nib-and-espresso-bean pedicure scrub. Enjoying that had been one of the highlights of my visit.

Just as I turned to leave Tomasz to whatever work had brought him to the bar's back room, I remembered something else.

I might as well take advantage of our growing camaraderie, I figured. "Hey, you have a good view of Carissa's cart." I nodded toward the warehouse's windows. At the moment, the twilight view outside looked . . . ghostly. "On the day Declan died, did you see anything suspicious? I know everyone's sure his death was an accident, and I know it probably was, but"—I broke off for every woman's secret weapon: a self-effacing smile—"well, I like to imagine myself sort of an international crime-solving chocolate whisperer, so I'm kind of investigating."

"Investigating?" Tomasz raised his brows. "Really?" I couldn't miss his patronizing tone. "Have you found anything?"

I'd be lying if I said his dismissiveness wasn't deflating. Looking into a (maybe) murder wasn't going to qualify me for a Nobel Prize anytime soon, but it didn't deserve outright scorn.

"Not yet." I raised my brows and crossed my arms. "Well?"

It took him a second to catch on—to remember that I'd asked him a question . . . one he'd left unanswered. *Hmm.* I didn't think Tomasz was stupid. He seemed really smart. Although I do get the appeal of a dense-but-gorgeous "himbo" now and then, a man who's short on intelligence *and* curiosity just doesn't do it for me.

"No." He seemed to be searching for patience. "I didn't see anything. Which is what I told the police when we all gave our statements and they decided that Declan had died accidentally."

"What time did Declan go into the trailer that night?" I pushed. "Did you see him? Did you see him the next morning?"

"No. No. And no. Look." Exasperation—and something else—crossed Tomasz's face. Even upset, he looked preposterously handsome. "If you only agreed to go out with me because you want to interrogate me, then do it now. Go ahead." He spread his arms, giving me a pugnacious look. "I'm an open book."

I was taken aback. "It's not like that. I like you."

What was I going to say? That he was a suspect? That would have played well (not). Plus, I needed to get out of there.

"Well, I like you, too!" Tomasz burst out. The hubbub grew louder in the bar's front of house. Someone yelled for him. Despite that, he returned his attention to me. "I had a bad breakup a while ago. Asking you out was a big deal for me."

Oh. The *something else* I'd glimpsed was interest. *In me.* Maybe self-consciousness and vulnerability, too, if

Tomasz was out of practice with dating. That explained his cheesy come-on, I figured. Showing me his antique roaster was the twenty-first-century equivalent of inviting me up to see his etchings.

"You're kind of intimidating. You know that," Tomasz added. "You keep everyone at a distance. I noticed that right away."

I scoffed . . . then realized he was serious. Right then and there, I felt my flirtation with him heat up by a few degrees. It was irrational but true. I didn't mind seeming aloof. Or intimidating. Those weren't qualities most people saw in me.

I didn't let on, though. I was too cool for that.

"Give me a chance. You might be surprised," I told Tomasz breezily. "But right now, there's someplace I have to be, so—"

"Right. I heard something about a chocolate tour?"

Oh yeah. I was going to be late for Chocolate After Dark. Never mind Declan's porno-worthy tour van; if I didn't turn up, *I'd* destroy my credibility. It wasn't like me to get distracted.

Sure, I might procrastinate on writing a consulting report now and then. But I *do* deliver excellent work. Without fail.

"Yep. I'm late. So, see you tonight!" I turned to leave.

Tomasz's tentative expression stopped me before I could.

"If you really want to know what time Declan was supposed to fill those tanks for Carissa, ask Austin. He'll know."

"Why's that?" I assumed he meant because Austin was crazy about Carissa. Chances were good he knew her schedule by heart.

Tomasz looked over his shoulder. I remembered there were customers waiting for him. "*He's* the one I saw lurking around that morning." We both knew which morning he meant. For a moment, the barman looked troubled. Then, "Austin's cart is nearby, though. And he was usually the one who filled the Dewars for Carissa, anyway, so it's probably nothing. I'm just trying to get into Sherlock mode myself. Forget I said anything."

As if I could. With a solid lead, a date, *and* a hiding place for Declan's iPad, I was feeling pretty good about my (unwanted) future as an amateur sleuth. I nodded at Tomasz.

"I won't say a word to Austin," I promised.

But I sure as heck was going to tell Danny thirty seconds from now, I promised myself as I made my getaway. Travis too. Because if Declan really *had* been murdered (and I still thought he had), I had several good ideas who might have done it.

My designated four minutes had long expired by the time I rounded the corner and all but skidded to a stop at Carissa's trailer. Danny was already there waiting for me. Arms crossed, he lounged in the *open* doorway, full of smugness and certainty.

If the Cartorama vendors hadn't already turned on their industrial-chic festival lights overhead, I would have missed the open doorway *and* Danny's expression. It was only around 7:00 P.M., but the cart pod was already shrouded in dusk.

Chocolate After Dark was aptly named, it turned out.

"You did it!" I squealed, happy my efforts to stage a fallback plan hadn't been for nothing. Also, high on the knowledge that I'd gotten a new lead *and* a date *and* a compliment on my intimidating levels of personal awesomeness. "Yay!"

"Way to be cool." My security expert glanced behind me as though looking for an excuse. "Here's a switch—*you're* late."

I laughed. "I bet you've been waiting years to say that."

"Years . . . and five minutes. Five minutes too long."

"Funny." I divined that now was not a good time to tell Danny about my date. I nodded at the open door. "Nice job."

Despite his acerbity, I could have hugged him. I'd been worried about getting access to Carissa's Airstream. On TV or in the movies, snooping around looks easy. In real life? Not so much.

For instance, right now, there were several vendors working at their open Cartorama carts. Plus a number of customers. Any one of them could have spotted me and sounded the alarm.

I felt ultraconspicuous. Danny could tell.

He motioned. "Get in here. We've got twelve minutes."

But with the door standing wide open, twelve minutes felt like an eternity. I took a moment to marvel at our success.

"And *you* said you didn't bring your lock-picking set."

Danny wasn't much for gloating. "I didn't. I never lie."

Well, that was true. At least . . . Danny never lied to me.

His dark gaze met mine. I sauntered to the trailer and met him at the open doorway. "I get it. It was already open, right?"

"No." He looked offended. "Look, the advantages of picking a lock are exaggerated. Usually, it's a lot easier to get inside another way. You break a window, you kick in the door—"

"But the windows aren't broken and the door is intact."

He looked around the cart pod. "There are other ways."

"Such as?" I shouldered past him and stepped inside. Even after I switched on the lights to push back the twilight, the trailer's interior felt gloomy and chilly, dangerous and dank.

I didn't like being inside it. Being in the space where Declan had drawn his last breaths—where Carissa had almost died—affected me in ways I hadn't anticipated. I felt sorry for Declan, sorry for his family and friends . . . scared for myself.

What if someone had rigged this place to be a death trap again? What if I suffocated like Declan? Or froze to death?

My nervous glance skittered to the twin liquid nitrogen tanks standing at one end of the trailer's approximate sixteen-by-seven-foot interior. Even though I knew Austin had already fixed the safety mechanism, they gave me the willies. They might as well have been two gigantic bombs. While I knew there were no such things as ghosts (of course), I couldn't deny feeling strange about stepping onto the spot where Declan had died.

"Such as getting a spare key from Lauren," Danny admitted as he followed me in, squashing my self-inflicted scare-a-thon.

Aha. Now I knew the Sweet Seductions vendor had a key. That meant that Carissa, Janel, and Lauren all had access. Who else?

Danny shut the door behind us. "I told her you needed to get some things out of Carissa's trailer for use on the tour."

I turned to him. "Really? And Lauren folded, just like that? She handed over the key?"

Danny studied the trailer's interior with a practiced eye, not drawn in by my incredulous tone. I wondered what he—a former thief—saw in the space around us that I didn't. Or couldn't.

"No wonder there was a murder here," I nitpicked, aware I was being pointlessly indignant—aware, too, of the key Tomasz had just given me to Muddle + Spade. Maybe I didn't want Danny and Lauren to be going steady, the way Tomasz had joked. "Cartorama's security practices are abysmal. Lauren just gave away Carissa's key, huh? What if *you* were a murderer?"

Danny's knowing gaze flicked to me. "Lauren and I have talked. We know one another. She doesn't think I'm a murderer."

"Well, *that* would be the best cover, wouldn't it?"

My security expert went silent. He roamed around the trailer, running his hands over its stainless-steel surfaces. The Airstream Classic had been customized for food-service with built-in prep tables, lowboy chilling units—one fridge and one freezer—to make up the bases of those tables, and nearby shelves for storage of cooking implements, aluminum individual ice-cream containers, recyclable spoons, spare spiroid paddles, and more.

It was a tight fit. There was barely room for all those things plus me and Danny. The trailer was clean and tidy, though. It was actually pretty cool, in a retro way. The stainless-steel backsplash and countertops were quilted; the storage areas were edged in the style of a 1950s diner, with aluminum groove-face nosing. If Carissa hadn't been in mourning for Declan—and *I* hadn't been inside on less-than-aboveboard terms—

I would have congratulated her on her well-thought-out ice-cream cart.

"We're getting together later, so stop it with the murder talk," Danny said. "I know what you're trying to do."

My search for proof of sabotage ground to a halt.

"We're not getting together," I disagreed, purposely misunderstanding so he'd tell me more. "I have homework to do for the chocolate tour. Once you crack Declan's iPad password—"

"Lauren. And me. We hit it off." Blithely, Danny pointed upward. "There's the intake register for the ventilation. We should definitely check that. It's the only one in here."

I didn't care. "You? And Lauren? Since when are you in the market for dates? What about that nice SFPD detective?"

"Somebody put the kibosh on that by uncovering a murder."

He meant me. "You didn't have to come here. I didn't ask you to," I reminded him, hands on hips. *Danny and Lauren were going to be a couple.* Well, it made sense. She *was* dishy. "Do you really think it's wise to date a potential murderer?"

Lauren was officially on my suspect list, after all.

Danny shrugged and pulled over an unopened cardboard box full of Dantifold Lowfold dispenser napkins. "It's one drink."

I recognized his improvised step stool for what it was. I grabbed an offset spatula, then took the initiative and stepped up onto the cardboard box before he could. Even packed full, a case of paper goods wouldn't begin to hold Danny's weight. Above me was the intake register for the trailer's ventilation system. "I get it. You're investigating Lauren, right? That's smart. I can use the help."

"What you could use is a screwdriver to take off that intake register." He steadied me with one hand on my thigh, making my leg tingle. "Unfortunately for you, I'm fresh out."

He was dissembling, not confirming that he was only dating Lauren to help me investigate. I frowned, even as I brandished my thin stainless-steel spatula. It was only four inches long or so, but it worked like a dream to remove the register's two screws. I handed Danny the spatula to hold, propped up the register with one hand, then dropped the screws into his palm.

"Working in a kitchen, you learn a few shortcuts," I explained, relishing the look of revelation on his face. I liked having an advantage with Danny. It didn't happen often enough. "Hold onto me so I don't fall. This is a little difficult."

"You should let me do it, then." But he complied.

Now both his big hands were holding me tightly. I'll admit, it was a little distracting. Danny is strong. Also (I may have mentioned) unfairly good-looking. I've had my moments of being drawn to his strength, his machismo, his loyalty, and his big heart.

Or maybe I was just feeling competitive with Lauren. Who knows? Either way, I got what I needed. A secure boost upward.

Carefully, I pulled off the intake register, then inspected it. I needed evidence of some kind, and . . . voilà. There it was.

"It's not even dusty." I handed the register down to Danny, feeling disappointed in Carissa. "I bet it's been moved recently."

That counted as evidence, right? The fact it was clean?

I wished I could have believed it *wasn't* incriminating.

"Or Carissa is a neat freak." It was nice of Danny to give her the benefit of the doubt. He peered up. "See anything?"

I didn't. Not really. The ventilation shaft was dark. Also, my viewing angle was awkward. The trailer's ceiling was probably only eight feet from the floor. My height, plus the box I was standing on, plus the distance to the shaft, meant that I had to stand on tiptoe and crane my neck just to see inside.

I caught a glimmer of something shiny. My heart leaped.

"Hand me those spring-loaded interlocking tongs, will ya?"

Nada. Danny gazed around the trailer in obvious bafflement.

"The things that look like giant tweezers," I clarified.

He still looked puzzled. "Yeah, it's been a while since I plucked my eyebrows," he cracked. "Point to what you want."

On behalf of my mom (who's prone to handing my dad a pair of pliers when he wants an Allen wrench), I felt vindicated.

I pointed. Danny handed up the tongs, then resumed his hold on my leg. His shoulder bolstered me, too, as he gazed upward.

"Here we go." I inserted the tongs into the ventilation shaft. It was narrow, but the tongs were long—the perfect tool for tossing a salad, flipping a roasted pepper, *or* withdrawing evidence of a murder. I held up what I'd found. "Plastic wrap."

To be specific, it was a scrap of commercial-grade clear cling film. The same crinkly stuff that Janel had sneaked out of Carissa's trailer. I'd only been able to reach it with my tongs—*and* my greater-than-Janel's height. Otherwise, I would have missed it for sure. I felt a distinct chill as I examined it.

Danny must have, too, because he frowned up at me. He didn't even admire my prize. "You got it. Now get down."

"This doesn't belong up here." I gestured with it—still on the tongs—toward the ventilation shaft. "There's no good reason anybody would shrink-wrap a ventilation shaft. *And* it's the same stuff we saw Janel with after she was in here." I couldn't help feeling victorious on behalf of my beleaguered friend. This was proof of sabotage for sure—but it wasn't proof of *Carissa's* sabotage. "That means *Janel* must have rigged the ventilation."

"Or Carissa did," Danny disagreed, "and Janel found it."

"The likelihood of Janel investigating is pretty slim."

"But not impossible. We're doing it."

"Yeah, but we're special. Right?" I didn't want to believe that Carissa had done anything wrong. My friend *wasn't* a cold-blooded killer. I would have known somehow, wouldn't I?

I didn't want to think my judgment was that skewed. Even if Danny and Travis both did. They thought I was too softhearted. I knew better. At that moment, for instance, I felt far from softhearted toward Janel. Especially if she'd killed Declan.

"You'd better come down." Danny signaled for me to step off the box and clear out of the trailer. "Let's get out of here."

I was too busy clinging to my hopes to do that. "Carissa couldn't have arranged something like this." Needing to believe it, I examined that scrap of plastic wrap. After seeing Janel, I knew there'd been much more of the stuff a few days ago. Enough to block the trailer's ventilation completely (and invisibly). Enough to allow the levels of liquid nitrogen to build up and ultimately kill Declan. "Even if she had, Carissa isn't stupid. She'd have had the sense to come back and remove it herself."

"She's been pretty busy pretending to be sad about Declan."

Danny's sardonic tone bothered me. "There *must* be another explanation." Reluctantly, I traded him my tongs for the intake register. I replaced everything the way we'd found it, then accepted his hand down. I watched as Danny put back the napkin box precisely in its former location, expertly hiding our tracks. "It's got to be Janel." I took back my tongs and scrutinized that scrap of plastic wrap. "I know it."

Danny shook his head. "The most obvious solution is usually the right one." He glanced at the time. "I know you don't want to think the worst of your friend, but you hadn't seen each other in person for almost ten years. People change. You've changed."

I had. I'd changed into someone who spied on my friend.

Well, as true as that was, I couldn't accept the rest— the part that suggested Carissa was guilty of killing her fiancé.

They said there was nothing so deadly as a woman scorned, I remembered (roughly). But I wasn't even sure if Carissa had been aware of Declan's extensive infidelity. As far as I was concerned, her ignorance was as good as proof of innocence.

"What about the liquid nitrogen tanks?" I persisted. "Austin said the safety wasn't working, but he fixed it before anyone could verify that for sure. That means *he* could have—"

"Tampered with it? To off his rival?" Danny strode to the two tanks. They gleamed like something out of a science fiction movie, silvery and metallic, with circular grab bars at the top and an assortment of valves and dials. Hoses snaked away from each one, enabling refills of the smaller vessels used in Churn PDX's individual ice-cream-freezing machines. "They look okay."

"You're not an expert," I pointed out. "Maybe one of the hoses has a leak? The liquid nitrogen is under pressure."

"If there was a leak, we'd be dead right now." Danny glanced up from his study of the tanks. "Do you feel dead?"

"Har, har." I plucked that incriminating piece of plastic wrap from the tongs. I tucked it into my purse for safe-keeping, then passed the tongs to Danny. He put them back on the stainless-steel countertop accurately—almost as if he had experience with conducting a search-and-find mission (aka a break-in). "What about Lauren?" I brainstormed. "After all, I'm pretty sure she pushed Austin into the path of an oncoming car."

Danny hadn't been at Declan's funeral. But I knew what I'd (almost) seen—and what I'd (definitely) heard. Lauren had grunted . . . while pushing Austin into danger to get rid of him?

Danny laughed. "There's no way Lauren could push Austin. He must have four inches and a hundred and fifty pounds on her."

"She had leverage. He was on a bike at the time," I informed him. "Plus, Austin's beanie had slipped. He couldn't see to defend himself. It was a perfect opportunity."

My security expert remained dubious. "Lauren didn't try to kill Austin. For one thing, she's not dumb enough to do it so publicly. She would have waited for a better moment."

"Nice." Worryingly, Danny didn't seem fazed by

Lauren's potential homicidal tendencies. "And you still want to date her . . . why?"

My echo of his skepticism about my belief in Carissa didn't hit its mark. His knowing smirk told me that much.

"You've seen Lauren, right? Tall, curvy, up for it?"

Ugh. "Try not to let 'little Danny' do your thinking for you," I suggested. "At least until we've solved this murder."

"Hey, *I* don't even want to be here in 'Murderville.'" Danny pulled a face at the new nickname he'd coined for Portland, then adjusted the tongs he'd replaced by a millimeter. Satisfied, he looked at me. "The least you can do is let me have some fun."

"Visit a brewpub. Have a beer. This *is* Beervana, you know."

I preferred *that* nickname. Or several alternatives I knew.

"There are better things in life," Danny said, "than beer."

Name one, I wanted to say . . . but I knew he would. In detail.

I didn't want to know that much about Danny's love life—especially his sexual shenanigans with Lauren. So I adjusted my purse on my shoulder, then headed for the trailer's door.

At the same moment, it swung open. Someone was coming in.

Eleven

It was a good thing I'd prepared a backup excuse for our presence there, I told myself. Unfortunately, in the heat of the moment, I couldn't remember what it was. Especially once I saw that it was *Janel,* my number one suspect, in the doorway.

It was growing darker outside. (I suddenly wondered how much time I'd wasted arguing "Carissa versus Janel" theories with Danny.) With the lights on in the trailer, I saw Janel clearly.

She saw us, too, and reared back in shock. Today she'd traded her usual slogan T-shirt for one with the Muddle + Spade logo, I noticed. I gawked at her, completely caught off-guard now that the crucial moment was at hand. (Hey, I'm not an expert, remember? What would you do?)

Danny brought up the rear behind me. He actually chuckled.

The cretin. Didn't he know how suspicious this looked?

Plus, as much as I liked Janel's blunt, boisterous ways, there was no denying her probable guilt. She had the means to kill Declan (liquid nitrogen dispensed in an unventilated trailer), a motive (unrequited love), and an opportunity (I glimpsed a key to Carissa's trailer in Janel's hand at that very moment). In my book, all those things added up to *guilty*.

"What are *you* doing in here?" she demanded.

Stuck, I got glib. "What does it look like we're doing?"

"It looks like you're getting freaky among the overstock supply of ice-cream cups." Janel's unswerving gaze darted behind me. *Low down* behind me. About hip height. "Next time, be a gentleman, dude," she advised Danny. "Bring something to cushion those stainless-steel countertops. They're murder on the hips."

I swiveled. Danny was stuffing his shirt in his low-riding jeans, giving a convincing impression of someone hastily getting dressed. His hair had gotten messed up somehow, too.

What the . . .?

Aha. That rat. Janel thought Danny and I had sneaked away for a romantic encounter in Carissa's trailer. Everyone knew it was currently unused. Churn PDX seemed to be on unofficial (indefinite) hiatus while Carissa dealt with losing Declan.

I didn't approve of Danny's diversionary tactic—but as rapidly devised excuses went, it was pretty good. I had to hand it to Danny. He'd covered us.

He'd had a plan B all along. I should have anticipated as much. Now Janel wouldn't know we'd (potentially) found proof of her sabotaging Carissa's trailer and killing Declan. I shivered. Even if Danny didn't agree that's what we'd done (his money seemed to be riding on Carissa), I was getting surer of Janel.

"Declan left me with some pretty wicked bruises a time or two, thanks to all that metal quilting and those stupid grooved edges," Janel volunteered with a lusty look. "I'm not sure he was sorry, actually. But I'm going to miss him all the same."

Great. More proof of what a dirtbag Declan was. For a spurned lover, Janel seemed pretty chipper about things. She was basically bragging about getting together with Declan in Carissa's trailer. I guessed that meant their relationship *hadn't* predated his romance (and engagement) with Carissa. He'd definitely been cheating on my friend, and he'd been doing it with Janel.

How else would Janel have had such a ribald story to relate about him? I'd never look at 1950s-diner-style stainless-steel countertops the same way again. Now they were nookie pit stops.

If Carissa had known about Declan's unfaithfulness (maybe because of Janel similarly bragging to *her*)—and reacted by forcing Declan to get a restraining order against Janel—then maybe there was something to Danny's and Travis's theories that my friend might be a different woman than I remembered.

A more vindictive woman. I'd assumed that Carissa had been pressured into that decision by her well-meaning parents. I mean, who *hasn't* had the experience of blowing off steam about relationship issues with friends, only to have those friends keep nursing a grudge later? Replace "friends" with "parents," and the dynamic held true. But if Carissa had *wanted* to keep Janel away from Declan by force . . . well, I couldn't really fault her. She wouldn't have been the first person ever to blame the cheated-with instead of the cheater when things got rocky.

Unaware of the rapidly churning wheels in my mistrustful mind, Janel ogled Danny. "Lauren won't like hearing about this."

He didn't even blink. "Lauren doesn't have to know."

His smooth willingness to (seemingly) collude with

Janel left me flabbergasted. I know I've hinted to you about Danny's sketchy past, but seeing the other side of him in action startled me. Even if it was for a good cause (and it was).

"What are *you* doing in here?" I demanded to distract myself. I nodded at Janel's key. "Carissa didn't give you that."

"You're right. She didn't." Carelessly, with no further explanation, Janel gesticulated to move past me. "Excuse me."

I didn't budge. "You didn't answer my question."

That's right. I can be pretty hard-nosed when pushed. Or when Danny was there to have my back. Or, you know, both.

Janel's acerbic gaze met Danny's. "This is how she is *after* she's gotten some? Whoa, dude. You must be pretty awful in the sack." Her attention zoomed past us. "I mean, on the counter."

Awful in the sack. Now both me *and* Danny were annoyed.

I folded my arms. "That's not an answer, either."

"Okay." Janel shook her head, muttering a swearword. "I'm only putting up with you because you didn't join the lynch mob earlier at Declan's funeral." I could have sworn her gaze thanked me for that kindness. She heaved a sigh. "I'm just here to pick up some napkins for Tomasz. He's fresh out at the bar."

Was it me, or was that sigh covering up a conscious pause? The kind of pause a person might use to concoct a bogus excuse?

Not waiting for me to decide, Janel squeezed past me. She spied the box of Lowfold dispenser napkins and approached it.

"I'll get that," Danny volunteered. Tricky. Deceitful.

And always chivalrous—that's my sometime bodyguard for you.

"No, thanks. I've got it." Expertly, Janel flipped over the box. Using its short side, she was able to pick it up. "See?"

I did see. So did Danny. We both saw that, positioned that way (the way we *hadn't* stacked it two minutes earlier), that box offered an extra several inches of height—height that could have been used by a short woman like Janel to reach the intake register for the trailer's ventilation system and cover it with plastic wrap, preventing fresh oxygen from getting in.

Warily, I edged backward. I couldn't help it.

I ran into Danny. He steadied me. Of course.

Janel groaned under the weight of the box. It was a good thing she was sturdily built. Good for her, not for Declan.

She refused Danny's second helpful gesture. "I've gotten pretty good at handling heavy boxes," she informed us. "Berk was nice enough to hire me part-time after Declan took out that—well, you know." *Civil protection order.* "Anyway, Berk knew how much I loved Cartorama. I was working on saving it from those developers at the time. I couldn't have continued if I wasn't allowed to be anywhere near Declan. But if I was working—"

"You *had* to be permitted to be here," I surmised.

"Something like that." Janel cracked a rueful smile. "I think nobody else wanted to do all the grunt work of putting up flyers and circulating petitions. Plus, I needed money. Still do. Otherwise"—her gaze turned faraway—"I wouldn't be here."

Because I'd be mourning Declan. Her subtext was clear.

But Janel wasn't the type to get bogged down in sentiment, apparently. Meaningfully, she nodded at me. "Hey, aren't you going to be late? You know, for the Chocolate After Dark tour?"

Uh-oh. I was. In all the excitement, I'd lost track of time. I scampered out of Carissa's trailer with Danny behind me.

Janel followed, awkwardly maneuvering through the doorway with the box of napkins. She aimed her chin toward the Sweet Seductions cart. "Everyone's already gathered over there." With unnerving cheerfulness, she added, "Catch you later!"

Then Janel trundled off to Muddle + Spade, leaving me and Danny outside our supposed love nest. Reminded of the excuse he'd made up, I shot my security expert a disgruntled look.

"Don't blame me," he objected with both palms in the air. He frowned toward Janel. "She was just bad-mouthing *my* ability to satisfy a woman. If anyone should be mad here, it's me."

Then he shut Carissa's trailer door behind us, shot my purse a significant look (reminding me of the evidence inside), and headed over to join the waiting tour attendees.

Regrettably, I couldn't follow Danny's lead and jump into action as Chocolate After Dark's fearless leader straightaway. I still needed Declan's iPad to check the client list, process late payments, and confirm the tour route before setting off to feast on triple-chocolate-chunk cookies, cocoa cream pie, house-made chocolate-hazelnut spread, and chocolate martinis.

This was where my plan B made things more complicated. I'd thought I would have more time to retrieve Declan's iPad—and (it occurred to me belatedly) to make sure Danny decoded it for me.

He saw me hesitate and doubled back. "What's wrong?"

"Declan's iPad. It's still locked. Even after I get it—"

"It's not locked." My security expert looked affronted.

"Are you sure? You barely had time to do anything with it." I gave him a stern look. "Don't screw around with me. I'm going to have to sneak back into Muddle + Spade to get it, so—"

"So I already broke the password." Danny still looked insulted. "Did you think I just picked locks and busted heads?"

I bit my lip. "Well . . ." I couldn't just say *yes,* could I?

"I'm not a caveman," Danny informed me with dignity. "I understand technology." He glanced at the gathered crowd. "Besides, Declan's password wasn't exactly complex."

"Let me guess. Was it . . . 'Carissa'?"

My protection expert rolled his eyes.

"'Declan'?" I deduced. "'Churn'? 'Chocolate'? 'PDX'? '123456'?"

I'd read somewhere that the latter number combination was one of the most common (and dumbest) passwords in use, right along with "password."

That kind of "cleverness" could get you hacked for sure.

We didn't have time to dawdle. Danny knew it. "Boobies."

I must have misheard him. "'Boobies'?"

"That was Declan's password."

"How in the world did you guess that?" I had to ask. I was ashamed of myself for delaying the tour any further, but I was unable to resist. "Why not 'butts'? Or 'thighs'? Or 'good personalities'?"

Danny laughed. "Have you seen Carissa, Lauren, and Janel?"

I frowned, perplexed. "Of course I have. So?"

"So . . ." He had the grace to look abashed—even as he directed a pointed gaze at my chest. "Declan wouldn't have dated *you*."

I caught Danny's drift and frowned. "That's short-sighted." To say the least. Not that I was sorry. I don't mind being less than well-endowed . . . and I didn't mind missing out on a loser like Declan. "I wouldn't have dated *him,* either. Just for the record."

"I know. You like your men tall, blond, and inaccessible."

Coincidentally, that described Travis to a tee.

"I don't have time to confirm or deny that." I looked to the waiting group of tour attendees. They weren't at the designated departure point (which was supposed to have been Churn PDX) but at Lauren's cart, Sweet Seductions, just as Janel had said. "I need to get Declan's iPad. Hold them off for me?"

Danny glanced that way, too. Or maybe he was looking at Lauren? Apparently, she wasn't just after Danny; she was after my job, too. Because she'd definitely co-opted my tour attendees.

"No problem," Danny told me with too much eagerness.

"Try not to get killed in the process," I warned.

I didn't trust Lauren. No matter how guilty Janel looked (or even Austin, given what I now knew from Tomasz about his A.M. activities on the day Declan had died), the siren of Cartorama looked guiltier still. She was even dressed the part of femme fatale, all dolled up in a leopard-print dress, black stilettos, and an Amy Winehouse–style beehive, plus all her tattoos. As usual, she should have looked ridiculous, but . . .

You can fill in the blanks by now. She looked fabulous.

Danny obviously agreed. He'd hinted that his interest in Lauren was purely physical, but the buoyant, boyish look on his face told me that Lauren might mean more than that to him.

He turned to me. Banally, he said, "Are you still here?"

That was my signal to scram. "Nope. I'm already gone."

Making good on my word, I headed across the busy, fairground-lit cart pod toward Muddle + Spade. As I left, Lauren's husky voice pursued me, trailing me across the lot.

"Declan *really* was one of the *best* people I've ever known," she was telling the waiting attendees, employing that uniquely pious tone people tended to use when speaking of the dearly departed. "I mean, he loved life *so* much! We *both* loved life. . . ."

I didn't want to hear more. But Lauren's lovey-dovey demeanor definitely sparked new suspicions about the likelihood of her sleeping with Declan. So far, that rumor hadn't been substantiated. Sometime soon, I intended to get to the bottom of it. Partly because, if Lauren truly was mourning the loss of her lover, then it wouldn't be wise for Danny to date her, would it?

Rebound romances never work out. Everyone knew that.

Not that saving Danny some heartache was my primary motivation, I assured myself as I slipped inside the busy bar and lost myself amid the crowd of people drinking, laughing, and listening to music. It wasn't. Mostly, if Lauren was Declan's killer, I wanted to catch her. But if things *also* weren't likely to work out between her and Danny for reasons other than criminal homicide, shouldn't Danny know that? Sooner rather than later, before he got in too deep with Lauren?

He did, I decided. But before any of those things could happen, I needed to retrieve Declan's iPad. And fast.

* * *

Just as before, luck was on my side. The front of the house was so busy that nobody was in the back. I cast a watchful glance toward the bar, caught Tomasz's eye, and waved to him.

Tomasz waved back. Despite my hurry, I couldn't miss the envious glances that a few ladies in his proximity sent my way. Say what you will about ego—it's an undeniable thrill to be noticed by an attractive man. There's no doubt about that.

In the small hallway leading to Muddle + Spade's back room, I picked up my pace. I couldn't believe I was cutting it so close with my tour guide responsibilities. Yes, I sometimes delay unnecessarily on taking action with my to-do list. (Just ask Travis. Or even Danny.) But garden-variety procrastination is different. It's semi-intentional. Even predictable. This thing that kept happening to me while investigating was . . . *trouble.*

A clump of several giggling women wearing tiaras clogged up the hallway as they spilled out of—or waited to get into—the ladies' room. Their satin sashes, worn over their going-out clothes with giddy pink enthusiasm, spelled out titles like BRIDE, MAID OF HONOR, BRIDESMAID, and MOTHER OF THE GROOM. They were clearly a group out celebrating a bachelorette party . . . just the way Carissa's friends were supposed to have done that weekend.

Trying to hurry past them, I felt a pang shoot through me. Their happiness was obvious; their smiles were infectious. But it didn't seem fair that one bridal party was allowed to celebrate an upcoming wedding while another had been stopped from doing the same thing by the most heartrending circumstances possible.

Prodded by that reminder of Carissa's predicament, I moved faster. The bar's polished-concrete floor felt slick underfoot. The music's bass reverberated through me as I kept going. It was one thing to play detective. It was another to feel the responsibility of trying to set things right. Just then, I felt the responsibility of it all. I wanted to make a difference.

Taking chocolates from "pretty good" to "ohmigod *amazing*" is a unique skill. I'll give you that. Not everyone has my talent for discerning what any given chocolate confection, cake, or cookie needs and then delivering it. But it can't *all* be dark versus milk, semisweet versus bittersweet, Criollo versus Trinitario versus Forastero. Sometimes it's got to be more.

On that deeply philosophical note, I almost stepped on the cart pod's cat. Again.

The poor feline yowled and flashed across the bar's back room in a streak of black fur and indignation. I jumped, too.

"Chow!" I put my hand on my heart, heard a clatter as the cart pod's resident alley cat delved behind some kitchen supplies to hide, and stifled an alarmed yelp of my own. "Sorry, kitty!"

One of these days, I was going to have to make friends with that cat. I knew I could do it, too. Animals liked me. Because I liked them. Someday I wanted a dog and a cat, a gerbil and a—

Fish. The instant I thought of it, I reconsidered. After Travis's story, I didn't trust those bloodthirsty creatures. Maybe I'd get a pet turtle, instead? Just something to welcome me home at night, whenever I (eventually) found a place of my own.

Feeling foolish for having been startled by a harmless cat, I veered toward the piled-up burlap bags of cacao beans sitting next to the roaster. The whole journey, from Sweet Seductions to the bar's back room, had probably taken only a few minutes. But to me, it felt like ages. I wasn't a natural secret keeper. It felt alien for me to approach the bags warily, glance over my shoulder, and then bend over, feeling around for Declan's iPad.

If anyone came in, I'd have *no* explanation for this.

My fingers touched sleek aluminum and glass. Declan's iPad.

I pulled. Just as that thin, squarish device came free, I felt a presence. I had a bewildering, sudden impression of two hands on my back. Then someone *pushed* me, fast and hard.

I couldn't hold on to Declan's iPad. It flew from my hand and skittered away. I gave a startled "oof!" and face-planted onto those burlap bags of cacao beans. They were so densely stacked I couldn't breathe. I tasted scratchy jute and inhaled chocolate.

It wasn't as enjoyable as you'd think. I awkwardly levered back and tried to gulp some cacao-free air, but the wind was knocked out of me. My knee throbbed, too. Confusedly, I realized I must have bumped it on the concrete floor when I'd fallen.

Disoriented by the surprise of finding myself suddenly on the floor, I took stock of my situation. It could have been worse, I knew. It could have been my head that I'd hit. I'd have a wicked case of burlap face tomorrow, that was for sure, given how hard I'd smacked into those bags. My chest hurt from a lack of air, too. But those things were infinitely better than a concussion. Better than *dead*. Unless I was slowly suffocating?

I dragged in a rattling breath, still struggling for air. I couldn't quite draw in enough. Shakily, I crawled backward from the bags of cacao beans. I got to my feet. I wanted to get Declan's hidden iPad and get out of there. Fast. If this was some kind of prank—some kind of Cartorama hazing—I didn't think it was funny.

I thought it was scary. Painful too.

I heard movement and remembered that shove. *Someone had pushed me.* It couldn't have been an accident.

Heart pounding, I whirled to confront my attacker, my trademark antimugging stance at the ready. No one travels the world without seeing trouble or being trouble. I've learned to be watchful, be smart, and (in the worst case) run. Thanks to some overprotective Spaniards, Italians, and one (especially memorable) Frenchman, I've also mastered some reliable self-defense moves. I knew I could take care of myself.

Except when no one was there. The place was empty.

Almost disappointed, I sagged, still trying to catch my breath. Then I heard that sound again. It came from my left, from within the rows of industrial shelving. It could have been the cat. But it wasn't. Because as far as I know, the average seven- or eight-pound domestic cat can't push a person—or shove over a detached metal shelving unit that's over six feet tall.

Uh-oh. The shelves closest to me swayed. The cans and bottles teetered in their places and then settled briefly where they belonged again, deceiving me into thinking I was imagining things. I stared, aghast, as they seemed to pause, just for a split second. A moment later, everything toppled toward me.

I didn't have time to think. I reacted instead. I lunged to the side, diving onto the cold concrete floor like an action-movie hero—*if* those macho guys ever squealed and flopped out of danger powered by pure motor reflex instead of bravery, that is.

Partway out of danger, my banged-up knee gave out. It refused to move me another inch. I collapsed and hit the floor hard, jarring my hip, my elbow, and my knee, too. Finding myself down so suddenly again was a bizarre sensation. I can't explain it. One minute, I was upright, moving on my own power. The next, I was crumpled on the floor, wondering what had hit me.

Except at that moment, *nothing* had. I felt relieved.

A heartbeat later, I heard a guttural sound not unlike the one Lauren had made before pushing Austin into traffic. Alarmed, I looked up to see the whole shelving unit sway horrifically forward before finally—*finally*—falling completely over.

Everything on its metal shelves slid and fell. Full boxes hit the floor and burst. Jars dropped like bombs, smashing one after another. As they erupted, I smelled maraschino cherries and olives, simple syrups and pickled onions, all gushing together in a malodorous wave. Juicy brines and sugar syrups splattered me. A deadly blizzard of glass shot toward me.

I think I screamed. I'm not sure. But I definitely closed my eyes. I ducked and covered my head. Bits of glass pricked my bare arms, my face, and my neck, ricocheting from the concrete floor in a thousand tiny shards. It felt like being caught in a sandstorm. I'd once been outdoors in Marrakesh in the late spring, when the sirocco winds come in from the desert. Then, I'd ducked inside before being abraded too painfully by the sand. In this instance, though, there was no escape from the glass.

Or from the shelving unit that came crashing down seconds later. It landed with a tremendous crash, shattering the items that hadn't broken already. I couldn't be sure. My eyes were still squeezed shut while I crouched amid the mayhem.

The resounding silence that followed made me open my eyes. Still suffused with adrenaline, I scooted sideways as best I could. It was a mistake. I put down my palms for leverage and instantly sliced dozens of paper-cut-like abrasions into my hands. I yelped and pulled them back, but it was too late.

Ouch. Shocked and sticky, I looked at the mess all around me. Shattered bottles oozed liqueurs, oils, and cocktail garnishes. Plastic-wrapped burger buns stuck to the floor, burst from a box that held even more. On top of all of it lay the metal shelving unit, its wired chrome shelves mashing everything beneath them. Near me, a fallen beer keg propped up one edge.

I'd been saved by beer. If not for that untapped keg, the shelf would have fallen right on top of me. At the least, my lower leg would have been broken. At the worst, my skull would have been fractured. Shaken, I scooted backward—this time using my feet to push with, instead of my hands—and encountered gummy glass.

A few pieces pierced my jeans and stopped me cold. I noticed too late that I was surrounded by lethal-looking shards, some of them pebbly, others as big as a spatula.

I looked down at myself. All the sticky liquids that had splashed me had basically glued glass slivers all over me. Cautiously, I lifted my bleeding hands. My hair was dusted with glass pieces, too. I probably looked very sparkly, but there was no one around to witness my glamorous glass-princess moment.

"Hey! Anybody?" My voice sounded quavery. "Help!"

I was afraid to move. As long as I stayed (mostly) where

I'd been when everything had come crashing down and/or exploded, I was (mostly) okay. If I moved, I risked more glass cuts.

I felt queasy with fear and shock. Just a second ago, I'd been harmlessly skulking around getting Declan's iPad. Now look at me. I was bleeding, hurting, and (maybe) unable to walk.

I frowned at my knee. It was useless. It had let me down at Maison Lemaître, too. I'd gotten injured while poking around. On the other hand, not much time had passed. My knee probably still hadn't healed. I was lucky it hadn't mutinied before now.

Well, it looked as though being stuck on the floor of the bar's back room was my new reality until someone wandered back there for another case of cocktail picks. Looking around, I spied my purse on the ground, covered in maraschino cherries and olives. My cell phone lay next to it, although it had escaped a similarly sloppy fate. I could *just* reach both items. I gripped my phone gratefully, ready to call Danny to come get me.

He'd have to abandon his tour-driving duties, I knew. But maybe Lauren could transport the tour attendees. It was likely that she'd already appropriated them and decided to run Chocolate After Dark's twilight tour herself, with or without Declan's iPad information. Although, I remembered, she'd been one of the few—unlike Austin and Janel—who'd *hadn't* volunteered their tour guide services. So maybe all Lauren had wanted was a chance to be near Danny . . . who was usually near me.

Except for times like this, when I *needed* a bodyguard.

Neither of us could have known I'd run into a killer shelf.

"Hayden!" Tomasz ran into the bar's back room, his face full of shock and dismay. He headed toward me. "What happened?"

I heard his dapper brogues crunch on the glass. I winced.

"I don't know. One minute, I was"—*sneaking out Declan's iPad*—"taking a picture of your antique cacao bean roaster for my Instagram feed. The next, everything was crashing toward me."

I decided to omit the distinct *push* I'd experienced before that. I didn't want to sound paranoid. It was better to look like a complete klutz than to suggest someone had attacked me.

I held up my phone for confirmation of my story, then gave a shrug. "Got it!" Trying to smile, I tucked away my phone in my purse before Tomasz could ask to see my phantom snapshot.

"You're hurt." Tomasz crouched beside me. He caught hold of my wrists, his dark brows arrowing down with concern. "Can you move? Is anything broken?" He crunched more glass, heedless of the potential for damage to his fancy shoes. "Did you hit your head? Do you remember my name? Or your name? I'll call 911."

His touch was ridiculously gentle. I swooned a little.

"Don't call. That won't be necessary, Rupert." I smiled at him. "I'll be fine. Nobody brings down Thumbelina that easily."

He gawked at me, not understanding that I was joking. I knew he wasn't Rupert (whoever that was). I knew *I* was *me*.

"Tomasz, I'm fine!" I suddenly hated being vulnerable and hurt, stuck on the floor amid all the mess. "I'm me. Hayden Mundy Moore. Superhot chocolate expert extraordinaire."

He widened his eyes. Then shook his head. "You scared me!"

I'd scared *me*, too. Given his good opinion of me,

I couldn't cry, though. Or show fear. I opted for breezy bravado, instead.

"Help me up?" I asked jauntily.

Tomasz did just that, carefully and powerfully hauling me to my feet. It was less an assist than an overtaking. But his hands were kind and his whole demeanor was concerned, and in my current (ouchy) state, both of those things were comforting.

"Oh, my god!" Lauren hurried in, her stilettos clacking. She stopped well short of the mess, protecting her high heels. "I was in the ladies' room when I heard something crash back here!"

Mmm-hmm. Suspiciously, I peered at her, craning past Tomasz's shoulder to do so. "Why were you using the bathroom in here?" I wanted to know. "There's a perfectly good Porta-Potty outside."

Lauren made a repulsed face. "Gross. Those are for customers, not us."

Bad-temperedly, I wondered what *else* she was too good for. Law and order, maybe? Letting Declan marry Carissa? I didn't trust Lauren—*or* her coincidental appearance at that particular moment. Before the shelf had fallen, I'd heard a sound—one that had sounded *a lot* like the noise I'd heard before Lauren had pushed Austin into traffic. That couldn't be happenstance.

What better way to hide, Danny would have said, *than right out in the open?* I was onto her. If I could have done it without crying or wobbling, I would have marched over to Lauren and let her know it. I settled for: "Too good for the Porta-Potties, huh? Typical. Anyway, I thought you'd be gone already."

As fiery ripostes went, I'll admit it was lacking gusto. Lauren blinked with pseudo innocence. "Gone where?"

Humph. "You know where. Chocolate After Dark. You want to take over my tour."

She glanced worriedly from me to Tomasz. "She's concussed, Tommy. We have to get her to a hospital or something."

"You'd like that, wouldn't you?" I hitched my purse higher on my shoulder. "I'm not going anywhere. Not until I—"

Find out who murdered Declan. Belatedly, I realized I should probably keep my mouth shut. Already someone had tried to crush me with an industrial shelving unit. They'd spackled me with glass shards and made me hurt my knee, my hip, and my elbow. There was no telling if they were still lurking nearby.

Of course, if the culprit was Lauren, she knew she'd failed. Mostly. Those zillions of glass pinpricks really hurt.

"You're not going anywhere, period," Tomasz interrupted before I could come up with a substitute rejoinder. "I don't think you're concussed, but you might need medical attention."

That was when Danny strolled in. I saw him blanch, probably at the destruction all around me. I'm sure I looked awful.

My bodyguard's gaze roamed over me, astutely taking in my glass-encrusted clothes, my bloody hands, my sparkly glass-dappled hair, and all the rest. His attention lingered on Tomasz's hand on my waist. Then he gave a brief frown. "Newsflash, genius. This isn't the ladies' room. I thought you were going for a pee break before the chocolate tour started?"

He sounded disgruntled. I *felt* disgruntled.

Where was the concern? The caring? The smoke screen?

Danny shouldn't have been looking for me at all. Not

if we didn't want anyone to know I'd stashed Declan's
iPad back here.

Reminded of my disastrous retrieval mission, I glanced
toward it. Danny noticed. I hoped he'd be smart enough to
grab it. And clean it. It had pickled cocktail-onion goo
all over it.

"Ooh," Lauren gibed, casting me an "I should have
guessed" look. "Too good for the Porta-Potties, huh,
Hayden?"

Well, I deserved it. I glowered at Danny, wishing he'd
come up with a better off-the-cuff excuse for my presence
there.

"I thought you were taking a picture of the roaster,"
Tomasz broke in, looking confused. "To Instagram it."

Oh, right. That's what I'd told him. I was really going
to need to step up my sleuthing game if this continued.

On the other hand, the last thing I wanted was another
suspicious death to look into. Two were two too many.

"Danny hates my Instagram habit. He's not much of a
tech guy." I frowned. "We were just arguing about that a
while ago."

Now it was Danny's turn to glower. He didn't like my
maligning his technical prowess. It served him right. *Pee
break?*

He had the last word, though. "I'll tell Austin he can
lead the tour after all," my security expert said. "He's been
waiting around with a clipboard, desperate to be the next
man up."

Oh, was he now? I couldn't help finding that suspicious.

Austin would have had no reason to suspect I might
not lead the inaugural Chocolate After Dark culinary
tour—unless he'd *created* a reason . . . say, by mimicking

Lauren and shoving something big and heavy (in this instance, a shelving unit) on top of me.

Austin could easily have killed me, then scampered outside with his clipboard and pretended to "hope" I didn't make it.

Weirder things had happened here at Cartorama—at least one death by liquid nitrogen–induced oxygen deprivation, for starters.

If Carissa had been around, I'd have had a trifecta of suspects—a superfecta, if I counted Tomasz. (If you don't follow horse racing, like my uncle Ross did, then you might not know that means either three or four suspects, all in order.) Either way, there was an abundance of people to consider. If Carissa hadn't been mourning Declan, she'd have been at the gate, too.

"If *someone* doesn't do it pretty soon," Danny put in, "Carissa's going to. She showed up five minutes ago, crying, and started 'networking' with all the people waiting for the tour."

Oh no. "I've got to go help her."

She had to be trying—however brokenly—to help Declan. Wanting to support my friend, I tried walking. My injured knee had other ideas. So did all those pinpoints of sharp glass. Cut short, I faltered, unable to hold back a pain-filled whimper.

Tomasz was next to me in an instant. His hand hovered near my shoulder. "I'm afraid to touch you and accidentally make all the glass dig in." He shot me an anxious look. "You've got to take off all these glass-filled clothes before you cut yourself."

Danny guffawed. "That's a new one," he said wryly.

I ignored his cynicism. "Do you have anything I can change into?" Oftentimes, restaurant and confectionary staff kept their civvies on hand in their lockers during their shifts. If one of Tomasz's Muddle + Spade workers would let me borrow some clothes temporarily, I'd be ready to go. "Because of all the glass, I'm afraid to sit down anywhere, least of all a car. I can give everything right back. I'll change, go straight home, change again, maybe get bandaged up, and come back to the bar."

Tomasz gave me a dubious look. "I don't think I have anyone your size. Janel was on duty earlier, but I gave her the night off. Aside from her—"

If he thought Janel and I were the same size, he needed a closer look. Or maybe glasses. For a man with a fine Arnys suit and *GQ*-worthy shoes, Tomasz seemed surprisingly clueless about women's clothes. Maybe he was only good at coaxing them off?

"I've got you covered, doll," Lauren interrupted, startling me. Aside from pondering Tomasz's sartorial weaknesses, I was also wondering why Janel had needed the night off. Lauren assessed me. "Everything I own is going to look weird as hell on you. But for tonight, at least, what's mine is yours."

"Thanks, Lauren." I wanted to help Carissa. If that meant playing dress-up in a potential killer's over-the-top glamazon wardrobe . . . well, I was up for it. "That's nice of you."

She flicked a flirtatious glance at Danny. "I'll get you all kitted out," Lauren told me in her raspy voice, "then we'll talk about what you can do to pay me back for my kindness."

I got it. She thought I would hand over Danny like a hunk on a platter. Fat chance, knowing my security expert and his lifetime stubborn streak. But I played along. I needed clothes.

Danny, typically, seemed oblivious to all the drama.

He poked his thumb over his shoulder. "I'm driving the tour van, so I've got to run. I'll check in with you later." He shifted a keen glance to Tomasz, winked at Lauren, and was gone.

That's when I realized . . . I wasn't safe anywhere. If *everyone* was at Cartorama tonight, then any one of my suspects could have just tried to kill me. Danny might not be worried, but I was.

I wasn't sure how many more "accidents" I could survive.

Twelve

Not much later, I stood in the bathroom of Lauren's small house—a bungalow handily located within walking distance of Muddle + Spade—staring with dismay at the pinup-worthy clothing she held out to me. "Don't you have anything normal?" I asked.

"Normal?" She wrinkled her forehead with bafflement. "You mean like normcore? If you're a devotee, I guess that *would* explain your wardrobe."

Whoops. I'd forgotten I was in hipster heaven. I wasn't looking for self-aware, intentional dullness (à la fleece tops, boxy khaki pants, and blindingly white athletic shoes), a trend that could have been born (and worn) in Portland as easily as Brooklyn. I realize I'm smack-dab in the Millennial demographic that's into that stuff. In the rest of the world, however, purposeful "theories" of ugly clothing don't say *trendy,* they say *tourist.*

"No, 'normal' as in something that's not straight out of a burlesque show." I was grateful to Lauren for her help, but the outfit she'd offered me was a bridge too far. For

one thing, it was strapless. I don't begin to have the goods
to hold up something like that.

"A 'burlesque show'?" She brightened with childlike
delight. "Good eye, doll! It *is* from a burlesque show. It's
from *mine*!"

I should have known. "You're a burlesque performer?"

Lauren nodded, eyes shining. "I used to be this super-
gawky, totally ugly teenager," she confided. "Now I'm
not. Give a girl a few years to grow into her curves, plus
a set of falsies and the right wardrobe, and voilà! Instant
bombshell!" She leaned closer, still looking tickled pink.
"Some of those boys who looked right through me when
I was younger are my best customers now. They don't
guess a thing. They tip big, too."

"Wow." I bet they did. "It was that dramatic a change?"

"You'd better believe it. My show is a huge hit!"

Confirming as much, Lauren smiled more broadly.
Coupled with her sophisticated look, her happiness was
incongruous . . . and all the more touching because of it.
Her naïveté sneaked right past my defenses. I couldn't
help it. Somewhere underneath all that scarlet lipstick and
leopard print was an innocent girl who'd transformed
herself from an ugly duckling into a swan.

Or a cold-blooded killer. I still wasn't sure which.

"If it's that successful, why don't you quit Cartorama?"

"Quit my cart?" She shook her head and disappeared
into the adjoining bedroom, giving me a chance to snoop-
ily examine her bathroom. Its skirted pedestal sink,
kitschy pink tiles, and profusion of toiletries suited her. "I
love Sweet Seductions. Anyway, it's all part of my brand.
My treats are dangerously delicious, and so am I." She
reappeared. "Presto! How's this?"

Well . . . *hoochie* came to mind. But given the various

options Lauren had trotted out so far, I didn't want to argue over this (relatively innocuous) choice: a pencil skirt and body-hugging Bettie Page sweater. Even if I didn't quite have the curves to fill out either of them, at least they wouldn't fall off me.

"That'll be fine. Thanks." I glanced at my brine-splashed flats, which I'd barely managed to rescue from the trash bag into which Lauren had stuffed all the rest of my glass-damaged clothing. "I think I can clean those and keep wearing them."

Flats plus a pencil skirt. Maybe it would add up to a chic Audrey Hepburn vibe? I needed to be able to move during Declan's tour. I still intended to rejoin Chocolate After Dark. Soon.

Fortunately, I'd changed out of my funeral clothes earlier, so at least I hadn't destroyed my all-purpose "fancy" black dress. I'd opted for less formal jeans and a knit button-up shirt for the tour—something that would have enabled me to crawl behind displays, wrestle with chocolatiering equipment, and/or tromp into a dusty wine cellar for the perfect Vin Santo del Chianti Classico to pair with a nice milk chocolate with nuts.

So long, favorite jeans, I thought now. Whoever had attacked me with that shelving unit had a *lot* to answer for.

Lauren hesitated, examining my shoes. After the tussle we'd had over tossing my clothes earlier, I expected a fight. Lauren would probably push a pair of sky-high stilettos on me, I knew.

"Good idea." She whisked my shoes from my hand. "I'll do it. You get started on your hair. There's a dryer right there."

Hm. Or maybe I was wrong. I grabbed the hairdryer on autopilot—careful of my now-bandaged hands, which looked like they belonged to the Invisible Man's mitten collection, they were so thoroughly covered—feeling taken aback by Lauren's kindness for what had to be the sixth time that day. I might have had her typecast all wrong, I reflected as I switched on the hairdryer and automatically went through the motions of styling my hair. Because so far, Cartorama's resident bombshell had been nothing but kind to me—at least since my accident at the bar, she had.

Maybe Lauren was trying to throw me off her (murderous) trail. Or maybe she was just hoping I'd talk her up with Danny.

But neither of those excuses explained why, earlier tonight, Lauren had cleaned and bandaged my hands herself, pooh-poohing my objections with a story about growing up as "the big sister" in her household—someone who'd spent part of her childhood "doctoring" her younger brother, Will. Or why Lauren had spread a plastic shower curtain on her bathroom floor, made me stand in the center of it, and then patiently combed glass shards out of my hair. Or why Lauren had shared her home, her shower, and even her (predictably vintage) silk chinoiserie robe, which I was still wearing after having gotten cleaned up.

I had to admit, those weren't the actions of a homicidal maniac. Lauren had been genuinely *nice* to me. After everything that had happened, I didn't know whether to double down on my suspicions of her, abandon them altogether, or wait and see.

Still trying to decide, I finished my hair and then got into Lauren's pencil-skirt-and-sweater combo. It was lightweight enough to be workable for springtime—especially a chilly Oregon springtime evening—but on me it lacked a certain va-va-voom.

"Are you decent?" Theatrically covering her eyes with her hand, Lauren edged sideways into the bathroom. "I just texted Danny to find out his location. I think we can still make the next stop of the Chocolate After Dark tour if we hurry, so . . ."

So hurry up was her not-so-subtle insinuation. I got it.

"I'm decent." I almost laughed as Lauren uncovered her eyes and then goggled at me. "Come on," I protested, feeling like a beanpole little sister next to her. "It's not that bad."

"No, but it's supposed to be a *look*. Maybe some lipstick?"

She came at me wielding a tube of fiery scarlet. I balked. "No, thanks. Really. You've done too much for me already."

I escaped into her bedroom with my lips thankfully bare and headed for the house's minuscule living room. Partway there, I caught a glimpse of something heart-shaped and sequined. A photo in a frame on Lauren's bedroom nightstand. I stopped, struck.

"Hey, isn't that Declan?" *And you?* In the photo, they were snuggled together like lovers. Lauren was giving Declan a lipsticked smack on the cheek while he laughed delightedly.

As I stared at it, transfixed, I felt Lauren's presence.

She was behind me. Maybe getting ready to stab me. Or bludgeon me. Or electrocute me with a hairdryer in the bathtub.

After the difficult day I'd had, I wasn't really up for a showdown. The fight had gone out of me at Muddle + Spade.

I thought about being found dead while wearing Lauren's clothes. I thought about the fact that she'd probably add some lipstick and false eyelashes to my corpse. I turned to face her.

But Lauren merely looked wistful, not criminally insane.

"Yes," she told me. "That's me and Declan, in happier days." I expected her to laugh off their cheeky pose as a joke, to hide the affair that I had suspected—and Janel had hinted about. "He never saw me as that ugly girl I used to be."

Oh. That was . . . okay, it was actually very sweet. It didn't mesh with the Declan I'd (kinda, sorta) come to know, though.

I played it dumb. "Oh, you two were an item?"

She nodded. So much for having to arduously sleuth to obtain confirmation of Declan's infidelity. I guessed sometimes my imagination got the better of me and made things seem more difficult than they were, because Lauren seemed to want to talk.

Maybe, it occurred to me, former ugly ducklings (and current man-stealing burlesque stars) didn't always have a ton of girlfriends to confide in. Especially when they were low.

I may have mentioned before—people tend to open up to me.

"Declan and I were . . . very close." Lauren picked up that photo. She grazed it with her fingertips, her expression an unreadable blend of emotions. Sadness. Nostalgia. *Remorse?* "We had a lot in common. Declan loved all the same things I did," she said in her husky, affecting voice. "Sushi, modern art, bungee jumping, muscle cars . . ."

The hairs on the back of my neck stood up. It was getting spooky hearing everyone's disparate images of Declan Murphy.

I butted in, unable to help it. "Movies?" I prodded.

For Janel, it had been Wes Anderson movies. For Carissa, romantic comedies. Austin hadn't mentioned films, per se, but he had said that Declan had shared his interest in gaming and Nintendocore. So far, Declan's supposed hobbies ranged from vegan ice cream to *tacos de lengua* to soul food, from anime to Broadway musicals, from shopping and doing DIY to going bungee jumping. It wasn't impossible one man had all those interests.

But it seemed pretty unlikely to me.

"French cinema vérité," Lauren confirmed with a nod.

That was pretty different from the other entertainment options Declan had supposedly "loved," but Lauren didn't know that. Her eyes got misty. Her hand trembled. She sighed.

I felt sorry for her. Whatever her shortcomings, Lauren seemed to have sincerely fallen for Declan. It couldn't have been easy to be in love with an engaged man. My sympathies still remained with Carissa, of course, but Lauren seemed so . . . lost.

A moment later, she snapped out of it. "I didn't believe him, of course. I mean, seriously? Cinema vérité? Please. That's pretty obscure." With a wry look, she pursed her lips. "But I was flattered, all the same. Declan went to a lot of trouble to get my attention—to get me to like him. He thought he needed to do that." She shrugged, elegantly. "He didn't know I'd be sympathetic to that feeling of not *quite* being good enough."

I recalled her ugly-duckling story about the boys she'd known growing up—the ones who'd ignored her then but had later admired the reinvented woman she'd become . . . all without knowing the effort Lauren had put in with clothes and makeup, hair and falsies, to become a bodacious burlesque performer. It was pretty clear that Lauren hadn't felt *quite* good enough, either.

She and Declan had had something in common, then. Something that had drawn them together—and maybe pushed them apart, too. Moments ago, I'd thought Lauren had meant that she'd found the admiration of those boys (now men) validating. Or pleasing.

But maybe she'd found it *infuriating*.

Maybe she'd secretly resented not being admired sooner.

"That's why Declan did it, of course," Lauren said. "Why he pretended to be everything to everyone. He wanted to be loved."

Yeah, by every woman he ever met, I thought. Carissa, Janel, Lauren . . . and probably others. But I couldn't say that.

"But most people morph into slightly different versions of themselves while dating someone, don't they?" Lauren broke into my thoughts with an easygoing wave. "Declan was no different."

"I'm not sure you *can* really be loved if you're not being yourself," I said. "Don't you have to be honest first?"

Another shrug. "Honesty isn't all it's cracked up to be."

"Hmm, maybe not." What did I know? I had three ex-fiancés and a pair of men in my life who couldn't get along with each other. I wasn't an expert. Plus, was I truly expecting a potential killer to agree with me that honesty was the best policy? "But isn't honesty a good starting point, anyway?"

Lauren surprised me with a slight smile. "My starting point with Declan was *completely* honest. He saved me from dying."

That wasn't what I'd expected to hear. "Really? How?"

Evidently, my (authentic) tone of amazement came through.

"I met Declan at a bar. Another bar, not Muddle + Spade," Lauren explained, catching my alert look. "At the time, those cocktails frozen with liquid nitrogen were all the rage. They *do* have that neat smoky effect, like a bubbling cauldron. . . ."

She trailed off, seeing my horrified expression.

"I know, ironic, right? Given the way Declan died?" Lauren glanced back at that photo, then shook her head. "Anyway, there I was, about to dive into a nice frozen caipirinha—"

She paused as though wondering if she should explain the drink she was referring to—a cocktail made of Brazilian cane-sugar hard liquor, sugar, and lime. I nodded to let her know that even if I didn't wear leopard print, I still got out some.

"—when Declan rushed over and knocked the glass right out of my hand! There was boozy lime juice everywhere—mostly on him." Lauren laughed and shook her head at the memory. "It turns out that if I'd taken a drink of that cocktail, I probably would have *died.*" She gave me an eager, macabre look. "Turns out, the bartender is supposed to pour the liquid nitrogen into a glass, swirl it around until it vaporizes and the glass is frozen, then pour in the cocktail. But Declan could see that the bartender had used too much liquid nitrogen. It hadn't vaporized yet. It was just there, floating in little droplets in my cocktail."

"Wow, that's pretty observant of Declan."

"He was looking at me pretty closely." Lauren appeared used to having that effect on men. Maybe my theory about her still being hung up on her ugly-duckling past couldn't hold water. "Anyhow, *I* thought Declan was just feeding me a line. But I gave him credit for a unique come-on and let him buy my next drink."

"And the rest was history?"

She nodded. Forlornly. "Complete with a tragic ending."

I must have given her a peculiar look—mostly due to my wondering where Declan's engagement to Carissa fit into this heartrending, epic love story she was weaving—because Lauren rushed to explain. "It wasn't just a line. I double-checked with Tommy later. If you drink liquid nitrogen, it freezes and expands inside you. It can, like, rupture your internal organs."

"And cause death by internal bleeding," I surmised.

I didn't need a *How to Kill with Liquid Nitrogen* manual. I'd done some research into how Declan had died. I'd wanted to make sure what little exposure I'd had in Carissa's trailer wouldn't cause a superslow death by asphyxiation. I was safe.

Sometimes I have more imagination than is good for me.

"Yes! Slowly and painfully, too." Lauren shuddered, plainly disturbed. "As horrible as Declan's death must have been, at least he wasn't awake for it," she said. "I mean, *drinking* that stuff sounds way worse than breathing it. I got away lucky."

"Thanks to Declan." I believed her story about how they'd met. Hooking up in a bar fit with the kind of approach an already-involved man would have taken. "Weren't you already both working at Cartorama, though? Wouldn't you have met there?"

"Oh, that was before Declan moved here. When we first met, we were both at Comic Con Portland." Lauren gave me a kittenish look. "I like a little cosplay now and then. How about you?"

I almost laughed. Me? Dressing up in an elaborate costume inspired by my favorite manga, anime, video game, movie, or graphic novel character? It was probably fun, but . . . "I can't even be bothered with lipstick, remember? I don't think I have the ingenuity for that. I usually go everywhere as me. Period."

"Hmm. Sounds boring. Life is better with a little adventure," Lauren advised me. "You should try it sometime."

Maybe. But I was more interested in the fact that Austin, Declan, *and* Lauren had all attended Comic Con. It was funny that, apparently, the one thing that Declan had authentically been interested in—geeky gaming—was the only thing he'd denied liking . . . publicly and vociferously. Hurtfully, for Austin.

"Maybe," I dodged, meaning *no way am I doing that.* "But if you meet someone in costume—the way you and Declan did—isn't it disappointing when you go back to being your real selves? What if you don't like each other without all the cosplay?"

Lauren gave me a tight smile. "If that happens, then I guess you get engaged to a prissy, preppy little bitch like Carissa and forget how much you liked your 'edgy' girlfriend's tattoos and piercings and 'extreme lifestyle.'"

Whoa. Lauren's sudden rancor gave me pause. Maybe she *wasn't* all sweetness and heart-shaped picture frames.

"Declan said that to you?" I asked, trying for a girlfriend-to-girlfriend vibe that might eke out the truth.

"He didn't have to." Decisively, Lauren put down that photograph. "When he skipped out on dinner with me, my little brother, Will, and my parents *and* got engaged to Carissa on that very same night, his actions pretty much said it for him."

"That *jerk*!" It just came out. I couldn't help it.

I was sorry Declan was dead, but sisterhood came first.

Lauren gave me the ghost of a smile. "Yeah, I wish I could have forgiven him for that. But I couldn't. And then he died."

I stood there, frozen, jolted out of our newfound just-us-girls solidarity by the awful implications of that statement.

Had Lauren *killed* Declan to exact revenge for his cruel treatment of her? Had she felt as betrayed as she still sounded and decided to get even with him? Had their very meeting—over almost deadly liquid nitrogen cocktails—given her the blueprint?

If so, did she feel okay about it, because she thought inhaling liquid nitrogen was a *slightly* less ghastly way to die?

I swear, the idea made me shudder with horror.

But Lauren seemed pretty cheerful. It was almost as though she felt perked up by all the girly camaraderie we'd shared.

"So," she said brightly. "Ready? Should we head out?"

To the Chocolate After Dark tour. In that moment, I didn't care about enlightening chocolate lovers about my favorite food. Just then, I wanted to get away from Lauren, but I was stuck.

I didn't have a car *or* the wherewithal to slowly make my way back to Cartorama on foot. My injured knee and hip hurt too much for that. For that matter, my sliced-up hands hurt too much for that. It was only thanks to a couple of over-the-counter pain relievers and the ample distraction of wondering if Lauren was an unrepentant murderer that they hadn't bothered me more.

I forced a smile. "Sure!" She wouldn't kill me on the way there. We were gal pals now, right? "Let's get going."

Three minutes later, I tucked my pencil-skirted, bandaged-up self into Lauren's sedate, four-wheel-drive Subaru.

"Buckle up!" she told me, moonlight glinting off the silver ring on her pierced, penciled eyebrow as she got ready to drive.

Then we headed downtown, with me hoping to arrive alive.

Not too surprisingly, I made it. Probably that was because there was no reliable way to commit vehicular manslaughter on someone who was *in* the same vehicle as you. Still, I heaved a sigh of relief as Lauren turned on her signal, ponderously changed lanes, waved courteously to another driver, waited for a pedestrian to pass, turned off her signal, and finally parked.

She was an *extremely* safe driver.

"Portland born and bred!" Lauren informed me proudly when I remarked on it. "There's no point arriving dead, is there?"

Her jolly tone put me on edge. I'd heard that same aphorism (more or less) from a Parisian taxi driver. From him, it had sounded a lot less menacing—and that had been *after* navigating the insane roundabout at the Arc de Triomphe de l'Étoile.

"Besides, old Subey won't let me down." Lauren fondly patted the dash of her practical car. She and that car were an absurd match. "My parents got me this car. We don't see eye-to-eye on much, but we all agreed on Subey. And on Declan."

I was back to feeling sorry for her again. Until I saw . . .

"Hey!" I peered through the windshield. "Is that Austin?"

It was. I glimpsed him through the lighted window of the chocolate tour's current stop, a shop selling cacao-based drinking chocolates, truffles, artisanal bars, and more.

Austin wasn't leading the tour, though. He was scarfing chocolate—specifically, a scoop of ice cream with an affogato-style shot of espresso and a generous pour of hot chocolate sauce on top.

It looked delicious. Deliciously *outrageous*. What was wrong with him? Leading a culinary tour wasn't about gorging on treats. It was about sharing, educating, clarifying . . . and yes, devouring the delicious goodies the sponsoring shops offered.

I was inside in a heartbeat, gimpy knee or not.

". . . which is why Declan wanted to start Chocolate After Dark," someone was saying as I came in with Lauren trailing me. The heady, delectable aroma of chocolate almost made me dizzy. "There are many, *many* devoted small-batch producers in the area, some of whom have developed very enthusiastic followings. At my own business, Churn PDX, lines develop around the block to taste the latest ice-cream flavors. Chocolate malt, chocolate with homemade marshmallow, chocolate vanilla bean—those are just some of our 'always on' flavors. Our seasonal items inspire equal dedication among our clientele. Our Twitter followers number in the hundreds of thousands. I understand that's unprecedented for such a newly established business in the Portland market."

Carissa. While Austin satisfied his ice-cream jones at the shop's window-facing bar counter, she was valiantly trying to continue the tour. Clearly, the effort of coming up with chocolate trivia on the fly was too much for her, though. She was dishing out business minutia, instead—probably things she'd committed to memory while trying to get Churn PDX financed.

Around her, the six people who made up the tour group stood by in courteous resignation, tuning out Carissa as they sipped their shot-glass-size portions of drinking chocolate. If you've never had drinking chocolate, it's fantastic. Made like a very thin ganache, drinking chocolate is ordinary hot cocoa's much fancier stepsibling: a mixture of chocolate, sugar, milk or cream, and flavorings, all blended and served warmed. Given the chocolaty fragrance on the air, I could see why Austin was so engrossed. If that blend was what was on his ice cream . . . *yum*.

Still, abandoning the tour was unforgivable.

Especially if Austin had tried to hurt me to lead it.

"Carissa is right." With a smile, I rushed to her rescue with some makeshift tour patter. "There are lots of unprecedented things here in Portland. For instance, there's no city sales tax—so buy all the chocolates you like!" A round of laughter greeted my interruption. "Also, you can't pump your own gas in Portland. You have to let an attendant do it for you—and you *can't* pay them in chocolate, either." It was a silly joke, but it earned another round of chuckles. Not bad for a woman who was wildly improvising. "Also, Portland is the only city to have a dormant volcano within its city limits. You never know when it might decide to wake up, right?" I motioned to the shop's wares. "So don't hold back on sampling chocolate tonight!"

There were a few more chortles and one nervous titter. As far as I knew, Mount Tabor had no plans to go rogue. I hoped I could say the same thing about Lauren as she sidled up to Danny.

The man I'd shanghaied into chauffeur duty seemed happy to see her. Either that or driving tour attendees all over town in the Chocolate Orgy van was secretly one of Danny's preferred activities. I wished I could have seen the attendees' reactions to Declan's artistically challenged tour van. Although I kind of hoped it had been too dark for them to see it clearly.

"I'm Hayden Mundy Moore, everybody." I gave a genial wave.

Oops. At the sight of my bandaged hands, two women shied away. One man looked alarmed. Two men ogled Lauren. The last woman . . . coolly turned away to eat a chocolate-covered caramel.

Well, it wasn't surprising that *everyone* wasn't engrossed. Austin was a dreadful tour guide. "I'm your guide for Chocolate After Dark. I had a little accident, but I'm fine now. Thanks to Austin and Carissa for filling in for me." I hugged my friend. She seemed startled to see me— and not quite as grateful for my help as I would have anticipated. "What do you all think of the drinking chocolate? Who's having which kinds? I'd love to know."

I spent the next several minutes finding out just that, meeting with each of the tour attendees, one by one. I wanted to build a rapport with them, however tardily. Fortunately, doing that isn't difficult. All you have to do is be interested in people and then sincerely listen to them. I am, and I do.

The last woman was a challenge, though. A redhead wearing tortoiseshell glasses, she dodged my every attempt to meet her.

I tried to draw her into a conversation about sea-salted caramels versus traditional caramels. I tried to answer her question to the shopkeeper about take-home drinking chocolate mixes. I even tried to corner her for an introduction near the bar where Austin sat finishing his ice cream, pausing only to shoot me occasional deadly looks.

It was possible that his aura of annoyance spoiled my efforts to be sociable. I didn't know. But I *did* finally wise up and wait near the tour van's side door as everyone headed to the next destination. If the enigmatic redhead wanted to continue the tour, she *had* to come face-to-face with me. No excuses.

I only wanted to be friendly. And thorough. That's all.

Austin got there first. "*You* shouldn't be here."

At his venomous tone, I jumped. "Austin! Hi."

"I had this under control," he informed me, using his bulky body as a bulwark between me and the van. "You should leave."

"Leave?" Even though I thought Austin (might) have killed Declan, I was taken aback by his hostility. "I just got here."

"I was doing fine without you. Just go! Don't come back."

Now he seemed almost pleading. I didn't understand. "You weren't 'doing fine,'" I told him as gently as I could. "All you were doing was eating ice cream. I know it's really good, but—"

"I was *connecting* with people. Just like Declan used to do. Just like he was good at." Austin took a distraught step away from the van, probably trying not to be overheard. He lowered his voice. "You never knew him, but Declan was *awesome* at socializing. That's why he started the tour."

"There's more to running a tour than chitchat," I debated. "There are facts to be shared. Chocolatiering techniques to—"

"I know, I know." Austin's gaze darted to the shop's window. Inside, Carissa chatted with one of the tour attendees. They exchanged business cards. Austin noticed. His frown looked fearsome, but his chin wobbled with hurt. "What Carissa loved about Declan was how 'out there' he was, no matter who he was with or what they were doing. It's the only thing *Declan* had that *I* don't. I finally figured it out. I *need* this tour."

Belatedly, I understood. Austin *was* carrying a torch for Carissa. He wanted to help with the Chocolate After Dark tour to be near her. To impress her. To finally—and openly—love her.

"Austin." I touched his arm, feeling bad for him. "I'm sorry for your situation. I really am. But you said yourself that you had your shot with Carissa." *All I got out of it was a chance to troubleshoot her equipment.* "You said if it was going to happen with her, it already would have. Remember?"

My reminder of our earlier conversation at my Airbnb foursquare house left Austin undeterred.

"That was *before* Declan died!" He gestured wildly, needing to make me understand. "Don't you see? Everything is different now. Carissa might change her mind."

Now that Declan is dead. But had Austin killed him?

I remembered Lauren's warning about how dangerous Austin could be if his feelings weren't returned. About how he'd already had "more than one run-in" with Carissa. I stepped back.

He saw me make that evasive maneuver and exhaled. A second later, he transformed back into the bearded, flannel-wearing teddy bear I remembered. His agility at doing that spooked me.

"Not 'different' in a 'Declan is out of the way, here's

my chance' kind of way!" Austin protested. "All I mean is, I was going to make one last effort at telling Carissa how I felt—*before* she married Declan. I even showed up early at the cart pod that day, just to tell her. But then you were there—"

That was why Tomasz had seen him? Because Austin had been on a mission to express his unrequited love for Carissa?

"—and then Declan was dead. It would have seemed pretty crass of me to jump in. But Carissa is already moving on," Austin told me urgently. "Soon she'll be *gone* if I don't act."

To me, it sounded as though he meant Carissa might be gone *if* he acted. Was Austin so committed to being with Carissa that he'd rather see her *dead* than have her reject him again? I just didn't know.

At that moment, Danny honked the van's horn. The Chocolate Beast revved up, destined for the next stop. Austin had to go.

"Please," he begged me as he headed for the van's side door. "Just call in sick or something tomorrow, okay? Tell Carissa your hands hurt. Whatever. I don't care. Just don't get in my way of leading Chocolate After Dark. I mean it."

Then Austin got on the van, Danny gave me a nod in the rearview mirror, and they all chugged away . . . leaving me to watch, wonder, and wait for Lauren to drive us after them in her (very *un*-edgy) Subaru. To make matters worse, somehow the mysterious redhead had sneaked onto the van while I'd been talking with Austin, too.

Tonight I wasn't exactly batting 1.000. But I was determined that would change soon. Because if someone thought they were going to scare off Hayden Mundy Moore with a killer shelving unit and/or a lot of veiled threats, they'd better think again. Danny wasn't the only one boasting a lifetime supply of stubbornness. I was, too. My inherent obstinacy was about to come to the fore . . . and help me catch a killer, too.

Because now, after everything else, this was *personal*.

Thirteen

It took me three days and three more tours to realize that Danny and Lauren were hooking up. I don't mean that in a euphemistic *"they were having lunch dates"* kind of way, either. I mean it in a down-and-dirty, naked-and-nasty kind of way.

That's three separate tasters of bittersweet *chocolat pots de crème* at one of the twilight tour stops, if you're keeping score. Three nibbles of fresh masa tamales with chocolate mole at another. Three swigs of minty cacao-nib mojitos and three (tiny) sips of habañero hot chocolate passing my lips—all before I caught on to the fact that my best platonic male friend was falling for someone, hard and fast.

Honestly, I wasn't sure how I felt about Danny and Lauren seeing one another. I'd gotten so many mixed signals from Cartorama's resident bombshell during our girl-talk chat, days earlier, that I didn't know what to believe. Danny usually had good instincts about people. I wanted to trust his judgment. But after the way he'd reacted to Lauren's overt va-va-voom, I wasn't sure my security expert was using all his upstairs faculties when it came to Lauren. If you catch my drift.

It took me almost as long to identify the mysterious redheaded woman I'd originally seen on Chocolate After Dark's opening-night tour. It wasn't for lack of trying, either. Even as I regaled my tour attendees with my far-flung chocolatiering adventures and entertained them with behind-the-scenes tales of how all the best chocolate treats are made while we tasted artisanal Fudgsicles and Belgian-style, sugar-studded *gaufres* with chocolate and whipped cream, I kept my eyes open for the woman in the tortoiseshell glasses. She never reappeared.

Interestingly, though, on the tour's second night, *another* mysteriously evasive woman appeared. She was black-haired, wearing owlish Harry Potter–style eyeglasses, and seemed to be obsessed with all things British. She wore Wellies and a Union Jack scarf; she said "cheerio!" and carried a handbag featuring an image of Queen Elizabeth with her famous corgis. I couldn't get close to that woman, either. She gave me the slip—possibly because Austin (naturally) chose the moment I almost had her cornered to badger me about *not* calling in sick for the tour.

As if I would. Who did he think he was dealing with? My reputation was on the line. Plus, I'd already promised to help Carissa. That's what I meant to do—even if she *was* behaving a little oddly herself. Rather than stay home to mourn Declan in private, my old college friend showed up on all the chocolate tours instead, insinuating herself into my conversations with the attendees and piping up at all the worst moments to wax rhapsodic about her dearly departed fiancé. I realized that Carissa probably felt a professional and personal obligation to explain Declan's absence. Maybe she needed the distraction, too. All the same, it was . . . awkward.

I felt for Carissa. I truly did. But I wished she could have trusted me just a little more. It wasn't as though guiding the attendees through Portland's best chocolate shops, bakeries, specialty retailers, and drinks emporiums was *difficult.* It was actually pretty fun. I learned about baking chocolate-almond cheesecake in the embers of a wood-burning oven to give it a smoky edge. I experienced chocolate thyme-infused olive oil drizzled on freshly baked bread. I tried Willamette Valley dark-chocolate Pinot Noir truffles and cupcakes filled with ganache that had been spiked with champagne-like brut made in the *méthode champenoise* style in the Columbia Valley, and I fell in love with Portland and its dedicated local producers just a little bit more with every slurp, morsel, and mouthful.

If not for the fact there was (potentially) a killer on the loose, I could have happily settled down in the Rose City. I could have snagged my own retro-modern post-and-beam Rummer, made peace with Portland's proclivity for drizzly rain, and spent my nonworking days hiking the Columbia River Gorge and exploring its scenic waterfalls with my dog and/or cat (Chow was slowly bringing me around to the appeal of felines) by my side. Maybe even with a hunky man by my side, too, if things went well with Tomasz. I'd postponed our first date on account of my injuries and the *very* long day I'd spent evading attempted manslaughter, but I was hopeful we'd get together after one of the tours.

Maybe even after *this* tour, I decided as I tuned back in to what I was doing—which was, not surprisingly, savoring something chocolate based and scrumptious. In this particular case, it was a chocolate-espresso dacquoise from a Stumptown baker who operated out of a rival food cart pod. If you don't know what a dacquoise is, imagine that you're eating an airy, sweetened cloud, and you're there. Technically, dacquoise is made of meringue and buttercream coated in chocolate ganache, but the cloud thing is all you need to know. In a good bakery? Try one.

While I'd drifted off momentarily, Carissa had taken over.

". . . that's why, at Cartorama—where we'll end up later, to give you your end-of-tour discounts and special goodie bags—we make sure to provide a covered place to enjoy our delicious treats," Carissa was telling the damp tour attendees. "That means that if you want ice cream in the middle of winter, there's no problem. Just visit Churn PDX for some chocolate-chunk rum-raisin ice cream with house-made hot-fudge sauce!"

She beamed at the attendees, some of whom smiled in anticipation. Others, though, looked baffled—probably by the fact that someone who *wasn't* their official tour guide kept butting in with anecdotes and sales pitches for Churn PDX.

I understood that Carissa was only trying to honor Declan's memory—that she was probably taking refuge in micromanaging Chocolate After Dark's start times, end times, and all the stops in between as a way to manage her grief and anxiety. But her odd behavior was starting to affect attendees' enjoyment of the tour. I was going to have to talk with her soon. I didn't want to, but I'd promised to help her launch the tour. If I didn't get it off to a successful start, I wouldn't have done my job.

That meant there was no time like the present, right? I inhaled for fortitude and stepped toward Carissa, intent on pulling her to the side for a private conversation. Almost there, I noticed Austin and the mystery woman huddled beneath the meager awning on one of the "other" cart pod's vehicles.

That wasn't surprising. It was raining outside, lightly but persistently, making the pod's overhead lights look misty. That's how Portland did rain, I'd realized. After spending almost a week in the city, I knew now why it was so green. Many of the tour attendees had temporarily dispersed to find shelter while they ate their treats. Their abdication was likely what had sparked Carissa's mini discourse about the superiority of Cartorama in general and Churn PDX in particular. She'd even reopened her ice-cream cart, I remembered, saying that it, too, was "to honor Declan's memory—he would have wanted it this way."

I had my doubts about that, but I'd been in no position to disagree. Now, though, I *was* in a position to notice something interesting. Austin and that unidentified woman (today, a blonde wearing horn-rim specs and vivid fuchsia lip gloss) were getting *very* cozy. You could almost say they seemed to be *conspiring* about something, there in the drizzly twilight.

I stopped and watched them, pretending to need more time to savor my allotted sliver of chocolate-espresso dacquoise.

I was trying to figure out what they were talking about when Lauren wandered over. She noticed what I was doing.

Well, it would have been hard not to, given my staring.

"Yes, you're right," Lauren said, glancing in the same direction. "That's a wig, all right. A pretty bad one, too."

"What?" Distracted, I switched my focus from wondering if Austin might have gotten interested in someone new (not Carissa) to the mystery woman's long, blond hair. "How can you tell?"

"Easy. It's too shiny." Lauren shook her head, studying the hairpiece in question with a practiced eye. "You need to wash synthetic hair before wearing it, or it looks like Barbie hair."

Hmm. I was sure that this newer, blonder mystery woman was the same person—the same redhead I'd noticed on the first day and the same brunette I'd noticed on the second. But why? Was she a chocolate competitor trying to suss out secrets? Another of Declan's long-lost lovers hoping to stay connected to him?

"Also, if you look closely, you can see where she's tried to use heat tools to restyle her wig," Lauren went on. "That's a no-no on anything but a high-end piece. It melts the fibers."

I squinted. "I think I see her wig cap."

"No, you don't," Lauren disagreed. "You just think you do, now that I've pointed out the wig. People see what they expect to see. When I'm performing, I count on that."

Now she sounded like Danny. I understood why he liked her.

"It's a common mistake," Lauren assured me with a friendly smile. "Trust me. I know artifice—I make my living at it."

I did trust her, in this instance. Not that I thought she ought to be bragging about being skilled at deception when there'd (maybe) been a murder in the vicinity. But I didn't have any proof of what Lauren (might) have done to Declan. I still needed more time, more information . . . maybe more protection, too.

I glanced around. "Hey, where's Danny?"

Lauren shrugged. "He disappears sometimes. He always turns up, though. He'll be back in time to drive us to the next stop."

She was right. That meant this presented an opportunity.

Maybe, it occurred to me, I ought to try bonding with Danny's . . . new girlfriend? Could I call her that? "Tell me about it," I cracked, hoping to do just that. "This one time in Fiji—"

My yarn ended before it began. Probably because that's when Lauren spotted a tall, dark-haired, handsome man near another food cart. Evidently, that was the only way they grew 'em here in Portland. Handsome. He wasn't Danny attractive. Or (my imaginary version of) Travis attractive. Or even Tomasz attractive. But he was still capable of drawing in the ladies. Lauren muttered something to me as an excuse, then hurried away.

Trying not to feel slighted, I resumed my unofficial mission. While all our tour attendees were busy nibbling dacquoise, I had the perfect opening to come to an understanding about the running of the chocolate tour with Carissa.

As it turned out, Carissa found me first.

"You might want to warn your friend Danny about Lauren." She crossed her arms. "They've been getting pretty cozy, right?"

"I'm sure it's nothing serious." I didn't want to get sidetracked. I needed to try to get through to her. She *didn't* need to help with Chocolate After Dark. "Listen, about the—"

Chocolate tour, I meant to say, but Carissa didn't give me a chance. She watched with obvious distaste as Lauren caught up with the handsome man. She touched his arm. He smiled at her.

Together they ducked behind one of the neighboring carts, out of sight. The whole thing looked incriminatingly intimate.

"See? She's up to her old tricks again," Carissa said.

Time to play dumb, I figured. "Old tricks?"

"Man stealing, of course." Carissa aimed a deadly glance in Lauren's wake. "Nobody's man is safe when Lauren's around."

"Oh, Danny's not 'mine,'" I demurred, purposely misunderstanding. "And I don't even know that guy, so—"

"She must be two-timing Danny with him," Carissa mused.

"No. *Really?*" I was trying to sound artless on purpose, but if Carissa was right, I'd have to karate chop Lauren, for sure.

I don't know martial arts, but I'd learn to avenge Danny.

Aaand I finally understood the urge to murder. Uh-oh . . .

"Isn't it obvious?" Carissa flung her arm toward Lauren. "She doesn't even bother to hide it." My friend scowled. "It's a good thing I'm moving Churn PDX soon."

Really? I wondered where she was moving to. And why. If she was leaving Cartorama, why reopen?

"The last thing I want," Carissa said emphatically, "is *another* man walking around with groove-faced butt prints after getting it on with a burlesque queen in *my* trailer. Gross!"

Eww. Did she really mean . . . Danny? "Who's been getting it on in your trailer? If it was Danny, I'm really sorry, Carissa. I swear, he knows better. It's just that he's crazy about Lauren."

"Yeah. I've heard that one before," my friend groused.

Then this wasn't the first time someone had buttprinted themselves on Carissa's 1950s-style diner counters. But how. . . ? Did she mean Janel? I'd thought Carissa didn't know about that.

"When did *you* see Danny's booty?" I had to ask about that niggling detail. "He's not shy about nudity"—I'd learned that to my discomfiture once or twice, most recently at Maison Lemaître, when he'd strutted around shirtless—"but usually he's more discreet than to have a sexy romp on someone else's property."

Carissa rolled her eyes. "Not Danny, dummy. Declan!"

Declan? "You and Declan got frisky in your trailer?"

I remembered that Declan and Janel had. In that case . . . *aha.* Carissa *definitely* knew about her fiancé's dalliances, then.

As the rain dribbled its way down and the tour attendees noshed, Carissa surprised me with a disgusted look. "What am I, stupid? Seriously, Hayden. I thought you were smart."

Her aggressive tone bugged me. "I thought we were friends."

She sighed. "We are. I'm sorry. It's just that I get a little bent when people act as if I'm stupid. It's my pet peeve."

I wished I'd never stumbled onto it. Maybe Declan had, too. Maybe he'd wished he'd never started the rumor that *he'd* developed Carissa's patented ice-cream freezing system. Maybe, as a result of it, Carissa had gotten "bent" in a whole new way.

No. Carissa wasn't a murderer. "I'm sorry I upset you."

"Declan used to act like I was an idiot, too. It was *so* annoying! Of course I meant Declan and *Lauren. They* got it on in my trailer. Lots of times. I suspected when I saw the telltale bruise on Declan's butt, but I knew for sure when Austin started getting all nervous around me." Her contemplative gaze traveled to the bearded candy-bar seller, all toasty in his usual beanie and flannel. "Austin is about as stealthy as a goldfish."

Given what I now knew about fish . . . that didn't reassure me.

"I'm sorry Declan and Lauren did that to you." I was even more unhappy that she'd known about it. There went my "ignorance is as good as proof of innocence" theory regarding Carissa. She was officially a woman scorned . . . and maybe out for revenge? "I don't see how Austin was involved, though. Unless—" I widened my eyes. "Were they having a threesome? In your trailer? Whoa, that takes the cake." *And a lot more space than Carissa's Airstream offered,* it occurred to me tardily. All three people would have had to be *very* bendy to get any action inside Churn PDX.

But by then, Carissa was already snorting with derision. "A threesome? *As if.* Maybe if Lauren put on a red wig and glasses so she could look like me, then Austin would go for it. But even as my doppelganger, I doubt that skank could pull it off."

Carissa knew about Austin's feelings for her, I realized with a sick feeling. But she didn't care. Most likely, she had never cared. Not about Austin. The spark wasn't there.

I didn't think Carissa had to be so mean about it, though. Despite everything, I still liked Austin. And Lauren had been kind to me. But speaking of wigs . . . I felt my gaze pulled back to the mystery woman. Something about her seemed familiar.

"Austin seems to have moved on," I remarked, watching them again. "So whatever guilt he felt about . . . things"—I still didn't know what *things,* exactly—"he seems to have changed direction now." I inhaled deeply, gathering my courage. I needed to be tactful. "Speaking of changing direction, Carissa, when you asked me to take over Declan's chocolate tour temporarily—"

I assumed that meant you wouldn't be micromanaging it.

She was beginning to upset the attendees. One woman had complained about Carissa's off-topic monologues. Although I'd noticed at least one or two receptive folks exchanging contact information with Carissa after each tour, so maybe it wasn't as bad as I imagined. Yet.

"'Things'?" Carissa repeated, mimicking me. She arched her brow, ignoring my lead-in about the chocolate tour. "Austin was covering for Declan," she informed me in a spiteful tone. "He was refilling the liquid nitrogen tanks for Declan. The whole time I was giving Declan credit for being so sweet and helpful, it was really Austin doing all the work—giving Declan loads of free time to get together with Lauren."

Oh. That explained a few things. Starting with Austin's emotional outburst at Declan's funeral: *It was my fault!* he'd wailed. *I shouldn't have let him. . . . I'll never forgive myself.*

He meant he'd never forgive himself for not *refilling the liquid nitrogen tanks that one final time,* I realized. On that last deadly night, Austin must have refused to cover for Declan for some reason. But had he murdered Declan?

But you had to go and get cold feet, Lauren had accused Austin after Declan's funeral. *Now Declan's dead and everything is horrible.*

Had Lauren been *that* upset about Declan's dumping her? Had she wanted him dead? Obviously, she and Austin had been working together to do something. But I didn't know what. It didn't add up. All I knew for certain was that Austin wanted Carissa, and Lauren wanted Declan. If they'd teamed up to help one another . . .

"I'm not dumb, you know," Carissa said. "I found out about all the women eventually. If not for Austin covering for Declan, he would have had a *lot* harder time cheating on me, that's for sure. I would have figured out what was going on even sooner."

I think you've done quite enough for Declan already.

No wonder Carissa was so mean to Austin. She partly blamed him for her fiancé's infidelity. I felt sorry for both of them.

"It's probably not Austin's fault," I hedged. "I mean, he's too nice to say no, that's all. Right? I understand Declan was a pretty charismatic guy, so if he asked Austin to do something—"

"What? Did *you* have a fling with him, too?"

I watched her eyes narrow with suspicion and wisely stopped playing devil's advocate. "*No.* You're right to be angry."

Carissa seemed mollified. "I was going to break off things with Declan, you know, the night before the engagement party," she confided in a pleasanter tone. "I even went there, to my ice-cream trailer, to do it. I figured I'd catch him with Lauren—or someone else—and that would be that. Easy-peasy."

"You didn't want to get married?" That was big news.

"Sure, I wanted to get married." Carissa shrugged, gazing at one of the alternative cart pod's trailers. "I'm just not sure I wanted to get married to Declan. Once it was almost time to go through with it, somehow that seemed crystal clear."

I was riveted. "Well, you did have a whirlwind romance."

"I know, right?" She smiled, seeming to feel that I understood. I didn't, but there was no way I was letting on. "It all happened so fast. By the end . . . well, I wasn't even sure I liked Declan very much. He hurt me a lot. I'd finally had it."

On that ominous note, I felt chills race through me.

Then Carissa added, "But then he died. And I was free!"

I swallowed hard, trying not to give away my sudden

uneasiness. Beneath my bandages, my palms started sweating. My cuts still hurt, but that was nothing compared with wondering . . . *Had Carissa been fed up with Declan enough to* kill *him?* She'd had a motive (multiple instances of unfaithfulness), a means (her own liquid nitrogen tanks, which—if her frequent reminders about her own intelligence were correct—she'd known like the back of her hands), and an opportunity (Carissa could have *definitely* gotten into Churn PDX on the night in question).

Danny had been right, I realized. More than anyone else at Cartorama, Carissa had had reasons to want Declan dead.

I suddenly felt I didn't know my old uni friend at all.

"Yes," I said in a parody of supportiveness. "*So* free."

Carissa nodded, gazing at me with pert interest. "So, a minute ago, you were telling me something about the tour?" she prompted. "Something about your taking over Chocolate After Dark temporarily?" She tilted her head inquisitively. "You're not trying to quit early, are you, Hay? Because I'm not done with you yet. Believe me, when I'm done with you, you'll know it."

Despite her smile, I felt *threatened.* I wished I could have been sure Carissa was joking. She sounded semi-serious. Suddenly, all I could think about was Carissa tiptoeing into my Airbnb house, finding me sleeping, bashing me in the skull with a fireplace poker, and then calmly putting it back before leaving. After all, everyone at Cartorama knew my temporary address. It had been posted on their shared social-networking group's site.

I didn't want to die at thirty. I hadn't even created my own original confection, tasted a rare 1926 Macallan whiskey, or found out if there was *really* a lifetime quota of passport pages (as I'd heard whispered about in gridskipping circles) yet. I didn't want to die before finding out what had happened to Declan, either. I'm obstinate that way. I wanted answers.

Serendipitously, that's when I got at least one.

Carissa looked at the time on her phone, then nodded toward Austin and the unidentified blonde. "We'd better round up Austin and Janel," she said. "It's almost time for the next stop."

I gawked at her. Then at the blonde. It was . . . *"Janel?"*

"Yeah, I think she's trying to circumvent the restraining order." Carissa sneered at her. "It's sad, really. As if I wouldn't recognize that sad-sack posture of hers. I think it comes from never wearing high heels. Anyway, I don't mind. Having a full house makes the chocolate tour seem superpopular." She sniffed, then raised her chin. "Ready?"

I wasn't. I was still stymied by Janel's appearance there.

I didn't think she'd gone undercover to evade the civil protection order against her. Because after all, that order technically prevented Janel from seeing Declan, not Carissa. Also, Janel wasn't stupid. She must have known her disguise wouldn't fool anyone who knew her well, like Carissa. Or Austin.

Aha. Now I knew why Austin had staged a confrontation with me at the first Chocolate After Dark tour. He must have been running interference for Janel, so she could board the bus.

I was embarrassed that his diversion had worked on me. I knew better. Wasn't attention to detail my bread and butter?

A little peeved, I studied the two of them. They were still hanging out together, talking in the rainy glimmer from the cart pod's overhead string lights. As I watched them, Austin said something. Janel laughed in response. Austin's face glowed.

Carissa noticed, too. "Ugh. Gross," she said, quickly looking away. "Nerds in love. They deserve one another."

It was obvious why Declan had hidden being a gamer geek. Carissa wouldn't have approved. But right now, Austin and Janel had it all over both of them. They seemed to be wholeheartedly being themselves—which was ironic, with one of them in disguise.

Maybe Lauren had been right, it occurred to me. Maybe she and Declan *had* had all the honesty they needed while cosplaying.

"I'll go get them," I volunteered, slightly afraid of what Carissa might do or say if she was the one who did it. My friend wasn't the woman she used to be. I didn't know if it was her grief talking (that seemed unlikely at the moment) or if she'd simply changed. "I'll meet you at the van in two minutes."

Then I headed over to where Austin and Janel were standing.

"Hi, you two!" I called. "Time for the next stop."

They broke apart. Austin blushed. Janel shot me a startled, cautious look. Now that I knew who she was, I recognized her blue eyes and slightly turned-up nose. I didn't let on, though.

I didn't want to. But I did wonder . . . if Janel wasn't hiding from Carissa (who'd recognized her) or Austin (ditto) or me (who'd been likely to catch on sooner or later, I told myself determinedly), then who was she hiding from? And why?

If I wanted to find out, I had to stick with it. After years of troubleshooting recalcitrant chocolates, I'm good at perseverance. So I trailed Austin and Janel to the chocolate-frenzy van, boarded right along with them, and stayed within listening distance all the way to the next stop.

Unfortunately, I didn't learn a thing.

I needed another bright idea, and fast. There was one place I knew I could get one. It was time to check in with Danny and Travis and find out what they'd uncovered about Cartorama's vendors.

Fourteen

Danny came home to our shared temporary accommodations early that evening. I'd had only time to brush and floss away some of the sugary chocolate goodness from my teeth (the result of a dental-related promise made to my dad when I'd entered into chocolate whispering), open the unexpected overnighted package that had been waiting for me on my front porch, and then . . . "Here." Danny threw something to me. "I got you something."

I caught it. It looked like . . . "My cell phone?" I cracked a smile. "That's sweet, Danny, but I didn't get you anything."

"Not *your* cell phone. Declan's. They're the same model."

I looked at it in bafflement. "Where did you get this?"

"You left it on the kitchen counter this morning, locked up tight." My security expert gave me a cocky look. "Didn't you wonder why you'd locked yourself out of your own phone?"

"I . . ." *Didn't want to talk about it.* I realized too late that I must have somehow snatched up *Declan's* phone from the back-room floor at Muddle + Spade the other day, not mine. Then I'd stashed them both in my bag and mistakenly pulled out Declan's when I'd been ready to use it later. "It's been a tough week. And anyway, *your* 'gift' can't hold a candle to Travis's gift."

Danny ignored my purposely incendiary remark. If I'd hoped to distract him from what I'd thought was an embarrassing tech mistake, well . . . I hadn't. That much was clear. He strode nearer.

"*I* wondered why you'd locked yourself out of your own phone." He sat on the chair nearest to my position—curled up on the sofa with my pashmina. He rested his brawny forearms on his knees and leaned forward, pinning me with an analytical look. Getting lucky agreed with him. "That's why I picked it up and had a crack at it. I figured it was a silent cry for help."

"What? I *never.*" Not that I'd admit, anyway. I valued my independence. As much as I think about wanting a hearth and home of my own, I could never give up globetrotting. I could never hang up my couverture spoons for good. "Anyway," I said eagerly, about to pounce on my own news, "about Travis's gift—"

"Last year," Danny reminded me brusquely. "Your laptop."

I scoffed. "I left the chewed-up power cord with that hotel concierge to mail to Travis for reimbursement. It wasn't a thinly veiled cry for help."

"Last month," he went on. "Your tangled necklace."

"That?" I gave a *pshaw.* I couldn't help it if Danny had clever, talented hands that were good at working knots out of fine gold links. "I just took it off and forgot it, that's all."

"In a pool hall? On the pool table? Before *my* turn?"

I shrugged. "You can't prove anything. Anyway, Travis—"

"Last week," Danny persisted. "Your locked wheelie bag, left on the floor of your hotel room—which adjoined mine."

There he had me. "*That* was an ethics test. You bombed."

But my bodyguard only laughed. "You need me. Admit it."

"I *won't* admit it, but I'll show you this fab gift. Look!" With great fanfare, I pulled out the thing I'd found in the express-delivered package on my porch. "It's my cross-body bag!"

Danny only harrumphed. "A purse doesn't trump a broken-into cell phone. There's no universe where that's true. Especially if that phone belonged to a dead guy who password protected it."

"It's a perfect replica." I hugged it, feeling all gooey and appreciative inside. "Travis had it made for me secretly last year, after I said how much I liked mine. He knew I might want a replacement someday, so he tracked down the vendor."

I couldn't *believe* how thoughtful that was. Also, ingenious. My bag had been one of a kind, bought from a street seller on the Bahnhofstrasse in Zurich. Travis was *amazing.*

I really had to make time to get up to Seattle to see him sometime. Privately, I thought the bag was an apology for the way Travis had creeped me out with that carnivorous guppy story when we'd last talked on the phone. If so, apology accepted.

I caught Danny's downhearted look and throttled my glee back a notch or two. "But cracking Declan's 'boobies' password again is great, too," I told him reassuringly, admiring the phone to demonstrate it. "I mean, Declan was a tricky guy."

He practically growled at me. "I don't want your pity."

"Plus, I really should concentrate, anyway." With effort, I peeled myself away from my new favorite bag. Seeing it had been like being reunited with an old friend . . . one who'd been given an expert face-lift. "I think I'm getting a handle on this whole 'Declan's murder' thing," I told Danny. "I talked to Carissa—"

"I think Travis is into you," he interrupted. "Otherwise, why set you up in such a huge place? Why send you gifts? Huh?"

Aw. His competitive streak was riled up. Poor Danny.

He could take it. I put on my best, most gushingly girly expression. It wasn't a natural fit, but Danny wasn't paying too much attention. "*Squee!* Do you *really* think Travis likes me?"

Danny's attention swerved to me. Held. "Very funny. I can promise you, if that shelf had squashed you the other night, *I'd* have been sadder to see you crushed to death. Way sadder than Harvard would have been. He's half machine. Speaking of which—"

"Speaking of Travis's bionic arms and robo brain?"

"No, speaking of your 'accidental' near maiming."

I didn't want to talk about it. Danny and I had had a brief review session afterward. That was enough. "We decided I'm not in any *real* danger, as long as I keep my eyes open. Remember?"

"No, *you* decided that. Because you're too stubborn to quit," Danny reminded me. "Every one of your suspects was nearby that night," he pointed out. "Anyone could have hurt you."

"The joke's on them, then. Because I'm *more* determined now, not less."

"Including Tomasz Berk," my bodyguard continued relentlessly. "Don't you think it's weird that Berk is *always* there, just hanging around, when things go wrong at Cartorama?"

"'Hanging around' at the bar he works at? No, I don't."

"Don't you think it's weird that he wears those shoes?"

"The good ones? No. Women like men with nice shoes. It shows he's grown-up enough to take care of his things. Probably grown-up enough to take care of a house," I said. "And kids."

"That's a lot to infer from a pair of fancy oxfords."

"You know what they're called! That's progress," I teased. "Next you'll be debating slingbacks versus espadrilles with me."

"Fat chance, Cinderella."

"Also, 'fancy' shoes aren't a luxury when you're on your feet all day working as a bartender," I reminded Danny. That's why Tomasz had excellent shoes but thrift-store clothes. "You're just being suspicious because I'm going out with Tomasz later."

While I appreciated overprotective Danny wanting to vet my dates for me, I didn't need help with my love life. I could handle myself. Besides, I still hadn't had a chance to reschedule that date, so debating it now was a nonissue.

"He talks too fancy for a bartender, too," Danny grumbled.

I laughed. Then I remembered Danny's wrong-side-of-the-tracks upbringing and got serious. My security expert might have two college degrees and more than his share of street smarts, but he still had a chip on his shoulder. Sometimes it showed.

"Portland is the capital of overeducated slackers," I told him lightly. "Around here, your barista probably has an MBA."

"I think Berk is playing you," Danny persisted. "All that stuff he said about you being 'intimidating'?" He shook his head. "Come on. That's a reach, and you know it."

I knew nothing of the kind. "I can be intimidating."

I liked the idea. It made me feel powerful. In charge.

"You like the idea of being intimidating. That's why Berk said it." Danny focused in on me. "It's a con. It works."

I scoffed. "You're just jealous you didn't think of it first."

"You're being gullible. Seriously, Hayden. Haven't you ever laughed at a guy's lame jokes or squeezed his biceps and let out one of those girly *'ooh!'* squeals, even if he was a ninety-pound weakling? Just to make him feel good? *This* is the same thing."

I grinned at Danny's over-the-top, demonstrative *"ooh!"*

"Women like to feel powerful," he told me in earnest. "They like to have that side of them acknowledged by someone else. It doesn't happen often enough. Not every woman, every time, but—"

"But *me*. This time. With Tomasz." I considered it. Then I shook my head. "He's a bartender. To him, I *am* intimidating! I have my own consulting business. I've traveled the world. I'm independently wealthy. . . ." Although Tomasz didn't, it occurred to me, seem especially interested in my income stream. "Hmm."

"'Hmm'?" Danny raised his eyebrows. "Hmm, what?"

"Tomasz doesn't care about my fortune," I said. "Most of the time, if a man is the least bit sketchy, he gets all bug-eyed when I flash a little cash. But I've been tipping *really* extravagantly for all my drinks and the rounds I've bought at Muddle + Spade. Tomasz has never even batted an eye."

"See? You were testing him," Danny said. "And he failed."

"Actually, he passed. I don't want to be wanted for my money." I hadn't even done anything to earn it. "I never have."

Danny looked away, obviously uncomfortable. We didn't see eye-to-eye on Uncle Ross's generous trust fund—*or* the hoops I had to jump through to get it. I told myself that Danny didn't resent my money, merely the unusual stipulations of my uncle's will. To keep my income stream flowing, I had to log at least six months' travel time per year—a provision that had to be verified by my sexy-voiced trustee (aka keeper), Travis Turner.

Any good friend would have resented seeing me always on the run, right? It wasn't that Danny begrudged me my good fortune. It was that he wished he could see me more often . . . see me *settled*.

"I still don't think you should date Berk," Danny said.

"I don't think you should date Lauren. So we're even."

We stared at each other. Were we really going there?

Nah. I looked at Declan's phone's screen. "Anyway, about Declan's phone. What did you find out after you cracked it?"

Danny looked indignant. "I didn't look at it."

"Mmm-hmm. Sure." I flipped through the screens, examining apps and email. It wasn't easy with my still-bandaged hands. After scanning innocuous apps and an in-box full of marketing come-ons, reminders for Declan to renew a porn site membership, and some spam from the PRODIGY GROUP (FYI, sending emails with all-caps tends to shoot them straight to the spam folder), I moved on to Declan's pictures. "Whoa!" I threw the phone, shuddering.

"What?" Frowning, Danny retrieved it. "What's wrong?"

"Declan was fond of selfies."

"So?"

"*Intimate* selfies." I grimaced, squicked out. "Now I hate my eyeballs for making me see that. Especially by surprise."

"Come on, you prude. It can't be that bad." But Danny didn't, I noticed, open Declan's photo gallery. He probably didn't want an eyeful of our murder victim's "equipment," either.

"There are a lot of texts on here." Danny thumbed through them, obviously having no compunction about snooping now that I'd had a chance to go first. "Ignored messages from Austin and Tomasz. Reminders about wedding stuff from Carissa. Your basic stalker-y threats from Janel . . ." He scowled. "*And* Lauren."

"Lauren couldn't have been stalking Declan. They were already seeing one another." I'd shared everything with him about my conversation with Lauren. "Plus, Carissa told me *how* they were seeing each other, with Austin as their cover story."

We had a few things to catch up on, Danny and me. Such as the news about Austin being the one who'd usually refilled Carissa's liquid nitrogen tanks for her—which meant Austin had a motive (rivalry with Declan), a means (those tanks he'd written the software for), and an opportunity (he'd admitted being right there at Churn PDX that morning). I also wanted to tell Danny about Janel attending the Chocolate After Dark tours in all those kooky disguises—especially since *Danny* hadn't recognized her, either. (That made me feel slightly better about my own oversight.) As of tonight, I reflected, Janel was my number one suspect. She was weird, unpredictable, and potentially unhinged.

Lauren, of course, had earned aces in every category,

too. *Motive?* Rejection by Declan, stirring up all her "not quite good enough" feelings. *Means?* Liquid nitrogen, which Lauren was more than familiar with after her improperly made cocktail incident. *Opportunity?* Well, obviously, Lauren had a way to get into Churn PDX, or she wouldn't have been able to meet Declan there.

Just then, though, Danny didn't seem up for strategizing. Especially about Lauren. He handed back Declan's phone.

On its screen were several mushy, suggestive texts from Lauren to Declan. I read a few, then frowned. "Sorry, Danny. But this is the past, right? Lauren has moved on. With you."

"Maybe." He looked at me. "She's been sneaking off with some other guy during the tour. They're pretty secretive."

Mr. Tall, Dark, and Handsome. I remembered him from today.

"It's probably nothing. I'm sure there's a reason."

Like plotting a murder, I thought darkly. *Or cheating.*

We lapsed into silence, Danny morose and me irate. If he had serious feelings for Lauren and she broke his heart, there'd be hell to pay. I'd make sure of it. You know, short of murder.

If nothing else, I'd *definitely* give her a talking-to.

Feeling helpless to make my longtime friend feel better, I decided distraction was the best policy. I searched my (soon-to-be-replaced) stand-in purse and pulled out my own phone.

Its screen showed a waiting message. Thinking it must be Travis getting back to me with the background information he'd promised to dig up on the Cartorama vendors, I opened it.

It was a text from Austin. I didn't know how I'd missed

it earlier—maybe because I'd thought my phone was "still" locked.

Janel hurt. Accident. At Providence Portland. Now. More

The message stopped in midthought, just like that. **More.** I shivered and stared at it for a second, feeling oddly numb.

It was possible I was in shock. It seemed likely that Janel's "accident" had been nothing of the kind. Austin had likely been too upset to notice he hadn't finished writing the message. I figured he'd sent it to everyone at Cartorama at the same time. But would "everyone" show up when Janel needed them?

I didn't know. But I did know *I* was showing up.

After the "accident" *I'd* had, I wanted to know more.

I showed Austin's message to Danny. "I'm going. I'll take my rental car. I'm assuming Providence Portland is a hospital?"

"I know where it is." He grabbed his jacket, not even bothering to give me a token argument about who was going to drive. I guess he could discern that it was me. I was in no mood to indulge in banter. I wondered how badly Janel was hurt.

We hurried through the dark night in silent unison. As we slid into my rented Honda Civic, my phone dinged, startling me.

I looked: **Don't worry about tour. Shutting down tomorrow,** Carissa had texted me. **It's too much. Already canceled w/attendees.**

I hoped she hadn't canceled with them via text message, the way she'd told me. I shook my head, feeling . . . confused. And kind of *used,* too, frankly. After all Carissa had gone through to strong-arm me into taking over

Declan's chocolate tour on an emergency basis, now she was *closing* Chocolate After Dark?

Just like that? With no warning at all?

She could have at least called me to break the news.

"I don't believe this," I blurted, handing the phone to Danny. "What about doing the tour 'for Declan'? What about not disappointing Declan's customers and investors? What about not wasting all the advance publicity he and Carissa had done?"

Danny looked grim. "What about the odd timing of this?"

"Huh?" I started the car and swerved out of my parking space. My foursquare was so old, it didn't even have a driveway. I asked Danny to direct me to the medical center, since he knew where it was. He was good with logistics. "What odd timing?"

"Carissa just happens to shut down the chocolate tour within an hour of Janel being taken to the hospital?"

I frowned. "Sure. That seems like a coincidence, but—"

"But maybe it's *not* a coincidence," Danny theorized. "Maybe Carissa killed her cheating fiancé, then tried to kill the woman he was cheating on her with." *Janel.* "Maybe after failing to kill Janel, Carissa decided to skip town in a hurry. Tonight."

I tossed him a doubtful look, tired of his various "Carissa is guilty" hypotheses. "Sure, she did—after canceling the chocolate tour and texting me and the attendees to say so. That's a pretty polite and informative getaway plan."

"I never said Carissa was a genius. Just a murderer."

"Don't let her hear you say that." I gripped the wheel, driving through the dark on rain-slicked streets. Fortunately, traffic was light, but pedestrians weren't. They slowed us down. "She'll go ballistic on you. She hates being called stupid."

"Stupid is as stupid does. If she tried to kill Janel—"

"We don't even know what happened to Janel," I protested, stopped at a traffic light and wanting to defend my friend. "For all we know, she got tangled up trying to take off her cheap wig and needed the Jaws of Life to set her free." I told Danny about Janel's various disguises during the Chocolate After Dark tours. "She might be fine now. It could have *really* been an accident."

Danny gave a doubtful sound. "Given the way things have been going around here? My money's on attempted murder."

"It was a hit-and-run," Austin told us with an anguished look. "Janel was riding her bike home after the chocolate tour. It was a little wet out, but nothing out of the ordinary."

We'd been at the medical center for ten minutes at the most. Predictably, no one else was there—and I didn't think it was because no one else had received Austin's emergency text.

In the waiting area, the lights overhead were ghastly and bright. The three of us stood serenaded by faraway beeping medical machines and coded emergency calls, both of which echoed off the cold tiled floors. There were chairs—those standard-issue armchairs upholstered in fabric that was more durable than comfortable—but none of us had any interest in sitting in them.

Austin paced, plainly upset. Danny and I listened.

"Janel has a good bike." Austin gave a choked laugh. "Well, she *had* a good bike—a one-speed fixie. I guess it's pretty well destroyed now." He meant a fixed-wheel bicycle, popular among urban cyclists. They were light and fast. "Janel wasn't used to it, though. She kept trying to coast. You can't do that unless you have a freewheel. Maybe she kicked her trailing leg and lost control." He wandered, then pulled off his beanie. He swore under his breath, looking down the hallway. "I don't know. All I know is, some asshole ran into her and then drove away."

I went to him. I hugged him. "I'm sorry, Austin. Have you heard anything?" I searched his distraught face. "How is she?"

"I don't know yet. It's bad. They're still working on her. I think she's in intensive care." He squeezed his beanie, then gave an agitated gesture. "First Declan, now Janel. What the hell, dude? I feel like I'm living in a freaking horror movie!"

"I know," I murmured, patting his shoulder. "Me too."

"I don't even know her family to call them," Austin told us. "I was trying to take it slow with her—trying *not* to get all 'I'm your boyfriend' too soon, like I did with Carissa." He rolled his eyes, struggling for composure. He gave a harsh laugh. "I picked a really great time to become Mr. Cool, right?"

His broken expression was heart wrenching.

"You couldn't have known this would happen." I remembered that Austin had gotten to know Carissa's family so well that he'd been the one to call them to come and comfort her after Declan had died. He probably didn't want to be friend-zoned again, this time with Janel instead of Carissa. "Hang in there, Austin. Janel is strong. She can come through this, right?"

"She wasn't a bad biker, you know." His expression begged us to believe him. "Other than that coasting issue, Janel was really strong. We went out together a couple of days ago, all around Washington Park—you know, the zoo, the Japanese Garden, all that dumb touristy stuff." He smiled wistfully, remembering. I couldn't believe I'd ever suspected him of killing Declan. He was too sweet. "Me and my old Trek CrossRip couldn't keep up."

I guessed that meant Austin *had* moved on from pining for Carissa. I *hadn't* imagined the spark between them earlier today.

Danny stepped forward. "Were you together when this happened? Did you see anything? Did you get a look at the car?"

If I knew my bodyguard buddy, he was trying to build a case that Carissa had ruthlessly mown down Janel with her car. I wasn't having it. "You don't have to talk about it, Austin. Not now."

"No," he told Danny, manfully squaring his shoulders and thwarting my plan to shut down Danny in the process. "I wasn't there. I was just the last number Janel had called on her phone, so they called me when she got here. I haven't even seen her."

The big man sniffled. He shook his head, gazing out the medical center's floor-to-ceiling windows as though looking for an answer. It wasn't possible to glimpse anything through them. It was too dark outside. All we could see was ourselves. We were all at loose ends, waiting to hear about Janel. I don't know what I expected Austin to say, but it wasn't what came next.

"Janel should have been wearing her favorite T-shirt," he told us in a choked-up voice. His gaze met mine, earnest and worried. "It's neon yellow. You know? That crazy color they make reflective tape out of. On the back of it, there's a slogan."

"Isn't there always?" I smiled, eager to comfort him.

Danny stood by, taut and muscular, having little patience for this. "You don't have to baby him, Hayden." He frowned at Austin. "Look, if you think someone did this to Janel on purpose, you should tell us," he told Austin. "We can help."

I shot Danny a *shut up* look. We couldn't promise that. Sometimes Danny can be *too* cocky about his abilities.

But Austin appeared not to have heard him. "The slogan was printed in reverse text," he said, brightening. "You know, like an ambulance? You can read it in your rearview mirror, but—"

"—but not in person." I understood. I patted him again.

"Yeah, anyway"—Austin broke off for a wobbly smile—"Janel's shirt said, 'Please don't run me over.' She though it was *hilarious*. You should have seen her face when she showed me."

Tears filled his eyes, then overflowed. I decided in that moment that Austin was way too softhearted to be a killer.

Danny was less convinced. He shoved a nearby tissue box into Austin's ample midsection. "Maybe whoever ran into Janel was too busy trying to read her T-shirt to watch the road."

His sarcasm didn't register with Austin. "Maybe. Yeah."

I'd been where he was—wanting answers, especially when something tragic had happened. I knew how comforting it could be to talk about the person who'd been hurt . . . the person you cared about. Austin wasn't so different from me. A lot shaggier and fonder of wearing hats, but aside from that, we were similar.

Danny caught a glimpse of my face and sighed. I knew what he was thinking—that I was being much too nice to a person I'd recently accused of killing Declan in cold blood. As far as I was concerned, Danny and Travis needed to quit being so cynical.

Just as I was about to tell Danny so, everyone arrived. Well, *almost* everyone, at least. Better late than never.

"What happened?" Tomasz strode into the waiting area, wide-eyed and slightly scruffy. Five-o'clock shadow agreed with him.

"Janel was hurt," I said, hoping to spare Austin the pain of reciting all the details again. I gave Tomasz a run-through, even as more Cartoramians filed in after him—Lauren included.

Conspicuously, Carissa was absent from the group.

"I'm so happy you guys all made it." Austin blew his nose. He smiled shakily, seeming cheered to have his food cart family nearby. "When I sent that text and didn't hear anything—"

He broke off, his chin wobbling with incipient sobbing.

"Of course we came!" Tomasz said heartily. He clapped Austin on the back. "We're a community. We stick together."

As Tomasz said that, I could have sworn several people's gazes swiveled to *me.* Suddenly, I felt like an intruder.

"We're just going to go, uh, grab a cup of coffee." I pulled Danny nearer. My accomplice. "Anybody want anything?"

A dozen revolted expressions greeted my offer.

Oh yeah. I was in the land of coffee snobs. None of them wanted hospital-cafeteria coffee.

"Okay, then! See you all in a while. Be strong." I held up my phone—*really* my phone. We'd left Declan's at my place. "Let us know if there's any news about Janel, okay? Thanks."

I made my escape, veering toward the signs that said CAFETERIA on them. Danny followed in my wake, his tough-guy boots clonking unconcernedly on the sterile and shiny hallway floors.

He caught up quickly. "You *know* Carissa must have done this," my bodyguard said in a harsh murmur. "She killed Declan, she took advantage of his business contacts, and then she took a parting shot at Janel on her way out of town. It all fits."

Maybe. Except . . . "Declan's business contacts? You didn't mention that earlier." At least if he had, I didn't remember.

"*That's* the riveting detail you're following up on?"

I nodded, still walking. I didn't really want coffee—especially not weak, hours-old, hospital-cafeteria coffee (I did have *some* gourmet standards of my own), but I needed to move. To think. "How did Carissa take advantage of Declan's business contacts?"

Danny tossed me an impatient look. "The tours were packed full of food service specialists—financiers and publicists . . . even a few franchise consultants. Declan wasn't messing around. He front-loaded Chocolate After Dark with all kinds of players."

"But why do that? Declan had already financed and publicized Chocolate After Dark. He certainly wasn't ready to expand." I shook my head. It hadn't occurred to me to wonder why so many people from my own industry had been on the tour—probably because I knew how much foodcentric types like trying new things. The foodies I knew were first in line for novel culinary experiences. "Besides, I met those people, remember? I talked with them. They were in Portland on vacation, not business."

Even the most high-powered executives like chocolate. There'd been nothing strange about having them on the culinary tour. Fancy-pants types generally wanted the best of everything, and they didn't have time to scout it out for themselves.

"Yeah—a vacation sponsored by Declan Murphy,"

Danny agreed with a curt nod. "*Paid for* by Declan Murphy. Lauren told me."

"But he couldn't afford that," I protested. I needed to talk to Travis about this. "It would have cost a fortune."

My security expert shrugged. We reached the medical center's cafeteria and found the coffee. I was too picky to drink it, but Danny had no trouble paying for an inky cup.

We strode to the self-service coffee station. I was lost in thought; Danny was interested in those institutional urns.

". . . it's a shame about that student," one of the residents was saying nearby as I waited for Danny to fill his cup. "Janel was one of the best volunteers around here. Always willing to do whatever grunt work was on hand, run samples over to the lab—anything you asked. A hit-and-run is pretty brutal."

I tuned in immediately, shamelessly eavesdropping. How many *Janels* could there be in Portland? It was an unusual name. I wanted a hint about her medical condition. Instead, I heard . . .

"Yeah. She's in bad shape," another resident confirmed. I peeked and saw him stirring his coffee. "It's kind of ironic, though. I mean, when I broke my arm last year, I could at least get some practical use out of the experience. But Janel is studying to be an ME. The only way she benefits is if she *dies*."

The other resident chuckled. I backed up, appalled.

They said people in medical and emergency professions—doctors, firefighters, first responders of any kind—sometimes need to develop a morbid sense of humor to cope with the horrors of their jobs. I was sympathetic to that, but . . . that was rough.

I glanced at Danny. He'd heard that conversation, too. He raised his eyebrows questioningly, silently asking if

I wanted to fabricate an excuse to get closer and eavesdrop some more. That was Danny for you—always willing to lend a hand with the subterfuge. Not every former bad boy was that generous.

I was too preoccupied to respond at first. That's because what the second resident had said was still whirling in my mind.

Janel is studying to be an ME? A medical examiner.

That explained her laptop and mountains of books. And her need for money. She'd mentioned being broke before—because of student loans? Money troubles would account for Janel's inexpert disguises on the tour. Not to mention her willingness to work at Muddle + Spade. Tomasz might be willing to pay her pretty well, given how much he owed her for keeping Cartorama together.

But it wasn't Janel's lack of funds that concerned me just then. It was something else I remembered. Something Austin had said on the day Declan had died, when he was explaining things.

With the proper protective gear and safety devices, it's fine, Austin had told me as he'd described the various properties and uses of liquid nitrogen. *Laboratories across the country use it with no problem. Even beginner medical students use it to work with tissue samples and things.*

Beginner medical students, I theorized, like Janel.

"I know who killed Declan," I told Danny. "And I know what happened to Janel, too."

Then I turned around, pulled out my keys, and headed for the door. If I was right, there was something important I needed to do.

Fifteen

"I was there," Carissa told me half an hour later, looking somber and harried. "I saw the whole thing. It was . . . *awful*."

My friend shuddered and went on filling the suitcase she'd been packing. It lay open on her pink floral comforter in the bedroom she occupied at her parents' house, half full of tops, underthings, and toiletries. Her face looked ghostly pale.

Given Carissa's obviously distraught state, it was hard for me not to comfort her. I felt pulled to offer a reassuring word, a hug, a justification—anything that would mean she *hadn't* done what I thought she had: purposely run down Janel with her car.

The stark likelihood of that was bad enough. I tried not to think about it too hard, knowing that what I needed to find out now was *why*. I thought I knew. That's what had brought me there.

Danny didn't agree with my strategy. He stood nearby, broad-shouldered and silent, looking unambiguously menacing while watching my flustered friend pack her suitcase. I knew my security expert thought Carissa's distress was all an act, but I wanted him nearby, anyway.

I'd learned the hard way (while in San Francisco) not to veer headlong into a showdown without backup.

In another part of the house—a well-kept multistory dwelling in a suburb of Portland—Carissa's parents were watching television. I could hear the sounds of one of those reality dance competitions playing on the set. Its exuberant music carried upstairs now and then, a surreal parody of normalcy.

Carissa had never moved out from her parents' home. Like many people our age, she hadn't quite gotten launched. Saddled with crushing student loans and a passion for entrepreneurship, Carissa had let her parents finance much of her life so far: Her housing. Her utilities and food. Even her food cart, Churn PDX.

It was because of Mr. and Mrs. Jenkins's generosity that Carissa had a business at Cartorama at all, I'd learned.

I watched Carissa stuff a pair of old wooly boots into her suitcase. They were clearly a comfort item, like sweats or slippers. A security blanket. I expected Carissa needed them.

"It's obvious you're upset," I said softly, doing my best not to startle her. "Why don't you tell me about it?"

Suspiciously, Carissa glanced at me. I gave her a commiserating look, then pulled out my phone. Sometimes people were more comfortable having a difficult conversation if they weren't 100 percent face-to-face with someone else.

I flicked open an app, then pressed *record*.

"Well . . ." Carissa sniffled, then shoved a scarf into her suitcase. She hastily wiped her nose. "It was dark out. Rainy. The streets were all slippery—you know how it is around here."

I nodded. I needed to get all of this, but I wasn't sure

I wanted to hear it. I shot Danny a skittish glance. He nodded.

Carissa inhaled. "I saw Janel, of course. She'd taken off her dumb wig, but I could still see part of it sticking out of her hideous messenger bag. Did you know she got that at a military surplus store? I mean, does she own *anything* decent?"

By "decent," I assumed she meant "girly." One look around Carissa's bedroom confirmed that my old friend still loved pink.

"I just got a new bag today," I confided. "From Zurich."

My overshare seemed to loosen up Carissa. "I'd love to see it sometime. You'll have to show me." By rote, she smiled. "Anyway, I saw Janel pedaling along in the bike lane downtown, looking like a hobo, for real, and that's when I—" Carissa broke off, looking ashamed. "You know, I *followed* her."

"You followed her." I hoped my recording app was getting this. "You followed Janel while she was riding her bike?"

Carissa rolled her eyes. "If you're going to get all judgmental about this, I'm not even going to bother."

"I'm not!" I forced a smile. "I just want to make sure I understand. You know I'm here for you, Carissa. Like always."

Unlike always, I wanted her to get help. *Serious help.*

"I still don't know why you didn't want to rush the sorority," Carissa mused. "You've got sisterhood down cold."

I shrugged, going for modesty. Danny looked out the window.

"Yeah, so, anyway, I was following her." Carissa studied her overflowing suitcase, then frowned. She added some socks. "At first, it was kind of fun. You know, just messing with her."

I couldn't speak. I was horrified. I managed a nod.

"I kinda revved up my engine behind Janel, crept up a little too close . . . that kind of thing. It was harmless," Carissa said. "You've got to understand, I wouldn't have been there at all if not for what she did. Janel *made me* act that way. I'm not proud of it, but it's the truth. I *hated* her. I hated her piggy little nose, her stupid T-shirts, her hair and her voice—"

"Okay," I soothed, holding up my hands. "I get it. But you were justified, right?" I was leading her. Not too overtly, I hoped. "After what Janel had done, what else could you do?"

"Right!" Carissa seemed vindicated. She pushed up her glasses, then strode to her closet to gather some jeans. She dumped them into her suitcase. I couldn't believe I was watching Carissa enact her escape. "I mean, I *saw* Janel that night—the night Declan died. I *saw* her go into my trailer with him."

"Really?" I felt goose bumps break out on my arms.

"I heard them arguing," Carissa continued. "It was really intense—like, they were shouting and throwing things. I wouldn't have been surprised if Janel punched Declan. She's crazy."

Danny appeared to have tuned back into Carissa's story.

I transferred my gaze from my protection expert to Carissa.

I nodded, trying to keep her talking. "Totally. What did you do?" I asked. I hoped I didn't sound as appalled as I felt.

"Well, I was *going* to go in there," Carissa confided in

a stalwart tone. "I mean, the only reason I was there in the first place was to call off the wedding and break up with Declan, like I told you. But I didn't want my final act in our relationship to be *me,* fighting over him with *Janel,* of all people. Are you kidding? She's not even worthy of that. Maybe Lauren, but—"

I tried to keep her on track. "So you didn't go in?"

"No, I turned around. The cart pod was closed for the night by then, so nobody saw me, thank God." Carissa grabbed some jewelry to take with her. "I would have *died* of embarrassment."

. I noticed Danny's mouth tighten. He was losing patience.

"So then what happened?" I asked, still recording (I hoped) on my phone. I wanted proof to bring to the police. Because if Janel died because of Carissa's "messing around" with her on those dark, slippery streets, that needed to be dealt with.

"But I didn't get away fast enough, because that's when I heard Janel." Carissa paused for dramatic effect. I had to hand it to her—she seemed undaunted by her own horrific acts. "'I'd rather see you *die* than married to Carissa!' she said." My friend flailed her arms. "*That's* what Janel screamed at Declan."

"That's a direct threat," I observed. "It's evidence."

"It sure is." Carissa nodded. "*And* it's proof that *I* won, after all. I was in Janel's head, see? She didn't beat me."

Hmm. That was disturbing, too. "And then?"

"Then I left." Carissa shrugged. "I'm assuming that's when Janel clobbered Declan over the head, broke the safety valve on the liquid nitrogen tanks, and left him for dead. I never dreamed she'd go through with her threat! But she's weirdly strong, you know. For a woman, Janel packs a wallop. I think it's because Tomasz took pity on her and hired her at the bar to work the roaster and haul around all those boxes for him."

I couldn't believe how casually Carissa was discussing all this. "I can't believe the way you've dealt with all this."

That much was true, at least, if awfully gruesome.

She busied herself trying to shut her crammed-full get-away suitcase. I knew either Danny or I would have to stop Carissa from leaving town somehow. It was a good thing he was there.

"It's been really hard for me," Carissa confided. "But I felt better about everything after today. You know, after that talk we had? It really helped. It made me realize that doing *anything* in Declan's memory was a waste of time. Why should I alter my life for that scumbag?" She finally shut her suitcase, looking somewhat perkier. "That's what made me decide to quit—"

The Chocolate After Dark tour, I expected to hear next. That would have explained what Carissa had told me so far. What she had texted me earlier, about canceling the chocolate tour.

You know, that *and* her pressing need to go on the lam.

"—following Janel," Carissa continued. "It wasn't worth it."

I blinked, disconcerted. "*Quit* following Janel?"

But didn't she mean *run over Janel?* That's why Danny and I had hurried there. To get to Carissa before she left town.

I could picture the scene. The gloomy night, the rainy streets, and lonely, frumpy Janel, pedaling along . . . unaware that Carissa was right behind her with her hate-filled face shrouded in darkness, gunning her car's engine, getting ready to strike.

Carissa had hit-and-run Janel as revenge for Janel

killing Declan, of course. That's what I'd told Danny on
the way from the hospital. Janel had murdered Declan
because he didn't want to be with her. Then she'd returned
to the scene of her crime later to remove the evidence:
the industrial plastic wrap on the single intake register
of the trailer's ventilation system.

I figured Carissa wasn't the only one who'd noticed
Declan having assignations in there. If Janel had "accidentally" caused Lauren to suffocate to death, too, well . . .
so much the better, from her perspective. Same if she'd
asphyxiated Carissa, instead.

Austin had covered Janel's tracks without even knowing it, because he'd been so eager to fix the broken safety
valve for Carissa. Everyone else had ignored Janel. No
one had been the wiser about her murderous scheme
except me, Danny . . . and Carissa.

Carissa had found out, I'd reasoned, because of Janel.
Because Janel had known how much Carissa hated her.
Her flying-middle-finger salute at Declan's funeral told
me that. Janel hadn't been able to resist taunting her rival
by showing up for every single day of Declan's tour as
one of Declan's Dozen.

While stalking him, Janel would have found out about
all of the women "slutty" Declan had been with. After
having been alerted to the possibility of Declan's infidelity when Austin started to get "nervous" around her,
Carissa would have, too.

Carissa would have recognized the redhead, the
brunette, and the blonde—the caramel lover, the fake
Brit, and the fuchsia-lip-gloss wearer. They were all repli-
cas, I was willing to bet, of women Declan had slept with
behind Carissa's back.

I'm not dumb, you know, Carissa had told me earlier,

with uncanny coolness. *I found out about all the women eventually.*

Those words had led me here tonight. Because the only reason Carissa could have been so easygoing about Janel's taunting was if she'd planned to get revenge. Say, in a hit-and-run accident on a slick, shadowy Portland street. It happened all too often, despite the city's "share the road" initiatives.

Carissa's story about the night Declan had died had only solidified my hunch about things. Although we hadn't known about that encounter until now, Janel's argument with Declan fit. So did her ability to knock him unconscious, rendering him less able to fight. Danny and I had seen for ourselves how strong Janel was. She could have murdered Declan. I believed she had.

Despite my inexpert sleuthing, *I* hadn't brought down Declan's killer. Carissa had. Literally, as it turned out.

Either way, Janel wouldn't be hurting anyone else—not now that she was in intensive care. That's what mattered. Everyone at Cartorama would be safe. Because even if Janel recovered, we had proof now of what she'd done to Declan. Along with that incriminating scrap of plastic wrap (which probably had Janel's fingerprints all over it), Carissa's eyewitness account had already been recorded on my phone to give to the authorities later.

It might be tricky to get Carissa to stay put and testify, of course. Especially if she'd suddenly wised up and re-alized she was implicating herself in Janel's accident by talking to me and Danny. I didn't know the legalities. I assumed that's why Carissa was suddenly pretending to have quit following Janel.

"Yes, quit following her," my friend confirmed, look-ing slightly confused at my question. "I quit following Janel just like I quit helping with Declan's tour. I'd already gotten all I needed out of the tour by then. As far as Janel was concerned—well, I guess she got what was coming to her without me, and way worse, too." Carissa smirked and hoisted her suitcase.

I stood by, feeling hopelessly bewildered.

"Janel 'got what was coming to her'?" I repeated.

"Yeah, when that MINI Cooper ran into her. I saw the whole thing, since I was still right behind her. I'd given up on messing with her, but there was too much traffic to leave."

I frowned and looked at Danny. He appeared lost in thought. He'd picked a heck of a time to get all daydream-y on me.

"Janel wobbled and lost control of her bike when coming to an intersection. The driver made a rolling stop, then just kinda bumped into her while making a right turn against the light. I saw her go down. Just *bang*!" Carissa pantomimed it. "Ugh."

She shuddered while Danny and I stared. I didn't know how to ask what I wanted to know. *Are you lying?* was too overt.

"I'm the one who called the police to report the accident. Ironic, right?" Carissa frowned as her mother called to her from downstairs. "I gave a statement describing the car and everything." In her pink bedroom, my friend winked at me. "One of the officers was pretty cute. I made him give me his number."

"Good for you," I said. I guessed she was ready to move on romantically. I might not be great at sneaking around, but I knew when a response was socially necessary. "What's his name?"

Carissa told me, while Danny paced around the room. I tossed him an apologetic glance. I hadn't needed his muscle, after all. Carissa wasn't a threat to anything except my peace of mind.

"Who was driving the MINI cooper?" Danny asked.

Carissa looked irritated. "Who knows? Not me, if that's what you're wondering." She exhaled, exasperated. "Maybe after I set up shop in L.A., I'll be able to afford one of those, though."

Danny nodded. "L.A., huh? That's my neck of the woods."

Like flipping a switch, he turned on the charm.

Carissa noticed. "Really?" She played with her long auburn hair, batting her eyelashes behind her glasses. "What part?"

He told her. "If you can drag yourself away from your new police officer friend, you should look me up sometime."

I stood by, befuddled. Why was Danny flirting? Why now?

Don't get me wrong—it was something to see. Even as a bystander, I felt kind of tingly. But I didn't get his strategy.

"I just might do that," Carissa cooed, examining my bodyguard's muscles and imposing presence with new appreciation. "I'm going to be in Santa Monica. On the Third Street Promenade. I found an investor to help me expand Churn PDX to California."

"That's a nice neighborhood to start in," Danny remarked.

I could have sworn he was ogling Carissa's legs. Whatever happened to his fling with Lauren? Geez, he was fickle.

It was a good thing *I'd* never gotten seriously involved with him. You know, in a romantic sense.

"I know. I'm pretty psyched," Carissa said. "I had my

pick of suitors, thanks to all the groundwork Declan did—thanks to him bringing everyone here. He had a lot of access through his Prodigy Group peeps. God knows, I wasn't going out for drinks with him and all those Seattle dude-bros for no reason."

Danny nodded. "You had a strategy."

"Of course. I'm the kind of girl who looks out for number one. I wasn't *crazy* about Declan." She laughed, giving Danny a flirtatious stroke on his bulging biceps. "I wasn't all mushy about him, I mean. Sorry, Hay," Carissa added in an aside to me. "I know how much you were into all the engagement party stuff, but I'm just as happy it never happened. All I wanted from Declan was his business contacts. He didn't know how good they were when he threw them over. I did. But I wasn't going to let him make it look as if *I* was being cheated on. I mean, *as if.*"

With an awful sense of disillusionment, I understood. Carissa *wasn't* the friend I remembered from college. She was a lot more grasping and a lot more ruthless. But she *wasn't* a killer. At least I'd been right about that much. *Yay?*

I couldn't help turning over what Carissa had said, though. *Prodigy Group.* That sounded familiar. I couldn't remember why.

The come-and-get-me eyes Danny was giving her didn't help.

"Declan didn't know how to handle you," he said.

"You've got that right." Carissa smiled at him. "I bet you do, though. I bet you're resourceful in all the right places."

"At all the right times," Danny confirmed in a husky tone.

I was starting to feel queasy. I had to get out of there.

"You're gritty. *Real,*" Carissa was telling Danny when I tuned back into their flirtathon. "I could use a little of that, after Declan. He was basically a glorified salesman. All the men in Portland are *so . . .*" She sighed, searching for an apt description. *"Tame.* Sure, they've got their beards and their boots, their flannel shirts and their growlers full of craft beer, but they're all so *sensitive.* Or geeky. Austin couldn't get through a single sentence without talking about some idiotic video game. He dressed up like comic book heroes! What a dork."

Her tone of derision was hurtful. I clicked off my app's recording function, then held up my phone. "I've got to get this."

As I'd intended, Carissa assumed I had to answer a call. Most phones these days had a silent-ring function. Mine probably did, too. I wasn't sure. I almost always used it for texting.

Carissa waved me off. I slipped downstairs, said good-bye to Mr. and Mrs. Jenkins, then stepped into the cool nighttime.

I looked at my phone, debating. Then I started texting.

I know what you're thinking—that I was texting Travis a cheeky *what are you wearing right now?* to cheer myself up.

Under ordinary circumstances, you might have been right. But these weren't ordinary circumstances. Things had changed.

I was technically unemployed now, for starters. I hadn't expected Carissa to pay me for conducting Declan's Chocolate After Dark culinary tours, but they had occupied a space on my calendar—a space that Travis would want to fill with something income producing and industrious. Just then, I wasn't up for it.

Hey, I'm leaving town soon, I typed out. Still wanna meet?

I deliberated for a minute, then glanced up at Carissa's

lighted bedroom window. I could see her and Danny laughing.

My sometime bodyguard really knew how to pick 'em.

I chose one of my contacts. A second later, my text whooshed through the Internet to Tomasz Berk. Our date was on.

At least it was, if *I* was half as lucky as Danny was. Seriously—*two* women, both hot to trot for him in the space of a week? He has his share of reckless appeal, but . . . wow.

Then I sent Danny a text and made him come out. Enough was enough. I wasn't in the mood to play wingman. Not tonight.

There was nothing but stony silence on the way back to our shared house. I was preoccupied; Danny seemed to be, too. In our defense, it had been quite a day. I didn't have any claim on Danny; that's not how our relationship worked. But I was still creeped out by the way he'd flirted with Carissa, after everything she'd said. I figured he'd done it out of boredom. Or perversity. Or maybe a desire to feel wanted, after having (maybe) been two-timed by Lauren with Mr. Cart Pod.

Danny was only human, I reminded myself. Neither of us was perfect. Both of us were given to retreating when upset. I was upset, too. I couldn't deny it—not to myself. I wanted to believe Danny was a better man than he'd seemed to be tonight.

I also wanted to believe I wouldn't let my own personal dramas trump the nightmare of what had happened to Declan and, to a lesser degree, to Janel. But I was doing exactly that as I drove toward my foursquare for the night.

I suppose I should have felt sorry for Janel, after what

she'd been through. I knew she might not make it. But she'd killed Declan. As much as I try to have faith in my fellow human beings, Janel had stepped over the line. Even *my* line. I might strive to think the best of people, but I'm no pushover.

My silence with Danny proved it. He knew it, too.

Traffic was light, so the trip was quick. We were arching across Portland's iconic Fremont Bridge, high above the city lights and the Willamette River, before Danny said anything.

"Just come out with it," he commanded. "What's wrong?"

I'm no pushover, but Danny can be a real bulldozer.

I kept driving, pretending a rapt interest in the steel bridge's tied-arch design. We were zooming along the lower of its two decks as we headed back home. "Nothing," I said.

My security expert laughed. "You're a terrible liar."

"In my world, that's a good quality." I shifted him a sideways glance as I changed lanes. "So, got a date now?"

He grunted. "That wasn't what that was about."

I decided to give him the benefit of the doubt. "Oh yeah?"

"Yeah. That was a tactic," Danny informed me. "You were running out of steam with Carissa—probably because you were horrified by how cold-blooded she was—so I picked up the slack. That's how we work. As a team. I'm better at gruesome stuff."

"*I'm* better at gruesome stuff," I rebutted automatically.

He didn't argue. *There.* I'd just successfully lied. *Take that, Jamieson.* I sped off the bridge toward home.

Then, "How did you know to use that tactic on her?"

Danny's sardonic face turned to mine. "Being friendly?"

"Making love to her with your eyes." I turned. "Yeah."

"'Making love'? Ew." He guffawed, giving me a look. "What are you, a walking self-help book? Who *says* stuff like that?"

I ignored that. He was trying to sidetrack me. "Well?"

Danny shrugged. "I wanted to make sure Carissa stayed in touch with me. In case you're wrong, and we find out later that Janel wasn't the one who murdered Declan."

We still hadn't heard how Janel was doing. She might still get out of the hospital. But not before we turned her in.

"Janel murdered Declan," I assured him. "Everything Carissa told us verifies it. Carissa might still flee, you know. If she does become a fugitive, why would she even contact you? How?"

"You know why." Danny waggled his eyebrows provocatively. "As for the how . . . Outlaw Meetup," he deadpanned. "You know, like Match.com or OkCupid. We all use it. Crooks have needs, too."

"You're not a crook anymore," I reminded him.

My security expert went silent. That worried me.

Then, "It's not a real dating site. You know that, right?"

No. "Of course." I waved blithely. "I knew the whole time. Just like I knew you weren't really interested in Carissa."

"Oh, I'm really interested in Carissa."

I gulped. Was I supposed to support this? I wanted to always be there for Danny, but—

Danny's laughter cut me off in mid deliberation. "See?" he told me assuredly. "You're too nice to track down killers. You should put away your gumshoe sign before it gets tarnished."

"I'm trying to, believe me." I felt better having talked to him. I don't like being on the outs with Danny. "If people would just stop dropping dead wherever I go, I'd have a shot at it."

"You've got to try harder," Danny urged. "Pretend those dead bodies are me, and you're giving me the silent treatment."

"Har, har." Anyway, it was beyond unlikely that I'd encounter a *third* murder victim. I didn't need advice on how to handle something that wasn't ever going to happen. "I think I'll call Travis and tell him you've finally gotten through to me."

"You do that," Danny suggested brashly. "I like the idea of Harvard knowing *I'm* the one who finally got you to quit."

Quit. He'd *had* to use that word, hadn't he?

I wondered if they'd had a bet going, Travis and Danny.

Well, I *was* quitting. For tonight, at least. I'd lined up the suspects and knocked them down, leaving us with Janel safely secured in Providence Portland, where she couldn't hurt anyone else, and all the rest of the Cartoramians accounted for.

"You'd better watch it," I warned Danny. "I'll go stirring up some trouble, just to keep things interesting. I promise."

He shot me a concerned look. Then his dark, rough-around-the-edges features softened. Knowingly. "You mean you'll flirt with someone, too, just to bug me. Yeah. Good luck with that."

How did he keep doing that? Reading my mind that way?

"Wouldn't you like to know what kind of trouble I'm headed for?" I tried to sound mysterious. "It could be *anything.*"

"It's flirting. I know it is." Danny studied me with disconcerting thoroughness—almost as if he *hadn't* known me forever. "Just don't do that thing you do with your teeth."

"What, you mean smile?"

"That's the one." He gazed out the car's window. "Don't do that one, or the poor sucker won't stand a chance."

I smiled. It was nicer when Danny's charm was aimed at me.

Then I drove us into our cozy neighborhood, past the rows of Eisenhower houses, all the way to our temporary home.

Sixteen

"You're not going to believe this," I told Danny the next morning. We'd both gotten up (relatively) early to hit up one of my favorite Stumptown coffee shops. It was misty outside, but we were warm and dry inside with a quad Americano (Danny) and a cappuccino (me), plus a trio of pastries. I hadn't been able to choose just one; my sometime bodyguard had urged me to throw caution to the wind. I knew there was a reason I liked him.

"Try me." With uncharacteristic lightness, Danny glanced at my laptop screen, where I'd been tying up loose ends relating to Portland and the Chocolate After Dark tour. If I hadn't known better, I'd have thought he was relieved that I'd survived our latest deadly adventure. But Danny never worried. "What's up?"

I nodded at the digital dossier Travis had sent me—before he'd known that we'd already pinpointed Janel for Declan's murder. I'd been idly going through it. It wasn't unthinkable for Travis to decide to quiz me later on its contents. He was pedantic that way. He'd dotted every *i* and crossed every *t;* he was particular. The dossier had an index, for Pete's sake.

Travis had clearly done a lot of work on my behalf. I didn't want to be unappreciative, so I'd been reading.

Okay, *and* I was curious. Pruriently curious. Travis had dug up skeletons that even the Cartoramians had forgotten they'd buried. His dossier made entertaining reading—especially when combined with a flaky marion-berry hand pie and/or buttery maple twist and/or scrumptious almond croissant. Or all three of them.

I know, they're not chocolate. So shoot me. Sometimes even *I* need a break from my dark and delicious specialty.

"Tomasz isn't your everyday sensitive and penniless bartender, after all," I told Danny, still reading. "He's—"

"Secretly a poet? A champion whittler? A cobbler?"

I smiled at my security expert's attempt at shoe-related humor. "He's a trust-fund kid from a superwealthy family in New York City." I kept reading, scanning faster now. "He's worth . . ." I paused, trying to tamp down my surprise. "He's worth *millions*."

"I knew it. Berk *is* your dream man, after all."

I wouldn't have gone that far. Especially since I knew Danny had an ax to grind against the affluent. But I couldn't resist teasing him. "Tomasz *might* measure up, I guess, but you never know. After all, I have some pretty *big* dreams."

"Ha. Don't make me crack a dick joke here. I'll do it."

I laughed, unfazed by Danny's ribald sense of humor. I was used to it. I sometimes indulged, too. Don't tell my clients.

"Tomasz did a really good job of hiding his wealth," I mused. I didn't know what to make of this new information. After all, usually *I* was the one downplaying my fortune. I'd never met anyone else who was interested in discretion when it came to throwing around the cash. "I really thought he was broke."

"He obviously wanted you to think he was broke."

"Me and everyone else. I never suspected a thing."

Wait. I had to take that back. I *had* suspected something was up with Tomasz's very fine Arnys suit—the one he'd worn to Declan's funeral. I'd obviously noticed his nice brogues, too.

"And that doesn't seem shady to you?" Danny asked.

I stopped pondering Tomasz's wardrobe and took a bite of my maple twist. *Yum.* I shook my head. "No, why would it?"

"Because he was deliberately keeping it a secret."

"You're just bugged because *you* didn't guess, either." I scanned Travis's digital dossier, reading the details. "Tomasz inherited his money." *Just like me.* "He's used to having it."

"What a problem." Danny's expression soured.

I gave him a *cheer-up* shoulder bump. "An inheritance has its share of problems," I reminded him. "For instance, sometimes I wonder if people want to hang out with me because they like me or because I can foot the bill for whatever we're doing."

"Hey, *I* paid for breakfast." His face grew darker.

I smiled. "Plus, having to report my whereabouts to Travis is no cakewalk. Do you think I like having a financial leash?"

It was ironic. For me, the main benefit of having access to all of Uncle Ross's cash was freedom—freedom that felt a tiny bit curtailed every time I had to check in with my sexy keeper.

"You could have turned down the money," Danny pointed out.

"What am I, crazy?" I laughed, hoping to ease the tension between us. I kept the details of my financial situation pretty well veiled. Danny knew the bare minimum—such as, I could afford to gallivant around the world . . . luxuriously, if I wanted to. I could afford to fly us both to exotic locations on a whim, then pay for everything once we were there. I could keep myself in Converse and cross-body bags for a *very* long time. Let's just say I'm comfortable and leave it at that. "Then I'd have to work harder—maybe even take on more clients. *Ugh.* Who wants that?"

The funny thing was, most of the time, Danny and Travis were more interested in growing my chocolate-whispering business than I was. I'm not lazy. It's just that I'm more attracted to the challenges of a particular consulting job than its lucrativeness—or its ability to net me a bigger fish down the road.

I'd stumbled onto chocolate whispering. Serendipitously. I liked it. I didn't want it to become *work* in the usual sense.

"You'd have to turn in your reports on time. Impossible." Danny shook his head, playing along. "You're right. It's better to be filthy rich." He finished his half of our (lip-smacking) almond croissant. "So, why is Tomasz hiding all his money?"

"Probably for the same reasons I hide mine," I guessed.

It was interesting that we had something else in common.

"*You* bend over backward to hide your moola because you're being nice to me." Danny watched the baristas. "I'm not that sensitive, you know. I can handle your undeserved windfall."

Right. The fact that he'd called it "undeserved" was a big tip-off. I was edging onto thin ice. My financial situation was a touchy subject between Danny and me. Usually, I avoided talking about it. I'd already put us on uncomfortable footing last night with my unanticipated reaction to Danny's faux flirting with Carissa. From here on, I just wanted harmony.

Apparently, my burly longtime friend felt the same way, because he chose that moment to peruse my laptop screen rather than continue our discussion of wealth and its drawbacks.

"What's that about Common Grounds?" Danny pointed to the itemized list of Tomasz's financial holdings. "Don't tell me Berk lucked into all that cash with a fancy-coffee dynasty."

Common Grounds. It did sound like a Starbucks-style enterprise—one that was too upmarket to serve ordinary java.

Then I remembered. "Common Grounds is Cartorama's landlord. They own the property that all the food carts are parked on."

"You mean *Tomasz Berk* is Cartorama's landlord?"

"I guess so," I said, feeling taken aback.

Danny was, too. We both sat there in the bustling coffee shop, watching the rain hit the windows, inhaling the delicious aromatic roasted coffee scents and listening to the muted thumps that sounded as the baristas struck spent espresso grounds from their portafilters. I looked at my security expert. He looked at me.

"I didn't see that one coming," I told Danny.

"Me either." He frowned. It was evident that he was mentally reviewing everything I'd told him about the cart pod's fight against development. So was I. "Berk isn't the entirety of the Common Grounds consortium, but for our purposes, he might as well be," Danny reflected. "He's the one who's *here.*"

I pondered that for a minute but turned up nothing. It seemed as though Tomasz being Cartorama's landlord *ought* to be a more meaningful revelation. After all, it was a *big* secret.

"This means that *Tomasz* was the one who refused to sell to developers," I told Danny, realizing it even as I scanned Travis's dossier for more surprises. "*He* was the one who refused to let the property become an apartment complex. Without him, all the food cart vendors would have needed to find new homes. Affordable parking spaces are getting scarce around here, too. But Tomasz saved them all." I shook my head, marveling at what he'd done. "He didn't want any credit for doing it, either."

That was admirable, partly because I had no doubt Tomasz could have realized a big profit if he'd sold the Cartorama property. I knew the vendors' rents were (relatively) cheap.

At the rate the Cartoramians paid, he wasn't getting any wealthier, that was for sure. "That is *remarkable,*" I said.

"Hold on. Back it up." Danny held up his palms. "Before you get all starry-eyed, remember we're not talking about Robin Hood here. It's not heroic for Berk to continue business as usual."

"It's heroic to turn down a humongous profit in order to continue business as usual." That's exactly what Tomasz had done when he'd refused to sell the Cartorama property. "Amazing."

Danny shook his head. "He's not a saint, Hayden."

"I'm going on a date with a saint!" I grinned, needling him on purpose. Just a little. "How's that for a going-away-from-Portland party? Never mind about Tommy's antique cacao roaster," I said, referring to my plans to see it in action with Tomasz later. "I'm going to go for the gusto."

"Humph." Danny grumbled. "If that's a euphemism—"

Ha. I'd known he'd make that racy joke eventually. "I guess we'll probably sit around comparing portfolios," I gibed with a nonchalant air. "We'll debate stocks versus bonds, and trustees versus butlers, then figure out who's richer, me or him."

Danny made a face. "Sounds like a real rager."

I laughed, then gave him a consoling pat. "Don't worry. At the end of the day, I'll always want to come home to your dirty jokes and unholy love of *Antiques Roadshow* marathons."

Confidentially, I thought Danny's binge-watching of that show was just a cover. Probably, he was doing research on things he could lift for profit. Or revisiting items he'd *already* stolen during his former mad-and-bad days as a criminal.

"I know you will," Danny told me, confident of the appeal of his dangerous ways and lovable heart. "I'm counting on it."

"Yeah, well—don't get too sure of me. I might surprise you one of these days." I finished the rest of my (perfect) cappuccino, then stood and slung on my (new/old) crossbody bag. *Ah.* Now everything was just as it was supposed to be. "I'm off to the police station. Are you sure you don't want to come?"

I was provoking him again. Danny has a well-known desire to avoid law-enforcement agencies. Even though he's clean now, he likes to steer clear. I couldn't say I blamed him. If I had a rap sheet like Danny does, I'd probably do the same thing.

I don't like being hassled, either—or feeling under pressure . . . both of which probably play into my long-time procrastination habit. Danny and I had that much in common, even if *his* avoidance tactic was chronic lateness, instead. It was one of his rare flaws.

His steely gaze met mine. "I'll let you have all the glory this time. Let me know how it goes. I'm there if you need me."

It said a lot about our friendship that Danny was willing to set foot in the police station if I wanted him to. "Thanks, but it should be pretty standard-issue stuff."

I'd made an appointment to speak with a detective about what we'd uncovered while talking with Carissa—and to turn over that scrap of plastic wrap. If I was right, the authorities would lift Janel's fingerprints from it. (And mine, of course, which I wasn't looking forward to explaining. I'm not exactly licensed to poke into suspicious "accidents.") That proof, taken together with what I'd recorded while at Carissa's last night, ought to be enough to get Janel arrested for Declan's murder.

She wouldn't be difficult to find; she was still in Providence Portland. I'd texted Austin earlier. He hadn't had any details—only that Janel's injuries were still considered critical. No one expected her to leave the hospital anytime soon.

I felt sorry for Janel, but I couldn't deny feeling relieved, too. At least now she wouldn't hurt anyone else.

"Where can I drop you?" I asked Danny, jangling the keys to my rented Honda. "The local men's shoe emporium, maybe?"

He laughed and almost choked on his Americano. Whoops.

I helpfully patted him on the back. Geez, he was muscular.

Shrugging off my attentive touch, Danny slung on his jacket. "If you're hoping I'll get a pair of those 'take care of a house and kids' shoes, you're barking up the wrong tree."

I widened my eyes. "Not even if they're nice monk straps?"

"*Especially* if they're nice monk straps."

I waited a beat, studying him. He'd grown his dark hair a little longer than his usual military-style cut, I noticed.

"You know that's a real style of men's shoes, right?"

"Of course." Danny cleared his throat. "I think Travis wears those monk shoes, especially when he's walking his dog."

Dog? I almost squealed out loud. "Travis has a dog? Since when? He never said anything to me about having a dog." My imagination ran wild. I couldn't help it. I pictured Travis walking his dog, throwing a Frisbee to his dog, teaching an adorable toddler how to pet his (harmless and lovable) dog. "What kind of dog is it?" I asked eagerly. "I've always pinned him for a golden retriever type, but you know accountants."

My dependable financial advisor was probably starting his pet-companion life with "affenpinscher" and ending it with "Yorkshire terrier," in perfect alphabetical order.

"It's a dog." Danny shrugged. "I don't know what kind."

I gawked at him. "What do you mean, you 'don't know'? Didn't you see it? Describe it to me. Do you have pictures?"

"I was interested in getting down to business, not making chitchat," my security expert complained. "What's the big deal?"

The *big deal* was that Danny had been up close and personal with my *extremely* private financial advisor and he hadn't even had the foresight to spy on him for me. Sadly, I shook my head.

"You're hopeless. You *know* I'm dying to know everything there is to know about Travis! It's been driving me crazy ever since he took over for old Mr. Whatshisname, my former trustee." I flung my hands in the air with frustration, feeling helpless. "You know how secretive Travis is. So why wouldn't you—"

"I'm not going to spy on Travis for you." Danny squared his shoulders, then headed for the coffee shop's door. I trailed him in a cloud of disbelief. "Maybe he's secretive for a reason."

"Maybe *you* just don't want us to get together."

"Get together?" Danny arched his eyebrows. "Really?"

I ignored his suggestive tone. "You know what I mean."

"Yeah. I do." He squinted against the rain. We were secure under the coffee shop's diminutive awning, but its protection wouldn't last. "That's why I'm not helping you. See you later."

I stamped my foot, still irked. Was Danny saying that he didn't want me to *get together* with Travis romantically? Or was he saying that he didn't want me to *get together* with Travis in a completely innocent, getting-to-know-you way? Or at all?

Were he and Travis in cahoots again or something?

Danny had known me long enough to understand that all I wanted was to be on equal footing with Travis. I didn't like that my (younger) financial advisor knew everything there was to know about me—my background, my finances, my whereabouts, my plans, the identities of all my friends—while I knew (almost) nothing about him. Unless, I guess, being aware that Travis liked to swim and run marathons counted as full disclosure.

I was here to tell anyone who'd listen: it *didn't*.

Not that those tidbits didn't provide me with a few entertaining fantasies now and then. I'll confess, they did. If you'd ever heard Travis break down an itinerary in that husky, supersmart, tell-me-everything voice of his, you'd spin a few daydreams yourself. You simply wouldn't be able to help it.

Just like me.

There on the coffee shop's stoop, Danny studied me with a distinctly perceptive glimmer in his eye. I noticed it when I finally snapped to again, surfacing from my thoughts.

"What fantasy is Harvard up to now? Doing your taxes?"

He waggled his eyebrows, suggesting that *was* a euphemism.

Hmmph. Danny didn't know everything about me.

"If that's what you want to call it. Sure," I told him.

Then I gave him a shove and breezed away toward my car. I wasn't exactly looking forward to visiting the police station, but it was the next step in putting Portland—and everything that had happened there—behind me. I might not love reporting in to Travis, but I *do* love being on the move. So I was ready to go.

Besides, anything was better than listening to Danny guffaw as he swaggered away, off to a destination that I belatedly realized I didn't know and now couldn't find out. He'd cleverly sidestepped my attempt to ask him—because *I'd* succumbed to making a dopey shoe joke, then forgotten to follow through.

Some detective I was, I thought as I hurried through the raindrops and got into my car. *I couldn't even interrogate my own best friend.* It was a good thing I was heading out for a new chocolate-whisperer–consulting job soon. Because even though I'd gotten lucky this time (and found a way to nab Janel), I had a long way to go before I could consider myself ready to deal with murder and mayhem on anywhere close to a full-time basis.

* * *

My penultimate day in Bridgetown was a busy one.

First I went to the police station, where I met with a very professional and attentive detective to turn in my evidence.

He asked me a lot of questions, had a good long perusal of my passport, conferred with his boss and some other police officers, copied the conversation off my phone, then returned.

"Thanks for your help, Ms. Moore." He offered his hand to me. "We'll be in touch if we need anything else."

I'd already given him all my contact details—my name, permanent address (Travis's office), Social Security number, passport, phone number, and more. So I accepted his handshake.

"Then you're going to get Janel? I mean, Ms. White?" This situation probably called for formality, I decided.

"We'll take care of everything from here." The detective skillfully maneuvered me toward the station's hectic reception area. "Don't worry about a thing. You've been very helpful."

Hmm. "I get the sense you're not taking this seriously," I pressed. "Is there something else you need as proof?"

"We'll examine the evidence you left. Thanks again."

His brush-off felt routine. "There might be fingerprints."

"We'll know that soon enough. Have a nice day, Ms. Moore."

I didn't bother correcting him about my name. (Clue: it always has three parts.) Afterward, I certainly didn't feel all warm and protected, though. Not to malign the brave people who protect and serve, but I felt I'd gotten the bum's rush.

Maybe that was part of the reason Danny avoided the police, I reasoned as I dashed outside and called Austin.

So far, the authorities hadn't been very receptive to my (amateur) efforts.

In my mind, I was Sherlock Holmes. In theirs, I . . . *wasn't.*

I had to leave a voice mail message for Austin. It felt weird. But while texting is efficient, it's too limited. It doesn't fit the bill for every situation—say, apologizing for thinking someone was a coldhearted killer, when they were really just a nerd.

"Hi, Austin! Yes, it's Hayden. Yes, I'm actually calling you on your cell phone. Yes, I *know* it's disconcerting to get an actual phone call, but—" I broke off, realizing too late that Austin might not even bother listening to his voice mail messages. Most of my friends didn't. "I wanted to apologize," I moved on anyway needing to have this said. "I'm sorry for"—*thinking you were a murderer*—"everything you've been going through. I hope I didn't make the situation worse for you."

I drew in a deep breath, pacing down the slick sidewalks of the Plaza Blocks. Here, tall old elms and ginkgo trees blocked some of the drizzly rainfall. Around me, city residents walked by with shopping bags or strollers, briefcases or backpacks. I passed a big bronze statue of an elk and smiled to myself. Even after everything that had happened, I still liked Portland. I might not miss it *immediately,* but I would miss it eventually.

"How's Janel doing?" I asked Austin in a deliberately chipper tone, continuing my voice mail. "I know you two were getting pretty close. I mean, you *are* getting close." Yikes. There was no point writing her eulogy already— although I knew the police would be closing in on her soon. "But even if Janel turns out *not* to be the one for you, hang in there, okay?" I felt compelled to say. "You'll find the right woman. And she'll *love* coffee and Nintendo-core and vinyl music, just like you."

I suddenly started to feel overwhelmed. Catching a killer was big. But dealing with the aftermath—even in a small way—was brutal. Austin would be better off without a murderer for a girlfriend, of course, but he'd still be upset for a while.

Thinking of men and girlfriends made me think of Danny and Lauren. I didn't know why Cartorama's burlesque queen appeared to be sneaking around behind Danny's back, but Lauren had never done anything except be kind to me. So I called her, too.

I was starting to see the (admittedly cowardly but undeniably time-efficient) benefits of voice mail by the time I'd left Lauren a similar *"nice to know you, sorry for all the sadness"* message. I figured Danny might have gone to visit her, in which case she'd be too busy to listen right away (if ever). But I'd done my part to help create some closure. That mattered.

I called Carissa, too, and delicately suggested she see someone. I thought a therapist could really help her. My old college friend would probably be too busy taking over the L.A. ice-cream world to deal with her mental health, but I hoped Carissa got some help, anyway. It was sad that we'd gotten back in touch, only to have tragedy (and change) pull us apart again.

Feeling lighter afterward, I walked past the green spaces of Lownsdale Square and Chapman Square, back to the street where I'd parked my car. I wanted to call Travis. Maybe I'd tell him about the Benson Bubblers, I thought. He'd appreciate the history of the iconic, old-timey bronze drinking fountains that a famous Portlander had installed throughout the city in the early twentieth century. Or maybe I'd tell Travis about the cocoa-balsamic drinking vinegar I'd sampled during the Chocolate After

Dark tour. I liked razzing my financial advisor about "weird" foods he'd never try. He was ludicrously squeamish.

Maybe, I mused as I pulled out my car keys and spied the spare Muddle + Spade key that Tomasz had given me, I'd tell Travis about the unique shop I'd found in PDX, which served the best chocolate-dipped profiteroles (*choux à la crème*) that I'd ever had outside of the septième arrondissement in Paris. *Mmm.*

In case you're not familiar with them, *choux à la crème* are usually filled with *crème pâtissière*. Then they're stacked as a pyramid, bound with threads of caramelized sugar, and served up as a *croquembouche* to "crunch in the mouth" (to paraphrase the French) for dessert at weddings, Christmastime, and parties. In Portland, though, the shop I'd found filled their *choux à la crème* with chocolate ice cream *and* topped them with two layers of chocolate, making them *choux à la glace à double chocolat.*

And making thinking about them (plus drinking vinegar and drinking fountains) my latest vehicle for procrastination.

Aha. My old (non)friend (procrastination) had reared its ugly head again. That explained why I was suddenly experiencing an urge to craft the perfect trivia-filled phone call for my financial advisor.

I recognized my impulse to tune out by phoning Travis for what it was and deliberately started my rented Civic's engine instead. Travis would have listened politely, of course, but he wasn't a foodie (another thing I didn't understand about him). He wouldn't appreciate the difference between *croquembouche*—my scrumptious pastry find—and *charcuterie*—basically, meat. Plus, he'd be annoyed about all the French . . . even though he understood it. I'd once sneaked in some frisky phrases during one of our phone calls, and I *know* Travis had gotten tongue-tied.

Remembering that, I felt another urge to call him. It was powerful, like an itch I couldn't reach. Teasing Travis sounded a lot more appealing than driving through traffic, going back to my (soon-to-be-abandoned) four-square house, and getting ready for my—

That's it, I decided. That was the root of my craving to procrastinate. I didn't want to leave the cute house Travis had rented for me. I liked being there too much. Just like my relationship with Chow the cat (which had blossomed lately), my comfort level with my adopted neighborhood had grown. I didn't want to stuff my pashmina into my wheelie suitcase, sequester my family photos in my duffel bag, and leave PDX for good.

Yes, that made sense. I wasn't completely lacking in self-awareness; I knew I only procrastinated when faced with doing something I didn't want to do. Something that caused me basic existential dread. Something like perfecting a temperamental chocolate soufflé. Controlling the fruit-forward flavors in a chocolate varietal from Ghana. Or sorting through receipts at tax time. (I knew *that* was fun for Travis—sorry, Travis!)

But the only thing left on my to-do list was to keep my formerly deferred date with Tomasz. What was there not to like about keeping a rendezvous to get up close and personal with a vintage cacao roaster and the man who owned and operated it?

Nothing . . . that's what, I reminded myself. Tomasz was (secretly) rich, (secretly) altruistic, and (openly) charming. He was also *really* good-looking, excellent at creating harmony (sometimes via well-timed boozy drinks), and devoted to everyone in his Cartorama "family." Plus, he wore good shoes and mixed a pretty amazing Cacao Negroni, too. In fact, I decided, there was no time like the present to just get on with our date.

You know . . . if it *was* a date. Although Tomasz had texted me back with a Come over anytime response, I still didn't know if we were getting together romantically— the way Danny thought I wanted to get together with Travis—or if we were just going to behave like food service colleagues admiring some nice equipment.

That (unintentional) double entendre reminded me of Danny again. If he'd been there, he'd have interrogated Tomasz about his undisclosed wealth. But I had no plans to do any such thing. I hadn't come clean about *my* fortune, either. It didn't matter.

I was going to close out my time in Portland on a high note, I told myself. All it would take was one trip across the picturesque Hawthorne Bridge, one meander up to the northeast side of town, and one quick jaunt over to Muddle + Spade and the Cartorama cart pod. I was coming for Tomasz Berk, all right. No matter how weird Portland got on the way there, I was coming.

I might even resist stopping to call Travis while I was at it, I decided. Because that's just how strong I felt.

After all, nobody told Hayden Mundy Moore what to do and got away with it—especially not her own procrastinatory tendencies . . . which were infamous in certain circles for good reason, after all. So I put my car in gear and just got going.

Seventeen

The first thing I noticed when I arrived at Muddle + Spade was that it was quiet. Although Cartorama was open, there wasn't much business at the cart pod. (I blamed the on-again, off-again rain showers for that. I mean, seriously, Pacific Northwest: just decide if it's raining or not, then *do* it!)

Tomasz's bar wasn't open to customers yet. Apparently, in my eagerness to get a look at his equipment (I'm kidding), I'd sped across town too quickly. The familiar A-stand wasn't even outside yet, luring in visitors with promises of house-made cocktails, artisanal herb- and fruit-based drinks, and beer.

In Portland, I'd learned, there was *always* beer.

Momentarily daunted by Muddle + Spade's generally deserted appearance, I hesitated with my car keys in hand. I looked over my shoulder, taking in the neighborhood's row of trees. They were dripping rainwater at the moment. As I stood there, those drops picked up speed. I watched for a second, perplexed.

Then I realized it was raining (again) and hurried to

the bar's door. I knocked, huddled against the struggling downpour.

Nobody answered. I considered texting Tomasz, but he'd said he might not hear my knock, hadn't he? So I took advantage of my exclusive access, unfastened that monogrammed key fob from its position affixed to my car-rental ring, and worked the lock.

Ah. Inside, it was warm and snug. Ordinarily, Tomasz's bar was packed with customers and throbbing with music. Most of the time, it smelled of beer and tequila, CHISELED! body spray and women's perfumes. Today, though, the only aromas wafting through Muddle + Spade were a hint of disinfectant cleaner and rosemary.

And women's perfume and hair spray. It was faint, but there. *Not* there (at least not in sight) was Tomasz. I frowned.

"Tomasz?" I called. "It's me, Hayden. I'm here!"

I gave a little ta-da wave, just in case he could see me from the back of the house. It would have been like Tomasz to stroll out with a bar towel over his shoulder, wearing something dapper and smiling at me. I felt unaccountably on edge as I stepped past the empty tables and booths, moving toward the bar.

I bumped into a chair and overturned it. *Real smooth.*

"Hey, Hayden." Tomasz chose that moment to emerge, looking as handsome and unruffled as he always did. His gaze shot to that upended chair as I endeavored to set it upright again. "Did you lock the door behind you? I have to keep it closed. Otherwise, the cart pod customers wander in before opening time."

"Oh, no problem." I wielded my personal key and did just that. *Presto.* Then I turned back to him, smiling as I showed off that familiar (to Tomasz) key fob. "I'm afraid this means we *won't* be going steady, though," I joked, referring to our earlier banter about the implications of accepting it. "I'm already booked on a flight out. That's why I'm here early."

Tomasz's face took on a stony quality. He seemed troubled. I hadn't realized he was so wedded to the idea of my being in Portland. It was flattering, but unnecessary. We hadn't known each other *that* well. Not beyond some mild flirtation, anyway.

"Maybe I can change your mind about that." Rallying, he nodded at one of the empty bar stools. "What's your pleasure?"

"Hmm . . . a lifetime supply of chocolate?"

"Sorry, no can do." Tomasz grinned and placed his palms on the bar, his arms spread wide in a comfortable pose. He looked like the king of Muddle + Spade. Of course, I knew he was. "Do you have a backup? For you, I'm willing to go pretty far."

Aw, that was sweet. "A lifetime supply of *noncaloric* chocolate?" I suggested. "My pants are getting tight, thanks to the tour." Ruefully, I tugged at my jeans' waistband. Usually, I managed to keep my weight down by running around kitchens, hiking around foreign markets and far-flung locales, and (if under duress) going running with Danny. "That would be super."

He appeared to consider it. "Nah, you look great to me."

I smiled, duly complimented. "So do you, to me."

It was true. Today, Tomasz had come to work in another pair of perfectly-fitted black pants, a white-and-black checked shirt, and a pair of black braces. He'd groomed his shadowy beard to perfection, left his hair perfectly tousled, and maxed out his hot-indie-guy appeal with vintage leather wingtips.

If not for the uneasy look in his pensive blue eyes, he would have been a poster boy for runaway rich kids everywhere.

Not that I knew he'd run away, I reminded myself

sternly. I didn't even know where that idea had come from. It was a major tangent. For all I knew, Tomasz was as stable as Travis was.

You know, on the inside . . . which was all that counted.

Deciding to appeal to that inner nice guy of his, I smiled. "It was good to see you bringing everybody to Providence Portland last night to see Janel. I know Austin appreciated it."

Tomasz nodded. "Did you really think so?"

Rather than take one of the bar stools, I strolled to join him at the bar. "Sure, I did. It was awful what happened to Janel. Austin was worried. He needed his cart pod family there."

Just steps away from Tomasz, I leaned against the bar. I've been inside enough bakeries, confectionaries, restaurants, and shops to feel comfortable in the front or back of the house.

"You really see us as a family?" Tomasz asked, touched.

I nodded. "You all seem very close. It's nice."

"Is it?" He gave me what I'd swear was a guarded look.

Was he really *nervous* in my presence? It seemed that way.

I was about to make my move when a noise from the back startled me. It sounded like a woman crying. Or maybe retching?

Was one of Tomasz's employees here? "Is there someone in the back?" I asked, uncomfortably alerted to the fact that we might not be alone. "Is she okay? If you want, I could help."

Tomasz grabbed my arm before I could get far. He loomed over me, tall and broad shouldered—and suddenly alarming.

"Is it?" he pushed. "Is it 'nice' that we're a family?"

I didn't understand his hostile demeanor. Frowning back at him, I yanked free my arm. "I just said it was," I told him in a sharper tone than I intended. I don't like feeling trapped. That's (abruptly) how I felt. "Look, if this is a bad time—"

"If you think it's so 'nice' here, why are you leaving?"

I'm not going to lie. I was getting a bad vibe from him. In my gridskipping life, a person learns to listen to intuition.

Right now, I reflected too late, my intuition was screaming that getting away from Tomasz was a good idea. Maybe it *hadn't* been reluctance to leave my cozy Airbnb four-square house that had pushed me into procrastination mode earlier. Maybe it had been an unacknowledged and indistinct reluctance to see Tomasz.

If it had been, it was sharpening up pretty quickly now.

"I'm leaving because it's what I do." I tipped up my chin, making sure to keep a few feet between us as I confronted him. "I have another job in another city. People are expecting me."

It was always good to let someone know that, I figured.

"But you told me you liked it here." Tomasz shook his head, giving me a tsk-tsk sound. "Maybe you were lying all along."

"I do like it here." *Not here in the bar, not at this moment,* I amended silently. But in general, Portland was fab.

"I don't think you do." Tomasz's modelesque good looks couldn't hide the resentment and disappointment he felt. "But maybe you just need more time. Maybe if you stayed longer . . ."

"I won't be staying longer." I hauled in a breath, knowing too late that this had been a mistake. I heard another heaving sound come from the back, followed by a feminine cough.

Who could be back there? A Muddle + Spade employee? Someone else? One of the errant tourists who tried to come in before the bar was open? A woman would explain the perfume and hair spray I'd detected. Maybe Tomasz had tied her up back there and—

—and I was getting carried away. This wasn't a movie.

"I'd like to stay," I fibbed, "but duty calls. You know."

Maybe I could buy enough time to make sure that whoever was sick in the back room would be okay. I couldn't just *leave.*

Besides, I could handle myself. I always have before.

"What if duty didn't call?" Tomasz asked, looking heartened. He put down his bar towel and regarded me squarely. "What if you could stay here in Portland forever? I know you like Cartorama. I know you like the vendors. You like Chow."

I *had* gotten close to the cat. I didn't think anyone else had particularly noticed me cuddling the kitty, though.

"I'm afraid 'full-time kitty cuddler' isn't very lucrative," I joked. "A girl's got to keep herself in brownies and hot-fudge sundaes somehow, right? It's been fun, though."

That was a gross overstatement. Of all the things I'd had in the Rose City, "fun" was not at the top of the list. Not this time.

But Tomasz seemed mollified. I dared myself to edge closer again, hoping I'd be able to see into the bar's back room.

After all, if no one had come to my rescue after the killer-shelf incident, I'd have been in pretty bad shape.

"What if you didn't need money?" Tomasz asked.

He looked sincerely interested in my answer. Maybe I

was overreacting. Maybe all the *murder!* in the air had me spooked.

I shrugged. Technically, I didn't need money. But Tomasz Berk didn't know that. I saw no reason to enlighten him.

I might make friends easily, but I don't do it by sacrificing my sense of safety or privacy. I'm kooky that way.

But apparently, I'd spent too long debating my answer, because Tomasz rushed in to give me one. "Because you *don't* need money. Not if you stay here. You could work at Muddle + Spade."

I almost laughed. I wasn't Janel. "I'm no good at staying put," I said, holding my mirth to a smile. "Thanks, though."

Tomasz's expression darkened again. "Do you think you're too good for Muddle + Spade? Too good for Cartorama? Is that it?" He advanced toward me. "Maybe I had you wrong from the start."

A wheeze came from the back. Then a moan. Concerned, I hooked my thumb in that direction. "Does somebody need help back there? I'm no nurse, but I've been hungover a time or two, so if that's one of your customers after a rough night, maybe I—"

"Yes, you *do* seem to have a drinking problem. We've all noticed." Attentively, Tomasz dropped his gaze to my hand. I was still holding the key fob he'd given me. "We were all talking about the rough days you've had since you've been here."

When I'd maybe been poisoned? Yeah, I remembered.

Also, enough was enough. I wasn't going to stand around and let Tomasz insult me. I drew in a breath and stepped decisively toward the back room to help. I didn't need permission to—

—run smack-dab into Tomasz's debonairly clad chest.

I gave a muffled exclamation. He glowered down at me.

"That's why nobody's going to think it's strange at all when they find out you let yourself in here alone," he said in an eerie tone. "Go ahead. Sit down. I'll mix you a drink."

"I don't want a drink." I added, "Thanks, anyway."

You know . . . just in case he was merely having an off day.

But he wasn't. Deftly, Tomasz slipped the key from my hand. "I'll give this back later. After you've had your drink."

"You can keep it. I don't need it anymore."

I almost said *I don't want it anymore.* Something told me not to. Probably, it was the same something that warned me when harmless-looking kids at the base of the Charles Bridge in Prague were really gangs of pickpockets. I stepped back.

I tried to peek around Tomasz's shoulder. I couldn't.

"I really wish you'd reconsider," Tomasz told me. He seemed genuinely distraught. "We have a lot to offer at Cartorama. You fit right in, too. I was hoping I could convince you to stay."

"By being extra creepy?" That's right. I'd had it. "Nope."

Tomasz only laughed. "You're feisty. I like that. That's why I thought this might work out. I'm the king of Cartorama—"

Whoa. I'd just had that thought a few minutes ago, before things had gotten weird between us.

"—and you can be its queen," Tomasz finished. *"Forever."*

"Well, I'm fresh out of tiaras, so I guess the answer's no." I stepped deliberately toward him. As I expected, he moved slightly to make room, allowing me behind the bar. It was a no-no to advance toward an attacker, but Tomasz wasn't dangerous to me. I hoped. "But you're already as rich as a king, right?"

If I'd hoped to set him off-guard . . . I failed.

He only smiled. "You knew about me. You guessed."

"Takes one to know one." I nodded at his clothes, uninterested now in making nice. "Your Arnys suit was a dead giveaway. That's not something that winds up in thrift stores."

Tomasz looked chagrined. "That suit is what I wear to funerals. I didn't even think twice. I just grabbed it." He glanced at me. "I was surprised you recognized it. You don't look like the type of person who appreciates the finer things."

"Why? Because I can't afford a bespoke suit? Think again."

"No." He gave me a fleeting smile. "Because you don't appreciate Cartorama and the community we've built here. I thought you did. I thought you understood. But you lied."

"Hold up. I never lied about anything."

"Just like Declan. He didn't care about Cartorama, either."

At Tomasz's unnerving tone, I got goose bumps again. "No?"

It was all I could manage. I was too disturbed to say more.

"No," Tomasz confirmed spitefully. "He brought his real-estate buddies here. He ruined everything. He told me they were supposed to help with Chocolate After Dark. But once they saw the cart pod property, they wanted more. They wanted *my* land."

"Well, they obviously didn't get it," I pointed out, realizing he meant the Prodigy Group. "No harm, no foul, right?"

"Not quite." Tomasz watched me. Coldly. "After that, I knew how Declan *really* felt about Cartorama. He had no loyalty at all. I value loyalty. It's the *only* thing worth having."

"I'm partial to love and chocolate chip cookies."

"This isn't funny." His dire expression sobered me up quickly. "I'm trying to give you a chance, Hayden. You're not making it easy on me. Be easy. *Please* don't be like Declan."

I assumed he meant, *Don't be dead like Declan*. Uh-oh.

I clutched the strap on my crossbody bag, wondering if I dared to reach inside it for my phone—for my recording app.

Tomasz saw my gesture. He scowled. "Why isn't anybody loyal anymore?" he growled, turning to pace a few steps. "Declan, Carissa, now you. It's getting to where I don't trust anyone. The whole reason I came to Portland was to find people to trust. People who *didn't* just want me for my money. People who *got* me. Did you think I was pretending to be a *bartender* for fun?"

At his scathing tone, I gulped. "Carissa?"

Was *she* who was in back, sick or hurt?

"She came here wanting to be reimbursed for her share of the cacao roaster. She said she needed money to bring her ice-cream cart to L.A." Tomasz looked angry. "I said no."

Oh no. My imagination took flight. Darkly. I imagined my old college friend, alone and hurt, with no one to help her.

"*You* pushed the shelving unit on me," I guessed too late, envisioning a similar scenario for Carissa. *Poor Carissa.*

Tomasz lifted his shoulder in a shrug. "I had to. Everyone kept coming in here to drink and complain about how you were snooping around. You were upsetting people. I couldn't have that. Not in *my* community."

He paused, seeming pained. "Don't you get it? This is the *only* place I've ever felt I belonged. I can't have that ruined—especially not because *you* want to pry."

I was feeling a little short on sympathy just then.

"Yeah, tough break. It's probably hard to make friends when you're busy trying to cripple them with industrial shelving."

"I wasn't trying to *cripple* you." Tomasz flashed a grin. "Just scare you, that's all. So you'd stop overstepping your boundaries. I knew I'd get a chance to explain. Here it is."

I didn't feel reassured. He was crazy. I didn't doubt it.

"I like you, Hayden," Tomasz said in a horrible imitation of the flirting we'd done. "But you have to stay in line."

I raised my chin a notch higher. "And if I don't?"

I felt torn between staying put (for Carissa) and running like mad (for me). But just as I hadn't been able to abandon my friend to her (supposed) grief after her fiancé's death, I found I couldn't leave now. Casually, I eased my hand into my bag.

My fingers touched the smooth surface of my phone.

"If you don't, you'll wind up drinking alone, I'm afraid."

I didn't understand. My frown probably revealed as much. I wished I'd asked the Portland police detective to put a rush on the fingerprints check on that piece of plastic wrap. Because I now felt certain that evidence would reveal Tomasz's prints.

Now they'd find that damning evidence too late. *For me.*

"Nobody likes drinking alone," I told him lightly, abandoning my quest for my phone. I needed a new strategy. "Why don't you join me?" I glanced at the bar stools. "You can tell me more about Declan. And Carissa." I smiled.

Sort of. It was the best I could do under the circumstances. "I'm a good listener."

Tomasz wavered. "It *might* be nice if you understood first."

First. I shivered, not wanting to think what he meant. Unfortunately, my overactive imagination had other ideas. I pictured myself shot, stabbed, and smashed over the head with that rare bottle of Macallan whiskey, all in quick succession.

"See, I really liked Declan in the beginning." Tomasz leaned on the bar, then casually rolled up his shirtsleeves. "He was funny. Not *too* bright. Good-looking enough to play wingman, but not cool enough to compete. You get the picture, right?"

I nodded, appalled by his flippant tone.

"I mean, Declan liked all the same things I did," Tomasz confided. "Slasher flicks, hot chicks, a nice Syrah, and a good lobster roll. He liked *me.* He liked the community I built here." He looked around the bar, momentarily distracted, then grabbed a pair of protective gloves. Slowly, he pulled them on. "But then Declan changed. He got engaged to Carissa. He started bringing over his old Seattle property-development buddies for drinks so she could mine them for contacts. You know there's nobody more connected than a real-estate professional, right? Especially those who specialize in commercial development."

Tomasz stopped, seeming briefly distracted.

I was, too. I was putting together the pieces of how Carissa had manipulated Declan into finding her investors for Churn PDX. Austin had told me that Declan had abandoned his old life in Seattle to woo and win Carissa, but the joke was on Declan. Carissa had only wanted him for his contacts, all along.

"Are you all caught up?" Tomasz inquired politely.

I shook myself and nodded. I had to get out of there. But first, I had to try to find Carissa and help her.

"The truth is, Declan betrayed me," Tomasz told me. "Worse than that, he betrayed the pod. He tried to unravel Cartorama, all for a share of the profits. I couldn't allow that."

I felt chilled again. Tomasz was *definitely* crazy. I hugged myself and looked around for an escape route, then remembered that the bar's locked dead bolt wouldn't open without the key. I was stuck. Stuck with an unbalanced killer.

I kept looking for a way out, hoping to disguise my scouting mission. My gaze lit on a tidy row of keys, hung near the mounted iPad that Muddle + Spade used as a cash register. That's when everything fell completely into place. Tomasz had had *all* the pod's keys.

He could have come and gone anywhere, anytime. He could have rigged Carissa's liquid nitrogen tanks and wrecked their safety mechanisms. He could have wrapped Churn PDX's ventilation system in industrial plastic wrap—which was used plenty in the kitchen area of the bar, I felt sure—and eliminated all of the oxygen in that cramped space. He could have killed Declan.

Who was I kidding? Tomasz *had* killed Declan.

"I know what you're thinking," he said in a blithe tone.

"I doubt that." I looked at him, horrified. "Seriously."

"You're thinking that I overreacted." Tomasz sighed, then pulled over two bottles of liquor and a mixer. He was making a margarita? "But it had to be done. I had to make sure no one else ever tried to destroy the pod. I had to set a precedent."

Killing Declan wasn't "a precedent." It was wrong.

But I couldn't say so. Because that's when I glimpsed

the thermos-size Dewar of liquid nitrogen on the bar. That's when I realized what Tomasz intended to do. That's when I remembered Lauren's story about having almost drunk liquid nitrogen.

I didn't want that stuff inside *me,* freezing on contact with my tissues, puncturing internal organs on its way through my system. I didn't want to bleed to death . . . slowly and internally.

"Ah," Tomasz murmured, watching my undoubtedly petrified expression. "I see you're familiar with the dangers of this stuff. At least your nosiness was useful, right?" He chuckled and grabbed my hands. Before I knew what he meant to do, he'd forced my fingers around the Dewar—undoubtedly leaving fingerprints to help enact his plan. I snatched them away before he could repeat the maneuver on the tequila and mixers.

He grabbed my hands again. Hard. "Cointreau or Grand Marnier?" His tone of polite inquiry was a terrifying sham.

I wrenched away. "This isn't necessary, Tommy."

At my use of that nickname, he paused. I felt heartened. Also, grateful to Lauren for her constant use of it. It looked as though she inadvertently might have given me a playbook to use with Tomasz—one that took advantage of his weakness.

I didn't think he'd been lying when he'd said he'd had a bad breakup. As far as I could tell, Tomasz had been ruined by rejection—ruled by his fear that it would happen to him again. Again and again and again. Not just with women, either. With everyone in his life. Including the people at Cartorama—the only "family" he seemed to have known or cared about.

"Don't you think I want to belong, too?" I asked. I looked away, pretending to be overcome with emotion. Really, I couldn't bear to meet his chilling gaze. "I'm gun shy, that's all. Geez." I forced a laugh. "Give a globe-trotting girl a break, will ya?"

He looked skeptical. "That was all a front? Just now?"

I chuckled. "Well, I wasn't like that before, now was I? We were getting along. But I had to be sure about you." I made myself step closer. "I mean, I had to know how far you'd *really* go to make sure I'd be okay here. I've been hurt, too, you know." I remembered how on edge he'd seemed while asking me out. "Just like you. I was involved with someone who let me down."

I heaved in a shuddering breath, pretending to be secretly heartbroken. In the process, I managed to catch sight of Carissa. She lay in a frightening heap just inside the bar's back room, almost as if she'd tried to run out the back door and had been overcome before she could. She moved, but just barely.

"I'll go all the way to protect you," Tomasz swore. His gaze locked on mine, his blue eyes searching. "I'll protect you, just the way I protected Cartorama. I've done it once—"

"When you killed Declan?"

He nodded vehemently. "Yes. I'll do it again, if I have to."

There it was. A confession. Proof that Tomasz had been the one who'd killed Declan—cold-bloodedly and without remorse. All because his new buddy had tried to break up Cartorama.

"You can be safe here," Tomasz coaxed. His eyes begged me to agree. If I hadn't known better, I might have fallen for it. That's just how sincere he seemed. "Safe with all of us."

His words put a new and chilling spin on the cart pod's close-knit community. I wondered if anyone else knew that Tomasz would kill to protect his "family"—had *already* killed to protect them. I wondered if I'd ever get out alive to warn them.

"Or," he went on in a resigned tone, "you can drink this margarita I'm about to make for you and stop worrying about it. Nobody will guess the truth. Just like with Declan, they'll all think it was an accident—even your friend Danny. I think he's a bad influence on you, by the way. I recognize the type."

I almost choked on bitter laughter. "Thanks for your concern," I said on a tidal wave of fear. "But I'm okay."

At that moment, I was anything but *okay.* I felt hysterical. Especially as I heard another pain-filled groan from Carissa.

Tomasz heard it, too. He rolled his eyes. "Austin and Janel will corroborate your 'drinking problem,'" he said soberly. "I know they'll be genuinely sad. If Janel makes it, of course."

I widened my eyes. "Did you—were you the one who—"

"No." He waved away my guess. "That was an accident."

I figured I might as well believe him—about all of it. He intended to kill me. What was I going to do?

"I'll be sad, too." Tomasz cast a mournful glance at the monogrammed key fob he'd taken from me. "I'll always regret having given that key to you. That's what I'll tell the police." He shrugged again. "But I couldn't have known you'd let yourself in here before opening time. I couldn't have known you'd try to mix yourself a frozen margarita"—his gaze shot to the Dewar of liquid nitrogen "—all unaware of its dangers. It's going to be *so* tragic." He paused. "You know, I think this will bring the whole community together. That will be a good thing for us."

I gaped at him, newly aware of how long he'd been

hedging his bets. Tomasz had given me that key days ago. He'd been willing to kill me—if necessary—almost from the moment we'd met.

Well, this (unfortunately) wasn't the first time that I'd faced down a murderer. I remembered everything that had happened at Maison Lemaître and tried to draw strength from it. I'd made it out of San Francisco alive. I could survive this, too.

I edged closer, then ran my hand along the bar's edge. I walked my fingertips up to the bottle of Grand Marnier. I slid my hand up the neck of the bottle, then looked up at Tomasz.

Just as I'd hoped, he was staring at my hand on the bottle. Conveniently, it was vaguely suggestively shaped, with a rich amber color and a sexy, curvy neck. I channeled my inner Lauren and gave that bottle a long, lascivious stroke up and down.

Tomasz's eyes almost bulged out of his head.

"If we're ever going to be together, Tommy," I purred, "I mean, *really* together"—I gave the bottle another stroke, feeling nauseated as I did—"you're going to have to learn to trust me."

Leaning forward, I let him look down my shirt. Yes, I know it's gross. But these were emergency circumstances. I wished I'd had the foresight to undo a few buttons. But then, I wished I'd had the intuitive farsightedness not to come there at all. Why hadn't I listened to myself? I'd *known* somehow I should be wary of him.

Wearing a dazed expression, Tomasz looked from my (meager) cleavage to my hand on the bottle. I might not have had the goods to attract Declan's bosom-loving attention, but Tomasz was hooked. "I want to trust you." He swallowed hard. "I do."

I leaned into him, then used my other hand to reach

lower. If Tomasz felt that surreptitious gesture, he thought I was reaching for something else—something that *wasn't* that heavy steel Dewar of liquid nitrogen, now held slackly in his grasp.

"Well, I'm afraid that would be a mistake," I told him.

Then, with a silent thanks to all my days of traveling—to all the miscreant pickpockets who'd inadvertently shown me the useful benefits of misdirection—I grabbed that steel Dewar and lifted it high. Then I bashed Tomasz on the side of the head.

I hit him as hard as I could. As hard as I could *imagine*. The solid *thwack* that hunk of metal made when it contacted his skull sickened me. But it worked. Tomasz staggered backward.

He gave a guttural howl of pain. But by then, I was already grabbing that monogrammed key fob and running for the door.

Unbelievably, it opened just as I reached it.

I ran into the first person who entered as I screamed about Tomasz being crazy—screamed about needing to call the police.

I was shaking all over. I realized I was crying, too. I couldn't breathe. But I *could* dizzily recognize Danny—and the lock-picking set in his hand? *Huh?* I was wrestling with my crossbody bag, simultaneously searching for my cell phone and waiting for Tomasz to come staggering after me like a horror-movie monster, when I began to make sense of what was happening.

I had to step aside to let all the police officers inside before I could say anything, though. There were a *lot* of them.

"Danny? Did you just *break in* to Muddle + Spade while the police were watching you?" I frowned, wanting to hug him, smack him, *and* yell at him at the same time. "What have I told you about going back to criminal behavior? It's bad for you!"

"I'm starting to think *you're* bad for me," my perennially tardy bodyguard said. "You keep bringing me into contact with criminal elements. That violates my parole. It's got to stop."

Then I *did* smack him. Gently. "You're not on parole anymore," I reminded him unsteadily, "and you know it."

"If I keep hanging around you, I might be sometime soon."

I hoped not. All around us, the police were busy with the work I devoutly hoped I wasn't imagining. They were arresting Tomasz, handcuffing him, reading him his rights.

"There's someone hurt in the back!" I yelled, pointing.

But they were already helping Carissa. I saw the same detective I'd spoken with earlier crouching over her, speaking to her in a low voice. He called for medical assistance for her.

That could have been *me,* I couldn't help thinking. Helpless. Alone. Slowly dying from a stupid deadly cocktail.

If I was ever going to die from a comestible, it *had* to be chocolate. No other food or drink would have the same significance. Not given who I am and what I do.

For a few seconds, Danny and I just watched all the hubbub. Eventually, I reasoned, we'd have to give statements. In the meantime, it was reassuring to be surrounded by people who knew what to do—whose job it was to catch killers, like Tomasz.

"How did you know to come here?" I asked Danny.

"I went to the police station to ask them to put a rush on the fingerprinting on the plastic wrap you found." He put his hands in his pockets and glared as Tomasz was led past us, head down, surrounded by armed officers. "It turned out they already had a fingerprinting job going. Its results had just come in."

I shook my head. "I can't believe you'd willingly go into a police station for me. That's like entering the lion's den."

"*For you.* That's the operative part." For a couple of breaths, Danny took in my face, my hair, and my fearful body. I wasn't proud that I'd run. But I'd planned to get help from one of the vendors and come back for Carissa. My dying wouldn't have helped her, either, I'd decided. Danny exhaled. "Anyway, the other fingerprinting job was on some plastic wrap that Janel had brought in. Once you did the same thing, they rushed it."

"She *was* investigating! Just like us."

Danny nodded. "Tomasz's prints were all over that stuff. Combined with what I knew about everything that had gone on here, plus your heroic work making sure Tomasz didn't get away—"

I managed a weak grin, recognizing his teasing.

"—led the police straight here. Justice done, et cetera."

I felt light-headed with relief. Also, doubtful. "Well, that's great, but what if it doesn't stick?" I asked. "After all, most people don't have their fingerprints on record."

Danny was ready for me. "Tomasz did, thanks to his filthy-rich parents. They had Berk fingerprinted as part of an anti-kidnapping measure years ago. My clients do it sometimes, too."

I'd forgotten he had other freelance security clients.

Also, that answered that, I guessed. Case closed.

"I was right," I told Danny. "Declan's death *was* a murder."

"No, *I* was right," he came right back at me. "You

should have left Portland. You almost died confronting that lunatic."

"Hmm. I suppose that means *Travis* was right, too. Just like you. Right? Wouldn't you say so? He wanted me to leave, too."

"Nah. I don't remember anything about that," Danny mused with pseudo seriousness. "I don't think it ever happened. I mean, me and Harvard working together? No way. Forget about it."

Then he gave me a grin and led me outside, ready to help me get some fresh rainy air, do what I had to do with the police, and prepare to (finally) leave Portland for good.

And this time, I really meant it.

Eighteen

Leaving Portland for good didn't mean leaving *right away,* though. I had time before my flight to go on a short field trip.

"Pretty good view, right?" I asked Danny the next morning, standing at the stone retainer wall at the Vista House, high above the Columbia River Gorge on a promontory called Crown Point. We'd driven out the historic old Columbia River Highway to see the views—and to decompress from all the *murder.* "I love it out here. There's something about being above it all that's so freeing—especially after everything that's happened."

Danny stuffed his hands in his jeans pockets and braced himself against the springtime breeze. I knew he'd rather have been hiking through the gorge or exploring all the waterfalls—including the most famous, Multnomah Falls—but we'd had to make certain concessions today. He squinted, peering at the view.

"Yeah. It's nice." My protection expert glanced behind us at the Vista House. Its Art Nouveau sandstone exterior looked oddly at home amid the windswept gorge. Inside, the place was full of marble and brass, with opalescent art glass windows and period details. But Danny wasn't looking for any of that.

I studied the wide, winding Columbia River Valley, drawn to the green hills, craggy rocks, and acres of evergreen trees. I might spend most of my time in kitchens and confectioners', but I like to get out and encounter the wilderness now and then.

"If I'd come out here while all the drama was going on, it might have given me a different perspective." I breathed deeply. "Back at Cartorama, it was easy to get carried away."

"You had reason to get 'carried away.' This time."

Danny was right. There really *had* been a murderer at the cart pod. I really *had* had a part in catching him, too.

Tomasz. He'd come to Portland and created the perfect community—at least for him. Once Declan had threatened the Cartorama "family," though, Tomasz hadn't been able to forgive him. He'd felt too betrayed by Declan wanting to sell out.

A brief perusal of Declan's emails from the Prodigy Group had confirmed Declan's interest in profiting from a cut of the cart pod property sale. But that wasn't a crime. He certainly hadn't deserved to die. I figured that Tomasz and Declan had argued in the back room at Muddle + Spade before he'd died. That would explain Declan's phone being there. He'd probably dropped it, then accidentally kicked it beneath the shelves.

After the police had examined it, I'd returned it to his parents. I figured they would have wanted it. They had.

"I can't believe Carissa was just using Declan for his contacts all along," I said, making myself keep talking before I started feeling too melancholy. "I didn't know she'd become so ambitious. She'd always been so nice to me, back in the day."

"She was trying to use you, too," Danny reminded me. "And your expertise. There was a reason she invited you to her engagement party weekend. Carissa was hoping you could hook her up with your chocolate-whispering peeps and help her franchise Churn PDX, just in case Declan's contacts didn't do the job."

Unwillingly, I nodded. Carissa was still in the hospital, being treated for the injuries she'd sustained after being forced to drink Tomasz's deadly cocktail of liquid nitrogen. I'd narrowly escaped similar injuries myself. Carissa had been in a lot of pain. She was lucky to have survived. Recuperating might delay her ice-cream dynasty for a while, though, I knew.

I hoped that forced delay gave her a chance to examine some of the things she'd done, like manipulating Declan and scaring Janel. Maybe Carissa would make better choices in the future.

Speaking of Janel . . . "Janel suspected Carissa all along, you know," I told Danny. "She knew Declan was alive when she left him after their argument that night." That's what Austin had told me, at least. Janel's prognosis had improved, but she was a long way from chitchat. "Janel saw Carissa in her car outside the cart pod. We know Carissa had been leaving after overhearing Janel's fight with Declan, but Janel thought Carissa was just arriving. She thought Carissa had rigged the trailer on purpose and had come that night to make sure Declan was dead."

Danny made a face. "No wonder she taunted Carissa with all those Declan's Dozen costumes on the tour." He shook his head. "Remind me not to piss off any short, stocky blondes, okay?"

"As if *I'm* going to get involved in your love life." I studied the gorge below us, watching the tiny-looking cars navigate the old highway. "Janel thought that reminding Carissa how much she knew about Declan might shake loose a confession."

"Hmmph. Carissa was way too frosty for that."

"Well, *we* know that, but Janel didn't. Neither did Austin." He'd been helping Janel investigate. That's why he'd run interference for her on the first night of the Chocolate After Dark tour. It was also how he'd come to fall for Janel—how he'd urged her to continue investigating. "If not for Austin, Janel might not have taken that plastic wrap to the police."

Grudgingly, Danny nodded. He looked at the Vista House again. He looked at me. "I still wish you hadn't confronted Tomasz the way you did. Someday, learn to wait for me, okay?"

"Hey, *I* didn't know there'd be any trouble," I said in my own defense. "Tomasz was really good at seeming normal. In fact, he's probably one of the most charming people I've ever met."

I hadn't been the only one who'd been affected by Tomasz Berk, either. Austin had let Tomasz talk him into refusing to refill the liquid nitrogen tanks for Declan on that fateful night. He'd told Austin that he needed to "stand up" for himself with Declan. He'd known that such a move would force Declan into the trailer alone, where Tomasz could enact his revenge.

Likewise, Janel had let Tomasz talk her into "stalking" Declan. He'd kept her going by saying that he had "inside information" from his good friend—saying that Declan was "tormented" by his engagement to Carissa . . . and secretly wanted Janel, instead. Janel hadn't been any crazier than any other jilted woman, I'd realized belatedly. She'd simply had her feelings whipped into a frenzy by a master manipulator: Tomasz.

He'd been setting up Janel to take the fall for Declan's murder the whole time, knowing that she'd look guiltiest.

I'd almost fallen for it, too. I was still sorry for that.

Making it a clean sweep, I knew now, was Lauren. The pierced and tattooed temptress of Cartorama had *not* been stepping out on Danny with that tall, dark, handsome stranger.

"You'd probably say the same thing about Lauren, right?" I elbowed Danny, grinning. "She's pretty charming, right?"

"Now that I know she's not looking over my shoulder for the next guy, sure," Danny agreed, giving away the bare minimum.

We'd discovered that Tomasz had gotten to Lauren, too. He'd learned of her closeness with her brother, Will (aka the tall, dark, handsome stranger with whom she'd been slipping away during the chocolate tours) *and* of Will's own struggling culinary-tour business. Tomasz had encouraged Lauren to spy on Declan's tour and report back to Will with hints for his own business.

I thought Tomasz had done it just to drive a wedge between Lauren and Danny, because Danny hadn't been part of the pod. As with me, Tomasz had advised Lauren to "steer clear" of my friend. He'd warned her that my security expert was "bad news."

As with me, Lauren *hadn't* taken that advice to heart.

Deliberately steering me away from Lauren and matters of the heart, Danny jutted his chin. "So, what are your plans now?"

I wasn't sure. "I think it'll be a while before I feel another yen to settle down anyplace." I smiled, letting Danny know I wasn't taking my nascent urges for hearth and home too seriously. "For now, my priority is going back to work. I asked Travis to look up some juicy consulting gigs to divert me."

I'd given my financial advisor the rundown on everything that had happened in Stumptown—plus a few sincere compliments to thank him for all the work he'd done to help. I wanted to keep Travis on my side. I was buttering him up for a future visit.

I hadn't given up on the idea of meeting him face-to-face. Not by a long shot. But for now, I just wanted to temper some chocolate, troubleshoot some bittersweet soufflés or cookies or cakes, and forget about murder for a week or two. At the least.

"What are you going to do?" I asked Danny. "Back to L.A.?"

He gave a noncommittal sound. "I might stay here for a few days." His gaze wandered back to the Vista House— just as a tall, curvaceous, flirtatious brunette emerged. Lauren, of course. She'd insisted on showing us her 'hood. She was the reason we'd come to the Columbia River Gorge at all. She waved. So did Danny. His smile broadened. "I think I can keep myself busy."

I didn't doubt it. I guessed this was how it was going to be between us for a while. Me, jetting off to the next international destination to make sure the world's chocolates were just as scrumptious as they could be. Danny, using my murder-related pit stops as a means to hook up with hot women.

It was just like my brawny longtime friend to capitalize on the situation. Danny was nothing if not opportunistic.

And, of course, chronically late. But I was used to that.

"You know," I hypothesized as I watched Lauren navigate the pathway in her high heels, "sooner or later, one of these women is going to want to keep you around longer than a few days."

But Danny only shrugged. "That won't matter. I won't do it," he said. "What I want isn't in any one of these cities."

"Right." I knew him too well. My wiseass tone said so. "What you want is in *all* of them. You don't fool me, Jamieson."

"I was never trying to fool you." His gaze met mine, serious for a minute. In a second, Lauren would catch up to us; then we'd be off to tour the rest of the gorge. Afterward, *I'd* be off to PDX—the airport this time, not the city. "Take care of yourself, okay?" Danny said. "You're not unbreakable, you know."

"I will if you will." I couldn't stay serious. Not with the wind in my hair and another adventure looming. I wanted to leave *and* I wanted to stay. But most of all, I wanted to say, "That's exactly the same thing Travis told me when I called him this morning—that 'unbreakable' business. That's a pretty funny coincidence, right? You and him having the same take on things?"

The same take on me, I meant. But there was no point rubbing it in too hard. Feeling cheered up, I gave Danny a saucy look and headed away, off to view the vista from another vantage point so I could give him and his new lady friend some privacy.

"Harvard and I are *not* the same!" Danny called after me in a husky, aggrieved tone. "We're completely different."

Didn't I know it. But before I got too wrapped up in either one of them, I had some *Theobroma cacao* to troubleshoot and some gridskipping exploits to enjoy. Because after what had happened to me in San Francisco and now in Portland, I was beginning to suspect that my unusual talents went way beyond chocolate . . . all the way to helping bring down killers. That was *big*.

From here on out, though . . . I was focusing on *chocolate,* I reminded myself. *Period.* I didn't think there was anything that could tempt me away from that sensible stance. But I didn't want to consider it *too* hard. Because if there's one thing I know about life, it's that chocolate is better than vanilla. And two is better than one. And exceptions are always the rule.

Okay, that's *three* things. I never said I was meticulous.

With chocolate, I'm methodical. With everything else? I was learning to be. That was a start.

From the other side of the promontory, I gestured to Danny and Lauren. "Hey, let's go!" I yelled. "I've got things to do!"

Then I led the way to Lauren's Subaru and reluctantly slid into the backseat. Next time, I promised myself, *I* was definitely going to be the one doing the driving.

Recipes

CHOCOLATE UN-CINNAMON ROLLS

8 tablespoons melted butter, divided
⅔ cup brown sugar, packed
5 tablespoons granulated sugar, divided
2 tablespoons cocoa powder
⅛ teaspoon plus ½ teaspoon salt, divided
1 cup mini chocolate chips
3 cups all-purpose flour, divided
1¼ teaspoons baking powder
½ teaspoon baking soda
1¼ cups buttermilk
1 cup confectioners' sugar
2 tablespoons milk
1 teaspoon vanilla extract

GET READY: Preheat oven to 425°. Grease a 9-inch round baking pan with 1 tablespoon of melted butter; set aside.

MAKE FILLING: In a small bowl, combine brown sugar, 3 tablespoons granulated sugar, cocoa powder, and ⅛ teaspoon salt. Stir in 1 tablespoon of melted butter until the mixture is like wet sand. Stir in mini chocolate chips, then set aside.

MAKE DOUGH: In a large bowl, stir together 2½ cups flour, remaining 2 tablespoons sugar, baking powder, baking soda, and remaining ½ teaspoon salt. In a small bowl, whisk together buttermilk and 2 tablespoons melted butter. Add the liquid to the dry ingredients and stir until the liquid is absorbed (the dough will look shaggy), about 30 seconds. Transfer the dough to a lightly floured work surface and knead until just smooth.

SHAPE ROLLS: Sprinkle clean countertop with remaining ½ cup flour, then pat out the dough into a 12- by 9-inch rectangle. Brush the dough with 2 tablespoons melted butter, then sprinkle with the chocolate filling, leaving a ½-inch border. Press the filling firmly into the dough. Using a bench scraper or metal spatula, loosen the dough from the work surface. Starting at a long side, roll the dough, pressing lightly, to form a tight log. Pinch the seam to seal. Roll the log seam-side down and cut it evenly into 8 pieces. Place 1 roll in the center of the prepared pan and then place the remaining 7 rolls around the perimeter of the pan. Brush the rolls with the remaining 2 tablespoons butter.

BAKE ROLLS: Bake until the rolls are light golden brown, 23 to 25 minutes. Cool 2 minutes. Use an offset metal spatula to loosen the rolls from the pan. Wearing oven mitts, place a large plate over the pan and invert the rolls onto the plate. Place the greased cooling rack over the plate and invert the rolls onto the rack. Cool about 5 minutes before glazing.

MAKE GLAZE: In a small bowl, stir together confectioners' sugar, milk, and vanilla extract until smooth. Drizzle over baked and cooled rolls. Enjoy!

NOTES FROM HAYDEN

Do you like cinnamon rolls, but wish they packed a little more *oomph*? Try these chocolate-filled rolls, instead! If you don't have mini chocolate chips, you can roughly chop regular chocolate chips or chunks into smaller pieces. If any filling escapes while you're rolling up the dough, just tuck it back in or sprinkle on top. These rolls don't have to look picture perfect to taste perfectly delicious!

NOW NOW NOW CHOCOLATE
SUGAR TOAST

1 tablespoon granulated sugar
½ teaspoon cocoa powder
tiny pinch flaky sea salt (optional)
½ tablespoon butter
1 slice good bread

GET READY: In a small bowl or ramekin, stir together sugar, cocoa powder, and (optional) flaky sea salt. Set aside.

Make the toast via your preferred method: toaster, toaster oven, grill, or broiler. Butter toast, then sprinkle evenly with sugar-cocoa mixture. Serve hot!

NOTES FROM HAYDEN

Okay, this twist on standard cinnamon-sugar toast is (admittedly) one of those treats you hardly need a recipe for. But it's useful to have in your back pocket when you need a chocolaty nosh fast (*now now now*).

The quality of the bread and butter is everything here, so spring for the good stuff! If you opt for the flaky sea salt, try natural Maldon brand. It's easy to find in most grocery stores. Or get fancy and try a vanilla bean flake salt from an artisanal purveyor (like Jacobsen Salt Co. in Portland).

CAN'T MISS HOT FUDGE SAUCE

8 ounces bittersweet chocolate, chopped
1½ cups heavy cream
2 tablespoons light corn syrup or golden syrup
¼ teaspoon kosher salt or flaky sea salt
1 teaspoon vanilla extract

GET READY: Place chopped chocolate in a medium heat-proof bowl. Have a lid or plastic wrap ready to fit the bowl.

MAKE SAUCE: In a microwave-safe medium container, combine heavy cream, corn syrup or golden syrup, and salt. Microwave until just simmering, about 3–4 minutes.

Carefully pour hot cream mixture over chopped chocolate. Immediately cover and let stand 5 minutes. Add vanilla extract, then stir until hot-fudge sauce is smooth. Enjoy!

NOTES FROM HAYDEN

Everyone needs a go-to hot-fudge sauce, and this is mine. You can use any kind of good-quality chocolate for this: bittersweet, semisweet, even milk chocolate. Or be a rebel and try very good quality white chocolate for a blond version! (In that case, look for cocoa butter listed first among the ingredients, to be sure you're getting an excellent product.)

This hot-fudge sauce will last for up to a week if kept carefully covered in your refrigerator. Your mileage may vary, however—mine never lasts that long!

This sauce will thicken when cold; just rewarm it gently to restore its silky, luxurious texture.

CHOCOLATE STOUT AFFOGATO

1 scoop chocolate ice cream
1 shot freshly brewed espresso
1 shot chocolate liqueur, like Godiva Milk Chocolate
½ cup chocolate stout or Guinness stout

GET READY: Place the ice cream in a small bowl or mug.

GO: Pour the espresso over the ice cream, followed by the chocolate liqueur and the chocolate stout (the chocolate stout will foam a little; that's okay). Consume immediately, before the whole thing turns into delicious, melty chocolate soup.

Notes from Hayden

Never had an affogato? You've got to try this one! An affogato is Italy's version of a root beer float—and this boozy version is especially delicious.

Don't try this one right before bed, though. I'm a huge chocoholic, but the espresso puts this treat in the afternoon-delight category for me.

(ALMOST) INSTANT HOUSE-MADE DOUBLE-CHOCOLATE PUDDING

3 ounces bittersweet chocolate, finely chopped
½ cup granulated sugar
¼ cup brown sugar, packed
⅓ cup cocoa powder
2 tablespoons cornstarch
⅛ teaspoon salt
2¼ cups milk
2 teaspoons vanilla extract

GET READY: Place chocolate in a small heatproof bowl; microwave at 50 percent power for 2 minutes, stopping to stir after 1 minute. If the chocolate is not yet completely melted, heat up to 30 seconds more at 50 percent power. After melting, allow to cool slightly.

MAKE PUDDING: In a medium heatproof bowl, whisk together granulated sugar, brown sugar, cocoa powder, cornstarch, and salt. Whisk in approximately ½ cup of the milk, stirring until smooth. Whisk in remaining milk.

Microwave pudding for 6-9 minutes, stirring every 3 minutes or so, until mixture comes to a complete boil. (Watch closely, or pudding may boil over!) Whisk in melted chocolate and vanilla extract. Pour pudding into individual serving dishes; cover each dish by pressing plastic wrap directly onto surface of pudding. Refrigerate until completely cool, approximately 2-3 hours. Serve and enjoy!

Notes from Hayden

You might be reluctant to use a microwave for this recipe
(and especially for melting chocolate), but as long as you
keep an eye on things, it's a fast and easy way to make
pudding (or ganache, or hot-fudge sauce). Feel free to
gild the lily with a dollop of Chantilly cream (which is
just a fancy way of saying heavy cream whipped with
vanilla and sugar) and shaved chocolate.